MARVELS

MARVELS

R. E. Harrington

Secker & Warburg
LONDON

First published in England 1985 by
Martin Secker & Warburg Limited
54 Poland Street, London W1V 3DF

Copyright © 1985 by R. E. Harrington

British Library Cataloguing in Publication Data
Harrington, R.E.
    Marvels.
    I. Title
    813'.54[F]   PS3558.A6295

    ISBN 0-436-19140-7

Typeset in 11/12½ pt Linotron 202 Baskerville by
Inforum Ltd, Portsmouth
Printed in Great Britain by
Mackays of Chatham Ltd

For Carolita: mi amiga, mi amante, mi vida

ONE

Seize the day!
Trust tomorrow
as little as you may.

Horace

1

Hucko Makes His Pitch

1908

WALTER HUCKO SWEPT OFF his hard-boiled derby before the handsome woman drying her hands on her apron in the doorway of the farmhouse.

"Miss, I spoke to your brother at the pig pens and he was kind enough to direct me up here where I was hoping to have a word with your mother."

"That was my son." The woman's grey eyes did not smile.

"Your *son*! You don't mean it!"

"What is it you're selling, Mister –?"

"Hucko. The Reverend Walter Hucko. I'm selling nothing. This *is* the Luther Marvel farm?"

"Surely my son told you that?"

"Can't be too careful. You see, Missus Marvel, your family's been selected by the Parson's Christian Products Company, out of St Louis, Missouri, for a free demonstration of the remarkable new Parson's Home Organ, and for a magnificent free gift."

"What church, exactly, is it that you're a Reverend of, Reverend Hucko?"

Hucko seemed not to hear, squinting into the fading August light. "Here comes the lad now. He kindly offered to help me carry the organ."

The boy was big-boned and gangling, his wrists sticking several inches out of his cotton work-shirt. His brown hair was cut so short his sunburned ears stood away from his head like vestigial wings. He'd overcome his initial shyness, when Hucko had talked to him at the pig pens, to ask how the truck worked, of which Hucko had only the faintest notion. But he had the impression that the boy, given time, might figure it out for himself. Despite his awkwardness and diffidence,

3

there was something about the way the boy looked at him with grey eyes that matched his mother's that had made Hucko uneasy without knowing exactly why.

A depression was raging in the country. Banks were failing. Many a farm Hucko had passed had a sheriff's notice of foreclosure nailed to its fence. He hadn't sold an organ in nearly three weeks, and his quota was four a week. He had a letter in his hat from his sales manager in St. Louis threatening him with dire consequences if he didn't start selling organs. He'd had doors slammed in his face, been cursed for a fool, and was even escorted from one farm at the point of a lethal-looking shovel. The week before he had begun to introduce himself as "Reverend." His sales hadn't improved since, but then neither had he been cursed nor driven off with farm implements.

To his surprise, the woman didn't object to having the organ brought into the parlor. She didn't exactly throw the door wide and dance a jig, but she didn't object. The Parson's Premier Home Organ was about the size of an easy chair, and weighed 150 lb. The boy wrapped his long arms around it, hoisted it effortlessly up out of the truck bed and, with Hucko trailing along behind with the organ bench, walked easily into the house and deposited it in the parlor without, as near as anyone could tell, taking a deep breath.

The demonstration went well for a change. Mrs. Marvel had once played the piano, although there wasn't one in the house. This was a great sales advantage. It was not unusual for Hucko to have to demonstrate to families who wouldn't know a flat from a sharp.

Mrs. Marvel played from the music book included in the price of the organ. After she'd gained command of the instrument by going through a few simple airs, Hucko turned the page to "Bringing In The Sheaves," and got mother and son singing along with him. The boy's voice was unschooled, yet it did not lack a certain hoarse sincerity. But the woman! Hucko had seldom heard the like of her sweet soprano for umblemished beauty.

At the end of the song, after the last wheezing open note had died, Hucko and the boy stood in a kind of reverent trance. Mrs. Marvel's cheeks were attractively flushed and her eyes shone with a joy that at that moment Walter Hucko would've given several years off his life to have been the personal instrument of. Emerging slowly from the fog of an erotic reverie that Mrs. Marvel's singing had enveloped him in, Hucko realized that the others' attention had shifted. The boy and his mother gazed beyond Hucko. He turned to find standing in the doorway to the parlor a fleshed-out, more care-worn version of the

4

boy. The man's face could've been quite handsome if it hadn't the stern set of one who knew right from wrong and didn't waste time arguing about it; and at that moment he was staring at Walter Hucko in a manner that left little doubt on which side of the moral equation he placed *him*.

"Oh, Luther!" the woman cried. "See what we have."

"I heard," the man replied, his eyes steady on Hucko's face.

"This is the Reverend Hucko," Mrs. Marvel said. "We've been selected by his company for a demonstration."

Luther Marvel extended a hand that swallowed Hucko's like a child's. "What church?" The man's pale eyes travelled over Hucko's houndstooth suit and came to rest on his yellow spats.

"Hard to keep a flock together in these times, so I accepted a position with the Parson's Christian Products Company, out of St. Louis, manufacturers of this wonderful organ – God's music-maker, we call it. Transforms a home into a house of worship, we say. Missus Marvel left out that you get a marvelous gift – a lovely Bible illuminated in four-colour chromolithography, bound in synthetic Moroccan leather, absolutely free . . ." Hucko was bolting his sales pitch in one agitated burst, but he couldn't seem to stop himself babbling under the man's unremitting gaze.

"We had a wonderful sing," the woman said.

Luther Marvel shifted his attention to his wife and his eyes softened. "You were in good voice, Elvira."

Hucko was dejectedly preparing himself for what he considered the inevitable, hoping only that he would have the assistance of the boy to get the organ back in the truck, when a most incredible thing happened. Mrs. Marvel took over the job of selling the organ! Hucko was so astonished by this turn of events that he didn't hear Luther Marvel's question the first time he asked it.

"I said, how much is the instrument?" Mr. Marvel repeated.

"Eighty-eight fifty," Hucko managed to stammer. "Normally we get a hundred, but we want to place a few with the most influential families, so . . ." But Hucko found he was wasting his breath. After he'd heard the price, Luther Marvel stopped listening and turned to his wife.

"You wouldn't have your trip to Chicago this winter," he said.

"We can always go to Chicago. But, Luther, to have music in the house!"

Marvel nodded gravely. "No reason hymns have to be confined to church."

5

"We can arrange a monthly plan," Hucko babbled. "Say twenty dollars now –"

"I pay cash," Marvel said. He withdrew a worn leather snap purse from his overalls, opened it, extracted a roll of bills, and counted off some. "Here are ninety dollars. I'll need change."

"In the truck," Hucko said. "I'll get it – and the Bible."

At the truck Hucko's hands were trembling so he had to calm himself with a quick nip from the bottle of whiskey he kept under the seat. His first sale in weeks! And at the sucker price, the one he always threw out first, expecting to come down as much as $20, to the company retail price; which meant he'd just made himself a $20 bonus above his commission.

When he delivered the change and the Bible, Mrs. Marvel said, "Won't you stay to supper, Reverend Hucko? We'll be sitting down in a few minutes."

"I wouldn't want to put you out."

"You won't be putting us out," Mr. Marvel said in a way that settled the matter.

The truth was Hucko was of two equally strong inclinations about staying to supper. He welcomed the opportunity to be a bit longer in the company of Elvira Marvel, but he was also afraid that he might, by some slip of the tongue or careless glance, reveal this to Mr. Marvel, the results of which, he had no doubt, would include his having to give the money back, and being ejected, probably bodily, from the house.

After Mr. Marvel had blessed the table with a long and sombre prayer the meal proceeded in silence. The food was wholesome and well prepared, and the appetites, except the boy's, all hearty, including Hucko's – he was not one to slight a free meal, no matter the internal tension of his conflicting emotions.

The boy, who Hucko had learned was called J.D., addressed his food with good manners, but he noticed a desultory and altogether woebegone air in his demeanor. This came to his attention not out of any interest in the boy, because, in truth, he was only interested in one other person in that room, but from Mrs. Marvel's solicitous glances at her son.

As she was clearing their dishes from the table, Elvira Marvel said, "Where do you plan to spend the night, Reverend Hucko? It's twenty miles to the nearest town, and dark out already."

"Why, to tell the truth, Missus Hucko, I generally bed down in the back of the truck when I'm out this far from a good hotel."

6

Elvira Marvel put an apple pie on the table and began slicing it. She shot a glance at her husband, who cleared his throat and said, "You're welcome to put your motor between the pump and the house. We haven't got a spare bedroom, but you can use our wash-house and the privy."

"Why, I'm much obliged," Walter Hucko said. "I surely am." Hucko told himself it was probably wishful thinking on his part that Elvira Marvel seemed to have prompted her husband to invite him to stay out of something more than Christian charity.

After they had eaten their dessert, they retired to the parlor where they sang hymns accompanied by Mrs. Marvel on the organ until eight-thirty, when Luther Marvel stretched his arms and said, "Bed time."

Hucko parked his truck where he had been directed and rolled out his blankets between the crated organs. He would have to uncrate another demonstrator tomorrow, but now he relaxed under the starry sky, sipping at his whiskey bottle and thinking delicious thoughts of Elvira Marvel.

It was after midnight, and a front of boiling black clouds had moved into southern Illinois to blot out the stars, when Walter Hucko was shaken awake by a gentle hand. He awoke startled, staring up into the turgid sky, to find the white orb of Elvira Marvel's face floating before his eyes like a lovely moon. Not knowing if he was dreaming or awake, and not caring in any event, he reached out to the vision before him only to have it withdrawn and his arms close on empty air.

Hucko sat up abruptly. Elvira Marvel knelt beside him in the bed of the truck. Her hair was formed in two braids that hung down her back. She hugged a blue cotton wrapper around her body. "May I speak to you?"

"Of course, dear lady." Hucko rubbed sleep from his eyes with his knuckles.

"Please – keep your voice down."

Hucko grinned at her, patted the floor of the truck bed until he found his bottle, and held it up to her. "A nip?" he whispered.

She shook her head.

"You don't mind if I do? The cold night air, and all . . ."

She shook her head again.

Hucko tilted the bottle against his mouth and took a long swallow. He wiped his mouth with the back of his hand. "You're not a farm girl," he said.

"No," she whispered. "I'm from Chicago."

7

"I knew it! I'm from Philadelphia, myself."

"You need an assistant, Reverend Hucko."

Hucko stared at her. "You –?"

"No, of course not! What do you do at the places where they don't have a man as strong and willing as J.D.? In any case, it seems to me you waste a lot of time getting someone to help you in with the organ. If you had an assistant you could carry it in straightaway."

"You don't mean the boy?"

"As you saw for yourself, he's strong. He's a good worker. He's also smart, and talks well. He can sing a bit . . ."

"Begging your pardon, Missus Marvel, and not doubting that all you say is true, but with things the way they are I have a hard enough time just keeping *me* in beans and bread."

"But that's the point, Reverend Hucko – with an assistant you could do much better. I'm sure you could."

Hucko thought for a moment. "I take it Mr. Marvel isn't exactly behind this idea?"

"If he found out he'd be very upset. That's why we have to keep our voices down." Hucko thought he saw her shiver.

"But if the boy went with me, he's bound to find out, and then he'd come after *me*." Hucko suppressed a shudder of his own.

"No, if he found out afterwards, he'd be too proud to follow. Believe me. I know him."

"I don't see why you want the boy to go with me in the first place."

"Does it matter that much?"

"Probably not. Especially since I can't take him along, anyway."

She sighed. "Next Friday he's to leave for his second year of theological school. He's not cut out to be a preacher, Reverend Hucko. He's miserable, but he's afraid to go against his father."

"Who wants a preacher for a son."

"It's what Luther wanted to be, but he had responsibilities very early in life."

"And you think he's cut out to be a travelin' man?"

"He needs to get away from here, before his life's ruined."

"Why don't you just take him over to the nearest train stop and put him on a train?"

"I haven't any money."

"Ah." Hucko got the picture. Luther had the money. And he didn't have money to send the boy anywhere but preachers' school.

"He has talent, Reverend Hucko. He has a good mind. He can figure things out – like machinery – quicker even than Luther. He

8

could be a help to you. A great help."

"He's awful young –"

"He's nearly nineteen."

"But – why did you pick me?"

"Because eventually you'll be going back to St. Louis. He needs to get to a big city, to have his opportunities. In the meantime, he can earn his way."

"You care a lot about this young fellow."

"He's my only one. I lost one two years after he was born – a girl."

"And maybe you remember what it was like when you were a girl in Chicago?"

"I'm happy with my life, Reverend Hucko." Hucko imagined her voice had a resigned tone. "But I want more for J.D."

"If that's so, why turn him over to a stranger?"

"I told you – he's to leave Friday. I don't know what else to do. And you are a man of the cloth."

"The last resort," Hucko said, but without bitterness. He held up the bottle. "Didn't this change your mind?"

"It gave me pause. But I guess lots of preachers drink. Everyone isn't a hard-shelled Lutheran."

Hucko took another swig and was silent for a long time, until, finally, Elvira Marvel said, "Won't you please take him?"

"You mean now, don't you?"

"Yes. He's up on the porch with his suitcase."

"I might take him. On condition."

"Condition?"

"Assuming we did make it to St. Louis, and assuming I had the money to do it, you'd come see him there if I paid your fare."

"Of course! Why wouldn't I –" she broke off with a little gasp.

"Now, now. Don't get the wrong idea. I'd just want a chance to see you. To talk to you."

"I'm a married woman."

"What's the harm?"

"You know what's the harm."

Hucko sighed heavily. "All right, damn it! I'll do it on one condition."

"I already told you –"

"Another condition."

"Yes?"

"That you call me Walter."

He thought he saw her smile. "Of course, Walter. I'll go and get J.D."

9

2

Hucko's Assistant

WHEN WALTER HUCKO took on J.D. Marvel as his assistant, he was thirty-eight years old. He'd spent his adult life, more than twenty years, as a "traveling man." He'd sold patent medicines from the back of a wagon. He'd sold Johnson's Granite Brand ("Endures Like The Rockies") cast-iron pots and pans door-to-door throughout the farm lands of Pennsylvania. He'd spent one summer as a pitch man for a cooch show in a carnival traveling through upstate New York until the Sheriff of Tompkins County arrested him and the four girls in the show, and he'd had to spend three days in jail, after which he was escorted to the county line by the Sheriff himself. He'd sold notions to dry-goods stores, portable forges to blacksmiths, and encyclopedias to housewives, the latter job landing him in Missouri, broke and out of work, where he had caught on with the Parson's Christian Products Company in St. Louis.

Parson's barely qualified to pluralize the third word of their name. They manufactured organs for sale, and they bought wholesale quantities of Bibles from a printer back east to give away as inducements to demonstrations of their organs. That was the sum of their "products." Although this was the most respectable job Walter Hucko had ever had, he held conflicting emotions about it. He was proud enough to be with a company of long standing and good reputation, but he was uneasy about all the restrictions Parson's tried to fetter him with. These were exemplified by the "Representatives' Rules Of Conduct" that Parson's had had printed on hundreds of cards to be handed out to their salesmen. Rule Seven, for example, said: "A Parson's Representative Never Touches Alcohol." To which Hucko had silently added his own amendment: "Except For Nervous Disorders." Hucko considered himself afflicted with a nervous disorder that periodically required curative treatment.

The first things Hucko gave his new assistant were one of the cards with the Parson's rules thereon, and a brief lecture on the Walter Hucko Sales Philosophy. He delivered the lecture while they were rattling along in the Ford truck over a rutted trail hardly suited for herding cows on. Elvira Marvel's assurances about her husband's pride preventing him giving hot pursuit aside, Hucko intended to put some distance between himself and the Marvel farm. So all of the remainder of that night and the next day they headed north, deeper into the heart of Illinois farm country.

The boy had a probing curiosity. He wanted to know all about Walter Hucko – where he was from, where he'd worked, how he got into selling organs from being a preacher. Hucko was flattered. He loved to talk, especially about himself. He found the hours spinning pleasantly by, while he regaled the boy with his story, edited here and there to gloss over his "preaching" experience and to make his life seem a bit more daring and successful than in fact it had been.

Just after noon they crossed the hills of southern Illinois that went by the grand name of the Illinois Ozarks and Hucko pulled the truck off the road to park it under a stand of bald cypress trees in a wild meadow bisected by a creek. They had a lunch of salt pork and hardtack from Hucko's provisions, washed down with cold creek water, while the truck rested from its ordeal of surmounting the Ozarks. After lunch they uncrated and began to assemble an organ for a demonstrator. Hucko found the boy a willing worker. In fact, he rather took over the assembly of the organ while Hucko sat on the ground in the shade of the truck and sampled a new bottle of whiskey that he'd removed from its storage place under the seat.

The boy was fascinated with the workings of the organ, examining the fittings and parts to deduce their function, and calling out each new discovery to Hucko, who exhibited at best a desultory interest. The storm clouds of the night and morning had given way to a porcelain sky and a merciless sun. When J.D. was finished with the organ, he descended from the bed of the truck and stood wiping the sweat from his face with a bandana he produced from his overall pocket while he looked down on Walter Hucko, sitting in his shirt-sleeves and braces, his hat on the ground beside him, the whiskey bottle in his lap.

J.D. took the Parson's Code of Conduct from his shirt pocket and read Rule Seven aloud.

11

Hucko squinted up at him in the glare of the sun, and said, "Except for nervous disorders."

The boy examined the card front and back. "I don't find that here."

"An amendment of my own. I suffer from a nervous disorder." He offered the bottle to J.D. "You look a might peaked, yourself."

J.D. took the bottle gingerly, carefully examined the label, uncorked it and took a tentative sip. Hucko had no trouble telling it was the boy's first taste from the expression on his face. J.D. handed the bottle back and went down to the creek for a drink of water.

The sun was an orange ball a few degrees above the horizon when the truck's radiator began to boil over. Hucko stopped at a farmhouse and asked permission of the woman who came to the door to use her pump. While they were cooling the radiator, Hucko said, "Maybe we should sell these good folk an organ. The lady seemed friendly enough." He was basking in a glow of confidence which selling the organ to J.D.'s parents had bestowed upon him; that Elvira Marvel had engineered the sale herself was now almost completely erased from memory by his optimistic mind.

J.D., who was manning the pump handle, paused to look around. "I don't think so," he said.

Hucko could scarcely believe his ears! It was one thing for the boy to evince a flattering interest in Hucko's life and times, and maybe he could throw an organ together faster than he imagined possible, but where did this puppy get off telling Walter Hucko where he could make a sale?

"We'll see about that!" Hucko said, and huffed off to the farmhouse to make his pitch. The friendly woman who'd granted them use of the well gave way to her decidedly unfriendly husband. Hucko was back in a matter of minutes, where he found J.D. had completed the job of cooling the radiator and was waiting patiently in the truck. Hucko got in the driver's seat while J.D. cranked the beast to life. They bounced out of the pasture and turned onto the road in silence. After they had gone a few miles, Hucko said furiously, "All right! If you're so almighty smart, *you* sell an organ."

Hucko thought this had squelched the boy's impudence once and for all. J.D. rode in silence, staring out at the cornfields that were marching by. Suddenly, he pointed. "There!" he said.

"What?"

"Turn in up there at the house."

"What are you talking about?"

12

"You said I should try to sell an organ."

"*All right!*" Hucko said grimly. "We'll just call your bluff!"

It was a neat little farmhouse, painted white, with a white rail fence around it. Down a sloping pasture stood a row of hog pens. Stubbled fields beyond attested to a recent harvest of corn. Hucko stopped in front of a gate in the fence. J.D. said, "I'll be back," and hopped out. He opened the gate, went to the back of the truck, heaved the demonstrator up in his arms and marched through the gate and up onto the porch of the farmhouse. A beagle came careening around the house, barking furiously, but at a word from J.D., dissolved into paroxysms of wriggling obsequiousness. J.D. bumped the door several times with his knee, and it opened to emit a shaft of yellow lamplight into the descending murk of twilight.

This was more than Hucko could stand. He leaped from the truck, grabbed the demonstrator bench, and trotted up to the porch while J.D. was still in conversation with the farmer who had answered the door.

"You mean Luther Marvel down in Johnson County?" the farmer was saying. He was a wiry, lean man in his fifties, his hands gnarled by years of hard work.

"Yes, sir."

"Why, how is Luther? I ain't seen him since – let's see – must be three years. It was the last Synod. Your daddy's an Elder. Guess I don't have to tell you that."

"He's just fine, sir. This is the Reverend Walter Hucko. I'm working for him. I wonder – could I put this down?"

"What in the world is it?"

"It's an organ, sir."

"Well, I'll declare. Where do you want to set her?"

"In the parlor, if it wouldn't be too much trouble. We'd like to show you how it works."

The farmer held the door for them and followed them into the parlor. J.D. put the organ on the floor, took the bench from Hucko and placed it in front of the organ. In an archway to the dining-room a hefty woman in an apron and two rangy boys and a squat girl in their teens gathered curiously.

"Sary," the farmer said. "This here is Luther Marvel's boy."

"You mean Luther Marvel down in Johnson County?" the woman asked. And when J.D. admitted that it was the same Luther Marvel, she said, "Well, I'll declare!"

The farmer offered a hand to Hucko. "Otto Gottschalk,

Reverend," he said. "You ain't Lutheran?"

"No, sir. Couldn't keep a congregation together in these times, so I went to work for the Parson's Christian Products Company, out of St. Louis, Missouri. I figure I'm still doing the Lord's work, though –"

"That's too bad," Mr. Gottschalk said, and turned back to J.D. "You have summer corn in?"

"Yes, sir. Eighty bushels the acre."

"You don't tell me! That's awful good for Johnson County. You hear that, Sary?" Sary was standing five feet away and could scarcely have missed it. "Luther Marvel got eighty bushel the acre out of that Johnson County hardpan."

"And how was your crop, Mr. Gottschalk?" J.D. asked. "Those pigs I saw looked mighty fat."

The farmer swelled a little with pride. "Near hundred bushel. 'Course we got the soil up here. It's easy to get hundred bushel."

"Mr. and Mrs. Gottschalk," Hucko said. "You've been selected for a demonstration of the Parson's –"

"That's easy to say," J.D. said. "But the other farms we passed didn't look near this prosperous."

"– Premier Home Organ, and for a wonderful gift –"

"What you doin' way up here?" Mr. Gottschalk asked J.D.

"We – the Reverend Hucko and me – are trying to sell organs."

Walter Hucko paled. That had done it! But then, he thought philosophically, it might do the boy good to be thrown out on his ear. Teach him humility.

"Is that right? Seems like a mighty hard job, times being what they are. Bank in Mt. Vernon rolled over and died last month. Not that I had any business with it. Don't believe in banks, never have."

"Neither does my daddy," J.D. said. "What we'd like to do is show you this organ, Mr. Gottschalk, and see if you wouldn't like to buy one."

"Well now, son – I reckon I just plain don't know what I'd do with an organ. If I feel the itch for organ music during the week I reckon I could just hitch up the team and drive into church and see if somebody wouldn't play some for me." He paused to laugh, a high-pitched cackle; Mrs. Gottschalk and the children joined in.

For the first time in his life Hucko was actually looking forward to losing a sale. The kid had made just about every mistake you could make.

J.D. joined in the laughter. "That's about what my daddy thought, too," he said.

14

"You don't mean to tell me Luther bought one of these contraptions?" Mr. Gottschalk asked.

"Yes, sir. As long as we got it here, would you like to see how it works?"

"Might's well."

J.D. discovered that out of the whole family only the plump girl had any musical training – she'd taken violin lessons once for a few months. J.D. seated her at the organ and asked Hucko to show her how to play it. Reluctantly, Hucko demonstrated a few simple chords, while J.D. opened the songbook he'd taken from the bench at "The Old Rugged Cross." Within minutes he had the family gathered around the organ singing. When they'd finished the hymn, Mrs. Gottschalk said, "Let me try it, Dotty," and took the girl's place at the bench, while J.D. turned the pages in the songbook to another hymn which the group sang even louder than the first. Then Dotty took over again and accompanied herself while she sang "School Days."

After Dotty was finished, the whole family began shouting out selections, but J.D. stepped forward with a hand upraised for silence. "I'm afraid we're going to have to be getting on, folks." There was a groan from the Gottschalk family.

"Can't you stay for supper?" Mrs. Gottschalk asked.

"We could have a sing-song after," Mr. Gottschalk chimed in.

"That's awful nice of you folks," J.D. said. "But we got to keep moving, if we expect to sell organs." He bent, put his arms around the organ, and lifted it.

"Now just a darn minute," Mr. Gottschalk said. "Where d'you think you're goin'?"

"Why, out to the truck," J.D. replied.

"How much did you say you wanted for it?"

"Eighty-eight fifty. Isn't that right, Reverend Hucko?"

Hucko swallowed hard and nodded.

"Twenty dollars down," J.D. said. "And you can pay the rest by the month."

"I'll bet your daddy didn't buy no organ on time," Mr. Gottschalk said.

"No, sir. He paid cash."

"Well, I reckon if a Johnson County hardpan farmer can pay cash, Otto Gottschalk can pay cash."

After he'd counted off the money into Walter Hucko's hands, Mr. Gottschalk said, "Now set that organ down, son, and you folks stay to supper. I reckon we can have us a sing-song after all."

15

"I reckon we can," J.D. said, giving Walter Hucko a big, infuriating grin.

"Pretty goddamn easy," Hucko raged. He laughed a bitter laugh. "Give me some yokel who goes to church with my old man, and I'll have him buried to his withers in organs before he knows it." They were careening down the road under a star-punctured sky. " 'My daddy got eighty bushels the acre,' " Hucko mimicked in a falsetto voice.

J.D., who'd been silent through the older man's tirade, said, "I feel bad about that."

"*Bad?* About what?"

"Actually, we got more like a hundred and twenty bushels."

Hucko stared at J.D. for a moment, and then a light of comprehension dawned in his eyes. "You made that old bastard think he'd outdone your Paw."

"I'm afraid so."

"You sold the organ," Hucko said reluctantly.

"Still, it *was* a lie."

"It wouldn't've mattered either way," Hucko said. "He was going to buy that organ if he had to arm wrestle you for it. A six-year-old imbecile could've sold it to him. It was a fluke, that's what it was."

But in the succeeding days Walter Hucko found out it was no fluke. He'd started out from St. Louis with eight organs in the back of the truck – enough, his sales manager had informed him, to last no more than two weeks before he would have to return for another supply. Within five days of selling the organ to Otto Gottschalk, J.D., with minimal assistance from Hucko, had sold the other six, four for cash, and all for the sucker price of $88.50. (Hucko hadn't bothered to tell J.D. that the company standard retail price was $20 less.) Hucko could no longer fool himself that J.D. was using some unfair advantage to make all those sales. Also, his self-interest was stronger than his pride. The boy was a born salesman, and Hucko figured the kid could make him rich. Hucko studied his technique. He came to understand that J.D. never visited farms that weren't well cared for, that didn't have a certain look of prosperity about them, whereas Hucko had been taught that canvassing a sales territory meant just that – you hit every place, plodding from one to the next. As a consequence of his selectivity, J.D. didn't waste time on prospects who couldn't afford to buy. Once in the house with the organ (and it

16

took a pretty cruel person to keep him standing on their porch with 150 lb of organ in his arms), J.D. made no bones about why he was there. He told them straight out he wanted to sell them an organ. He never mentioned the free Bible, or their being selected for a demonstration. He got the family singing. But the clinchers were when J.D. would mention that some other farmer in the neighbourhood (Gottschalk, for example) had bought an organ, and then to make as though to take the organ away. Hucko also came to understand that J.D.'s appearance made a difference. In his overalls and faded blue workshirts, he was one of the people. He saw that his own hard-boiled hat, houndstooth suit and spats were a handicap.

For each organ that was sold for cash, Hucko got to keep his standard commission of $10, plus the extra $20. For the two sold on time, he would get to keep $10 of the $20 down-payment, and the Parson's Company would pay him the remaining twenty out of the time payments the farmers made. So it was that he found himself having earned $200 cash, and $40 on the company account, in just a week. He'd never made so much money in so short a time in his life.

After they'd sold their sixth organ, and were parked along the road while J.D. assembled the last one, Hucko said, "I been thinking about what I ought to pay you. I figure I can either put you on salary or commission."

J.D. stuck his head over the edge of the truck bed, to peer down at Hucko sitting in the shade with his whiskey bottle. "How do you mean?"

"Thirty dollars a month or two dollars on each organ we sell."

J.D. thought a moment. "That mean on commission you'd owe me fourteen dollars?"

"That's right."

"I'll take commission."

Which is just what Hucko had hoped. He wanted the boy motivated to sell organs. By giving him a choice, he'd got his mind working on the decision, rather than studying about what was a fair price. He told himself he still knew a thing or two about selling.

The morning after they'd sold their last organ, Hucko said, "Well, I'll be heading for St. Louis."

Excitement sparked the boy's eyes.

"You want to come along?"

"I thought that was agreed to."

"It was agreed to on condition."

"Condition?"

"I'm not running any trolley, here. If you're going to stick with me, why, I reckon I'll take you along to St. Louis. If you aren't you might as well get out now."

"How do you mean – stick with you?"

"I'm going to St. Louis to pick up some more organs and have a day or two of rest. Then I'm heading back out on the road. If you want to do that, okay. If not, say so."

The boy thought about it for a moment, and then gave Hucko that look of his, his head tilted and his grey eyes wide. "How long do you mean?"

"Well, I don't mean for ever. Nothing's for ever. One more trip, and we'll see after that."

"Fair enough."

Hucko headed the truck east.

3

Wanda Agronsky and the Genius

1910

THE ONLY GIRLS that J.D., at twenty, had known were those of the farm country where he grew up. They were a sturdy lot, made robust and hale from farm work and heavy diets, their calloused hands shaped more for pitchforks than parasols. So when he first set eyes upon Wanda Agronsky's delicate beauty in the lobby of the Blackstone Hotel in Chicago it couldn't have seemed more alien to him than if she'd just stepped out of Jules Verne's moon rocket.

It was noon and the dust of their travels was still on their clothes as J.D. and Hucko crossed the lobby, carrying their battered Gladstone bags, J.D. gawking at the vaulting grandeur of the marble columns and the crystal chandeliers glittering over their heads. A banner was festooned over the desk bearing the message: "Welcome Parson's Sales Agents." This was a new program for Parson's, the first time in the two years J.D. had been with them they'd so honored their top salesmen, and J.D. was excited at the prospect of three days of luxury at the expense of the company. Then, as he and Walter turned from the desk after signing in, he saw her.

She was emerging from open double doors that connected to the lobby. Through the doors J.D. caught a glimpse of rows of folding chairs and, beyond, a small stage. She was walking at the head of a group of men dressed uniformly in dark suits and vests. They were middle-aged men, portly, well-fleshed, their ample waists anchored side-to-side by large gold watch chains, and they were bending their heads toward the girl as she talked – those farther back trying to get closer – so that she had the appearance of being swept along before a wave of black wool crested with florid faces. She was dressed in a white shirt-waist and a navy-blue skirt that fit her hips and waist tightly and then flared out and down to just conceal the tops of high-laced patent-leather shoes. Her long yellow hair was pinned at the back of her head in an upsweep, and seemed to J.D. to give off golden flashes in the light of the crystal chandeliers. She was talking as she walked, and making gestures with her hands, her head held high, her eyes meeting those of the men around her boldly. She wasn't very tall, but slender, with delicate wrists and a long neck that supported her well-shaped head. She might've been taken for a mere girl if it weren't for the sure way she carried herself and the bold, questing look in those wide-set blue eyes. Her walk was fast and sure, her whole being informed with a kind of determined purpose, toward what or whom J.D. couldn't say, but which, the minute he set eyes on her, he longed to know.

J.D. sort of froze to the spot when he saw Wanda Agronsky that first time, just stood there like he'd grown roots, with his old Gladstone in one hand and his room key in the other, while the girl and her entourage passed not ten feet from him – and as she went by the girl's eyes met his. It was only for a moment, a glancing contact, but J.D. felt as if sparks had been struck from his eyes. He watched her and her escorts until they disappeared through the doors of the hotel dining-room on the other side of the lobby. He was suddenly painfully aware of his dusty clothes. Hucko and he had been in the middle of Indiana selling organs when the word came about the convention, and they'd only just had time to put the truck on the road to Chicago. The Ford had broken down twice and J.D. still had grease on his clothes and hands from fixing it the last time. That yellow-haired girl had given him one quick look and that was all, and he knew why: no girl that pretty would give anyone who looked as he must a second glance. And she might never look at him again, but he promised himself that while he was in Chicago he would be ready if she did.

The Blackstone Hotel was one of the most modern in the country. J.D.'s room had another, smaller room connected to it that contained a sink, a toilet and a bathtub. After he'd unpacked his Gladstone he stripped down, drew a tub of hot water, and soaked the road grime out of his pores. Then he dressed in a new suit he'd bought in Indianapolis. It was made of grey Buchanan's English worsted with a navy-blue Italian-silk lining, cut to the latest fashion. The coat was four-button, tube-shaped, with narrow lapels. The trousers tapered to brush the tops of his gleaming black congress boots. Under the coat he wore a blue Cassimer vest, silk shirt with detachable cuffs and collar, and a maroon cravat. A derby hat of black nutria with a maroon silk band crowned all. In the closet hung an overcoat that he'd bought along with the suit. It was tall, with sweeping skirts, double-breasted and

20

made from a soft navy-blue material that the salesman had called chinchilla cloth. The outfit had cost him nearly $200 and now, as he stood in front of the mirror in his room putting his hat on, he told himself it was worth it.

The first meeting of the convention was scheduled for three o'clock that afternoon. J.D. used the time to get a haircut and a shave in the hotel barbershop. Lying back in the barber's chair with hot towels soaking his beard, feeling the silken touch of his shirt against his skin, he promised himself that he would never ever again be poor. Oh, he might have to dress as if he were in order to sell organs, but he would have only the finest when he wasn't on the road. The finest clothes, the finest hotels, the finest food. He wanted to add, the finest women, but then he remembered the cursory and uninterested sweep of the yellow-haired girl's eye across him, and suddenly all his fine clothes and all the cash in his money belt now locked in the hotel safe were as nothing.

That first sales meeting seemed to J.D. more like one of the tent revival shows that used to set up once in a while in a field at the county seat back home. The sales manager of Parson's gave a rousing talk to the assembled salesmen that rivaled that of any hell's-fire preacher J.D. had ever heard. Then songbooks were passed out and they sang words about Parson's and their organs that had been set to popular tunes, with the sales manager himself playing a Parson's Home Organ and leading the singing. The last song was set to the tune of "Yankee Doodle":

> A Parson's agent went on the road,
> Canvassing all the houses;
> And there he sold to all he saw,
> Premier Home Organs.
> Parson's Agent, keep it up;
> Parson's Agent, sell 'em;
> Mind the demo and the pitch,
> And you will make your quota.

As childish as the words were, J.D. was surprised at the strong feelings aroused in him by singing them. It was a cross between patriotic zeal, religious fervor and avarice. And looking around him at the faces of the other salesmen, he saw he was not alone. When they were discharged from the meeting for dinner at six o'clock they burst forth into the lobby like a troop of Rough Riders charging San Juan Hill.

21

Across the lobby, the meeting-room from where he had seen the yellow-haired girl emerge was open and unoccupied. Instead of following his comrades into dinner, J.D. slipped into the room. Wooden folding chairs were arrayed in neat rows before a small stage shielded from his view by a curtain. J.D. went up the steps at one side, pushed the curtain back, and stepped behind it. In the dim illumination shed by a light backstage he saw a strange collection of machines. He studied them, ran his hands over them, twisted a dial here, pushed a button there, but for the life of him he couldn't figure out what they were for. All he could determine was that they operated on electricity (there was a tangle of cords and plugs running across the stage floor) and that somehow they used or produced (or both) cards with holes punched in them.

"Are you finding what you're after?"

J.D. spun, banging his elbow against the metal case of a machine, to find the yellow-haired girl regarding him with the curtain in her hand where she'd come through it. Her eyes were cold, and her voice had an edge of anger to it.

J.D. removed his hat. "Didn't hear you come in. Hello."

"Who are you working for?" the girl asked. "Pidgin and Hunt?"

"No, ma'am. Parson's Theological Products."

"Of course you are," she said. "What did P. and H. pay you to steal our designs?"

He was struck dumb by her accusation. She moved closer.

"I've seen you before," she said. "Was it at the Census Bureau?"

"Actually, I've never been –"

"You were there with Pidgin when he was trying to undercut our contract."

"Only time I ever saw you was in the lobby of this hotel, around noon today." J.D. was beginning to get mad.

For the first time a look of doubt appeared on the girl's face. "The lobby?"

"You went sailing by me with a pack of old men baying at your heels."

"The dusty man with the long hair?" She looked at his new suit.

"Minus the dust and some hair."

She was embarrassed now. "I apologize."

"Accepted. Miss – ?"

"Agronsky. Wanda Agronsky." She held out a hand.

J.D. said his name and took her hand.

Her grip was strong.

"Who is this Pidgin?"

"A competitor. May I ask what you're doing back here, Mr. Marvel?"

"Curiosity. My company's meeting just across the lobby."

"You said theological products?"

"We sell organs."

"To churches?"

"To homes. Small organs."

"You see, we're in a very competitive business. Our competitors would love to steal our designs."

"I couldn't make heads or tails of these machines."

"Tabulating machines. In fact, that's the name of our company. The Tabulating Machine Company."

J.D. shook his head. "I don't know any more now than I did before. What's your job with this outfit?"

"I'm a tab operator. I demonstrate the machines. Perhaps you'd like to see a demonstration."

"Indeed I would!" J.D. replied enthusiastically.

"I'll be conducting one with our president in the morning at ten o'clock." She produced a card from her handbag. "Here's an invitation."

"I'll be there."

The next morning at breakfast J.D. told Hucko he wasn't going to the Parson's meeting.

"But you've got to!" Hucko protested.

"I've other things to do."

"They're going to present us to the meeting," Hucko said. "I wanted it to be a surprise. They're giving us an award –"

"You accept for both of us," J.D. said.

"But, J.D.!" Hucko found himself talking to an empty chair.

J.D. presented his invitation to the attendant at the door and took a seat in the back row. The curtains had been opened to reveal the machines. In repose they seemed to J.D. to exude some mysterious and awesome power. The audience was composed of those same dark-suited middle-aged men. A stout man with greying red hair, a huge walrus mustache, and watery blue eyes behind tiny wire-rimmed spectacles stepped onto the stage and faced them.

"Gentlemen," he began. "This is our final demonstration. In a moment the operator will perform a detailed cost-accounting procedure. The Pennsylvania Steel Company has been using this procedure for the past five years. The Philadelphia and Erie Railroad, the Buffalo and Allegheny Railroad – the Pennsylvania Railroad itself – have all installed our machines using them for cost accounting, payrolls, daily distribution of labor costs. I could go on. Studebaker Brothers at South Bend keep an inventory of their lumber supply with our help. Pope Manufacturing, the bicycle-makers, have used our machines for years. There is hardly a major industry in the United States that hasn't found use for our equipment.

"Now, I am not a salesman. I am an engineer. I do not employ salesmen for the very simple reason that our equipment sells itself. It is the best equipment available – the latest design, the most reliable, the fastest to do your work. If that, coupled with the obvious applications for these machines, won't sell you on them, well . . . a bunch of grinning, back-slapping drummers certainly can't." Wanda Agronsky came onto the stage and stood by one of the machines. "Yesterday," the man with the walrus mustache continued, "you saw payrolls, inventories, shop order costs, and labor distributions. In this audience are executives from railroads, steel mills, and automobile manufacturers. Everything we've demonstrated, including the cost-accounting routine we will show you today, can be quickly adapted to your particular businesses. At the conclusion of the demonstration four of us from the company will be available to answer questions and take orders. I must advise you that there is a six months' backlog."

There was a murmur from the audience. "Miss Agronsky, please begin."

J.D. had never heard a sales pitch, if it could be called that, like it. The walrus-mustached man had delivered his little lecture in stern tones. His attitude seemed to be: Buy my machines or be damned. And yet, if J.D. was any judge of sales prospects, much of the audience seemed primed to buy, leaning forward in their seats to listen intently.

Much of what followed was beyond J.D.'s comprehension, yet he was dazzled by it all. Wanda Agronsky's movements among the machines had a kind of balletic quality. Her slim hands flew unerringly to buttons and levers. At her touch thousands of cards spun into machine pockets so fast that they appeared to be a continuous ribbon. Paper chunked through print carriages in a clatter of rising and falling type bars. She ripped paper from the printer, removed cards and stacked them in boxes and, twenty minutes after she had begun, was done. She shut off the machines and passed through the audience handing out sheets of paper that had been printed, while the walrus-mustached man stood on the stage explaining what had been accom-

24

plished. J.D. stared uncomprehendingly at the sheet of paper Wanda handed him while the man's voice droned on in what for J.D. might as well have been a foreign language. He used strange terms that J.D. had never heard. Terms like "cross-footing," "plug-boards," "automatic sorters," and "key punches."

J.D. waited until the meeting-room was nearly cleared before he approached Wanda Agronsky.

"How did you like the demonstration?" she asked.

"I didn't understand the half of it, but I liked it."

She smiled. "How can you like something you don't understand?"

"That will take some explaining. Could I buy you lunch?"

She looked at a Lavalière watch. "It's only just eleven. I've got to see the machines packed for shipment back to Washington."

"You're going to Washington?" J.D. felt a sudden emptiness.

"No. Dr. Hollerith has assigned me to the Chicago office. It's just a small staff now – I'll be the only tabulating-machine operator."

"Dr. Hollerith? Is he the fellow with the big mustache?"

"Yes. Herman Hollerith. You mean you haven't heard of him?"

"No." For some reason he felt like a fool admitting it.

"I keep forgetting that not everyone is in this business. Would you like to meet him? He's the inventor of those machines."

"I'd like that a lot."

Hollerith fixed him with his little blue eyes. "Marvel. What line of work are you in?"

"I'm a sales agent for Parson's Theological Products."

"The ones having the convention here? I don't hold much with religion, myself. Now, science – there's something a man can have logical faith in."

"I agree," J.D. said. "About not holding with religion, I mean. I don't know much about science."

"Then what in the world are you doing with a theology outfit?" Hollerith asked.

"I sell organs to farm folk."

"That's the extent of your theology?"

J.D. grinned. "We sing a hymn or two when we demonstrate the organ."

Hollerith chuckled. "Did Wanda tell you we're staffing a new office here? Only our second branch office. The other's in New York. We're looking for bright young people to work for us."

"I'm afraid what I know about those machines of yours wouldn't fill the brain of an ant."

25

"Excellent! Just what I'm looking for. I want young people I can train from scratch, who don't have their heads full of the wrong stuff. I want bright, presentable people. You're certainly presentable. And if you're a friend of Wanda's, you have to be bright."

"I'd be interested in finding out more about it."

"Good! I'll be in our Chicago office this afternoon. Come by at three. Wanda can tell you how to get there." He turned to two workmen who were lifting one of the machines between them. "Careful! That's not a sack of potatoes you've got there." He strode towards the stage.

After the machines had been loaded into a truck, Wanda Agronsky went to lunch with J.D. Over salad she said, "Now tell me about this contradiction."

"Well, on the one side I know very little about those machines of yours. On the other, I have this itch to know. It seems to me that there was something important happening in there this morning."

"Important! That's not the half of it. Let me tell you something, Marvel –" she pointed her fork at him. "Those machines have revolutionized business and government. Yes, a revolution! And ninety percent of the people in this country aren't even aware it's going on, so don't feel bad that you didn't either." She looked up into the red face of Walter Hucko, who had approached hurriedly as she spoke.

"J.D.!" Hucko cried. "Where have you been? The sales manager's been lookin' high and low for you."

J.D. introduced Wanda to Hucko. Hucko nodded absentmindedly at the girl and returned to J.D. "He was mighty upset you didn't show for the presentation. I told him you were sick in your room, but then he went up there to see if he could help out and found you gone. I tell you, J.D., he's fit to be tied."

"Listen, Walter – Miss Agronsky here is a tabulator operator."

"A what?"

"Tabulating machines. I'm trying to learn something about them."

"We're organ salesmen, J.D. The best there are! What are you –" Then Hucko took another look at Wanda Agronsky. "I see."

"What is that supposed to mean?" Wanda Agronsky asked icily.

J.D. stood and took Hucko by the elbow. "I'll be back in a minute," he said to Wanda.

He led Hucko away from the tables. "Look, Walter. I'm onto something big."

"We *got* something big, J.D.," Walter said desperately.

"How long do you think we can sell organs?"

"I don't know. Years! How much money did you make this last year?"

"That's not the point. This lady, and her boss, their company, are manufacturing machines like you never heard of. They do fantastic things. Accounting, arithmetic . . ."

"I *bet* I never heard of them! Ten thousand! That's what you made last year. You know there're presidents of companies don't make ten thousand? You know that?"

J.D. nodded patiently. "I know we made ten thousand apiece last year. I know we're making more than a lot of people. But that's not enough for me, Walter."

"Look, J.D. Have your fun, okay? She's a tasty piece, I grant you. But don't ruin what we got. If I hadn't promised the sales manager you'd straighten up for the rest of the convention, I swear he was about to fire you."

"How can he fire me? I'm his best salesman."

"You hurt his pride in front of the rest of the agents. He can't stand for that. What do you mean ten thousand isn't enough for you?"

"I mean it's not just the money. I want to get into something with a future. Organ-selling is going to be the past, very soon, Walter. The day of the drummer is about gone. Pretty soon every farmer will have a car and telephone. How're you going to keep him in the parlor singing hymns when that happens?"

"Okay," Hucko said. He took a deep breath. "Okay. So you have to look into this new-fangled business." He paused, struck by a thought. "It's not a medicine machine?"

"Medicine machine?"

"Sends out electrical waves that cures rheumatism, gout, that sort of thing? I got hooked into such a thing once. Dr. Wizard's Health Magneto. You grabbed this knob with one hand, turned the crank with the other –"

"It's nothing like that, Walter."

"Well, that's good. Because that thing didn't work worth a damn. Damn near got shot once, and left one county just ahead of the sheriff. Promise me this, J.D., that you'll attend the rest of the meetings, and lay a little sugar on the sales manager. If you get fired, I – well, damnit, J.D. – I don't want to have to break in a new partner."

"New partner? Listen, Walter. Whatever I do – you're my partner."

"I appreciate that. Just remember – we know how to sell organs.

27

We know we can make good money doing it."

"I'll keep that in mind."

"Now, will you come over and spread a little honey on the sales manager?"

"No, I won't. If the sales manager wants to fire me, after all the money we've made for Parson's, let him. We'll go onto better things. You'll see."

Hucko shook his head sadly. "I'll try to smooth it over. At least come to the meeting this afternoon."

"Can't. Got an appointment."

Hucko moaned piteously. "That tears it. He'll fire you for sure. And I'll have to quit."

J.D. patted Hucko's shoulder. "Trust me, friend."

Back at their table, Wanda Agronsky said, "What did that little man mean, Marvel?"

"Mean?"

"Don't play the innocent. I suppose you fancy yourself a gold-plated cad. I've run into your type before."

"No, ma'am, I don't. You want to know the truth, I haven't had a girlfriend since high school, and she milked cows a lot better than she courted."

"*Cows?*"

"I was raised on a farm in the southern part of the state. Since I left home I've been traveling farm country selling organs and, let me tell you, the opportunities to be a gold-plated cad are few and far between."

"That's a mighty fancy suit for a farm boy."

J.D. grinned. "You should see me on the road. Overalls and clodhoppers. If I showed up at a farm in this outfit I couldn't sell a bucket of water in a drought."

"Listen, Marvel. Don't lose your job on my account. Not everyone is cut out for the tabulator business. Don't give up a sure thing for a pipe dream."

"I won't lose it on your account, I promise you. You see, Miss Agronsky, I was fed up with the organ business a long time before I saw those machines of yours. Walter and I've managed to put aside a bit of money, and I'm looking around for something else for us to do. The tabulator business may be a pipe dream, I don't know. But right now it sort of looks like the business of the future to me."

"You're right, Marvel! You don't know how right!" Wanda

28

Agronsky leaned earnestly over the table. "Do you know what our essential business is?"

J.D. thought a moment. "Calculations?"

"Not calculations. Not payrolls. Not cost accounting. It's information! Sure, we do payrolls. But from the payroll process, along with writing the checks, I can have the tab punch out cards that go into our labor-distribution routine. It provides managers with labor costs by product or activity. Information! From the cost-accounting routine I can create data cards for the inventory routine which can then be used to automatically replenish stocks. Listen to this, Marvel. When I was in Boston recently I talked to an engineer at MIT who thinks it would be possible to calculate a thing called 'economic order quantities' on the tabulator for our inventory runs. That could save a large business thousands – maybe millions – by reducing the expense of inventories. Information! That's the business we're in."

"How many clerks will one of those machines replace?"

"It depends. I recently installed four machines, along with sorters and key punches, in the payroll department of a steel mill. They took the place of fifty clerks."

"And how much money was saved?"

"The rental on the machines is a bit over eight hundred a month. The cost of the clerks was nearly four thousand."

J.D. whistled. "My God! Are you sure you're charging enough for the machines?"

"That's up to Dr. Hollerith. But think of this, Marvel. That eight hundred a month will be coming in for years. After the cost of the machines are paid for some time in the second year, it's all profit."

"And with a few hundred places like that steel mill –"

"Hundred? Thousands! Do you realize how many businesses there are in this country?"

J.D. shook his head admiringly. "That's no pipe dream, Miss Agronsky."

"Wait till you talk to Dr. Hollerith before you burn your bridges, though, is my advice, Marvel."

4

The Modern Woman

THE CHICAGO BRANCH of the Tabulating Machine Company occupied two cramped offices in a run-down building on south Clark Street. Herman Hollerith sat at a desk piled with papers and books. J.D. took the only other chair in the room.

Hollerith leaned back in his swivel chair and gazed at J.D. through his steel-rimmed spectacles.

"We are an expanding company, sir. It is a simple business to describe. I and my engineering staff in Washington design the machines, my shop on 31st Street in Washington puts them together. We ship them to customers. We provide maintenance to the machines after they're installed. And that's the business. It is in the running of the machines themselves, adapting them to the work of particular customers, where you might, after proper training, be of use."

"Seems like something's missing, Dr. Hollerith. What about selling the machines?"

"If the machines are any good they will sell themselves. We have a backlog of orders, which is our biggest problem. I spend far too much of my time trying to expedite parts for assembly. Gradually, we are taking on the manufacture of the parts ourselves. If you ever run a manufacturing business, Mr. Marvel, take my advice and make yourself independent of sub-contractors."

"I'd say you're mighty lucky to have products that sell themselves."

"It's not luck, sir! It's engineering skills! Our machines are the best, and they were the first. I see you joining us as a tabulating-machine operator trainee. You would work with Miss Agronsky for six months." He held up a pamphlet. "We have the training program spelled out here." He leaned across the desk to hand the pamphlet to

30

J.D. "After six months, assuming you performed as one would expect, you would become a Tabulating Machine Operator, Grade One. You can rise as high as Grade Four. Miss Agronsky is a Grade Three. A remarkable woman! She's been with us only eighteen months. You might also get into management. We expect the Chicago office to expand. Or we might require your services in New York, or at Headquarters in Washington. The opportunities are boundless."

"Does that mean you're offering me a job?"

"It does."

"Well, sir, there're two things –"

"Yes?"

"I've a partner. We've been together a long time, and we made a pact to stick together."

"By all means, let us speak to him. Can he come in today? I'm leaving in the morning."

"I think he could."

"Excellent. We need earnest, bright young men."

"Well, he's not quite as young as I am."

"How old is he?"

"Ah, I expect Walter is in his thirties somewhere."

"That is older than we generally consider."

"I can't take the job without him."

"Well, I'll talk to him. You said two things."

"The second is salary."

Hollerith bridged his fingers under his chin. "I think you'll find that a pleasant surprise. Our employees are among the highest paid in the country."

"I wonder if I could get some specifics, Dr. Hollerith?"

"Of course, of course. As a trainee you, and your friend, if he came with us, would start at a hundred and fifty dollars a month. That would rise to one hundred and seventy-five dollars at the end of the six-month training period, provided you met our standards. It is no secret among the staff that Miss Agronsky makes two hundred and twenty-five dollars a month."

Hollerith chuckled. "Well, sir, I can see that took your breath. It takes some getting used to, to think that you could be making nearly three thousand a year within the next couple of years."

"I'll tell you the truth, Dr. Hollerith, it *would* take some getting used to. I don't think I could do it."

"What's that?"

"I made ten thousand this past year."

31

"I find that hard to believe! Why, no one in this company makes that kind of money!"

"Aside from you?"

"Yes, of course, aside from me. What I make is no concern here. After all, I am the inventor of the machines we sell."

"Don't take me wrong, Dr. Hollerith. I'm sure you deserve every nickel. But, since the only job in the company that pays more than I make now is filled, it doesn't look like I'd be giving myself much of a future by coming with you."

"And let me assure you that we wouldn't want you, with that attitude. But if you think selling organs has a future, I think you're in for a rude surprise." He stood.

J.D. got to his feet. "Oh no, sir. You, and the demonstration by Miss Agronsky, have convinced me that this is the business for me. I'm just going to have to get in an end of it that pays more."

In the outer office J.D. found Wanda Agronsky at a desk. "Well, Marvel?"

"We couldn't strike a deal."

"I hope you're not disappointed. I tried to tell you that Dr. Hollerith offers jobs to very few."

"Yes, you did. I wonder, Miss Agronsky —" J.D. paused. "I appreciate your help, and I wonder if I might buy you dinner."

"That's not necessary, Marvel."

"I know it's not necessary, but —" J.D. could feel his face burning. "I'd like to do it."

Wanda Agronsky looked at him for a moment. "All right," she said. "I'll be finished at six."

Back at the hotel J.D. found a distraught Walter Hucko pacing the lobby.

"Well, that cracked it," Hucko moaned. "You're axed. And I got so goddamned mad, I quit."

"Good for you, Walter."

"Good for me! Good for me! I just threw away the best job I ever had."

J.D. took his elbow. "You look like you could use a drink, Walter." He guided him toward the bar. They took a table and ordered beer.

Hucko massaged his eyes. "What a mess!"

"Listen, Walter. We're better off out of Parson's. We're going to do all right, you'll see."

Hucko peered at him from red-rimmed eyes. "You got the job?"

J.D. shook his head. "It wasn't the right deal. But it's the right business."

"How do you mean, not the right deal?"

"They wanted someone to demonstrate machines, and to wire them up for customers. Nothing wrong with that. I'd like to learn about it. But they pay peanuts for that kind of work. I've been thinking – the end of this business we need to get into, the end that can use our talents the best, and where we can make big money, is the selling end. Unfortunately the man I talked to doesn't believe in selling."

Hucko laughed tragically. "Let me tell you something, J.D. I'm a drummer. Those folks you been palling with aren't even in the same country as me. How the hell am I going to sell something I don't know the first thing about?"

J.D. sipped his beer. "I'm going to show you that you know more about it than you think. Miss Agronsky told me they put some machines in the offices of a steel mill. They charged eight hundred a month for them. But the machines replaced clerks that cost the steel mill four thousand a month."

Hucko stared at J.D. "You mean to tell me it saved the steel mill thirty-two hundred a month?"

J.D. nodded solemnly. "What do you think of that, Walter?"

"I think they're idiots! Why, if they just split the savings, the steel mill ought to be happy."

"I had the very same thought." J.D. gripped Hucko's arm. "There are thousands of businesses in this country, Walter – each one ripe for those machines."

"There are other companies?"

"Must be."

"But this fellow Hollerith has the best machines. So he claims."

J.D. looked at him in surprise. "Where did you hear that?"

"I picked up one of their pamphlets in the lobby. It was written in high-falutin' language, but it was pretty convincing. This Hollerith invented those machines, it claims."

"He did."

"Well, how're we going to go up against that? No wonder he doesn't need salesmen."

"Let me ask you something, Walter. Who invented the organ? You don't know, and neither do I. Who has the best home organ on the market? There aren't two ways about it – it's Wurlitzer, isn't it? Their organ will play rings around a Parson's. But how many Wurlitzers did we run into out on the road? Very few! Why?"

"They don't hire drummers. You have to buy them in a store."
J.D. nodded. "See my point?"

"I see it. Only, these machines aren't organs."

"No, they aren't the same. But I'll bet the principle's the same. No matter how good the product, you have to get out and sell it."

"Marvel," Wanda Agronsky said. "If you'll buy a chicken, I'll cook it at my place. You can't get a good meal at a restaurant in this town for under a dollar." They were standing on Clark Street in front of the Tabulating Machine Company offices. The wind off the lake was icy.

"It's a deal," J.D. said.

They caught a trolley to Wanda Agronsky's neighborhood in northeast Chicago. It was an area of small homes and modest stores. They stopped at a grocery store. She selected a chicken, and J.D. paid for it.

Wanda Agronsky rented a three-room bungalow that had a grade school on one side and a vacant lot on the other. The living-room sported a small fireplace with a gas log and sparse but tidy furnishings.

"You light the log," Wanda said, "and I'll get the chicken started." Wanda returned to the living-room with a bottle of wine, a corkscrew and two glasses. "Open this while I get rid of our coats."

When they were seated on a spindly Empire couch with their glasses of wine, Wanda said, "I hope you like stewed chicken."

"I like it a lot," J.D. replied.

"You didn't tell me the truth," she said.

"I didn't?"

"You said Dr. Hollerith hadn't offered you a job."

"You assumed that."

"He thinks you might have exaggerated what you make selling organs."

"He's wrong."

"You actually make ten thousand a year?"

"Last year, I did. This coming year I expected to make more."

"Expected?"

"I'm no longer associated with Parson's."

"I feel responsible for that."

"I'd made up my mind before I saw Hollerith to get into this business of yours."

Wanda studied the color of her wine in the light of the glass log. "I don't know where you'll make that kind of money."

"Oh, I don't have to, starting off. I just need to know that the possibilities are there."

"Dr. Hollerith said you wouldn't work without your friend."

"That's right."

"The one in the dining-room?"

"Yes."

"Frankly, do you think he's the type? We have to present a conservative, business-like appearance."

"Walter can learn. I'll have to learn myself."

"But spats? Checked suits?"

"He can buy new clothes."

"It's not that. It's just that he's so obviously a drummer."

"I don't go anywhere without Walter. He's my partner. If it weren't for him, I'd be graduating from theological school next spring."

"Theological school!" Wanda stared at him.

J.D. grinned. "Believe me, it wasn't my idea."

"Your mother?"

"My father. It was Mother who arranged for Walter to take me on as his assistant."

"I admire your loyalty, Marvel. I hope it's not misplaced."

J.D. studied her profile in the firelight. It was sharply etched: long forehead, small nose, full red lips. Her blonde hair was pulled back over her ears and caught at the back of her head by a clip. He imagined he could almost feel the texture of her smooth, pale flesh under his fingers.

She turned and studied him solemnly. "How old are you?"

"Does it matter?"

"I suppose not. Sometimes I think you're about my age, and other times, like now, you look like a choirboy."

"I didn't ask *your* age."

"I didn't mean to offend you. I don't mind telling you my age. I'm twenty-five."

There was a heavy silence that played on J.D.'s nerves. "Okay," he said finally. "I'm twenty."

She nodded. "I thought so. It's those clothes that make you look older. Can I give you some advice?"

"Sure," he said stiffly.

"Always dress well. It pays. I'll bet you laid out a pretty penny for that suit."

"I suppose I did."

"It gives you character. Attracts respect. And you wear it very well.

Never go for the bargain clothes."

"Okay. Anything else, Professor?"

She smiled. "That's all for now."

They ate their dinner on a card table in front of the fireplace. Wanda Agronsky's cooking skills would never threaten great chefs. The stewed chicken was stringy, the potatoes underdone, but J.D.'s farm-bred appetite overcame the meal's culinary deficiencies. At least the coffee was good. J.D. pushed his plate back after disposing of his third helping.

"You're a pleasure to cook for, I must say, Marvel."

"It was fine."

"You're not a very good liar."

"Well – it was plentiful."

"That it was. I don't usually go to much trouble. It's not worth cooking just for myself."

"I would've guessed you had lots of fellows."

"Men are attracted to my looks. But before long they usually find me too strong for their taste."

"Strong?"

"Most men are looking for a simpering girl who will swoon over their manly frames."

"You are about the most outspoken girl I ever met."

"I'm not a girl," she said. "I'm twenty-five years old, remember? I'll bet you were raised to think that women were like delicate plants, to be mollycoddled, but never, never to be treated as if they had a brain in their heads."

"Oh, I don't know," J.D. said. "Although, most of the girls I knew acted like they didn't have a brain."

"And who do you suppose taught them to act that way?"

"I haven't the foggiest notion."

"You didn't have sisters, I take it?"

He shook his head. "Or brothers, either."

"Well, then – your mother?"

"No. My mother has brains, and she isn't afraid to show them."

"I'll bet your father made the decisions, though. Like your going to theological school."

"He's a strong man. Once he makes up his mind, that's it."

"And your mother had better go along."

"She has her ways of getting around him."

"But why should she have to!"

Her face was attractively flushed by the heat of her emotions.

36

"I don't know why she has to," he said honestly.

Wanda Agronsky smiled suddenly. "You know, Marvel, you're not a bad sort. Perhaps even rare – I don't know. I think I'm going to like you."

After the dishes were cleared away, and J.D. had folded the card table and returned it to its place in the hall closet, Wanda brought a bottle of brandy and two glasses from the kitchen. She took a hand-carved wooden box from the mantel, opened it, and offered it to J.D. It contained cigarettes. He refused. He couldn't help staring as she took one and lighted it.

"I suppose you've never seen a woman smoke."

"I can't say as I have."

"Do you find it offensive?" she asked as she let smoke trickle from her nostrils.

"No."

"What then?" She asked with a touch of defiance.

"Curious. Interesting."

She gave him a little smile. "Why shouldn't women smoke?"

He shrugged. "Beats me."

"I mean, men smoke wherever and whenever they please."

"That's true."

"You're saying it doesn't really matter?"

"Not to me."

Her smile broadened. "You know, Dr. Hollerith was furious that you turned him down." She chuckled. "He's used to having his own way."

"I imagine he's a little tough to work for."

"Oh, no –" she grinned. "Not as long as he stays in Washington."

"He did tell me one thing that almost made me take the job, cut in pay or not."

"What's that?"

"He said I'd be working with you for six months."

She tossed her cigarette into the fireplace. "Would you like to kiss me, Marvel?"

"Yes, I would!"

She stood and held her arms up. "Then why don't you?"

He stood, stepped between her arms, and put his hands on her slim, supple waist. He placed his lips on hers very gently. But she brought her hands to his neck and crushed her mouth against his. He could smell the delicate odor of the soap she used, feel her tongue dart between his lips, her lips working against his, the brandy coursing through his veins . . .

She pulled back to look up at him. "Are you all right?"

He nodded.

"You're trembling."

"Yes?"

"No wonder. It's stifling in here." She stepped to a window and opened it. "Take your coat off."

They sat on the couch together. She took his arm, placed it around her neck, and held his hand.

"Did you ever live in a city, Marvel?"

"I've hardly ever been in a city, except St. Louis."

"How did you like St. Louis?"

"I don't know. Walter and I were only there for a day or so every couple of months."

She very gently ran her fingernails over the back of J.D.'s hand in a way that made him shiver with pleasure. "And I've never been on a farm. I was born in the city. On the south side."

"Do your parents live here?"

"Yep. My mother has given up on me, though."

"Given up?"

"She thinks I should be married with six kids underfoot. Married to a good Polish Catholic boy. And then when I'm fifty, like she is, I can have rheumatism and chilblains and nervous headaches from trying to take care of them and my oaf of a husband, like she has."

"You don't mean you father's an oaf?"

"Sure he is. He's no different than any of the other Polish men on the south side, or the Italians, or the Jews, or any of them. They're dumb, Marvel – just dumb, not malicious."

"You've told your folks this?"

"And a hell of a lot more. That's why my mother's given up on me. She has six other kids; I'm next to youngest. All the others are married and have families. The boys are oafish husbands, and the girls are aged before their time from trying to keep track of all the kids they've got. My father's a butcher at the stockyards. All three of my brothers work there. They come home every night covered with animal blood. And you can guess who gets to do their laundry. One of my brothers-in-law is a laborer for the city. Shovels horse manure all day. Another is a trolley driver. One is a policeman. And get this, Marvel – *he's* the pride of the family. A dumb oaf of a flatfoot who'll have to pay someone to take the Sergeant's exam for him and, at that, he'll probably be a flatfoot the rest of his life – that's the guy my mother brags on about all the time. 'My daughter Sylvia,' she'll say. 'Married to a police officer!' You know what I had to do to finish high school? I had to lie and sneak around. All the Agronsky girls quit school after ninth grade. Why would a woman need any more? Does it take higher education to change a diaper, or wash your man's underwear? I told them I had a job. Which I did, but it was afternoons, in a flour-sack factory. Piece work. Sewing bags all afternoon until ten o'clock at night. My folks thought I worked all day and all night. That was fine with them. They never questioned, not so long as I brought the pay check home every Friday.

"When I graduated I moved out. You'd have thought the world ended. No Agronsky daughter, in the history of the Agronskys, ever moved out, except to live with a husband. I went on at the bag factory, except now I didn't turn my paycheck over to my old man. I enrolled in business school. Went for two years. They made me shift supervisor at the bag factory, gave me a raise. I was making twenty dollars a week, and damned glad to get it! That was five dollars a week more than I'd been averaging on piece work. And all I had to do for it was work an extra sixteen hours a week. They didn't hire men at the bag factory, because no man would put up with it.

"After business school I took classes at the University of Chicago. Two years ago I got my degree."

"How did you happen to go to work for the Tabulating Machine Company?"

"After I graduated I began to look for another job. They could've *given* me that damned bag factory, but I still wouldn't have gone back. You should see the faces of those women, row upon row of them, pale and hopeless.

"Anyway, I first heard about tabulating machines in college. The University has an installation. But only the grad students get to fool around with the machine. I knew a grad student, and he got me in at night to work with them. I knew right then that I wanted a job wiring and running tabulators. About six months after I graduated, Dr. Hollerith came to town looking to staff a Chicago office. I heard about it, and went down to the hotel where he was staying to apply. The fact that I'd had some experience with his tabulators was a strike against me, although, of course I didn't know it, or I wouldn't have mentioned it. He likes to train his people his way. But I had two off-setting assets. My degree, and the fact that I was a woman."

"A woman?"

39

"Surprising that that could be an asset, isn't it? But Dr. Hollerith is an innovator. He likes to be different. It tickled his fancy that he would have one of the few – maybe the only, for all I know – women tabulating-machine operators. Of course his innovative streak doesn't extend to offering me the manager's or the assistant manager's job."

The window rattled, the gas log hissed. Wanda snuggled closer to J.D.

They kissed, long and passionately. Wanda broke away, stood, and took his hand. "Come with me."

He followed her to the bedroom. She turned, kissed him again, and said, "I'll be a minute." She left the bedroom, closing the door behind her. The only light came through the curtains at the windows, a pale white luminescence. When his eyes adjusted he could see the quilted comforter on the bed, a mirrored dresser and a highboy. He was in a state of high agitation. His knees began to tremble, so he sat on the edge of the bed.

When Wanda came back into the room she was naked.

"What have you been doing?" she whispered, her voice trembling. "Get those clothes off."

She lay on the top of the bed and watched him while he undressed. When he was ready, she extended a hand to him. "Put this on."

He held out his hand and she pressed an object into it. It was a condom. He recognized it because Walter Hucko carried a supply and had explained their function to him. "But – " he stammered.

"Not buts!" Her voice rose. "I'm not getting pregnant."

He managed to get the thing on. Wanda pulled him down beside her. She guided his head to her breasts. He took an engorged nipple in his mouth and felt her shudder of pleasure. Her hands caressed his body, stroked his sheathed organ. He kissed the firm flesh of her stomach, the golden wiry hair between her legs. She pulled him on top of her, guided him inside her, and raised her legs to encircle his back. He was now far beyond the boundary of his experience, but his instincts were sure. He was gentle, but forceful. Her hips rose to meet his thrusts. An animal sound came from deep within her throat. Quite suddenly an enormous shock coursed through his body, from the top of his head to his toes, and he wondered briefly if he were dying, yet somehow didn't care. The shocks continued for a long time, one after another, finally coming less frequently, with less force, until they subsided to an occasional twitching spasm in his groin. He lay stunned on top of Wanda Agronsky, her hair tangled in his mouth. Atavistic cries of ecstasy lingered in his memory and he realized with a

40

little shock of wonder that they had come from him.

"I wish you could stay the night," Wanda said. "But there's a neighbor across the street who calls the cops if my lights are on after midnight. If she saw you coming out of here in the morning, she'd send for the marines."

He was sitting on the edge of the bed in his trousers and shirt. She was lying under the covers. Their initial encounter had been the prelude to three hours of exhausting love-making. He began to pull on his shoes. He felt a light-headed, delicious languor that he'd never experienced before.

"Can you find the trolley stop?"

He nodded. "You go to sleep." He stood, bent and kissed her chastely on the forehead. She reached out and grabbed his head and kissed him passionately on the mouth. His lips were numb.

"Listen," she said. "There's a company called Peerless Cash Registers. Its headquarters is in Iolus, about twenty miles from here. Their salesmen make the kind of money you're talking about – the good ones do."

"Cash registers? I don't know –"

"They're getting into the tabulating-machine business. Homer Medville Cranston owns the company. He's a tough old rooster, and hard to work for, I hear. I know someone who worked for him. I'll introduce you."

"Are they competition?"

"Not yet. Some day, maybe. Don't thank me. I've got an ulterior motive."

"Yes?"

"I'd like to keep you around."

"I'd like to be around."

"When can we get together again?" she asked.

"Soon, I hope."

"Will you come to a lecture tomorrow night?"

"Lecture?"

"Victoria Woodhull is speaking."

"I see."

"She doesn't get to the country very often. She lives in England now, you know. I could introduce you to my friend who worked for Cranston. He'll be there."

"I'd like to go," he said.

As he walked the chill, deserted streets to the trolley line he stopped

41

suddenly, struck his thigh with his fist, and said under his breath, *Gold-plated cad!*

5

Tales of the King

THE LECTURE WAS GIVEN in a hall on West Carroll Avenue located across the street from the E.Z. Polish factory, a graceful ferro-concrete building that had been designed five years earlier, in 1905, by Frank Lloyd Wright.

It was a long two-transfer trolley ride from the offices of the Tabulating Machine Company, where J.D. met Wanda Agronsky at six o'clock, to the lecture hall. By the time they got there the lobby was milling with people waiting for the doors to open for the lecture, which was scheduled to begin at seven.

"There's the fellow I was telling you about," Wanda said and, standing on tip-toes to wave, she called, "Shawn! Paul Shawn!"

A stocky, fair young man made his way through the crowd to them. Wanda introduced them. Paul Shawn had an open, friendly face. J.D. liked him at once.

"Are you one of Wanda's converts?" Shawn asked.

"Converts?"

Shawn gestured to the crowd. "To the cause of modern womanhood?"

J.D. and Shawn were practically the only men there.

"Now, Shawn," Wanda said. "Don't scare him off before I've had a chance to work on him."

"Ah," Shawn said. "Then it's your first meeting?"

"I'm afraid so," J.D. replied.

"Well, she chose to start you off with the powerhouse, Victoria Woodhull. She worked me up more gradually, but I must admit that I'm thoroughly hooked and landed."

"Marvel is interested in the Peerless Cash Register Company, and I told him you knew all about it."

"More than I'd care to know, actually," Shawn said with a rueful grin. "But I'd be happy to tell you anything I can."

There was a stir in the crowd as the doors to the lecture hall opened. "Why don't you have supper with us after the lecture?" Wanda said to Shawn.

"I'd be delighted!"

Victoria Woodhull was a grey-haired elderly woman with a narrow, saturnine face, and a mystical air about her. Her voice was so weak that J.D. had to strain to hear. The audience listened in hushed reverence. What she had to say was a mixture of politics and spiritualism. J.D. had certainly never heard anything like it. Victoria Woodhull advocated suffrage for women, abortion and the licensing and medical inspection of prostitutes. She excoriated the double standard in the workplace and in society. She asked rhetorically why it was that a man who was a successful seducer was considered a "jolly chap" by his fellows, while the women he seduced were reviled and cast out by "decent" society. She spoke of birth control, and "free love." The oratory was punctuated by mystical references. She "saw" the future of mankind. A coming Golden Age when women and men would be regarded as equals in the workplace, in the bedroom, and in politics. J.D. kept sneaking glances at Wanda and the other women near him for signs of embarrassment or shock, but they all gazed upon the old woman with rapt and adoring expressions. Victoria Woodhull finished her speech with a call for action; she exhorted her audience, as best she could with her frail voice, to organize their efforts for the reform of the inequities in the social and legal systems of the country.

After the speech was over, they took a trolley to a café that Shawn and Wanda knew of. It was a scruffy little place on south State, but Wanda said the coffee and waffles were excellent.

"What did you think of Victoria?" Wanda asked J.D.

"Interesting," he said.

Shawn smiled. "That's right, Chappie, be noncommittal, or Miss Suffragette here will give you her two-dollar lecture."

Wanda smiled thinly. "Am I that bad, Shawn?"

"You're not bad, dear," Shawn said. "Just committed."

"What's wrong with that?"

"Not a blamed thing, as long as you realize not everyone thinks the same."

"If they don't," she said flatly. "They should."

"Well," J.D. volunteered. "I can see the logic in what Mrs.

44

Woodhull was saying. But I don't think you can always change things on the basis of logic."

"Very cogent, Chappie," Shawn said. "You've put your finger on the problem. Trying to change people's sexual prejudices is not unlike trying to change their religious beliefs." He made a motion like turning a key in his forehead. "All locked away from the light of reason . . ."

They spent the rest of their supper discussing the speech and the reform movement. J.D. was curious about what they had to say, and he saw the justice of their convictions, but it all seemed remote from him personally.

As they were settling the bill, he brought up the reason Wanda had wanted him to meet Shawn.

"Why don't we have lunch tomorrow?" Shawn said. "My business is downtown – office equipment. Typewriters, adding machines, and the like." Shawn mentioned a restaurant, told J.D. how to get there, and they agreed to meet at noon.

"I'd like to bring my partner, if it's all right."

"By all means, Chappie!"

On the trolley, Wanda said casually, "You'll stop by, won't you?"

He had told himself he wouldn't when he'd set out for the evening. He didn't – he couldn't – love Wanda Agronsky, and without that he would be doing something he knew he would suffer agonies of remorse for, but as he looked down into her expectant face, he remembered the look and feel of her body, and he took her hand, raised it to his lips, and said, "Of course."

J.D. and Hucko were still at the Blackstone Hotel, although for the past two nights they, not the Parson's Company, were paying the bill. At breakfast, the morning after Victoria Woodhull's lecture, J.D. told Walter about their appointment with Paul Shawn and the reasons for it.

"Cash registers?" Hucko said.

"The main thing is that they're starting up a data-processing division."

"Process what?"

"Data processing. That's what it's called."

"What the hell does it mean?" Hucko asked irritably.

"Well, it refers to information, and what the machines do to it. Data – information. Processing – machines."

Hucko nodded glumly. Then he brightened. "Say, I don't mind the sound of cash registers. That's something a feller could get his teeth into. Think of all the places could use one. As a matter of fact, they have a big fancy one at the desk out in the lobby."

"I've seen it," J.D. said. "I took a closer look at it this morning when I was waiting for you, and found out it's a Peerless."

"That's the outfit in – where?"

"Iolus. About twenty miles west of here."

Hucko drummed on the table with his fingers. "How long do you think we can stay in this place? With the room and meals and all, it's costing me over five dollars a day."

"We've got the money, Walter. And right now I think it's important that we have a good address. We don't want to look down and out."

"At least let's ask about weekly rates."

"Good idea. Speaking of money –" J.D. broke off awkwardly.

"Yeah?" Hucko gazed at him expectantly.

"I think we ought to buy you a new outfit this morning."

Hucko's jaws stopped working and he stared at J.D. "A new outfit?" He turned his gaze down to his houndstooth checked suit. "What's the matter with this one?"

"Not a thing," J.D. said. "Only – well, you know how come I wore my old overalls when we were on the road."

"So the folks would know you for one of their own."

"Exactly. If we're going to land jobs, we've got to dress like the folks who are going to hire us would expect."

Hucko nodded. "I get it."

"In fact, I'm going to buy another outfit or two myself."

"I've got four of these suits. Seems a shame. Two of 'em are hardly broke in."

J.D. could scarcely keep from staring at Walter Hucko. He looked a different person. He was dressed in a dark-grey suit with a black vest, crisp white shirt, and blue tie, over which he wore a pearl-grey chesterfield topcoat. On his head was a black derby. They rode side-by-side on a trolley bench looking, Walter had said, like a couple of undertakers on their way to pick up a customer.

Paul Shawn was waiting at the restaurant when they arrived. They took a booth and ordered beer.

Shawn launched into his dissertation on the Peerless Cash Register Company. "Forget the name 'Peerless,' " he said. "That company is Homer Meville Cranston, and no other. You know what he's called?"

The King of Iolus! The town is utterly dependent on the Peerless factory. Once, the city fathers down-zoned a section of the town that included property owned by Cranston. He shut the plant down until they rescinded the zoning order, which they did in damn short time, since Peerless *is* the economy in Iolus."

"What did you do there?" J.D. asked.

"I was Assistant Sales Manager when I left, or, I should say, got the boot."

"Assistant Sales Manager!" J.D. was impressed. He didn't figure that Paul Shawn was much older than he.

Paul Shawn shrugged. "It didn't mean much. Oh, I'm a good enough salesman, but the old man changed sales managers and their staffs about the same way he changed shirts."

"Can you make money working for Peerless in their data processing?" J.D. asked.

Paul Shawn shook his head. "Not when I left. That was six months ago, and I doubt it's changed much. The data-processing division is a pet project of the old man's. Peerless make a cash drawer that they sell to banks. They've about got a monopoly with eastern banks. So old Homer figures, why not sell them data-processing machines to do their back-office work? It's a natural, he figures, since his salesmen already have an in with the banks."

"It makes sense," Walter said.

"The problem is that Homer went about it in his typical way. He wants the division to be making him millions before he puts much into it. He bought a license to manufacture tabulating machines designed by a man named Ansell Farnsworth. Farnsworth is a queer chap, but he seems to me to know his apples. The equipment is top drawer. Problem is, old Cranston won't let the division do the things they need to do to sell. He got jealous of Farnsworth. But, he couldn't fire him because he had to give him a piece of the business to get his license."

J.D. frowned. "I was hoping to hear something different. Walter and I want to get into the data-processing business."

"If you want to make money, cash-register sales is hard to beat."

"But it didn't work out for you," Walter said.

"I lasted nearly two years. And I made a heap of money. If you can put up with Cranston, Peerless is the place to be. At least around here. I like what I'm doing now, though. I don't make nearly the money, but my ulcers love the job."

"Do you suppose that if we started out in cash-register sales we

47

would work our way into the data-processing business when it got better?" J.D. asked.

Shawn shrugged. "*If* it got better. And if Cranston doesn't scuttle it. With him, you never know. 'Management by whim' seems to be his motto."

"But the money's good?"

"Let me put it this way," Shawn said. "I was Assistant Sales Manager for the last six months I was there, and during that six months I made nearly twenty-five thousand."

Hucko gasped. "You don't mean it!"

"The sales manager made around two hundred thousand a year."

J.D. shook his head in wonder. "I see what you mean about good money. It's a wonder anyone ever leaves Peerless."

"You wouldn't think it was such a wonder if you knew Homer Medville Cranston."

"Is he some kind of monster?" Hucko asked. "Because I could put up with about any kind of flesh and blood feller for that kind of money."

"You couldn't expect to start out making that, but at the rate the old man fires his top people, you might say the opportunities for advancement are unlimited."

"Why does he fire them?" J.D. asked.

"You have to understand I'm kind of prejudiced on that subject, since I'm one of the victims. But, if Cranston has any reason behind his axing people, it's because they're too good."

"Too good!" Hucko said disbelievingly.

Paul Shawn took a sip of his beer. "It's like this, Chappies. The old man really does think of himself as king of his domain. He thinks of himself, with some justification, as the best manager, and the best salesman, in the company. And when someone comes along who (a) does an outstanding job, and (b) gets to the point where he isn't totally dependent on the old man, then Cranston up and fires him. Oh, he finds excuses. In my case, he said there'd been customer complaints about a Jew being in management, and he couldn't very well ask me to step back to being just another salesman, not that he asked me, and not that I would've taken it."

"A Jew?" Hucko stared at Shawn.

"A lot of us are blond and rosy-cheeked."

"It seems like a hell of a thing to get fired over," J.D. said. "Surely Cranston knew you were a Jew when he made you Assistant Manager."

48

"Oh, he did!" Shawn replied. "And believe me when I tell you that I don't think Cranston has a prejudiced bone when it comes to business. Anything that will make him money, and keep him on the throne, is okay with the old man. And no customer is going to tell him how to run his business, assuming he actually got complaints. No, Chappies – I got fired because my boss and I got too good, and too independent."

"The sales manager was axed at the same time?" Hucko asked.

"Yep. Good man."

"There are two things I like about what I've heard," J.D. said. "The fact that their data processing is just starting out, so a fellow might get into some ground-floor opportunities, and the money to be made in the cash-register business in the meantime. D'you think we'd have a chance of getting jobs?"

"Officially, they aren't hiring right now," Shawn said. "The bad times have affected them, though not as much as most businesses. But, Cranston can and will change stated company policy, if he wants to."

"I don't suppose you'd be in a position to give us a recommendation?" J.D. asked.

Shawn smiled. "I'd give you one in a minute, but it would do more harm than good."

"How do you advise us to go about getting on with Peerless?"

"You'd have to get to the old man directly, because no one else has authority to hire right now."

"Is it possible to get to talk to him?" J.D. asked.

"I'd say it's difficult, but not impossible – once you get in, you'd better have something to say that will catch his ear, or he'll throw you out on yours."

"Suggestions?"

Shawn grinned. "You chappies are salesmen. It's a selling job."

J.D. turned to Walter. "Want to give it a try?"

"Listen," Hucko said. "I've delivered a pitch looking down the business end of a shotgun, and I don't reckon this Cranston feller can be much tougher than an Illinois hardscrabble farmer. Damn right I want to give it a try!"

49

TWO

We all have the same eight notes to play with.
Arthur Sullivan

6

A Visit to the King

A HARD SNOW was pelting down on that December day in 1910 when J.D. and Walter Hucko descended from the train and entered the station at Iolus. At the curb before the station entrance they found a span of elderly horses hitched to a sleigh presided over by a grizzled driver. When they enquired about the Peerless Cash Register Company the cabbie pointed vaguely to the sky in the south and they looked above snow-packed rooftops and skeletal pines to see upon a long rise of ground perhaps a mile away what appeared to be a fortress lowering over the little town like a grand seigneur over his vassals.

The cabbie agreed to haul them there for a quarter and they set off amid the creaking of harnesses and steaming horse breath.

At the offices they entered an anteroom where they shook and stamped the snow from themselves, and then passed through another set of doors into a lobby with a floor of black and white tiles presided over by a stern-faced middle-aged woman sitting behind a desk and dressed in a striped seersucker blouse and black string tie, her grey hair gathered in a bun from which sprouted yellow pencils. Above her desk was a sign that said, "Spend Time With Care."

"Mr. Cranston, please," J.D. said.

"Mr. Cranston is not seeing anyone," the woman said.

"Could you take him my card, please?" J.D. asked.

"I have *told* you, Mr. Cranston is not seeing anyone."

"I believe he'll see us."

The woman gave J.D. a look, from his shoes to his tie, taking in, along the way, the hat that he held in his hand. "Mr. Cranston does not see salesmen."

J.D. smiled pleasantly. "I'm not here to sell," he said. "I – my partner and I – are here to dispose."

53

The woman frowned. "Dispose?" she said. "Of what?"

"Of Peerless cash registers." J.D. took one of his cards from his vest, and a fountain pen from his coat. He leaned forward to use the edge of the desk to write on the back of the card. He waved the card to dry the ink while he smiled down at the woman. "Take this to Mr. Cranston."

She read what J.D. had written on the card, turned it over and said, doubtfully, "There's no company name."

"We are not a company," J.D. replied. He had had the cards made just that week. They simply gave his name. "We represent ourselves."

"Well," the woman said dubiously, rising. "Wait here."

She walked to a door marked "Private," her sturdy shoes clacking on the tiles, opened it, and disappeared through it.

"Are you nuts?" Walter said in a tense whisper. "*Buy* cash registers? Us!"

"In a manner of speaking, Walter – that's exactly what I'm proposing."

"And what are you proposing to use for money – in a manner of speaking?"

"Why," J.D. smiled broadly. "I thought we'd ask Mr. Cranston to loan us some."

Walter looked at him as if he'd lost his mind.

The woman appeared at the door marked "Private" and beckoned to them. "You may go in."

They stepped into another anteroom of wainscoted walls and lush carpeting. A young man in a dove-grey suit, white shirt, celluloid collar, and black tie sat at a desk before a typewriter, pounding away on the machine at a furious pace. Beside the desk was a closed, unmarked door. On one wall was a sign that said "Time Is All You Have." J.D. cleared his throat. "Wait!" the young man said, without missing a beat. In a moment, the bell on the typewriter dinged, the young man pressed a lever with his left hand while he snatched the paper from the platen with his right in a gesture that a magician producing a rabbit from a hat might envy, and swiveled his chair to look at J.D. and Hucko.

He picked up J.D.'s card from his desk. All of his movements were graceful, somehow dramatic. He had long tapering fingers, slender, graceful wrists, and a small head crowned in yellow curls that spilled onto his forehead.

"Mr. Marvel?" the young man said.

"Yes. And this is Mr. Hucko."

"Mr. Cranston will see you in a moment. He is terribly busy, so I

54

must ask you to be brief. While you're waiting, would you like to see our catalog, or do you already have in mind the models you want?"

"We'd like to see the catalog," J.D. said.

The young man took a booklet from one of his desk drawers and handed it to J.D.

"And your name?" J.D. asked.

"Sorry – I'm Jamie Ryan, Mr. Cranston's personal assistant."

Hucko and J.D. sat side-by-side in upholstered chairs and looked at the Peerless Cash Registers catalog.

"I didn't know there were so bloody many," Walter whispered. "I mean, a cash register's a cash register, isn't it?"

"Apparently not," J.D. said. "Here we have one that will keep ten totals."

"What for? All you want to know is the bill, isn't it?" They were talking in low voices. In any event Jamie Ryan couldn't overhear – he had inserted fresh paper and gone back to battering his typewriter.

"These extra totals are kept in registers – see the little windows? So you can keep track of up to ten items of inventory. Some of the models are fancier than others – don't seem to do more, but have more brass and nickel."

They waited for forty-five minutes. Finally, a whistle came from a speaking tube resting on a hook on Jamie Ryan's desk. He picked it up, listened in an earpiece for a moment, and said, "I'l take you in now."

He opened the unmarked door and allowed J.D. and Walter to precede him into a large office furnished with a huge black leather couch, several club chairs, a walnut conference table surrounded by massive straight-backed seats, a small fireplace in which a log blazed, and a roll-top desk that sat against a long, high bank of windows overlooking the town. Above the couch a black-framed sign proclaimed, simply, "Time" in gilt letters.

Seated at the roll-top was a man who, when the door opened, swiveled his chair to face them.

"Sir," Ryan said. "Mr. Marvel and Mr. Hucko. Gentlemen – Mr. Cranston."

Cranston was in his early fifties, with thick grey hair swept back and up in a sleek pompadour that had the effect of thrusting his features forward from his head. He had a strong, rather handsome face, with a square jaw, deeply dimpled chin and, under a narrow long nose, a military mustache. His face was florid, as if he'd just come in from the weather. Seated he appeared to be of average height with massive chest and arms bulging in the coat of his dark-brown wool suit, and a more than ample stomach encased in a vest and anchored from side-to-side with a heavy gold watch chain. Cranston's eyes were close-set, dark and intense, behind pince-nez that reflected the firelight in sharp flashes as he turned his head.

He ordered his visitors to sit. They took club chairs facing Cranston. One of his hands rested on his knee, holding J.D.'s card. "Which is Marvel?"

When J.D. admitted that he was, Cranston said, "You wish to purchase one hundred cash registers?"

"No, sir."

"This *is* your card?"

"Yes, sir. But you'll notice I said nothing about *buying*."

The color in Cranston's face deepened. "What kind of flummery is this?"

"Not flummery, sir. I meant every word. Mr. Hucko and I can dispose of one hundred of your machines."

"And just how do you and Mr. Hucko propose to go about doing that?"

"Why, by selling them."

There was a tense silence, broken only by the snap of the fire, as Cranston stared at J.D. with his piercing eyes. Finally, Cranston said in an unbelieving voice, "Do you mean to say you two came in here to hit me up for jobs?"

J.D. nodded. "Yes, sir. That's it exactly."

"How long do you propose to take to rid me of these hundred cash registers?"

"Well, sir," J.D. replied, "I don't exactly know. But I do know that Walter and I could do it in jig time."

"Come, come, Mr. Marvel. You mean to say you crash my office with all the effrontery of an army mule, saying—" he held up the card, and read from it, "saying: 'Would like to take 100 cash registers off your hands,' and you have no idea how long it will take?"

J.D. shifted uncomfortably. "A month?"

Cranston did not answer, just stared.

J.D. swallowed hard. "How about a week, then?"

Cranston laughed. "A *week*? Did you say a *week*, Mr. Marvel?"

J.D. pulled at the knot of his tie. "After all, there are two of us . . ."

"Do you know what the record is, Mr. Marvel? The most cash registers sold in one week, ever?"

"Can't say that I do."

56

"Eighty-six, Mr. Marvel! Eighty-six cash registers in one week! And you know what kind of man set that record?"

"No, sir."

"A man who spent a lifetime becoming one of the best – no, by God! – *the* best salesman in the country. Maybe in the world. And he sold eighty-six. There's a plaque in our sales school commemorating that, and the name on that plaque is mine, not that you'll ever see it. I only tell you so that you can appreciate the magnitude of your ignorance; to come in here and tell me that you and Mr. Bucko can sell more cash registers together than the best salesman who ever worked a territory."

"Well, sir – I'm pretty ignorant, and I admit it. Mr. *Hucko* here is an experienced salesman, but I've only had a couple years at it, and neither one of us ever sold a cash register, or even tried. So, naturally, I didn't know what the proper number for us to sell would be. But I do know this – we want to work for Peerless because we heard you were the best. We're hard workers and we learn fast. We also heard you've got yourself a data-processing business and if things worked out in the cash registers, we'd like to maybe get into that business later on. I apologize for getting in here by trickery, but we figured it was the only way to get jobs, since we heard it wouldn't do any good to apply through regular avenues."

"You're right about one thing," Cranston said. "We're the best." He shook his head in wonder. "I'm sitting here about to have you thrown out, and you've already got your whole career with us mapped out."

"Let me make you a proposal, Mr. Cranston," J.D. said. "Mr. Hucko and I would be willing to work for nothing to learn the business. Then, if you aren't satisfied, you can let us go, and no hard feelings."

"Mr. Hucko doesn't seem so sure about your offer. What do you say, Mr. Hucko? Are you fool enough to work for nothing?"

"I go along with J.D.," Hucko said. "He and I been together two years, and I've never proved a fool going along with him."

"I don't think we're fools," J.D. said quietly. "Unless, of course, you're saying the Peerless Cash Register Company isn't all we've heard it is."

Cranston smiled. "A sharp point, neatly put, Mr. Marvel. Let us give you the benefit of the doubt."

"Which is?"

"That you aren't fools at all, but simply young men with enough self-confidence to invest in yourselves."

"How do you mean?" Walter asked.

"Our salesmen's training school lasts four weeks, followed by a field apprenticeship of three weeks."

"We have enough savings to support ourselves for seven weeks," J.D. said.

"Ah, if that were only all," Cranston said sadly. "There's the school itself."

"The school?" J.D. asked.

"Yes. Since, as you noted, we haven't been hiring, the school has closed down. Are you prepared to pay the cost of opening it up for the sole purpose of training you two?"

"What would it cost?" J.D. asked.

"I should think two hundred a week would cover the direct costs, assuming I threw in the classroom and the heat."

"Eight hundred, then," J.D. said.

"That's correct. Mr. Hucko seems to be choking on something."

"We'll do it!" J.D. said.

"And you, Mr. Hucko?"

"I told you before, sir – I'm with J.D.," Hucko said staunchly.

Cranston regarded first Hucko, then J.D. under hooded eyes. The snow continued to fall past the windows behind his desk. Finally, he said, "How old are you?"

"Twenty," J.D. replied.

"Thirty-nine," Hucko lied. He'd turned forty the month before.

"What sales experience do you have?"

"We've been selling organs," J.D. said. "To farmers in the southern part of the state."

"What went wrong with that job?"

"Nothing," J.D. said. "We were the top salesmen in the company."

"They didn't pay enough?"

"Enough for our needs. More than we could spend."

"Then why the deuce aren't you still selling organs?"

"Because we want to get into something with more future."

"If you think selling cash registers is anything like selling organs, you're much mistaken."

"No, sir – we don't think –" Hucko began.

"Just because you may have been hot-shots down on the farm, doesn't mean you can toe the mark in our field."

"Well, we're willing to learn –" J.D. said.

"First," Cranston replied. "You have to *un*learn."

"Unlearn?"

"Everything you've ever known about selling. There aren't any *born* salesmen, and don't ever let anyone tell you different. Give me a reasonably bright young man, who's willing to work, and who doesn't know a thing, and inside six months I'll teach him all he needs to know to be a top-notcher."

"*We'd* certainly like to learn the business," Walter said.

Cranston snorted. "You can learn the business from any one of a half dozen of my competitors."

"But," J.D. jumped in. "We can't learn to be top-notch cash-register salesmen anywhere but at Peerless!"

Cranston rose from his chair and walked to the conference table and leaned on it with his fingertips. With that simple act his presence seemed to fill the room. His powerful shoulders thrust his head forward. His eyes seemed to acquire light from the overhead electric fixtures and then give it off again. "Don't," he said, "try your cheap organ-salesman's tricks on me."

"I only meant . . ."

"You only meant to flatter me," Cranston said. He pointed to the sign on the wall. "Time," he said. "More precious than gold. Time! It's all we've got. And you have the brass-balled effrontery to waste mine."

There was a heavy silence marred only by the faintly heard rattle of Jamie Ryan's typewriter in the next room, and Walter Hucko's heavy breathing.

"I'm sorry," J.D. said, meeting Cranston's gaze levelly. "It was stupid of me. You can be sure I won't do it again."

"Tell me one reason," Cranston said, "why I should waste any more time on you?"

"I think we might make good salesmen for you," J.D. said. "I don't know it for sure, but we have one thing in our favor."

"What's that?"

"We want it bad," J.D. said. "Bad enough to bet our whole stake on it."

Cranston smiled. But it was a stormy smile, that did nothing to soften his eyes. "Do you think I care about your 'stake'? By the time I was your age I owned one of the most successful retail stores in Indiana. By the time I was his age –" he nodded toward Walter, "I'd been bankrupt twice, and was worth a million dollars. So don't tell me about your 'stakes.' Tell me why *I* should give a damn if you work for me or not."

"I can only think of one reason, Mr. Cranston."

"Well?"

"An experiment."

"Experiment?"

"To see if you can take fellows like Walter and me – fellows that have been contaminated by learning ways other than yours – and turn them into valuable Peerless salesmen."

"Supposing I succeeded – what would I prove?"

"That your methods were even better than you thought they were."

Cranston stared at J.D. for a moment and then he put his head back and laughed. It was a rolling, full-bodied laugh that seemed to well up like a geyser from his capacious stomach. Finally his laugh died and he said, solemnly, "I'm going to give you a chance."

"Thank you, sir," J.D. said.

"You won't be sorry," Hucko said.

J.D. and Hucko got to their feet.

"I'll let you know when I'm finished!" Cranston said. J.D. and Walter sat again. "The school is closed," Cranston continued. "But it will be opening up again next week for a new class."

"Does that mean we won't need the two hundred a week?" Walter asked.

"No, you won't need the two hundred a week," Cranston said. "You'll go into the school on the same terms as all the trainees. Twenty dollars a week, room and board. When, and if, you successfully complete the school, you'll be put in territories on draws against straight commission." He paused. "Now clear out of here. Time's wasting."

7

Graduation

On Wednesday morning, January 11, 1911, in their final week of training, Walter Hucko read aloud to J.D. from the *Chicago Tribune* that the average weekly income of those Americans fortunate enough to have jobs was $15.

"So?" said J.D. who was peering into a mirror over the chiffonier in his room while he tied his tie. It was eight o'clock, the beginning of another bone-chilling day such as had been visited on Chicago for the past eight days.

"We're making five dollars a week over the average," Hucko replied. For the past seven weeks, since their training had begun, he'd been trying to find a bright side to their circumstances. Even though they weren't making a tenth part of what they'd made selling organs, Hucko was at least grateful they hadn't had to pay their own expenses, or those of the school at Iolus, as J.D. had proposed to Cranston. The school had ended just before Christmas and, after a week's break for the holidays, they had been assigned to the Chicago office for field training. They had taken rooms in a rooming-house on Garfield just around the corner from the Peerless branch office on State Street.

Their principal endeavour at Iolus had been learning and practising the Peerless Pitch, a 450-word sales talk said to have been written some ten years before by none other than Homer Medville Cranston. Sales-school mythology had it that this was the very pitch that had helped to garner the title of World's Best Salesman for Cranston. The Peerless sales literature and the many plaques commemorating notable landmarks in Peerless history that were strung about the halls of the school attested to the infallibility of the Pitch.

In the field, the trainees were assigned in pairs to experienced salesmen for practical experience. J.D. and Walter were taken in hand by a tall, long-faced man of Scottish ancestry named Thomas Finch. The work day started promptly at eight-thirty, when twenty-eight salesmen and six trainees of the Chicago branch gathered at the office which occupied the ground floor of a three-story brick building.

The space was divided into a small private office for the branch manager, a stocky, florid man named Patrick Carney who was given to wearing a gardenia in the lapel of his dark suit, and who was rumored to be in line for a headquarters sales job; a narrow, long work room at the rear of the building for the field mechanics, and, looking out on State Street through high arched windows, a common room for the sales force. Six rows of desks jammed end-to-end paraded across the linoleum floor. Cranston dictated that all branch offices should be situated in such a way that his salesmen could be viewed by passersby. He thought this discouraged loitering in the office. He wanted his salesmen out in their territories, selling cash registers, not languishing at desks. One desk tucked away in a far corner was that of the data-processing salesman. He was a wiry, nervous little man with thinning hair and thick black eyebrows that nearly joined at the bridge of his nose whose name was Leland Prescott. In the nearly three weeks J.D. and Walter had been working out of the Chicago office J.D. hadn't found a chance to talk to him. Prescott kept to himself, which wasn't difficult, because he was generally ignored by the other salesmen who regarded him and his job as useless appendages to the office. "It's a fad," Thomas Finch said of data processing when J.D. asked him. "Give it a year or two, it will die out."

Finch's sales pitch was straight from the can. He never deviated a syllable from the famous Peerless training-school oration, and if a prospective customer interrupted with a question out of sequence Finch simply took up at the break and plowed on. In his dry, humorless way, he was quite a closer. His technique was simple: he wouldn't take no for an answer. He kept boring in, repeating appropriate parts of the pitch, until often the prospect, exhausted beyond resistance, would sign to get rid of him. The least a prospect could expect to get by with from Finch was a maybe, which he would live to regret, because that meant Finch would be back on his neck at some future date, going again through the whole long pitch.

"I wonder," J.D. asked Walter one night near the end of their training as they were sitting in the parlor of their rooming-house after dinner, "if Thomas Finch wasn't stamped out and assembled at the plant at Iolus."

"I'll bet the bugger looks up the right procedure in the Peerless policy manual before he kisses his wife," Walter replied.

On Saturday, January 14, 1911, J.D. and Walter spent their last day in training. All the Chicago employees gathered in the salesmen's room at quitting time for a little ceremony. The branch manager, Patrick Carney, a fresh gardenia in his lapel, gave a short speech and handed each of the five surviving trainees that had been assigned to the Chicago office a leather-bound pocket notebook which had stamped on it in gilt letters "Time Is Gold."

Later, as they walked back to their rooms, J.D. said to Walter, "How about a celebration tonight? We could call Paul Shawn, cook up a party –" J.D. stopped talking as a peculiar look passed over Hucko's face.

Hucko took a deep breath as if about to plunge into icy waters, and muttered, "I – I have plans." Then he blurted, "Damn it, J.D.! I've been seeing Wanda."

J.D. stared. "Agronsky?"

"I – I hope you don't mind."

"Me! Why should I mind?" J.D. meant it. Yet he couldn't help wondering why his voice cracked when he said it.

On Monday morning Carney, the branch manager, parceled out territory assignments to the five new salesmen. When it came to his turn Carney called J.D. into his office and said,

"I'm giving you a grand opportunity, Marvel."

"Thank you, sir."

"I'm giving you Elmhurst."

"Elmhurst?"

"What's the matter, Marvel?"

"I'm sorry, Mr. Carney. I don't know where Elmhurst is."

"You don't know –" Carney seemed shocked.

"I'm from the southern part of the state, you know –"

Carney stood, spun around, and, with a snap of his wrist, unrolled a map of northern Illinois from a tube that was fastened to the wall behind his desk. "Here," he said, tapping the map with the back of his hand. "About sixteen miles west of here. Fine little town. They incorporated last year."

J.D. rose, leaned across the desk, and squinted at the map. "It doesn't look very big."

"Well, it's not Chicago, if that's what you mean," Carney said jocularly. "But it's got better'n four thousand people. Stores. Bars. A limestone quarry. Elmhurst College." Carney made it sound like a metropolis. He glanced over his shoulder at J.D. and frowned. "What's the matter, Marvel? You don't seem too happy."

"Well, sir – I was just thinking what they told us in sales school, about the number of cash registers we should expect to sell per one hundred population."

"Two!" Carney held up two fingers.

"Which means Elmhurst has the potential for eighty, if they don't have *any* right now."

"See here, Marvel," Carney said. "I'm giving you your own town, man! Most salesmen would fall over themselves for their own *town*. And you're giving me sales-school statistics."

"Sorry."

Carney turned back to the map and swept his finger in a circle around Elmhurst. "Besides," he said. "You'll have the surrounding area. Here," he jabbed his finger at the map. "A lumber yard. Here. A hotel and café. Site of the original Cottage Hill tavern, where farmers from the Fox Valley west of there used to stop over when they were making their way to Chicago with their wagons loaded with crops. Historical country, Marvel! Historical!"

"Yes, sir."

"You still have doubts, my boy?"

"No, sir – only –"

"Spit it out! Let's get it all on the table."

"I was just thinking that Mr. Cranston sold eighty-six cash registers in one week. At that rate, Elmhurst would be saturated in less than a week."

Carney stared silently at J.D. for a long moment. Finally, he said, "I'll tell you what. You sell eighty cash registers in Elmhurst in one week, and I'll give you my job."

Walter was on the front steps of the building, smoking a cigar. "How did you do?"

"Elmhurst."

Walter stared. "Jesus!"

"You mean you've heard of it?"

Walter nodded. "Some of the fellows were talking about it."

"What did they say?"

"That whatever assignment we have it could always be worse – it could be Elmhurst."

64

"The bottom of the barrel, huh?"

Walter shrugged. "I wouldn't pay much attention to it. Should we walk over to the rooming-house? I have to pack a suitcase. I've been assigned Cicero."

They began to walk toward the rooming-house. "What's your quota?" J.D. asked.

"Four a week," Walter said.

"Four!"

"Yours?"

"Two."

They walked in silence for a moment. "Do you think Carney has something against me?" asked J.D. finally.

"No."

"Look at the territory he gave me. Did he give anyone else anything like it?"

"Finch told me Carney didn't make the assignments for our bunch."

"But that's the branch manager's job! If he didn't, who did?"

"Finch said it was Cranston himself."

It was snowing when J.D. got off the train at the Chicago and Northwestern station in Elmhurst at one-thirty that afternoon. He had two suitcases with him. The rest of his possessions he'd stored in a basement space he'd rented from the landlady of his rooming-house in Chicago.

Inside, in the tiny waiting-room, J.D. telephoned for a taxi. The rooming-house that had been recommended to him was across town from the station so J.D. had a chance during the journey to see quite a bit of Elmhurst. What he saw did not lift his spirits. It was a picturesque town, with brick cottages nestled among elm-lined streets, but obviously it was not one of the dynamic forward-looking places which had been depicted in sales school as the typical hunting ground of the Peerless salesman. The business district was three blocks long and two blocks wide. The largest establishment was a general store. There was a bank, barbershop, a couple of saloons, two or three grocery stores, dress shops, and a hardware store. J.D. sighed gloomily as they left the business area and passed into a residential section of larger homes. It was at one of these that the cabbie deposited J.D. – Schenley's boarding-house.

Mrs. Schenley was a thin, nervous woman with a deep, bronchial cough. Mr. Schenley was large and fat with a livid complexion. They greeted J.D. with bored indifference. Mr. Schenley took the $15 J.D. gave him for the first month's room and board quickly enough and then showed him to a narrow room with an iron double bed, a rickety wardrobe, and one chair, all of which so filled the available floor space that J.D. had to lean over the bed to allow Mr. Schenley to leave the room.

The room had one small window through which J.D. had a view of a side yard. The snow was falling heavily now, but J.D. considered the outdoors no less appealing than this cell of a room. He picked up his leather zipper briefcase that he'd unpacked and that contained his Peerless salesman's kit, put his overcoat back on, and went downstairs, out of the house, and began to walk toward the business section of town. He figured that calling on a few prospects would dispel his gloom.

The Elmhurst Mercantile Store occupied a huge, drafty old frame building that had been built forty years before by the founder of the business, Albert French, who had left it to his son, Albert French, Jr., when he'd died five years ago. J.D. was directed to Mr. French's office by a plump saleslady presiding over a counter of gaudy ribbons. He was encouraged that not a single cash register was in sight.

The office was on a mezzanine at the back of the building. He found Mr. French seated at a desk that looked out upon the vast expanse of the store below. Albert French, Jr. was a tiny man of about forty with a thin, black mustache and patent-leather hair parted in the middle. He was coatless, dressed in a red-candy-striped white shirt, with celluloid cuffs and collar, and a navy-blue bow tie with red polka dots. On the sleeves of his shirt were black arm garters. A pair of rimless octagonal spectacles perched on his short nose. He peered over his glasses as J.D. introduced himself.

"Peerless?" Mr. French said, placing a limp, wet hand in J.D.'s. "You mean the cash-register people?"

"Yes, sir." J.D. took a deep breath, and launched into the Pitch: "I'm here to help you make more money, Mr. French. Before I'm through, I guarantee you – notice I did not say 'assure,' or 'demonstrate,' or any of those –" Mr. French was holding up a tiny hand. "Or any of those weak words employed –"

"Whoa!" Mr. French said. "Just slow down there, son. I'm not buyin' one of your things."

"But, sir." J.D. said, "I will guarantee to make you more profit and to prevent dishonest employees from taking –"

A bell rang somewhere over J.D.'s head, there was a rasping noise, and a shiny brass cylinder with rubber ends dropped into a basket on Mr. French's desk. "Now," French said, "I'll show you why I've no use for your contraption." He picked up the cylinder, twisted it so an opening appeared in one side, and shook out a slip of paper that was wrapped around a $5 bill. He held them up for J.D. to see. "Sale in yardage goods." He consulted the slip. "Two dollars and eighty-one cents." French flipped open the lid of a grey metal cash box that stood on his desk. He put the $5 bill in, carefully counted out change, put it in the cylinder, closed the cylinder, attached it by a hook on its side to a ferrule on one wire of a network of wires that were over his desk near the ceiling, gave it a flick, and the cylinder sped off into the vast expanse under the roof. J.D. and French watched it go. It sailed along, suddenly dipping down a wire at the far side of the store to alight in a basket on a counter behind which stood a waiting sales clerk. She picked up the cylinder, opened it, and gave the customer on the other side of the counter her change. In the meantime, another cylinder had arrived at French's desk.

French smiled at J.D. "What were you saying about preventing dishonesty among my employees?"

"Yes, but our cash registers keep perpetual inventories," J.D. said, leaping pell-mell into the sales pitch.

"Let me show you something," Mr. French replied. He picked up the sales slip that had come in the first cylinder, opened an account book lying on his desk, took up a pen, and made two entries. He closed the book and deposited the slip in a box that contained a stack of similar slips. "There," he said. "Perpetual inventory all up to snuff." He gave J.D. a smug smile. "Not only that, but I entered my cash journal which I keep on the opposite page to the inventory. So you see, my accounting is practically all done."

J.D. signed. "I don't guess it would do any good to point out that you're spending a lot of valuable time that could be better spent figuring ways to improve the business." The Pitch was now totally shot. J.D. was speaking for himself.

"Not a bit. There's nothing I could do that would be any more productive." He surveyed his store serenely. "You see, every clerk and stockboy down *there* knows that Albert French is up *here*."

"Sort of like God."

French chuckled. "You're wasting your time in Elmhurst, young man, as you've probably found out."

"You're the first call I've made."

67

"Let me save you time, then. We're not much taken to new geegaws around here. You'll find everyone is pretty much like me. We like to look after our own businesses, not have some machine do it for us. Was never a machine invented that could replace the judgment, common sense, and just plain prudence of your good businessman. So I'd suggest you take your wares over around Chicago. They got plenty of flash-in-the-pan businessmen in Chicago who would go for your fancy machines."

J.D. sighed. "Problem is, Elmhurst is my territory."

"Oh dear!" French said. "That is too bad."

J.D. flushed. "I intend to lick it, Mr. French!"

"Well, I admire your spunk." He offered his limp hand.

J.D.'s first stop the next morning was Welch's drugstore. Bill Welch was a spry, elderly man with a bony bald head and a walrus mustache who, J.D. had been told by his landlord, was president of the Rotary Club. Welch pumped J.D.'s hand vigorously when he told him why he was there. "Rotary meets on Wednesdays for lunch at the Cottage Hill Café. Why don't you come along tomorrow and see how you like us?"

His next stop was the Elmhurst National Bank. J.D. had also found out from his landlord that Everett Small, the president of the bank, was also the president of the Chamber of Commerce.

J.D. was ushered into a wood-paneled office where Small sat behind a walnut desk framed by a halo of light from a leaded glass window at his back. He was a sad-faced, friendly man of thirty-five with thick black hair, heavy eyelids, and a drooping large mouth.

"The Chamber is quite active in Elmhurst," he said. "We work hand-in-glove with the mayor and the council to put things right in this town. I believe you'll find this one of the better-run towns in the state, if not in the Midwest. And I must say that the Chamber has had a good deal to do with that."

"The mayor?" J.D. asked.

"Porter Frawley. Owns the limestone quarry."

"I'd certainly be interested in joining the Chamber," J.D. said. "How do I go about it?"

"Not much to it. Get a member to propose you. I'll do that myself. In fact, tonight's our monthly dinner. Would you like to come along?"

So it was that J.D. became a member of the Elmhurst Chamber of Commerce and the Rotary Club. It turned out that many of the members of one were members of the other. Porter Frawley was past

68

president of both, and was a man widely liked and respected. He was a fat, tall man in his late forties, with a bulbous red nose, small eyes, and a kind and amiable personality. J.D. liked him immediately.

He was made to feel welcome by both organizations. Members bought him drinks at the Cottage Hill bar and welcomed him informally to Elmhurst. His spirits were soaring by the time he'd been dropped at his boarding-house by Bill Welch after the Rotary Club meeting. He washed up, collected his zipper briefcase with his sales kit in it, and set off downtown. Everywhere he went he was greeted amiably. When he returned to the boarding-house at five o'clock he'd called on three businesses, had his pitch listened to courteously all the way through by one and all, and hadn't made a single sale. He hadn't even got a commitment from anyone to think it over. Every turn-down had been flat and unequivocal. His depression of Monday seemed downright jocular compared to the way he felt as he plodded heavily up the stairs to his room.

"By God, I'll tell you!" Walter exclaimed. "Cicero is something! Bars. Gambling. Women. More damn fun per square block than any place I ever been, and that includes Saint Looie!"

It was Friday lunchtime, and they were sharing a table at Jiggs Muldoon's. J.D. had taken the train to Chicago that morning and had an appointment after lunch with Patrick Carney, which he dreaded, to review his first week as the Peerless representative in Elmhurst. "So, how did the week go?" J.D. asked casually.

Walter shook his head morosely. "Only sold two cash registers. How about you?"

"Zero. Not a sniff."

"Jesus!" Walter exclaimed. "That's rough, J.D."

"Not only that," J.D. said. "I don't even have a lead."

"Christ!" Walter said. "Elmhurst must be one son-of-a-bitching territory!"

J.D. laughed bitterly. "I joined Rotary and the Chamber of Commerce – the total of my successes."

"That'll get you in good with the businessmen!"

"Who do you think I've been calling on this week? Those same businessmen, my fellow club members."

"It's not fair!" Walter said vehemently. "I'll bet Cranston himself couldn't sell Elmhurst."

"It's not just a tough territory, Walter. It's an impossible territory. This morning I had coffee with Tom Finch. A fellow who owns the

69

drugstore in Elmhurst thought a Peerless salesman called on him several years ago. I asked Finch about it. He remembered. Seems they were having trouble with some salesman out of the Chicago office. Drinking on the job, fooling around with the wife of a customer. Problem was, he was a hot-shot salesman. One of the Quota Busters year after year. So they sent him out to Elmhurst and starved him out. Took him about two weeks to quit, Finch said."

"I thought Carney said they'd never had a salesman out there."

"This was before Carney's time. And even if he knew about it, do you think he'd tell me a story like that?"

Patrick Carney leaned back in his chair, drummed his fingers on his desk, and stared at the ceiling as though trying to decide if it had been properly installed. "Not a very good beginning, Marvel," he said.

"In any other territory, I would agree," J.D. replied.

"Excuses don't sit well at Peerless," Carney said sternly.

"That's not an excuse," J.D. said. "It's a fact. Elmhurst doesn't deserve the name 'territory.' " J.D. had sat silently in Carney's office for five minutes, while Carney read the report of his first week.

"Joining the Chamber and Rotary were good moves," he said.

"Mr. Carney," J.D. said. "May I ask you a frank question?"

"Fire away," Carney replied.

"Do you think I or any other salesman could make it in Elmhurst?"

"Certainly!" Carney said indignantly. "I wouldn't have given it to you, otherwise."

"As I understand it," J.D. said levelly. "You didn't."

"What are you talking about?"

"The rumor is that Mr. Cranston handed out the assignments for my class."

"Rumor! What the hell are you listening to rumors for?" Carney blustered. "You should be spending your time making sales, not listening to rumors."

J.D. noticed, however, that he did not deny it. "That's what I intend to do," he said.

Early next morning J.D. rousted Walter from his room and took him to breakfast at their favorite diner. Over hotcakes and bacon he said, "What I must find is the key."

"Key?" Walter asked sleepily.

"I know those folks in Elmhurst could do better with Peerless cash registers, but they can't realize it because they have a built-in prejudice against anything new. They're smug. They think they have it all over Chicago, for example, because they don't have office buildings and prostitutes and everyone goes to church on Sunday."

Walter shook his head. "Sounds impossible."

"Nothing's impossible, once you have the key. I can't put my finger on it, though." He blew on his coffee. "I mean, all the sales points we learned at Iolus, and from watching Finch operate; I've used every single one, in the Pitch, without the Pitch; nothing works."

After breakfast they walked to the office. J.D. spent the rest of the morning at his desk. It took him hardly fifteen minutes to complete his paperwork. He had no orders to write, few expenses to report, and his plan for the coming week was simply to call on as many businesses in Elmhurst as he could. He spent the balance of the morning studying Peerless sales manuals, making copious notes, and trying to figure, without success, what it was he was doing wrong.

At mid-morning J.D. took a break. A small table at the back of the room contained a hot-plate and coffee-pot. Around it were arranged several chairs where the salesmen could sit while drinking their coffee. J.D. found Leland Prescott, the data-processing salesman, seated there alone. J.D. poured himself a cup of coffee.

"I envy you, Mr. Prescott," J.D. said.

Prescott looked startled. "What do you mean?"

"I'd like to be in your end of the business."

"Believe me, you wouldn't feel that way if you tried it."

"Why do you say that?"

"Peerless is only in the business because they can't get out of it."

"Can't get out of it?"

"Yeah." Prescott paused to light a cigarette. "Ansell Farnsworth, the guy who invented the equipment I sell, has old man Cranston by the short hairs. Cranston can't sell the business without Farnsworth's approval. And he can't get rid of Farnsworth, because the patents are half his."

"So Cranston neglects the business? Seems like he's only hurting himself."

"Well, he's hurting Farnsworth, too."

"Trying to starve him out?" J.D. was beginning to see that as a favorite Cranston strategy.

"Yeah. But Farnsworth is a stubborn old coot. He doesn't care that much about money anyway. All he cares about is working on his inventions."

"Where does Farnsworth work?"

"He lives in De Kalb. He has a big old house out there. His lab is in the house."

"Say, I'm working Elmhurst. That's only fifty miles from De Kalb. Have you seen his lab?"

Prescott shook his head. "Nope. Farnsworth is an eccentric cuss. Doesn't like visitors. I'm told he once ran Cranston off with a shotgun."

J.D. grinned. "That would've been worth seeing."

8

J.D. Hatches a Plan

J.D. SLEPT UNTIL NOON, an old habit – trouble a soporific – and awoke refreshed and, if not ebullient, at least with the determination to get on with his life. His train to Elmhurst left at two-fifteen.

Before he left for the station J.D. found Walter in his room packing his bag. "When are you delivering the two cash registers you sold?" J.D. asked him.

"Wednesday. I'm thinking about buying a car and the garage that has it is loaning it to me. I'll drive in Wednesday morning to pick up the units."

"I want to ask you a favor, Walter." Quickly, J.D. outlined what he had in mind.

Walter's eyes widened. "Jesus, J.D.! If we got caught –"

"We won't."

A wild light danced in Walter's eyes. "Just like old times –"

J.D. grinned. "Will you do it?"

"Hell yes! What have we got to lose?"

J.D. was in front of Bill Welch's drugstore Monday morning when Welch arrived to open it. J.D. helped Welch set out his displays of patent medicines and corn plasters while he explained what he wanted.

Welch wiped his bony bald head with a large gingham handkerchief. "I don't have to buy anything?"

"I guarantee it." Welch's clerk, a hefty blonde girl, came in the store, went in the back room, and emerged again wearing a green smock. "Cm'ere a minute, June," Welch said.

The girl listened till J.D. was finished, frowned, and said to Welch, "I dunno – what if I can't?"

73

Welch said, "If you can't, it doesn't matter one bit."

"Well, I guess I could try," she said. "If that's what you want me to do." And Welch said it was and she went off into another area of the store with a feather duster and began dusting shelves.

"Don't worry," Welch assured J.D., combing his big mustache with his thumbnail. "She's really very bright."

Walter arrived at Welch's drugstore at ten-thirty Wednesday morning to find J.D. waiting on the curb, bundled in his topcoat and blowing into his hands. It had snowed the night before, but now the sky was clear and the temperature just above freezing. Walter parked the Oakland touring car he was driving next to the curb. In the back seat was a shiny new Peerless cash register, its fat front gleaming with nickel and brass.

"This is for a saloon," Walter said. "Told the customer there was a delay at the factory, but I have to have it to him Friday, without fail."

"You will," J.D. said, hoisting the cash register from the back seat. "Nice car."

"Runs like a top," Walter said. "I'll probably buy it if I can get the feller down to four hundred."

They set the machine on the counter at the back of the store and J.D. instructed Welch and June how to use it. They drove in the Oakland to the Cottage Hill Café and had lunch. As usual, J.D. found a good many of his fellow Rotarians and Chamber of Commerce members there. He made it a point to stop at each table, introduce Walter, and in the course of the conversation mention that they had just come from installing a cash register at Bill Welch's drugstore.

Albert French was sitting with Porter Frawley, the mayor of Elmhurst and owner of the limestone quarry. French gave J.D. a supercilious look and said, "I thought Bill Welch had better sense."

"Why don't you fellows drop by and look at it?" J.D. asked.

Frawley frowned. "Don't reckon it would do me much good. I don't do enough retail to shake a stick at."

"Wouldn't matter if you did," French sniffed. "Doesn't do a thing that a person can't do better for himself."

"You've had experience with our cash registers, then, Mr. French?" Walter asked innocently.

"Can't say as I have," French admitted. "Not that it matters."

"No," Walter said solemnly. "I guess not. No need to clutter up your opinions with facts."

Frawley laughed, and French flushed. "Maybe I will drop around

74

and take a look at your contraption," Frawley said.

"I wish you would," J.D. said. "We've found them useful in wholesale businesses, particularly cash-and-carry, like yours."

When they were seated finally at their table, J.D. grinned at Walter and said, "You gave old Frenchie a good shot."

"He asked for it."

"Funny thing is," J.D. added. "He could use more cash registers to better advantage than anyone in town."

He took a menu from the waiter. "It's funny. Here I am feeling on top of the world, and all I've done is convince a fellow to take something for nothing."

J.D. was at the drugstore a few minutes before closing. Bill Welch was in the back filling a prescription for a customer. June gave him a smile in greeting.

"How was it, June?" J.D. asked.

"It was fun," she said. "It makes such a grand noise, the bells and all."

"What about the boss?" J.D. nodded toward the back.

June giggled. "He'd never admit it, but I think he was taken with it too. Several customers commented on it."

"Favorably?"

"Oh, yes. The mayor even said he was glad to see someone in town was getting modern ideas."

"Porter Frawley was in?"

"Right after lunch, with Mr. French."

"Is that right?"

"Don't think Mr. French thought much of it, though."

J.D. helped Welch close up. Then they sat together at the table in back that Welch used for a work bench when he was filling prescriptions and went over the cash-register tapes. It only took a few minutes, and when they were through Welch had a complete inventory on the ten items he'd chosen to keep track of, as well as a cash-transaction journal from the tape.

"All you need now is to count the money in the register and reconcile it," J.D. said.

Welch brought the cash drawer from the register and when he counted the money found that the total reconciled with the tapes.

"I have to admit," Welch said. "I usually don't reconcile my cash box on the first try."

"Well," J.D. said. "You couldn't expect that every time with a cash

75

register, either. Usually the first few days that a place has a register everything reconciles because no one's used to the thing yet, and they're being extra careful."

Welch nodded amiably and passed a hand over his bald head.

"How do you like the inventories?" J.D. asked.

"Good," Welch said. "I'm not buying a cash register, though, J.D."

J.D. smiled and winked. "Wanted to make sure you liked what it did, though, in case anyone asked."

Walter got to Elmhurst on Friday in time for lunch. He looked around the Cottage Hill Café from their table, and said, "Not that I'm complaining, but is this the only place around to eat?"

"Just about," J.D. replied. "Certainly the best."

"When do we pick up the cash register?"

"Right after lunch."

"Good. Welch know we're coming?"

"He will when we get there."

Walter grinned.

Bill Welch came out of his back room with his mustache quivering with indignation. "Here!" he said. "What do you think you're doing?"

"I told you we'd have to take it back, Mr. Welch," J.D. said.

"Yes, but damnit, you didn't say so soon."

"It's been sold," Walter said.

Welch looked alarmed. "In Elmhurst?"

"No. An establishment in Cicero."

"This is damned embarrassing, J.D.," Welch stammered.

"Embarrassing?"

"Quite a number of my customers just assumed that – well that that was my damned cash register."

"Gee, I'm sorry, Bill. But you can see we have to take it."

"Suppose I bought it?"

"That would be grand, Bill," J.D. said. "But you couldn't have this one. I'd order you one. It would take about a week."

Bill Welch combed his mustache with his thumbnail. "What would I tell my customers?"

"Tell them I've taken it in for an adjustment," J.D. said.

"You wouldn't sell another in Elmhurst until I have mine?"

"I won't deliver another one until I deliver yours," J.D. assured him.

"Okay," Welch said decisively. "I'll take it."

The next morning J.D. was stopped on the main street of Elmhurst by the woman who, with her husband, owned the hardware and feed store. She asked when he could come by the store, and J.D. said how about now. When they got there he discovered that the couple had made up their minds to have a cash register after seeing the one in Welch's drugstore and J.D. doubted anything he could've said would've talked them out of it, even if he'd wanted to.

On Sunday he called Walter at the rooming-house in Chicago. Walter sounded sleepy, although it was nearly noon.

"Listen, Walter," J.D. said. "What did you decide about the Oakland?"

"I offered the feller four hundred, but he's holding out for four-fifty."

"How about if I go in with you?"

"On the car, you mean?"

"Yeah."

"What do you have in mind?"

"I'd only need it a couple of days during the week to pick up registers."

"You mean you've sold that many?"

"I've sold one since I saw you. But I'm going to put them in every business in this town."

"I'll call the guy now and let you know."

Walter called back in ten minutes to say they had themselves a car.

On Monday morning J.D. took the first train to Chicago where he delivered to Patrick Carney the two orders he'd sold plus three others that he'd made out to dummy names and addresses in Elmhurst.

"What happened?" Carney asked.

"What do you mean, what happened? I sold cash registers. Isn't that what a Peerless salesman is supposed to do?"

"Of course. It's only – it's just that last week you seemed so dead certain Elmhurst was a rotten territory."

"It is a rotten territory," J.D. said.

By the time he left Chicago on the afternoon train J.D. had talked Carney into placing all five orders on the priority list, which meant he could pick up the machines himself at the factory in Iolus on Thursday.

On Tuesday he called on Porter Frawley in his office at the quarry. Frawley listened good-naturedly to J.D.'s proposal, and then said, "If what I hear is true, this is the way you hooked Bill Welch into buying one of your machines."

"You're right," J.D. replied. "But I didn't mesmerize him. He bought it because he wanted it."

Frawley laughed, and said, "Okay. You can stick one down in cash accounting, and we'll see what happens."

The manager of the Cottage Hill Café wasn't so amiable. Getting a cash register into the café was important to J.D. Although Rotary didn't allow members to make sales pitches to other members, most of them ate lunch at the Cottage Hill Café, and the meetings of both Rotary and the Chamber of Commerce were held there. However, the manager was so stubborn that J.D. thought for a while he might have to offer to *pay* him to get a machine into his establishment. But finally J.D., in a last desperate effort, told the manager that even the staid restaurant in the Blackstone Hotel in Chicago had a Peerless cash register. Amazingly, the manager acquiesced without another protest. J.D. promised to deliver the machine on Thursday.

On Thursday morning J.D. took the early train to Cicero and picked up the Oakland at the hotel where Walter was staying. He put the top down – it was a clear, icy day – and drove to Iolus bundled in topcoat, scarf and gloves, revelling in the feel of the wind in his hair. He even startled a few birds by breaking into song.

He got to Iolus shortly after the factory had opened, parked the Oakland at the loading dock, and went into the shipping office. The shipping foreman looked at J.D.'s invoices for the five machines and then sent a stock clerk into the warehouse with a hand truck. While they waited he gave J.D. a cup of strong hot coffee from a pot that rested on a stove in the office.

"Got a note here about you," the shipping foreman said.

"Yes?"

"They want you to stop by the office before you go."

J.D. frowned. "I wonder why."

"Says here Mr. Cranston wants to see you."

9

The Baron of Takeovers

HOMER MEDVILLE CRANSTON was sitting at his roll-top desk wearing a dark-grey suit and vest, and pearl-grey spats. He was smoking a long cigar and his heavy brows were knitted.

"Sit down," he said.

J.D. sat. A fire roared in the fireplace.

Cranston examined the ash on his cigar with all the concentration of a surgeon examining an incision. "I understand," he said, "that you sold five units in less than two weeks in Elmhurst."

"Yes, sir."

"To whom?"

J.D. told him. The three fictitious names seemed to stick in his throat.

"Elmhurst is a difficult territory," Cranston said.

"It certainly is." The combination of the heat and cigar smoke was making J.D.'s stomach queasy.

"Not impossible," Cranston went on. "But challenging."

"Mr. Cranston," J.D. said. "I would call it impossible for ninety percent of the salesmen you've got working for you."

"Young man," Cranston said. "You've sold five cash registers! It remains to be seen if you are half as good as you seem to think you are."

"You're right, sir. I haven't proved myself. But I intend to."

"A certain amount of self-confidence is essential to the successful salesman," Cranston said. "But over-confidence has destroyed more salesmen than booze."

J.D. remembered Cranston's own words from one of the sales manuals: "A Peerless salesman is never cocky, but he must have all the confidence in the world – the right kind of confidence. That inner

79

strength of which one can never have too much."

"At any rate," Cranston continued, "I wanted to congratulate you on your fine start. At this pace, you have a good chance of getting to the Quota Buster's convention. It's in New York this year, you know."

"Yes, sir," J.D. said. "I intend to be there."

Shortly after that Cranston dismissed him with a brief handshake. J.D. was glad to be back in the clear, icy air and away from the cigar smoke, heat and piercing eyes.

Driving back to Elmhurst with the five cash registers on the back seat, J.D. tried to figure out why Cranston had called him into his office. The old man certainly didn't have a reputation for congratulating apprentice salesmen every time they sold five units. There was something underlying Cranston's words – some hidden tension – that J.D. couldn't quite put a name to.

On Saturday the manager of the Cottage Hill Café stopped J.D. as he was leaving after lunch and placed an order. He liked the cash register well enough, but J.D. suspected he was more convinced by the fact that the Blackstone Hotel's restaurant had one, than by the cash register's features, handy as they might be.

The following Monday he went to see Porter Frawley who not only bought the machine installed in the accounting department but placed an order for two more.

J.D. took Frawley to lunch at the Cottage Hill Café and was approached in the middle of his club sandwich by Everett Small, the president of the Elmhurst National Bank.

"Say, J.D.,' he said. "Am I poison, or something?"

"Why, what do you mean, Everett?"

"I seem to be the only business in town you haven't given a cash register to."

Of course this was an overstatement – there were plenty of businesses J.D. hadn't got around to yet. But he understood Everett Small's point – the bank was perhaps the most important enterprise in town, financing, as it did, much of the commerce. But there was a very good reason why he hadn't called on Small. Peerless made a special cash drawer just for banks. And Small's bank was the only one in town. There was no way for J.D. to write a dummy order for a bank machine.

He explained it a little differently when he called on Small that same afternoon.

"Trouble is, Everett," J.D. said. "We don't have demonstrators for banks."

Everett Small pondered this. "I have three windows," he said. "Suppose I bought one of your machines and tried it out? Then, if it goes good, I can buy the other two. If not, maybe you could find a place for a used machine. At a discount, of course. Does that make sense?"

J.D. agreed that it made eminent sense.

Everett Small didn't have his Peerless Bank Drawer for a week before he'd ordered the other two. Everett Small was not only president of the bank but also president of the Chamber of Commerce, and after he had his three machines installed the rest of the businesses in Elmhurst of any size at all were stepping all over each other to get on the bandwagon. By the end of his first four weeks J.D. had taken orders for fifty-three cash registers. Since the Quota Buster's convention was due twenty-five weeks after J.D. started his territory, he had qualified if he didn't sell another cash register until the convention. J.D.'s commissions for the four weeks came to over $1300.

On Tuesday evening, February 14, 1911, his fifth week in the territory, J.D. came home to his boarding-house to find a long, black Cadillac parked at the curb with a uniformed chauffeur at the wheel, and its owner waiting for him in the parlor.

His first impression of Joseph Falk Whittier was of shades of grey and black – grey hair, dove-grey chesterfield with black velvet collars, light-grey vested suit, and black spats. He was a thin, elegant man in his middle forties and when he introduced himself J.D.'s mouth fell open.

Joseph Falk Whittier had been dubbed the "Takeover Baron" by the *Wall Street Journal*. He was famous for the daring way in which he bought and combined the assets and talents of seemingly disparate businesses and created thereby enterprises significantly more profitable than their separate parts had been. And he didn't always bother to get the consent of the parties involved beforehand.

In somewhat of a daze J.D. offered him a seat. Whittier crossed his elegantly clad legs, took a silver cigar case from his coat pocket, opened it, and offered it to J.D., who declined.

Whittier talked as he clipped and lit his cigar. "Young man," he said. "I've been hearing about you."

"May I ask how?" J.D. said.

Whittier shook a match lazily to extinguish it and aimed a stream of

81

cigar smoke at the ceiling. "From the Peerless Cash Register Company, of course. You are aware that I'm on the board?"

"No, sir."

Whittier smiled. "Well, take my word – I am. And your name came up at our meeting last Friday, so here I am, to take a look at the marvelous Mr. Marvel."

"I'm flattered," J.D. said.

"You look puzzled. Let me guess – you're wondering what is so grand about selling fifty or so units your first month on the job that it would attract the attention of the board of directors. Am I right?"

"Yes, sir. That's it exactly."

"After all," Whittier went on, "although it is an outstanding accomplishment, you're not the first salesman to do such a thing."

"I expect not."

"You see, there are two things that make you unique." Whittier held up two fingers. He gripped one in his other hand. "Elmhurst had always been considered by the company to be impenetrable. And," he gripped the second finger. "Homer Medville Cranston."

"I beg your pardon?" J.D. said.

Whittier smiled. "It is a custom of the board to review the assignments of Peerless trainees. We consider, quite rightly, that the trainee program is the very life blood of the company. If we don't keep a constant stream of excellent men coming into the sales force, why, we will atrophy, and our considerable competition will devour us. Do you know that the used cash-register business in this country last year equalled the total sales of the Peerless company?"

J.D. shook his head.

"Every fly-by-night huckster with a salesroom and a screwdriver for reconditioning seems to have moved to Chicago, New York, Philadelphia – the population centers – and opened up a used cash register business.

"But," Whittier went on, dismissing the used cash-register business with a wave of his cigar, "that's another topic. Where was I – oh, yes. The board. We review the sales-trainee placements very carefully. And there was something very odd about the class you graduated with."

"You mean that Mr. Cranston made the assignments himself."

Whittier looked up sharply. "How did you know that?"

"Rumors," J.D. said. "You mean it's true?"

"It would seem that it's impossible to keep anything from our sales

82

force. Yes, Homer made the assignments. In my five years on the board he'd never done such a thing. It is the purview of the branch sales manager, as I'm sure you're aware. So naturally, this piqued my curiosity. Homer would say nothing before the board, but in private, just the two of us, he let slip a hint or two that was enough for me to deduce that he made the assignments for one reason, one reason only, and I can tell by the look of anticipation on your face that you probably know that, too."

"I can guess," J.D. said. "He wanted to give me Elmhurst."

"A good guess. Of course, he hoped that the whole thing would remain between himself and the Chicago branch manager – is it Barney?"

"Carney," J.D. replied. "Patrick Carney."

"Either Carney let it slip, or someone made a damned good guess."

"Why give me Elmhurst?" J.D. asked hotly. "The last salesman they had out here lasted two weeks, and he was experienced."

"Precisely. And I can't imagine you don't have a guess or two about that, as well."

"Well, all I can think of is that I offended him when I applied for the job in the first place. I'm afraid I was pretty brash."

"He said you were. But that wasn't the reason – not if my deductions are correct, and I believe they are." He looked around the room. "Is it possible to get a drink in this house?"

"I'm afraid not," J.D. said. "I could ask Mrs. Schenley if she would make coffee."

Whittier sighed. "If that's the best we can do."

J.D. found Mrs. Schenley in the kitchen and she put one of her daughters to making coffee.

When J.D. returned to the parlor, he asked, "Why did Cranston send me out here?"

"Fear," Whittier replied with a small smile.

"I'm afraid I don't know what you mean, sir."

"When he looked at you, Mr. Marvel," Whittier said slowly, "he saw himself thirty years ago. Oh, I don't mean physical resemblance – I mean the eagerness, the intelligence – above all, the sheer will, which you amply exhibited by the way you had yourself and your friend hired."

"He told you that?"

"Of course not! Homer would never say such a thing. I doubt he even thinks it to himself. But that doesn't make it any the less true. Ah, the coffee. Thank you, my dear."

After the girl who brought the coffee had left, J.D. asked, "Does Mr. Cranston know you're here?"

"A very shrewd question," Whittier said, sipping his coffee. "Of course he doesn't. And he must never know."

J.D. nodded. "Then may I ask why you *are* here?"

"I assume you know who I am – or, at least, who the press claim I am." J.D. nodded again. "The 'Takeover Baron,' they call me. The vision is of some rapacious octopus reaching out tentacles to wrap them around unsuspecting little companies. Not a vision original with me – Thomas Nast did a cartoon of me just so ten years ago.

"What all the financial pundits and the cartoonists miss, however, is the real business that I'm in. I am not in the business of acquiring companies, or factories, or rolling stock, or the like, although what I do acquire entails those things. No, what I acquire are *people*. Men with ideas. Men with vision. I wouldn't give a plugged nickel for the biggest company on God's green earth if the *people* who were in that company didn't excite me, didn't have the talent and the brains and the drive to do far-reaching things. You see, Marvel – what I provide is opportunity. I find men who have been shackled by the petty little rules of lesser men and I buy their companies and I *remove* the shackles."

Whittier held his cigar over the ashtray on the table beside his chair and delicately flicked off the ash with his little finger. "Succeeding in the people-finding business is not dissimilar to, say, the horse-buying business." He smiled suddenly. "Wouldn't the pundits at the *Wall Street Journal* love to hear me say that. 'Whittier Calls People Animals,' the headline would read.

"Nevertheless, there is a similarity. To make the wisest selection in regard to horses one can only go by two factors: breeding and performance. Of course, when a horse is a mere yearling it has no performances to speak of, so one goes entirely by breeding. Later, if the horse performs really well it becomes very dear, if not impossible, to acquire. Do you follow my little analogy, Mr. Marvel?"

"I think so. You want to take a look at my confirmation."

Whittier gave J.D. a delighted smile. "Are you a horse fancier, then?"

J.D. shook his head. "Just raised on a farm."

"Well, you're quite correct. I did come out to look you over."

"And if you like what you see you'll go back and make Cranston an offer?"

Whittier laughed. "I like a man with a sense of humor. No, there is

84

where the analogy breaks down. We stopped buying and selling people in this country some fifty years ago. But, I do like what I see."

"So?"

"So, I propose that we take an interest in each other."

"How do you mean?"

Whittier took a pigskin wallet from his coat, opened it, took out a card and extended it to J.D. "I propose that we stay in touch," he said. "The telephone number on that card is for my apartment in New York. I travel a lot, but there will always be someone at that number who can tell you how to reach me.

"If you ever need advice, call me. Let me know how you are from time to time."

"I'd like that," J.D. said.

Whittier stood and J.D. helped him on with his coat. "You will be coming to New York this summer for the Quota Buster's convention. Let's have dinner one evening."

J.D. stood in the doorway and watched the long black car until it disappeared. When it was gone, he took out the card Joseph Falk Whittier had given him and looked at it to assure himself that it hadn't all been a dream.

THREE

If chance will have me king,
why, chance may crown me . .
William Shakespeare

THREE

10

The Baron's Lair

WHEN JOSEPH FALK WHITTIER said he had an apartment in New York he understated the case considerably. He actually had one half of a large duplex in the 1100 block on 5th Avenue. The building had been designed by Hardenbergh in the grand Renaissance château tradition. Each of its three stories was done in a different architectural style: the first, the strong Tuscan; the second, the more decorative Ionic, topped by the graceful Corinthian. The entryway in Whittier's part of the building was a long, high, narrow room with walnut-wainscoted walls and covered by an intricately coffered walnut ceiling. This opened into a gallery from which two staircases, one on each side, ascended to the second floor in sweeping arcs. The polished oak floors of the entryway and the gallery were partially covered by rich Persian rugs in age-mellowed blues and reds.

J.D. stood in the gallery where the butler, after taking his overcoat and hat, had placed him. While the butler went to announce him to the master of the house, J.D. made a slow turn, drinking in the surroundings. He was examining a tapestry on the wall that depicted a cowled ascetic-faced man reaching out a hand to grasp the stem of a rose in whose bloom was the visage of an enchanted girl, when Joseph Falk Whittier appeared beside him.

"Do you like it?" Whittier asked. He was wearing a maroon smoking jacket with black silk lapels over a dress shirt, black tie, and tuxedo trousers.

"I don't know," J.D. replied. "I think so."

"It's called 'The Pilgrim In the Garden,' by Burne-Jones, woven at Merton Abbey.

"Come along now," Whittier said. "We have time for a drink."

J.D. had arrived three days before on the Broadway Limited with its valets, library car, white linen, crystal and silver. Walter Hucko had seen him off in Chicago. Walter, although doing well in his territory in Cicero, hadn't qualified for the Quota Buster's convention.

J.D., however, had fulfilled his year's quota in not quite four weeks, and gone on to wring Elmhurst dry of cash-register prospects. According to Homer Cranston's formula of one cash register per one hundred population, Elmhurst had been good for no more than eighty units, but by the time J.D. boarded the Broadway Limited he had sold 176. Counting bonuses for going more than three times over his quota for the year, he had made nearly $5000 in commissions, which meant he'd earned at about the same rate as he had selling organs.

This was certainly more money than J.D. needed to live on, and to live quite well, and to send some home to his mother, too, but he was not content. In fact, he was worried. He'd saturated Elmhurst with cash registers, even Albert French had finally succumbed – French's mercantile store sported seven shiny chrome Peerless cash registers – and unless J.D. could get a new territory his days with the Peerless Cash Register Company seemed numbered. He had tried to discuss the situation with Patrick Carney but had got the brush-off. When J.D. had pointed out to Carney that unless an application could be discovered for cash registers in barns and outhouses he was out of business, Carney just gave him a fish-eyed look and changed the subject.

Joseph Falk Whittier led J.D. to a tall room lined with bookcases on three walls. Leaded casement windows were open to the hot, heavy night. A black Bechstein grand piano stood on thick lathed and pedestaled legs on one side of the room. Whittier seated his guest in a dark walnut armchair with a slatted barrel back, upholstered in pale-green silk.

"What'll it be?" Whittier asked.

"Whatever you're having," J.D. said. The butler had appeared at the open door, and Whittier sent him for drinks.

Whittier took a silver box from a trestle table, opened it, and held it out to J.D. The box was lined in cedar and contained cigars, Prince des Galles Perfectos: long, thick, made in Havana. J.D. had never smoked them, but he knew what they were. He took one and held it appreciatively under his nose.

"Homer Cranston smokes these," he said.

Whittier passed a gold cigar-clipper to J.D. "I introduced him to them."

When they had their cigars going Whittier took a seat opposite J.D. Between them was a low table holding a crystal ashtray and a statuette of a gnu in bronze, its rough shaggy head turned toward the windows behind J.D. The butler appeared and deposited a silver tray on the table. The tray held a bottle of Scotch, a siphon, an ice bucket and two glasses. Whittier prepared the drinks, passed one to J.D., leaned back in his chair with his glass in one hand, his cigar in the other, crossed an elegant leg over a knee and smiled at his guest. J.D. suddenly felt awkward. His arms seemed too long, his hands too large.

"How's the convention going?" Whittier asked.

"Fine. I enjoyed your speech." Whittier had addressed a plenary luncheon session just the day before.

"Hardly deserves the title. More of a chat. I leave the hortatory outpourings to fellows like Cranston." Whittier blew smoke at the ceiling. "What do you think of the Plaza?"

"It's the finest hotel I've seen," J.D. said.

"Cranston does not stint when it comes to celebrating the stars on his sales force. Remember that. It's a good lesson."

At that moment one of the double doors slid silently back and into the room walked the most incredibly beautiful woman J.D. had ever seen. She paused for a moment, and then walked over to stand beside Whittier's chair. In her raven-black hair she wore a tiara of gold sculpted leaves encrusted with pearls and diamonds. Her gown was lavender velvet, worn off one creamy shoulder and caught at the other with a gold brooch. She moved sinuously but unselfconsciously, her lithe body informed with the feral grace of a cat.

"My dear," Whittier said, rising. "Allow me to present Mr. J.D. Marvel." J.D. got hurriedly to his feet. "Mr. Marvel, Madelline Yates."

"Pleased to know you," J.D. stammered.

"Mr. Marvel. Don't you have a first name?"

J.D. blushed.

"He is called 'J.D.,' " Whittier said.

"And those initials stand for nothing?" Madelline Yates asked.

"Jesse Dinsmore," J.D. said.

"Ah, Jesse!" she said. "Let me see – the father of David, wasn't he? Do you aspire to be the father of a king, Mr. Marvel?"

Whittier laughed. "He aspires to be king himself, don't you, my boy?"

J.D.'s blush deepened. The rude habiliments of the farm seemed to cling to him like some reeking disease, announcing loudly the hayseed that he was. Suddenly the suit that he was wearing, his best suit, the grey English worsted with its Italian silk lining, that he'd paid nearly a hundred dollars for in Indianapolis and had been so proud to wear before Wanda Agronsky, turned to an ill-fitting lump of graceless cloth as Madelline Yates' glance brushed it with what J.D. perceived as a critical eye.

"Father sent me to discover what time dinner is. He's in his room trying to stab himself with his studs."

Whittier laughed. "We'll dine at eight. Please invite him down for cocktails first, and, of course, my dear, come yourself."

Madelline Yates wrinkled her nose. "As much as I'm tempted, I'll join the ladies for sherry and idle talk, though I'd much rather listen to you men hatching your plots."

"Ah, how you over-rate us. Dull fellows, we businessmen."

"See you at dinner, Mr. Marvel." Madelline Yates made her way out of the room.

"A lovely woman," Whittier said.

J.D. cleared his throat. "Yes."

"I think you'll find her father interesting – not as interesting as Madelline, I daresay. Do you still have your curiosity about data processing?"

"Very much so."

"Arnold Yates is in the business." Whittier leaned forward to flick an ash from his cigar. "Do you remember my telling you that used cash registers were giving Peerless a bit of competition?"

"Yes. I even experienced it myself. There're several used cash-register shops in Chicago."

"Yates has applied the same practices to data-processing equipment. He buys up used stuff, refurbishes it, and sells it for about half the price of new. He's made himself a millionaire doing it. Not so long ago Arnold Yates was bankrupt. Today he's worth five million."

Whittier consulted a thin gold wristwatch. "It's time I put on my dinner jacket." He stood. "Enjoy your drink, finish your cigar. I'll return directly."

When he was alone, J.D. rose and examined the room. The books were leather-bound. There were matched sets; the works of Shakespeare, Molière, Ben Jonson; Marvell, Wordsworth, Whitman; encyclopedias, atlases, thesauri; novels, histories, biographies. The arrangement of the volumes on the shelves seemed to be according to some decorative scheme incorporating the color of their bindings rather than one of cataloging. He discovered a copy of *Pride and*

Prejudice, his mother's favorite novel, and when he held it in his hands he saw that the end leaves were uncut and he remembered something his mother had said upon one of the rare occasions she had spoken words of defiance to his father, who had called a dime novel he had caught J.D. reading a "bad book". "The only bad book," his mother had said, "is an unread book."

J.D.'s thoughts were interrupted by the appearance of a man in a dinner jacket who introduced himself as Arnold Yates. He was a short, rotund man of late middle age with a little rose-bud of a mouth hidden between great rosy cheeks and a rim of white hair above which loomed a large, smooth dome of bald head. He reminded J.D. of a woodcut of Friar Tuck that was in one of his mother's books – a Friar Tuck caparisoned in black tuxedo, crisp white shirt and black tie.

As Arnold Yates prepared himself a drink he said: "You're the young feller works for Cranston."

"Yes, sir."

"What d'you do for him, if you don't mind my asking?"

"I'm a salesman, in Illinois."

"Ah! Sales!" Yates raised his glass in salute. "Backbone of the country. As I tell my own sales force, they – people like you – keep America goin'." He went to the trestle table, opened the silver box, and began to rummage among the cigars until he found one that met his requirements, bit the end off, and stuck it in his mouth. "D'you have any idea – Mr. Marvel, was it? D'you have any idea what would happen to this fine country of ours if every salesman stopped work tomorrow?" Yates pointed his thumb at the carpet. "She'd go to the bottom faster'n the *Maine*."

"Mr. Whittier told me that you are in the data-processing business."

"That I am."

"I'm interested in that business," J.D. said. Briefly, he recounted his meeting with Hollerith.

"Perfect example of what I'm talking about!" Yates exclaimed. "Herman Hollerith couldn't sell a jail passkey to a convict. Oh, he's a genius with thinkin' up the machines, true enough. But it takes a different kind of genius to sell 'em. And if you can't sell 'em, there's no need to think 'em up, is there?" Yates chuckled and puffed on his cigar. "No, sir, there's no need to think 'em up. Take me, for example. Got no idea how those machines work. I mean, how their innards work. I have an understanding of *what* they do; it's the *how* that leaves me in a quandary. But I know *sales*. And I saw a market and a product

93

– and how do you put the two together? *Sales!* That's the ticket! The product was *used* data-processing machines." He tapped his temple with the unlit end of his cigar, and winked. "*Marketing* brains, that's what it takes. I saw, on the one hand, that there were a hell of a lot of machines floating around that didn't have a home. Machines that had been replaced by newer models, or machines that had worn out, machines from businesses that had come a cropper. On the other hand, businesses are always looking to cut costs. Then there are the firms that won't go into something new, no matter how good the idea, until they think they're getting the cut rate. So I buy up the used machines, renovate them, and rent them for a considerable amount less than they cost new."

"You don't sell the machines?" J.D. asked.

"No, sir," Yates said emphatically. "Lots of companies can't pay cash on the barrel head."

"On the other hand," J.D. added. "If you sell you get your money now."

"I'm fifty-eight years old, my boy." Yates said. "I want a secure old age." He chuckled. "My policy has served me well. Money comin' in every month. You can ask our host if it hasn't. I've taken most of the data-processing business away from Peerless."

"I didn't know that," J.D. said, surprised. But now that he thought about it, he could recall Leland Prescott, the Peerless data-processing salesman in Chicago, muttering about used machines undercutting his business. He hadn't paid much attention at the time, because Prescott was usually muttering darkly about something.

"Yes," Yates continued. "The reason I'm in town is to persuade Joe to see the light."

"The light?"

"I've said too much. Strictly confidential, if you don't mind, my boy."

They were interrupted by the arrival of their host, who had changed his smoking jacket for a black tuxedo, and the other guests. At dinner J.D. was seated between Madelline Yates and Mrs. Whittier. Mrs. Whittier fell into a conversation with Mrs. Yates, a tall woman of regal bearing on her other side, and J.D. found himself the exclusive object of Madelline Yates' attention. Her eyes held a strange expression; they seemed to hold, deep behind the outward façade of civility, a kind of mocking invitation. She told him she lived in an apartment in Manhattan, worked as a commercial artist and spent occasional weekends at her parents' home on Long Island. The time flowed.

Much too soon J.D. found himself back in the library with the men, over cigars and brandy.

At ten o'clock Arnold Yates stretched mightily, and said, "I'm for bed, gentlemen."

J.D. got to his feet. "I'd better be going too –"

Whittier put a hand on J.D.'s shoulder. "Stay for a bit."

Yates shook J.D.'s hand and Whittier escorted the little man to the door and closed it after him. Then he replenished J.D.'s brandy and sat across from him.

"Did Yates give you his speech about sales being the backbone of the country?"

"He mentioned something about it, yes."

"He wants to buy out the Peerless data-processing business." Whittier examined the ash on his cigar. "Let me tell you a bit of a story. About five years ago, not long after I joined the Peerless board, I met a man named Ansell Farnsworth. You know the name?"

"The man who invented the data-processing machines for Peerless?"

"Not quite. He'd already invented his machines before he and Peerless ever heard of each other.

"At any rate, I met him. He was a professor of engineering at a little backwater college in Pennsylvania. Since he'd done the work on the machines while he was a professor, the school owned the patents. Farnsworth is brilliant, in his field, but he's one of the most eccentric and contrary men you'd ever want to meet. I was convinced that the machines could give Hollerith and his outfit a run. I put together a deal that I took to the Peerless board. Cranston was skeptical, principally because, in order to get into the data-processing business, we not only needed the patents, we needed Farnsworth. The sorter and the card-punching machines he'd invented were fine, but the tabulator still needed work. At first, Farnsworth wouldn't come unless, after we bought the patents from the school, we assigned them exclusively to him. What we finally worked out was a co-ownership of the patents. Farnsworth and Peerless, fifty-fifty.

"As it turned out, it was a disaster. Farnsworth's hard-headedness is only exceeded by one man I've known and that is Homer Cranston. To say they didn't get along is like saying Caesar and Brutus had their differences.

"Well, Farnsworth finally got the tabulator running, and we had a fine line of equipment. But Homer was only half-heartedly supporting it. Then a couple of years ago along came our friend Arnold Yates. He

95

and his used machines took away most of what little business we had.

"Now Arnold has come to us with a proposition. He wants to buy Peerless's fifty percent interest in the Farnsworth patents. He's ready to branch out into new machines. He figures, probably rightfully, that he can manufacture them at his renovation plants."

Whittier rose, went to the trestle table, got the cigar box and brought it back and offered it to J.D., who declined. Whittier carefully selected a fresh cigar and clipped and lighted it. "Any questions so far?" he asked.

"If the business is so bad, why would Mr. Yates want to buy it? Couldn't he find some other company or, better, some inventor, to design him machines?"

"Yates wants the Farnsworth outfit for a number of reasons. One: it still has a fine reputation in the business as a manufacturer of reliable equipment that can do more than even the Hollerith machines. Two: difficult as he is, Farnsworth is a genius, and his inventing days are far from over. In conjunction with someone who could get along with him, he *might* make them both fabulously wealthy. And, finally, and most important, Mr. Arnold Yates would love to see me humiliated, and, believe me when I say that if we have to sell to him for the pittance he's offering, I *will* be humiliated. The reasons for that are ancient history and not germane to our topic. But they are present in everything that Yates does in connection with this deal."

Whittier paused to puff on his cigar. "So – what do you think of all that?"

"Sir?"

"How would you advise us to go?"

"I'd stay with the data-processing business, but I'm not a very good one to ask."

"And why is that?"

"I'm sold on data processing. The reason I went to Peerless was because I thought there might be a chance to get into the field."

"I agree data processing is one of *the* businesses of the future. But if things go on the way they are, the data-processing business of Peerless won't be worth one of Mr. Arnold Yates's shirt studs."

J.D. thought for a moment. "I don't see what choice you have, then."

"We could take the business back from Mr. Arnold Yates."

"But if Peerless won't get behind the data processing, how could that be done?"

"You mean if Cranston won't get behind it." Whittier rose to refill their glasses from the brandy decanter. "He's backed into a corner now, though. The board's on his tail to get the division profitable – we can't even sell it for what we've got in it, the condition it's in now. Yates would be stealing it, and his is the only offer we've got."

Whittier gestured for J.D. to rise. He took his arm and guided him out into the hall where the butler shortly appeared with J.D.'s hat and topcoat. While J.D. was putting them on, Whittier said, "I want you to think over what we've talked about tonight. Then let me know how you'd approach getting the business back from Yates. And remember this – we've got to act fast. Also, and this is just between you and me, I want a plan that will not only get our business back, but that will finish Yates. D'you follow me?"

"Yes, sir," J.D. said.

"Fine!" Whittier smiled and offered his hand. "Let me know by tomorrow night if you've come up with anything." He opened the door and before J.D. knew it he found himself alone on the cold porch of Joseph Falk Whittier's mansion.

11

The Challenge

J.D. WAS TOO FIRED UP by his talk with Joseph Falk Whittier to sleep. He had a pot of coffee delivered by room service and while he drank it he paced his room. The question that Whittier had asked plagued him: Did he want to win badly enough? He thought he did, but until he was tested he wouldn't know. He tried to imagine the extremes to which he might be forced to go to win. Whittier wanted Yates ruined. Could he ruin a man to win? Well, if the man were trying to ruin him, of course.

He remembered Yates' monkish, jolly face; his blustering but somehow kind interest in J.D. He remembered Yates' breathtakingly beautiful daughter and his regal wife with the kind eyes. He imagined these people overflowing with grace and human kindness, and then asked himself if he could bring them to ruin, and decided: Yes! By God, if Yates were knowingly in his way – Yes! He struck his fist into his palm.

By the time the dawn broke over the monuments to the Grand Army of the Republic in the plaza in front of the hotel, J.D. was sitting on the bed in his room with his shoulders against the wall, a notebook propped on his knees, writing furiously. Joseph Falk Whittier wanted a plan, and J.D. intended to give him one.

He showered, dressed and went downstairs in time for the first meeting of the day of the Quota Buster's convention. He hurried from the last meeting at six o'clock that night, to a lobby telephone. He was buoyed by an excited optimism that overrode his body's need for sleep. After J.D. had given his name, the butler summoned Whittier to the phone.

"I'd like to hear your plan," Whittier said. There was a pause. "I'm going to the opera tonight. Why don't I stop by your hotel about an hour from now? Meet me in the bar off the lobby."

When Whittier arrived in the bar J.D. was waiting at a table.

Whittier removed a black topcoat with velvet lapels and a top hat and placed them on a vacant chair. He was wearing tails.

After they ordered drinks, Whittier said, "Tell me about your plan."

J.D. removed several folded sheets of notepaper from his coat pocket. "I've written it all down." He offered the sheets to Whittier, who waved them away.

"Tell me about it," he said.

J.D. took a breath and began. He referred from time to time to his notes. It took him half an hour. When he was finished, Whittier signaled the waiter for another round of drinks, took a cigar case from his pocket and, after he had lighted J.D.'s cigar and his own, sat puffing, looking broodingly at J.D.

Finally J.D., unable to bear the silence any longer, said, "How do you like it, sir?"

"Your sales plan?" Whittier waved a dismissive hand. "The best I can say for it, is it's naive."

"For my instruction," J.D. said stiffly, "I wish you'd tell me its failings."

"Happy to," Whittier said, accepting his drink from the waiter. "The main failing is it won't get the job done. You remember what the job was?"

"Yes, sir." J.D. chafed under the edge of sarcasm in Whittier's voice. "To take the business from Yates' used machines."

"That was half of it," Whittier said, and paused expectantly.

"And to – to 'finish' Yates."

"That's right," Whittier said mildly. Then he leaned over the table and said in a cutting voice, "You don't really think this custard-pudding plan of yours could tackle a tough job like that, do you?"

J.D. felt the heat rise to his face. "Yes, sir," he stammered. "I did. Or I wouldn't've wasted your time with it."

Whittier leaned back in his chair. "Well, let's review it and see what you think. You want to send salesmen into every business that has Yates equipment. You want them to give demonstrations of the Farnsworth equipment, showing how superior it is to theirs. Then you expect them to fall all over themselves to pay forty percent more to change it over to new equipment at great inconvenience and expense, and to be happy while doing it. Do I understand your plan correctly?"

"There were some other things –"

"Oh, yeah. Some ribbons and frills. Like installing machines free until they got dependent on them –"

"It worked in Elmhurst. And you left out the reference selling."

"Can't reference something that doesn't exist," Whittier said. "We've got hardly any business left."

"I meant, that the machines you install free you use as reference."

"Listen, J.D. This is not cash registers we're talking about, and it's not Elmhurst, Illinois. This is the major leagues, my boy."

"Well, damnit! I believe it would work. I believe I could make it work, Mr. Whittier!"

"All right, all right! You're probably right that *you* could make it work. And let's suppose you sold more machines than anyone in the history of the business, which I'm also prepared to believe you might do. That still wouldn't accomplish the job I want done. One salesman can't do it."

"But I could teach others –!"

"How bad do you want to work for me, Marvel?"

"How bad –!" J.D. stared at the other man. "I was up *all night* on this thing. I haven't been to bed yet."

Whittier looked at his watch. "I have to make this quick. Do you trust me? If I say you're going to work for me, and that this will be the biggest break in your life so far – maybe ever – will you believe me?"

It didn't take J.D. a moment to reply. "Of course."

Whittier patted him on the arm. "Good lad! Now. You go back to Chicago when the convention is over. When you get there, you will be rather ignominiously fired by your manager – what's his name –?"

"Carney. But what –!"

"Remember! Trust! The minute you are fired by Carney you begin work for me. What are you making a month in commissions?"

"About eight hundred."

"Your salary with me will be fifteen hundred for starters. Is that satisfactory?"

J.D.'s mouth was open. He shut it and said, "Yes, sir."

"You'll have to move to New York." He looked at his watch again and stood. "I've got to go. I'll be in Chicago next week and we'll continue this."

J.D. stood too. "But, sir –"

Whittier was striding away. Then he spun and hurried back to where J.D. stood. "One other thing, Marvel. Begin to think about a staff. You'll need twenty, thirty, I should imagine. Choose them with care. Go-getters like yourself, who want to win above all else. Don't say anything to them until we have a chance to talk again. I'll see you in Chicago." And then he was gone, leaving J.D. staring after him.

J.D. was fired the first morning the convention attendees were back. Patrick Carney had never liked J.D. Carney, as a matter of policy, didn't like those whom Homer Medville Cranston didn't like, and he had good reason to believe Cranston didn't like J.D. So it was with a certain relish that Carney carried out his instructions.

The main office was crowded with salesmen making up their plans for the day when Carney walked out of his cubby-hole and pretentiously cleared his throat to get silence.

Then he fired J.D. in front of the whole office.

He said he was doing it that way as an example (in fact he'd been instructed to do it just that way, but of course he didn't say so). He said that J.D. had been guilty of unethical practices – he'd installed cash registers that hadn't been paid for. He'd lied to customers, telling them that it was the policy of the Peerless Cash Register Company to allow them to try out cash registers for nothing. Finally, and, judging by Carney's tone, the worst crime of all – J.D. had diverted new machines meant to be delivered to paying customers, to non-paying customers.

Of course, every charge was true as far as it went. J.D. longed to leap to his feet and tell them that every single cash register he'd installed on a non-pay basis had been bought – the company hadn't lost, but had gained! He would've loved to have shouted in Carney's face that if the dumb Mick had a brain in his head instead of firing him he would adopt J.D.'s sales practices throughout the office! But he remembered what Joseph Falk Whittier had said, and held his tongue. Red-faced, he packed up his briefcase and left the office, with Hucko close on his heels.

"What in Christ's name is that little prick doin'?" Walter asked.

"Don't worry about it, Walter," J.D. said.

"Don't *worry* about it!" Hucko exploded. "The bastard can't get away with it. You're top man in the whole office, for God's sake!"

J.D. stopped and turned to his friend. "Look, Walter. I can't tell you what this is about right now, but I will – soon. Just take my word that it's okay."

"You mean you knew this was coming?" Hucko asked.

"Yes. But that's all I can say."

"I can't go back there and work for that son of a bitch!" Hucko exploded.

101

"Maybe you won't have to for long. But for now, for my sake, go on back, will you?"

J.D. stood at the windows of the Prince Albert suite of the Blackstone Hotel and looked at a pewter Lake Michigan under a lowering sky.

Joseph Falk Whittier came into the sitting-room carrying a tray upon which were a pot of coffee and two cups and put it on a coffee table.

"Have a seat and some coffee," he said.

J.D. sat across from Whittier and poured himself a cup of coffee. Whittier took an engraved silver cigarette case from the smoking jacket he was wearing.

He smiled through the smoke at J.D. "Well," he said. "I hear you were drummed out of the corps pretty thoroughly. Epaulets stripped, and all."

J.D. smiled ruefully. "Carney enjoyed every minute of it."

"Always remember two things," Whittier replied. "The little, petty men with no talent will always be jealous. And, they're not worth the effort to stamp on. Ignore them. They suffer enough just being who they are."

"I'll try to remember that."

"I admire your restraint, J.D."

"What do you mean?"

"Well, after all that's happened, with Carney and so on, you must be dying to leap over here and grab me by the lapels and demand to know what's going on."

J.D. smiled. "So, what's going on?"

"You are sales manager of a new company." Whittier paused. "The company's called the Renovated Data Processing Company. RDP for short."

"I never heard of it."

"Not surprising. It's only existed for a couple of days." Whittier smiled. "Should I go on?"

"Please."

Whittier poured himself more coffee. "This company is wholly owned by the Northeast Fiduciary Trust Company."

"Never heard of that, either."

"That one's been around for quite awhile, but it's still not surprising you haven't heard of it. It's a holding company. It's only business is to own other companies.

"Now for the dénouement of this little chain. The Northeast

102

Fiduciary Trust Company is wholly owned by the Empire State Investment Company of which I –" he bowed, "– have the honor of being majority stockholder."

"Ah."

"Ah, indeed."

"But why the runaround?"

"Because it wouldn't be wise to have the Renovated Data Processing Company too closely connected with the Peerless Cash Register Company."

"Why?"

"Let's just say that the marketing policies of RDP might be considered – ah, unfair in certain quarters."

"I think you lost me."

Whittier waved a hand. "Don't worry about it. All you need know is that you are sales manager and an officer of RDP."

"We'll sell used data-processing equipment?"

"Yes."

"Where will we get it?"

"RDP has a contract with Peerless for machines."

"Peerless has *used* machines?"

"A few. They'll have more – all you'll need."

"We're going to go head-to-head with Yates?"

"You are going to. This is your baby, J.D. Have you thought about staff?"

"I have several in mind."

"Hire them."

"What should I pay them? What should I tell them the job is?"

"Pay them what you have to. The job is to replace every Yates account with RDP equipment."

"I see," J.D. said. "RDP exists to go against Yates."

"Absolutely."

"This is beginning to feel familiar."

Whittier leaned forward and served them more coffee. "What do you mean?"

"When I was assigned to Elmhurst there was only a limited market there. When I'd sold the market, I was out of work."

"To find yourself in a new position making a hell of a lot more money."

"Am I to take it then that if I do this right I'll not work myself out of a job?"

"J.D. – you said you wanted to be in the data-processing business.

103

Well, now you are. Beyond that – trust!"

"When do I start?"

"You already have." Whittier stood. "Get out there and hire your men. Here –" He took a folded sheaf of papers from the drawer of a desk. "This is a list of Yates' customers. They're pretty well concentrated in New York and Chicago, with New York having about twice as many. Also, here's your price list. When you get to New York, let me know. I've rented an office for you." Whittier stuck out a hand. "By the end of this year I want Yates out of business."

J.D. went back to the rooming-house in a daze. He went up to his room and looked at the sheets of paper. He estimated that there were over a thousand Yates customers on the list. He looked at the price list. There were three basic pieces of equipment: sorter, card punch, and tabulator – with a few optional devices. Although he knew little about the business, the prices for the machines seemed low – very low.

He sat down at the desk in his room and made a list of things to do:

1. Hire salesmen.
2. Move to New York. (Get stuff from Elmhurst, pay bill.)
3. *Learn data processing*.

Leland Prescott said, "I don't know if I should be seen talking to you." He sat across from J.D. in the bar at Jiggs Muldoon's. It was six o'clock and the bar was filled with office workers.

"You mean your job with Peerless is that good?" J.D. asked.

"No. But it's the only one I've got."

"I want to talk to you about a new one. A good one." J.D. signaled the waitress for more beers.

"Why would you want me?"

"Jesus!" J.D. exclaimed. "You're full of self-confidence!"

"Try working as a Peerless data-processing salesman for two years and see how much self-confidence you have."

"I need you, Leland," J.D. said, "because you're experienced. You know the equipment. I haven't got time to train people."

Prescott sipped his beer. "Tell me again. This is *used* equipment?"

"Yes. And we'll be going after specific customers – those now in the hands of the Yates Used Equipment Company."

Prescott looked at J.D. in astonishment. "Are you nuts! That's our major competitor."

J.D. nodded.

"They've practically driven Peerless out of the business!"

J.D. nodded again.

"What makes you think you can do any better than we have?"

"Look, Leland – how much support has Peerless given you? What is it you're always moaning about?"

"How is this new outfit of yours going to do any better?"

"We're going after the business." J.D. took the RDP price list from his pocket and put it on the table between them.

Prescott bent over the price list, and then looked up at J.D. "Are you serious?"

"That's the price list, Leland."

Prescott shook his head in wonder. "Tell me again about this company."

"We're owned by the Northeast Fiduciary Trust Company."

"Never heard of 'em," Prescott said.

"Have you heard of every company there is, Leland?" J.D. asked.

Prescott shook his head. "Pardon me for saying this, J.D., but you're kind of young to be sales manager of a company. I just want to make sure everything is on the up and up."

"Why?" J.D. asked, letting his irritation show. "Have you got such an almighty good job now? Listen to me, Leland. Here's a chance to do what you're always complaining that Peerless won't let you do – compete in the market place. But, man! You've got to take a chance. You can't sit on your ass in your little corner in that office all your life and expect to make anything of yourself."

Prescott stared at J.D. for a long moment and then said, "Okay. Tell me the deal."

"Eight hundred a month, if you fulfill your quota. If you can't sell a hundred between now and the end of the year, you aren't trying."

Prescott had gone pale. "Eight hundred –! Are you serious?"

"I figure," J.D. said, "that you couldn't be making much more than three hundred now. But, damn it, Leland, you're worth eight hundred! Let me guess what you're thinking. You're thinking that if this kid can offer someone like you eight hundred a month, then you know he's nuts and not to be trusted. Am I right?"

"More or less."

"Well look at it from my angle for a minute. You've had years of experience in the data-processing business. How many people have? You know all the Yates accounts in the Chicago area. I'm sure you know people at those accounts on a first-name basis. And, given the chance, I think you could be a hell of a salesman."

Prescott pointed at the price list. "At those prices you wouldn't have to be any kind of a salesman."

105

"So, are you knocking *that*?"

"I just don't see how anyone could make money at those prices."

"No one's asking you to see. That's the business of the people who are putting up the money for the company."

"It's my business if I take the job and then the company sinks under me."

J.D. threw up his hands. "Christ, Leland! I thought from all the complaining you do that you'd jump at this." J.D. picked up the price list. "I guess I was wrong."

"Wait," Leland Prescott said. His mustache twitched. "Damn it!" Prescott exclaimed, striking the table with the flat of his hand. 'I'll do it."

Walter Hucko was easy to convince. "Hell, yes," he said, when J.D. offered him the job, even before he'd got around to mentioning pay.

"A thousand a month," J.D. said. "And commissions."

"A thousand –!" Hucko became, for the moment, speechless.

"We'll have to learn data processing, and learn it damn quick, Walter."

"Hells bells, I'd learn to talk Turkish for a deal like that."

"Have you seen Wanda lately?"

"Night before last, matter of fact. Why?"

"I want to hire her. We need someone to make the machines work for the customers. Besides that, she'd be the perfect one to teach us."

"I dunno," Hucko said. "She likes workin' for Hollerith."

"But I wonder if she likes the pay."

"It's true the old man doesn't pay her a fourth what she's worth."

"And I wonder if she likes being passed over for some young fool who doesn't know half what she knows."

Hucko grinned. "You got me sold, J.D. All you have to do now is sell Wanda."

J.D. had lunch with Wanda. She knew from Walter that he wanted to hire her and her resistance was already in place. It quickly crumbled when J.D. offered her the job of Assistant Manager and $1000 a month.

"Christ, Marvel!" she said. "You take my breath away. What do you figure I can do that's worth that much?"

"Run the technical end of the business while I'm out selling."

Wanda passed a hand over her eyes. "I'd – I'd have to give two weeks' notice."

"Oh, no! I need you Monday."

"But that wouldn't be fair to Hollerith."

"Has Hollerith been fair to you?"

She stared at him for a moment, and then said, "No! No, he hasn't. Monday it is, Marvel."

J.D. grinned. "Shake on that, Agronsky."

By Monday J.D. had added Paul Shawn to his employees. He'd also made an offer to Thomas Finch that the cautious Scot was thinking over. He rented a meeting-room at the Blackstone where he had installed a sorter, a card punch and a tabulator that the Renovated Data Processing Company had bought from Peerless.

At seven o'clock Monday morning Wanda started a class for three students: J.D., Walter and Paul Shawn. She told J.D. that the beginner's class normally took a week. He replied that he wanted it over by Tuesday evening. In the event it was over at five o'clock Wednesday morning because Wanda worked them all night Tuesday.

By the time they were done the three men could wire the plug-board on the sorter to do a complete repertory of different sorting operations; they could operate the card punch at a respectable rate; and they could wire the much more complex plug-board on the tabulator to do a number of fundamental accounting jobs.

On Thursday, Thomas Finch made up his mind to join J.D. He gave Peerless a week's notice and Wanda gave him an armload of manuals to study at night until she could train him properly.

Finally, on the Saturday evening of July 22, the five of them got on the Broadway Limited, leaving Leland Prescott behind to open the Chicago offices of RDP.

12

The Quest

THE DISAPPOINTING HEADQUARTERS of the Renovated Data Processing Company occupied a small warehouse on a dreary street a block from the East River in the Bronx.

"You won't be here enough to have it matter," Whittier said to J.D. They had arrived a few minutes earlier in Whittier's chauffeured Hispano-Suiza, and were now standing in the only office in the building – a dusty cubicle containing a battered desk, two file cabinets, and a chair.

Whittier led J.D. into the warehouse where crates were piled haphazardly. "This is your inventory. More is coming." He handed J.D. a bill of lading.

J.D. studied the paper. "This is new equipment!" he said.

"It won't be when you sell it," Whittier replied matter-of-factly. "Run them for awhile before you deliver them. Scratch up the cases."

J.D. examined an uncrated tabulator. "Is this a mistake?"

"Why?"

"This plate – it says: 'Renovated by Yates Used Equipment, Inc.' "

"It's no mistake."

"What does it mean?"

"It's a knocker. You'll have twenty or so to begin with, more if you need them."

" 'Knocker'?"

"My boy, you've a lot to learn about business. What are you going to do if Yates starts to meet or beat our prices?"

"Can he afford to?"

"He might, for awhile. The idea being that later he could raise the prices again. So if you run into that situation you tell the customer that

108

if Yates equipment is what he wants, you'll let him have it for half the price Yates is offering."

"Half –! And where do I tell him I got Yates equipment?"

"Why, you've taken them on trade, and they're so inferior you're glad to be rid of them. Then, if that doesn't convince, you deliver him one of these little dandies."

"And they don't work too well."

Whittier smiled. "They might tend to break down rather often."

Whittier put a hand on J.D.'s shoulder. "There are big things ahead for you. Now, let's get out of here and go to lunch. I have reservations at Sherry's."

Louis Sherry himself greeted them at the door and led them to their table where Madelline Yates was seated.

"Madelline insisted on seeing you," Whittier said. "You've made a conquest." He turned away to consult with the *sommelier* over the wine list.

Madelline smiled and said, "Joe tells me you've hired a number of people."

J.D. was confused. He couldn't imagine why Whittier had discussed their business with the daughter of the man he had sworn to ruin.

"I'm only going to have a cocktail with you," Madelline Yates said. "I know you have business to discuss, and I have a luncheon engagement."

She was dressed in a white middy blouse with a dark-blue scarf at her slender throat, and a dark-blue blazer. Her eyes were even more luminously violet than J.D. had remembered, and when he looked into them he experienced a kind of vertigo. His hand trembled as he accepted a cocktail from the waiter.

J.D. tried to keep up his end of the conversation, but Madelline Yates's presence had unnerved him. She finished her cocktail. "I must go. I'm having a small dinner party tonight and wondered if you'd like to come?"

"Yes. I would."

She took a card from her purse and handed it to him. "My address. Shall we say about eight?"

Whittier turned in his chair to watch her walk from the restaurant. "That girl has one of the most pleasant walks, don't you think?"

"She knew about the people I'd hired," J.D. said.

"I probably mentioned it to her."

"Is that wise?"

"I try not to do the unwise," Whittier said drily.

"Then I guess I don't understand. Isn't it her father that we want to put out of business?"

"Not 'want' – are going to. Yes, it is her father." Whittier sighed and put down the menu to look at J.D. "You have to understand that things are not quite so simple in the circles you are now in."

"As simple as down on the farm, you mean?"

"No need to get testy, my boy. It is no fault of yours that you don't have experience among the – shall we say, sophisticated? But you shall. You shall." He signaled the waiter with a curt nod.

After they had ordered, J.D. said, "How old is she?"

"Madelline? Let me think. She must be thirty, or close to it."

J.D.'s surprise showed.

Whittier smiled. "Doesn't seem that old to you? It's a fact that the women we are smitten with are often seen by our love-clouded eyes at the age that will give us the best chance for their favours. Now, if I were enamored of la Yates, I'm sure I would be seeing her as *over* thirty. See what I mean?"

"But I didn't say I was 'enamored' of her."

Whittier laughed. "You didn't have to! The writing is plain."

"If that's true, what a fool she must've thought me!"

"Not at all. Madelline was quite taken with you, believe me. Your age is an advantage, if anything."

"Why do you say that?"

"When a woman attains the dreaded age of thirty, or approaches it, she looks with a great deal of favor upon the attentions of a younger man."

After they'd finished their meal and were having coffee and cigars, Whittier said, "Do you have the accounting?"

"Yes, sir." J.D. drew a set of papers from his pocket. "You'll see it's all as I discussed with you, except for the office in Chicago. I had to give three months' rent in advance to get the lease."

Whittier glanced through the sheets, looked at the totals, folded them, put them beside him on the table and took a sheet of paper from his coat.

"I'm going to give you more authority. I can't keep authorizing every expense. If you'll sign this, you can write your own checks. I'll want you to give me a budget of what you expect to spend, of course."

J.D. studied the paper. "What is this?" he asked. It was couched in legal language. "It looks like a contract."

"By signing that you agree to be Chief Executive Officer of the Renovated Data Processing Company. Along with that, of course, comes the power to act for the company. Makes everything a lot simpler."

"Why don't you just put me on the authorized list at the bank?"

Whittier smiled. "Because, when you make a decision you want to be able to make it stick, without having someone second guess you, don't you?"

"I hadn't thought about it. Who might second guess me?"

"How about Homer Medville Cranston, for one?"

"He's on the board of RDP?"

"He's on the board of the Empire State Investment Company, which is more to the point, don't you think?" Whittier watched him with an amused light in his eyes. "He also has reservations about this venture. I don't want him to torpedo it before you've even left port."

"I don't know –"

"Oh, for God's sake, J.D.!" Whittier exclaimed impatiently. "It's standard practice. You're going to have to learn about these things, boy. You can't expect me to take up valuable time tutoring you."

"I'm sorry to take up valuable time," J.D. said angrily. "But I don't understand this, and until I do, I don't guess I'll sign."

Whittier sighed dramatically. "I wasn't going to tell you until later. The board wanted to give you something for the work you've done so far. They wanted to recognize your potential to the company. They wanted to make you the top man in this company. Along with all that went a raise. As soon as you had signed that paper you would've been making two thousand a month."

"Two thousand!" J.D.'s eyes widened.

"I have spent a considerable amount of my time convincing the board of the wisdom of this move. The board thought you were too young, they thought you needed testing. I've finally convinced them that you ought to have the authority and the pay that goes with it." He picked up the paper. "I don't know if you realize how humiliating it is to go back to them now and tell you turned me down and we'll have to look for someone else."

"Wait!" J.D. said. "I didn't realize! I'd like to sign, if it's not too late."

Whittier put the paper back on the table, removed a pen from his pocket, and held it out to J.D. "Of course it isn't too late! You're my choice, and have been all along." He picked up the paper, examined J.D.'s signature, and stuck out his hand.

"Congratulations, Mr. Chief Executive."

*

111

All the New York employees of RDP were staying at the Windsor, an inexpensive but clean hotel on the east side of Manhattan. J.D. called a meeting that afternoon in his room. Paul Shawn and Wanda sat in the only two chairs, Walter and Thomas Finch sat on the bed, and J.D. stood while he addressed them.

"Here's a list of Yates customers in New York. Most of them are in a ten-mile radius of Manhattan."

Thomas Finch whistled. "How did you get hold of that?"

"Mr. Whittier gave it to me," J.D. said. "How he got it, I don't know. I've divided the list into five. As we hire more people, we'll share our lists with them." He handed out the papers.

Wanda looked skeptically at her list. "I don't know," she said. "I've never tried selling door-to-door."

"It's hardly that," J.D. replied. "We'll be welcomed with bouquets and kisses, I should think, with the deal we've got."

"Wanda should be welcomed like that, anyway," Walter said. She gave him a smile.

"It will only be for a few days," J.D. said to Wanda. "As soon as we have business, we'll pull you off to run the installation of equipment."

"What about new business?" Walter asked.

"Avoid it for now," J.D. said. "We have enough to do calling on the Yates customers. Any questions?"

"I don't know enough to ask a decent question," Paul Shawn spoke up. "That's what worries me."

"Look it up in your Peerless Data Processing manual if you get stuck," J.D. said. "I know it's tough. With the exception of Wanda, we're beginners, and we'll just have to learn as we go. But with the story we've got to tell – the price, the performance – I don't think we can miss."

J.D. took his watch from his vest and looked at it. "It's nearly four. Let's begin bright and fresh tomorrow morning."

Madelline Yates's apartment was in a three-story whitestone building in Greenwich Village. When she opened the door she was dressed in a black sheath dress with a square neckline and a long double loop of pearls that came nearly to her waist. Her hair was pinned up by pearl-studded combs. She looked at J.D. for a long moment and said, "Oh." Then, after another look, "Oh, my."

J.D. stood there in his new tuxedo and knew he had made a fool of himself again. Madelline Yates's look said it all.

"Well," Madelline said, recovering, "don't you look nice." She

112

stepped into the hall and pulled the door to behind her. "Listen, I should've told you the party was informal."

"I'll go change," J.D. stammered, his face burning.

"I know!" she said. "You've just come from a wedding!" She took his arms and pulled him into the apartment.

There were half a dozen people in a small living-room that featured a bow window that overlooked the street. A low-slung couch of leather and steel was at one end of the room, a grouping of two chairs and a coffee table at the other. The walls were decorated with prints and posters in wild profusion, most of them unframed and held to the walls with thumbtacks. A trestle table stood under shelves of books and held an ice bucket, glasses, and a bottle of spirits.

Madelline introduced J.D. to the guests. The men wore a variety of casual attire. Madelline explained that J.D. had just come from a wedding.

"Really?" a woman exclaimed. "Anyone we know?"

"I doubt it, dear," Madelline said smoothly. "Midwesterners."

"You from the Midwest, Mr. Marvel?" A turtleneck-clad man asked.

"Illinois."

"Mr. Marvel's accent is charming," a woman said.

Madelline brought J.D. a glass. "Scotch – right?"

"Thanks."

"What's your racket, J.D.?" asked a beefy young man with thinning black hair and a massive jaw.

"I'm in the data-processing business," J.D. replied.

"Say," the man said. "Isn't that the same racket Mad's daddy's in? You work for the old boy?"

"No. Different company."

Madelline served a buffet dinner on a sideboard in the small dining-room: a fish casserole, rice and salad, with a cheap Italian red wine. They ate in the living-room, sitting on couches or chairs or the floor and balancing their plates on their knees. The members of the group had obviously known one another for a long time, so that they had achieved that kind of relaxed family feeling from which J.D. felt very much excluded. The talk involved people and places he didn't know, common experiences he had no way of sharing.

He sat on the floor under the bow window with his back against the wall to eat his meal. Madelline moved over from the couch to sit beside him.

"How are you liking New York, Mr. Marvel?" she asked.

113

"Fine, what I've seen of it."

"You're working for Joe, aren't you?"

"In a way, I guess you could say that," he said cautiously.

She laughed. "Don't feel you're telling tales out of school. Joe told me you were working for him."

Later, as it turned out, J.D. was the last to leave.

He held out his hand. "Thanks. It was a fine evening."

She took his hand in both of hers and looked up into his eyes. "Stay a minute, won't you?"

They sat on the couch and drank coffee. Being close to her and alone made J.D. ache with desire. Again, he sensed in her eyes a hidden challenge, a mocking question that gave another, deeper layer of meaning to her words.

"You cut a handsome figure in your tuxedo, Mr. Marvel."

"Frankly, I feel like a fool, Miss Yates."

"Please, call me Madelline. Or Mad, if you prefer."

"Thank you, Madelline. My friends call me J.D."

"I remember. Jesse Dinsmore."

He was fatuously pleased that she had remembered.

"And you have no cause to feel like a fool. Do you think everyone but you is born knowing about dress customs?"

He grinned. "Since you put it that way –"

"You have a nice smile. I'm puzzled."

"About what?"

"You. When you're serious, I think you're near my age. Then, when you smile, as you did just now, you look about eighteen."

"Would you like to know?"

"I'm not sure." She smiled. "The mystery is pleasant. But, yes! I suppose I must."

"I'm twenty-one."

"Ah." There was an uncomfortable silence. "You *are* a gentleman."

"Why do you say that?"

"You didn't ask me to reciprocate when you had every right to. But I don't mind saying, if you'd like to know."

"Please."

"I'm twenty-eight. Twenty-nine next month, so I'm a year away from thirty."

"Twenty-eight, twenty-nine next month, is a lovely age."

"Why, J.D.! You've a silver tongue."

"I don't know about that."

"You're also very appealing when you blush. Do you think two

114

people of such widely varying ages could be friends?"

"I don't consider the difference much at all."

"You *are* charming."

He shifted uncomfortably. "What does a commercial artist do?"

"Nothing very exciting, I'm afraid. Layouts for newspaper ads. Illustrations for technical books. In fact, I'm doing some illustrations for Jacob Kettleman's new book."

"Jacob Kettleman?"

"The professor you met tonight. He's written a book on color."

"Do you work for a company?"

"I'm free-lance. In a way, I'm a small company. I have a secretary and an assistant."

J.D. looked at the pictures on the walls. "Did you do any of those?"

She laughed. "No. I'm afraid I deal in a different kind of art. Oh, at one time I had pretensions to be a painter. But I didn't have the talent."

"I'd like to see where you work."

"Why, then you shall! We're agreed then, that we'll be friends?"

"Yes."

"It's late and I have to be up early for work," Madelline said.

J.D. stood. She stood beside him. The bridge of her nose came just to his shoulder. Although he'd never considered such matters before, he found himself observing that hers was the perfect height for a woman.

"Would you like to kiss me goodnight?" she asked, gazing up into his eyes with that veiled, mocking look.

He bent and brushed her lips with his own. It was a dry, brief kiss, chaste in every respect, yet it sent a shock through him to the very soles of his feet.

As she let him out the door, she said, "Call me when you want to see the office."

It was a warm night, the air heavy with summer. He decided to walk back to his hotel. Although it was two miles, he hardly noticed.

It was over a week before J.D. saw Madelline Yates again. He thought of her every day, but Renovated Data Processing kept him so busy that he hardly had time to eat and sleep. In fact, he did very little of either.

At the outset, the sales campaign was a success. Every Yates account that they called on agreed to throw out Yates and take on RDP. It was seldom necessary even to demonstrate the equipment to the customer. They already knew about the advantages of data processing, since they'd been using it. Very few hadn't heard about Peerless equipment and its reliability. And at the prices they were offered by the RDP representatives, even the fact that the Peerless equipment was represented as used, couldn't dampen their eagerness.

By the end of the first eight working days, they had sold to 112 customers in New York and J.D. was starting to think it wouldn't take them until the end of the year to finish the job.

Leland Prescott, with whom J.D. spoke on the phone every morning, had hired several salesmen and in the same period the Chicago branch of RDP had racked up almost seventy Yates accounts.

Finally, Madelline Yates called *him*.

"I thought you were going to come and see my office," she said.

"I want to, Madelline – but I've been going almost day and night." It was eight o'clock on a humid August evening when she'd called and J.D. had only returned to his hotel for a clean shirt and to grab a sandwich before setting out for a customer in the Bronx where RDP equipment was waiting to be wired up. The demand had got so heavy that, even though Wanda had hired assistants, everyone was having to pitch in and work nights to get the equipment installed and running.

"Surely you eat lunch."

The truth was he hadn't that day. "Listen." he said. "I'll be working in Manhattan tomorrow. How about then?"

"Wonderful! Come by my office about eleven-thirty, can you?" She gave him the address.

When J.D. finally got back to his hotel room that night it was past midnight. He wearily let himself into his room to find the desk lamp on and, sitting in one of his chairs, a glass of whiskey in one hand, a cigar in the other, the portly figure of Arnold Yates.

13

Victory

YATES POINTED TO THE TOP OF THE DRESSER where a bottle, glasses and a bucket of ice stood.

"Have a drink."

"You seem to have made yourself at home," J.D. said. He went to the dresser and prepared himself a drink. "Do you mind telling me how you got in here?"

Yates held up a thumb and two fingers and rubbed them together. "The bell captain liked the color of my money. Now don't go gettin' pissed off at him. I told him I was a friend of yours." The little mouth grinned.

J.D. sat wearily on the bed, pulled the knot of his tie down, and unbuttoned his collar. "What do you want?"

Yates lifted his glass. "To have a drink with you, and a little talk."

"I'm listening."

"You look beat to a whey, boy."

"Look here, Mr. Yates. I've worked sixteen hours today. If you don't say what you want to say pretty quick, you're going to be talking to an unconscious man."

"Why, goddamn me, boy, if you don't talk awful high and mighty, for such a young shit."

J.D. focused his weary attention for the first time on the little man and saw that his mouth was grim, his little eyes mean slits, his great jowls quivering with indignation. In a kind of wonder he noticed the dome of Yates's head was glowing red.

"But," Yates continued, "I guess you and me don't have to go through the social niceties. We can get to the point, you and me." He leaned forward a little in his chair and said, "What you tryin' to do to me, boy?"

"Take away your accounts."

Yates stared at J.D. for a long moment. "But how're you doin' it? I'll tell you how. By sellin' stuff at prices that no one on God's earth could make a profit on."

"I expect that's our business, Mr. Yates."

"Now that's where you're wrong, mister. It's not only my business, but it's the business of the courts. What you're doing is against the law."

J.D. said, "I doubt that."

"You hear of the Sherman Anti-Trust Act, boy, or didn't they teach you anything in that piney wood where you grew up?"

"That only applies to big businesses," he said. "Standard Oil, and the like."

Yates snorted. "It applies to you and your fly-by-night outfit just as much as it does to Andrew Carnegie."

"I don't believe it," J.D. said.

"Well," Yates continued. "Don't matter what you believe, it don't change the law. And what you believe isn't going to get your ass outa jail, when it's put there."

"Jail!" J.D. very nearly laughed. "You aren't serious?"

"Never been more so." He pointed his cigar at J.D.'s head like a gun. "You better believe it!"

Yates stood. "Lookee here, boy. You go find out first thing tomorrow if what I say isn't true. Then you call me." He took a card from his wallet and put it on the dresser. "If I don't hear from you tomorrow, I'm goin' to the Justice Department the next day."

J.D. was at the door of the law library at Columbia University the next morning when it opened. He read the Sherman Anti-Trust Act from end to end. The part that worried him most said:

"Every . . . conspiracy in restraint of trade or commerce among the several States is hereby declared illegal."

Reading the criminal penalties section didn't exactly assuage his worries, either. For each violation of the Act the miscreant could be fined up to $5000 and imprisoned for up to one year.

J.D. couldn't determine for sure if RDP's methods were in violation of the Act. But two things were certain: RDP met the interstate condition of the Act, since they were operating in both Illinois and New York; and if they were in violation of the Act, J.D.'s neck was on

118

the line. He considered trying to find a lawyer to talk it over with, but rejected the idea because he wasn't ready to tell anyone else about it – not yet, at least.

He left the library with one conclusion – whatever happened, he wouldn't allow the "knockers" in the warehouse in the Bronx to be used.

From a public phone he called the number on the card that Arnold Yates had left him, and Yates himself answered. "Thought you'd call," he said. "Let's have lunch."

"I can't," J.D. replied.

"I'm a busy man, and you're not in any position to set the tune. I'll meet you for lunch at Delmonico's at twelve-thirty." The line went dead.

J.D. called Madelline Yates' number.

"I'm disappointed in you, J.D.," she said. "I thought I might take precedence over some business engagement."

"Normally you would. But this engagement is with your father, and he wouldn't take no for an answer."

"My father! Why are you seeing him?"

"Business."

"But I thought you were in competition with him."

"I am. No reason we can't have lunch, is there?"

"Listen, J.D. I'd like to see you tonight. Can you come to my place?"

"Should I wear my tuxedo?"

She laughed. "Only if it'll make you feel better. It will be just the two of us for dinner. Shall we say eight?"

"Fine."

"Oh – and try not to let business pre-empt me."

"You've got my word."

Next, J.D. called Whittier, who answered the phone himself.

"Don't worry about it," he said, after J.D. had told him his experience with Yates. "You're not going to jail, and neither is anyone else. Have lunch with the bastard. But don't tell him a thing. Play it close to the vest, understand?"

"Yes, sir."

"I'm leaving for Europe Saturday. Be gone a couple of months. So you're on your own."

"What if I need to get in touch with you?"

"I'll cable from time to time. Don't have an itinerary, so I'll let you know as it develops. Oh, and another thing, J.D. –"

"Sir?"

"Make sure the little bastard picks up the check."

Arnold Yates was far more affable than he'd been the night before.

"Been waiting long, boy?" Yates said when he puffed into Delmonico's twenty minutes late. "I'm glad they went ahead and put you at my table. What you drinkin'? Scotch? I'll have one of those, too, Leo." The waiter glided off for the drink.

Yates rubbed his hands over the table as if it were a fire and said, "Well – come to your senses, did you?"

"I'm prepared to listen to what you have to say."

Yates threw back his round head and laughed. "*You* ain't in the driver's seat! *I* am."

"Granting that," J.D. said. "I still don't know what you want, do I?"

Yates accepted his drink from the waiter. He took a gulp and looked at J.D. "I want you to get me back the accounts you stole."

"Is that all?" J.D. asked.

Yates didn't take notice of the sarcasm. "No, it's not. Then, I want you to raise your prices up to what they should be. We both know that's new equipment you're selling. It should be near twice the price of mine. Either raise your prices up, or get out of business."

"You don't want much."

"It's not so much, when you consider what I'm offerin' in return."

"Which is?"

"To keep you out of jail."

"You're sure you can put me there?"

"I'd lay odds on it."

"Then why offer me a deal at all?"

"Because it could take time to get you in jail, what with all the flim-flam the lawyers and courts go through. And that wouldn't get back the accounts you stole."

"Is that all?"

"That's the whole ticket, boy. What do you say?"

"I'll have to think about it."

"You don't have much time. Tomorrow morning I go to the Justice Department. Waiter! Let's order lunch. Should we go Dutch?"

J.D. accepted a menu from the waiter, and then smiled at Yates. "Since it's your party, Mr. Yates, I don't mind letting you pick up the check."

*

120

J.D. called Whitter after lunch. "The little bastard didn't want much, did he?" Whittier said. "You did the right thing."

"What should I do now?"

"Ignore it."

"But what if he goes to the Justice Department?"

"He won't."

"You think it's a bluff, then?"

"Likely. Forget it, and concentrate on your job. If you continue to takes Yates's accounts at the rate you have been, there could be a nice bonus for you."

"Yes, sir."

"By the way – did you stick Yates with the check?"

"Yes, sir."

Whittier laughed. J.D. wished he felt like joining him.

Madelline Yates greeted him at the door of her apartment attired in a long flowing dress with a swooping neckline that left J.D. feeling short of breath.

Candles burning on the low table in front of the couch and on the trestle table against one wall were the only illumination in the apartment.

She seated him on the couch and sat across from him in a chair. On the table between them were, besides the candles, two glasses and a bottle of French wine. Madelline poured.

"Tell me," she said, "about this incredible business that keeps you occupied night and day. If I were the suspicious type, I might suspect it was some kind of feminine business."

"Just the dull kind."

"Meaning you'd rather not talk about it."

"I talk about it sixteen hours a day."

"Very well. No business talk, for now." She raised her glass. "To the evening." They touched glasses.

"I hope you like spaghetti," Madelline said.

"Love it."

"I'm afraid I'm not much of a cook." She smiled. "You don't have to argue with me about it. I wasn't fishing. I really am not a very good cook, or a very good housekeeper. I'm afraid my idea of an ideal domestic scene is one populated with cooks, maids, chauffeurs and butlers."

"Like Joseph Falk Whittier."

"Exactly." She sighed. "Unfortunately, the pay of a commercial

121

artist won't support Hispano-Suizas, not to mention servants."

After dinner they took their coffee and cognac into the living-room where Madelline opened curtains to reveal a french door beyond which lay a small balcony.

"This is why I took this apartment," she said, throwing open the French doors. The balcony just had room for a tiny round table and two canvas-backed chairs. The view was of alleys and roof-tops. The late August air was balmy and heavy with the complex odors of Greenwich Village – cooking, flowerbox plants, and the street.

"I'd like to clear up a misconception," Madelline began. "It's about my father."

"Yes?"

Instead of continuing, she took a teak box from the table and offered it to J.D. Inside were lavender cigarettes with black tips. He took one, and lit hers and then his own. "Do you object to a woman smoking?" she asked.

"No. I have a ladyfriend who smokes in public."

Her eyes widened. "Hardly a 'lady,' do you think?"

"You'd have to know her," he replied. "It's a point of honor with her."

"Ah," Madelline Yates said, breathing smoke out through her nostrils. "One of those."

"One of what?"

"You know. The battle-axe crowd. Suffragettes. Free-lovers."

"I suppose," J.D. said. "You were going to tell me about your father."

"It's not easy for me."

"You don't have to –"

"I want to. First of all, Arnold Yates is not my father. I guess legally he is. He adopted me. But, really, he's my step-father. My mother married him when I was seventeen. My father died the year before, on San Juan Hill.

"My mother is a lady. It's hard for people to understand how Arnold Yates could have convinced her to marry him. But you have to realize that my father left us practically penniless. He had had a comfortable inheritance that he'd spent on adventure. He was a great one for getting up an Arctic expedition, or an African safari. And, of course, he helped finance them. This love of adventure finally killed him. He couldn't resist the war. Teddy Roosevelt was an old friend of his – they hunted together in the Rockies. So it was easy to enlist father in the Rough Riders.

122

"There was my mother, a sixteen-year-old daughter on her hands, who had never worked a day in her life, and in fact, until my father was killed, had always had servants and a summer home on Long Island – there she was, penniless. Along came Mr. Arnold Yates, riding the crest of one of his lucky streaks, and younger than you see him now – I must say rather charming in a kind of primitive way – and swept her up and married her." She paused and looked at J.D. in the dim light. "You're probably wondering why I'm telling you all this."

"A bit."

She leaned intensely over the table. "I hate Arnold Yates!" she said. "He is nothing but a pig!"

J.D. was momentarily taken aback by the force of her venom.

"The moment my mother and he said their vows, the charm fell away from Arnold Yates like a snake sheds its skin. But my mother has the old-fashioned notion of honor and marriage. She sticks to her bargain."

"You visit her?"

"I try to choose times when Arnold isn't there."

They smoked their cigarettes in silence. Finally, Madelline said, "I told you so you'd understand I'm on your side."

"My side?"

"I know what you're trying to do. Joe told me."

J.D. stared at her.

"I mean it when I say I'm on your side."

"What did he tell you?"

"Everything."

"Why?"

"Because he knows how I feel about Arnold. Joe has been a good friend to my mother and me. He's like an uncle to me. I know about what Arnold's trying to do to you. The threats."

"How could you –?"

"Joe called me this afternoon. Listen to me, J.D. – Arnold can't do anything to you without doing it to himself."

"What do you mean?"

"How do you think he built that business in such a short time? He did the same thing you're doing. He undersold the competition. Then, when he had them beaten down, he bought them. Why do you think there aren't any large companies other than Arnold's selling used data-processing equipment? He bought them all up – all of those that amounted to anything."

"You mean he used the same method –?"

123

"And more. He not only cut his prices, he sold machines that had the competition's name on it – equipment that he made sure was no good."

"Is there proof of this?" J.D. asked.

"I can get it. I know a man who used to work for Arnold. I'm sure he'd be willing to give a sworn statement about what went on. There are bound to be others."

J.D. thought for a moment. "Do you know the names of any of the companies he ruined?"

"ABC Tabulating, Johnson and Blake – those were two of the largest."

"And this former employee – do you think he'd mind if I used his name?"

"How?"

"With Yates."

Madelline smiled slowly. "J.D. – I think he'd be delighted. His name is George Evans."

Not long after that, J.D. left. Madelline let him kiss her good-night and this time there was nothing chaste about it.

The following morning J.D. had an early appointment to give a sales pitch to a Yates account. But before he left the hotel he called Yates.

"Thought you'd come to your senses, boy," Yates said sleepily.

"That's not why I called. Do you remember a man named George Evans?"

"What the hell's that got to do with anything?"

"Or a company called ABC Tabulating?"

"Listen here, Marvel – did you get me out of bed to play some kind of joke?"

"How about Johnson and Blake?"

There was a long silence broken only by the crackle of static on the long-distance connection to Long Island.

Finally, in a husky voice, Yates said, "You think you're pretty goddamn smart, don't you?"

"How about 'knockers,' Mr. Yates? Ever heard of them?"

"All right, goddamn it – you made your point! What do you want?"

"I want you to stop making ludicrous threats. I want you to stop breaking into my hotel room. I want you to stop wasting my time."

"This is gonna be a battle, boy. Two can play that game, and I know ways to play it you never heard of."

"You're wrong, Mr. Yates."

124

"Oh, I am!"

"Yes, sir. This is not going to be a battle – it's going to be a war." J.D. slammed the earpiece into its hook.

That afternoon, he delivered his first knocker.

Arnold Yates struck back. J.D. and his team started to run into resistance at more and more Yates accounts where they found that Yates's salesmen had preceded them and lowered the prices on their equipment below that of RDP. Leland Prescott reported the same thing happening in Chicago. During the first week in September, 1911, RDP won a total of eighteen accounts in Illinois and New York.

"How long can that son of a bitch hold out?" J.D. asked Walter Hucko as they were having a late dinner at a café near their hotel. J.D. had been trying for ten days to get in touch with Whittier, without success. His New York office said that he was motoring through the French countryside "incommunicado."

"Maybe," Walter said, "he figures he's going to lose everything if he sits on his hands, so he'd rather go down fighting. Can't blame the man."

"Yeah," J.D. said wearily, and reflected that if Walter had ever met Arnold Yates he might not be so sympathetic.

"Can we cut our prices?" Walter asked. "It's the only way to lick him. The rate we're going, we'll be down to zero sales next week. I sold one account today out of twelve calls."

"We haven't got the cash to keep going if we cut anymore. We have to pay Peerless the full rate for their machines. I *have* to talk to Whittier –"

Madelline was sympathetic. "You'll figure a way, dear," she said. They were sitting on the couch in her living-room, the French doors open to catch the vagrant breeze. J.D. had his arm around her and her head rested on his shoulder. Occasionally, she would lift her mouth to nibble his neck. He could feel the hard nipple of her breast pressing against his hand through the thin material of her lounging-gown. Although they'd seen each other almost every night for two weeks and during that time had kissed and caressed and murmured foolish endearments, Madelline had yet to allow him the ultimate intimacy. He left her apartment usually around midnight, seething with sexual frustration. During the day he was assaulted with another, no less powerful, kind of frustration. The business which, less than two weeks ago, had been more than he and his team could handle working

125

sixteen-hour days, had dwindled to nothing.

Finally, in the middle of September, Whittier called from Biarritz.

"I thought we'd discussed this," he said irritably, in a tiny, far-away voice. "Cut below his prices!"

"We don't have the money," J.D. shouted. "We've got more going out than coming in, and the reserve is about gone."

"There's another million dollars in reserve. Tell Parkington at the bank, and he'll start drawing it down in hundred-thousand increments."

"I didn't know –"

"You do now. Get cracking!"

The next day, RDP cut its prices twenty percent below Yates's. Immediately, sales accelerated. By October 1 they were back on sixteen-hour days. They hired two more assistants for Wanda, experienced tabulator operators, which relieved the pressure enough so that J.D. could stop wiring machines himself and concentrate on managing what was becoming a very large business.

During the last week in October, a strange thing happened. Sales suddenly and precipitously dropped off. It was like entering the eye of a hurricane.

"We're out of prospects," a grinning Hucko said. "We've done it, J.D.! There aren't any more Yates accounts in all New York!"

J.D. called Prescott in Chicago, and found he and his team were still working long hours. "But it'll be over soon," Prescott reported. "I figure we got another week to go."

Since his last phone conversation with Yates, J.D. hadn't seen or heard from the little man. Now he began to be curious about him. He figured the resources of Yates Used Equipment must be about exhausted; there was no more income. He asked Madelline.

"I don't know, darling. He's gone into hiding, I guess. Mother hasn't seen him for days. A blessing, if you ask me."

"Where could he be?"

"Licking his wounds, I expect," she said in an off-hand manner. "He owns a hunting lodge somewhere in Virginia, a rude cabin, without plumbing. Just the sort of thing for a beast like him."

J.D.'d worked himself out of another job. RDP couldn't continue on its present course. At the rental rates it was charging its nearly one thousand customers it would take ten years to pay off the equipment it had bought from Peerless. It would be worn out, if not rendered obsolete by the advance of the technology, long before that. J.D. called

126

Whittier's office only to be told that the financier remained incommunicado somewhere in Europe. The RDP team in New York was showing signs of restlessness.

When Leland Prescott reported in early November that the last Yates account in Illinois had been converted to RDP, J.D. told him to come to New York for a meeting, and to bring as much of his workforce as could be spared.

The warehouse in the Bronx was nearly empty. J.D. had it swept out, chairs and tables installed, hired a caterer. RDP had grown to thirty-one employees and twenty-eight were at the meeting, three having been left in Chicago to mind the Illinois business.

J.D. stood at the head table and looked over his employees as they filed into the warehouse and found seats, and came to the conclusion that, somehow, he was going to keep this team together. Everyone in the room had been hired with his approval. He considered them an élite corps. A kind of Rough Riders regiment of the commercial world, equipped with training in the most advanced business machines, their dedication proved over the arduous months. And, although the cut-rate prices of the equipment they'd sold had been an enormous edge, he couldn't help feeling that his group, given the right product and organization, could sell with the best.

J.D. told them the condition of RDP. He showed them flip-charts with the financial projections, and voiced the obvious: RDP couldn't survive long under the present circumstances. Then he threw the meeting open for discussion.

"Why don't we raise the rental we charge?" Leland Prescott asked.

"That's right," Paul Shawn said. "Most of my customers know they're paying below cost for the machines."

"And with Yates sunk," another voice added, "the cut-rate competition is gone."

"I agree," J.D. replied. He turned to another flip-chart. "Here's a plan I doped out for raising the rates gradually over eighteen months until we're where we ought to be. You can see from these figures –" he flipped over to a new chart, "that the equipment is paid out in three years, including three percent interest. If, in the meantime, we could increase our customer base with full-paying accounts, we could turn this company profitable in a couple of years."

"When do we start?" Walter Hucko asked.

"Soon. One thing – whatever we do, we won't coerce any of our customers into staying with us by saying they've no place else to go, now that Yates is out. We want satisfied customers – customers that

127

will be with us for years. When we go into a company and put their most vital transactions on our equipment, we are entering into a trust. They are placing in our hands the welfare of their business: the profits, the jobs of their employees."

"Peerless has the best data-processing equipment on the market," Thomas Finch said.

"That's true," Wanda Agronsky agreed.

"So," Finch went on, "there's no reason we shouldn't be able to compete at fair prices."

"Assuming we can buy Peerless machines," one of the Chicago men added. "What's to prevent old man Cranston from refusing to sell us equipment? After all, we've established a damned broad customer base for Peerless. Why shouldn't Cranston keep that business for himself?"

This brought a murmur from the audience.

"That worries me, too," J.D. replied. "All I can say is that Joseph Whittier is on the board of Peerless. I'm sure he thought of this when he set out to take the Yates accounts. But I don't know what he plans. One possibility, of course, is that they'll offer us jobs with Peerless."

"It would have to be a different deal," Leland Prescott said, "for me ever to go back. I'd forgotten what it was like to work for an outfit that was behind you."

"Why can't we be the data-processing division in Peerless?" a man asked. "Just the way we are? Hire a few more folks, maybe? You oughta be the vice-president, general manager."

There were shouts of affirmation from the audience. A few clapped. J.D. said, "I appreciate that. And I wouldn't mind it at all. But it's not up to me. We'll just have to wait and see what Whittier has to say when I hear from him, which I expect will be any day now."

The formal part of the meeting broke up soon afterward, and the caterers came in to serve drinks and lunch. There was a feeling of cameraderie among the twenty-eight, a kind of fraternal bond, as if they'd been through a war together which, in a way, they had. There were war stories, too: the accounts of the strategies employed to win the tough sales, the funny stories of mistakes made, opportunities lost and regained.

After lunch they went their separate ways, the Chicago contingent to catch a train, the New Yorkers to call on customers. J.D. stayed in his dingy office and worked on the details of his plan to make RDP profitable. He was still at it at seven o'clock, his head bent into the

128

pool of light from a goose-necked desk lamp, when Joseph Falk Whittier walked into his office.

For a moment J.D. couldn't believe his eyes. It was like seeing a ghost, and Whittier didn't help this illusion by standing in the half shadows of the office just beyond the light of the desk lamp. J.D. switched on the overhead light, and said, "I thought you were in Europe!"

"Got back last night on the *Lusitania*. Fine ship. The Brits know how to build 'em." He took a cigar from his pocket and busied himself clipping and lighting it.

"I've been calling your office every day. They said you were still in Europe."

"I'm not officially back, yet. Wanted a few days before I get back in harness." He blew smoke at the grimy ceiling. "A few months in Europe is very restorative, my boy. You should try it."

J.D. nodded, only half hearing him, organizing the sheets of paper scattered about his desk. "This is good timing, sir," he said. "I was just working up a plan for RDP –"

Whittier waved aside talk of plans with his cigar. "Plenty of time for that later. I see the warehouse is practically bare."

"Yes, sir. We've won every Yates account in the country."

"Had a little party, did you? I noticed the tables."

"A meeting, yes, sir. Of the staff. They're a bit nervous about what's going to happen now."

"What did you tell them?" Whittier asked.

"Couldn't tell them much. We were all waiting to hear from you."

Whittier perched a hip on the edge of J.D.'s desk and examined the ash on his cigar. He was wearing a black overcoat with velvet lapels and a rakish black Borsalino hat.

"Would you like to take the plan I've worked up to read later?" J.D. held the papers out to Whittier.

"That won't be necessary," Whittier replied.

"But, sir – the company is losing money! I've got a plan that will fix it. I figure we can turn profitable in eighteen months – two years at the outside. We have a really fine organization. I'd stack them up against the top sales and technical staff in the country. It would be a pity to just let it all go, now, after all the work –"

"You've done a fine job," Whittier interrupted. "I promised you a bonus, and you'll have it."

"Does that mean you're dismissing me?"

"No, no. Mentioned it in passing. I thought it might cheer you up."

129

"I'm in fine spirits."

"You haven't heard about the investigation, then?"

J.D. stared. "Investigation?"

"The Justice Department has started an investigation of RDP. I only heard about it yesterday myself."

"The Justice Department!" An icy finger touched J.D.'s spine.

"It was the Yates thing that set them off."

"You mean what we did to his company?"

"No," Whittier said slowly. "He has a hunting cabin. They found him there the other day. He'd been dead for some time."

"Dead! How –?"

"Shot himself," Whittier said. "Between the eyes."

14

The Spoils

J.D. DIDN'T GO TO THE FUNERAL. He'd considered it, until Madelline said to him, "It would be the acme of hypocrisy if either of us went."

J.D. wasn't sure about that. He couldn't get out of his mind an image of the little round monk's face, with the white tonsure-like hair, a bullet hole between its staring eyes.

The morning of the funeral Madelline let him make love to her for the first time.

He'd gone to her apartment for breakfast. She'd taken the day off in the event her mother needed her. J.D. was feeling low. Guilt over Yates's death haunted him. The Justice Department investigation filled him with anxiety – he'd been unable in the two days since Whittier had told him about it to find out anything else. He'd called the United States Attorney's office in New York and got exactly nothing from the man he'd talked to who said, vaguely, that cases under investigation were confidential.

Madelline prepared Eggs Benedict and a wonderful South American coffee from beans she ground herself in a hand-cranked grinder. But J.D.'s appetite was as low as his spirits. Madelline wore a sheer white silk dressing-gown that J.D. had never seen her in. She removed his jacket and his tie, sat him in a chair and took off his shoes. After they had eaten she cleaned the table and came and sat on his lap.

"Do you know," she breathed in his ear. "That you are very appealing when you're sad?"

"Brings out the mother in you?" he murmured against her neck.

"Hardly," she said, and ran her hand inside his shirt and down his chest.

Madelline stood and held her hand out to him. The old mysterious challenge was naked in her eyes now. She led him into the bedroom.

131

They undressed each other slowly, savoring each revelation of the other with hands and lips. When they finally lay naked on the bed Madelline took him in her arms and gently guided him into her body. She orchestrated all that followed, taking him now gently, now rapaciously, until his body and mind seemed fused into an entity that had no purpose or function beyond that of receiving and giving pleasure.

When, at last, they were finished, they lay spent in each other's arms and J.D. drifted into a gentle, restorative sleep. How long he slept he didn't know. He awoke to the caress of Madelline's kisses on his chest. This time they coupled eagerly, almost violently, and it was over quickly. Her climax thrust her to the heights of an exquisite agony; she moaned deep in her throat and arched her body against his, and finally collapsed to pillow his heaving chest against her damp and yielding flesh.

J.D. was sitting in his office at the warehouse talking to Walter Hucko and Thomas Finch about what the future might hold, when the Marshalls came. Finch had stated the opinion that Cranston would take them into Peerless. Hucko felt they didn't need Peerless. What they would do by themselves, he wasn't sure, but he was full of optimistic if vague plans.

"We can strike out on our own, J.D.," he suggested.

"With what? We don't have the kind of money to start a data-processing company," Finch said.

"We could raise it," Walter countered. "We got the organization. We got J.D. to lead it."

"All true," Finch said. "But hardly the collateral you can borrow money against."

Then the Marshalls walked in. They were large, quiet men, with expressionless eyes. They identified J.D., handed him a warrant, and gave him a moment to read it before they ordered him to his feet.

"If we have your word you won't try anything, we won't put the cuffs on you," one of them said. J.D. stood, his face had gone white.

"What is this!" Hucko cried.

"It's okay, Walter," J.D. said. "They've got a warrant."

"Can you tell me where you're taking me?" J.D. asked.

"The Federal Building."

As the Marshalls led him from the office, J.D. turned to Hucko: "Call Whittier."

"We'll get you out!" Walter called after him.

*

In the basement of the Federal Building they fingerprinted and photographed him. Then he was put in a tiny room with a wooden bench, no windows, and a door of steel bars.

An hour later a different Marshall came, manacled his hands, and led him up a long flight of stairs to a courtroom where he joined four other handcuffed men standing before an empty bench. Walter Hucko sat in the spectator section beyond a railing.

A moment later the judge entered. J.D.'s case came up second. A man in a dark suit at a table in front of the bench argued that he should be held without bail. Barring that, he argued the bail should be $100,000.

The judge asked J.D. if he understood the charges against him. "Yes, sir," J.D. replied hoarsely. The warrant had said it all; almost word for word from the Sherman Anti-Trust Act as J.D. remembered it.

"Considering the defendant's age," the judge pronounced, "and that there is no record of any prior arrests – the bail will be five thousand dollars."

J.D. stood stunned, not really understanding what the judge had said, until the Marshall who had brought him led him over to the clerk of the court who sat at a table in a far corner. "Would you like to pay the bail?" the clerk whispered.

Walter appeared. "I'll pay it," he declared, took a wallet from his pocket, and began to pull bills out.

When they were in the street, J.D. took a deep breath. It was late afternoon and the lowering sun wheeled spokes of dusty light down the canyons of Manhattan.

"Thanks, Walter," he said.

"Nothin' you wouldn't do for me," Walter replied, holding up an arm to hail a cab.

"Where did you get the money?" J.D. asked.

"Went to the bank, Finch and me, and drew out all we had. Sure glad that judge didn't go for the hundred-thousand bail. I only had twenty-five."

When they were in the cab, J.D. said, "Did you call Whittier?"

"Finch is at the hotel tryin'."

At the hotel Finch met them in the lobby.

"Thanks for the bail," J.D. said.

"I've been trying to call Whittier," Finch said. "Nobody knows where he is."

133

J.D. took a shower. Jail had made him feel dirty. He put on a clean suit and set off to find Whittier.

At the duplex on 5th Avenue the butler answered the door and left J.D. standing on the stoop. He returned a full five minutes later and led J.D. to the library where he found Whittier sitting in his smoking jacket with a cigar in one hand, a drink in the other, talking to Madelline Yates.

"What are you doing here?" J.D. asked her.

"What's wrong?" Madelline asked. "You're white as a sheet."

"I guess jail does that to me," J.D. said.

Whittier rose. "Here, my boy. Have a seat. Let me get you a drink." He went to a tray and began preparing a drink. "What's this about jail?"

"Didn't you get Finch's message?"

"I got a message that Thomas Finch wanted to see me." He handed the drink to J.D.

"Why didn't you talk to him?"

"I told you that I wasn't seeing anyone for a few days."

"Mother is upstairs," Madelline explained. "The doctor gave her a sleeping potion. Joe has been kind enough to let her stay here."

"As long as she likes, my dear," Whittier affirmed. "Now," he said, turning to J.D. "What is all this?"

Briefly, J.D. described the events of the afternoon.

"That's terrible!" Madelline said.

"I doubt you have much to worry about," Whittier said calmly.

"That's easy for you to say," J.D. replied tensely. "You didn't have to sit in a jail cell."

"Now, now, my boy," Whittier countered smoothly. "Let's not lose perspective. I'm sure this will all work out."

"But jail, Joe!" Madelline Yates said.

Whittier puffed on his cigar. "Let me give you the name of a very good lawyer –"

"We're in this together," J.D. said.

"Oh, no," Whittier replied. "Indeed we aren't. I intend to do all that I can to help you, but let us get one thing clear, J.D. This is your problem."

"But everything I did was with your knowledge and on your orders."

"Hardly, my boy. As your friend, I may have made a few suggestions –"

"Friend! You owned the company!"

134

"Let's clear that up, too, while we're about it," Whittier said. "The Renovated Data Processing Company is solely the property of Mr. J.D. Marvel."

"What about the Northeast Fiduciary Trust? What about the Empire State Investment Company?"

"If you had a bit more experience in these matters, J.D., you would know that it is not at all unusual for investment companies to provide venture capital for new firms. You must see that, in fairness and in fact, under the law, they can't be held responsible for the actions of the principals of the companies they invest in."

J.D. stared at Whittier, the truth finally spread before him. "My God!" he stammered. "I've been had."

"So melodramatic! You made a calculated gamble. You haven't lost yet."

"What happens to RDP now?" J.D. asked. "And the employees?"

"Well, I can't tell you what will happen to your own company. But I can guess that, unless you can come up with a sizeable transfusion of money, it will go into receivership."

"You mean bankrupt!"

"Yes."

"And the employees?"

"There I can help you, I think," Whittier replied. "Those that want it can be absorbed into a new company I'm forming."

"New company?" J.D.'s mind reeled.

"I and a few associates are acquiring the data-processing business of Peerless."

When J.D. got back to the hotel he found almost the entire New York staff of RDP waiting for him in the lobby. They crowded around him.

"Did you see him?" Hucko asked.

J.D. told them what Whittier had said.

"Jesus!" Hucko said. "He's leaving you out on a limb, J.D."

"He can't get away with it!" Paul Shawn declared.

"He has," J.D. replied flatly.

"What are you going to do?" Wanda asked.

"I'm going to fight it."

"We'll fight it with you!" Hucko cried, and the rest voiced their assent.

J.D. went wearily up to his room, and fell exhausted into bed. His old habit of untroubled sleep when he was most worried served him well

135

now. He awoke at seven o'clock the next morning refreshed.

Madelline Yates was at work over a drawing-board in her office when J.D. walked in. She wore a paint-spattered smock over a skirt and blouse and her hair was disarrayed in wisps around her face.

Madelline said, "Why don't we get some coffee?"

There was a small coffee shop off the lobby of the building that held her office. They took an out-of-the-way booth.

After their coffees were served, J.D. said, "You and Whittier must think I'm a prime fool."

"Why do you say that?" she asked.

"You played me like a fish. He took care of the business end, and you made sure my head was spinning with romance."

"It wasn't like that, J.D."

"What do you get out of it?" he asked bitterly. "Money? Is that it?"

"Let me explain –"

"Or was it simply revenge? You wanted Arnold Yates hurt. And, boy, did I take care of that! Did you ever imagine I'd do such a good job of it?"

"Do I get to say anything?"

"I'm listening."

"I admit that Joe asked me to be your friend. He was afraid that you were too green. He thought you needed a friend who could, well – guide you."

"You were perfect!" J.D. said harshly. "You had me believing Arnold Yates was Attila the Hun. I actually thought I was doing a service to mankind running him out of business – ruining him – causing him to –"

Madelline covered his hand with her own. "Listen to me. I agreed to help Joe before I ever met you. I agreed for a number of reasons. Joe said he would be forming a new company and that he would give Mother and me stock. I desperately wanted to find a way to free Mother from Arnold. I knew if he was down-and-out he would sink to new depths. Mother would once and for all have to leave him. And, if the new company succeeded, she'd have the money to live on."

"You'd have money, too."

"Of course! Do you think I like living in a hole in the wall? Do you think I enjoy watching every penny I spend?"

"A lot of women have to."

"I'm not a lot of women!" she said fiercely.

"No," he agreed.

Her face softened. "That was the plan. But complications arose."

136

"Complications?"

"I fell in love with you."

J.D. stared into her lovely eyes and felt the foundations of his soul shift. He put his hands to his eyes.

"You love me, too," she said softly. "Don't you?"

He nodded, his hands still over his eyes.

Gently, she took his hands, and removed them. She smiled. "Don't look so miserable. People who are in love are supposed to be happy, darling. You'll win your battle in court. I'm going to be there with you. I'll always be with you."

Parkington, the bank manager, was coolly polite. The RDP bank account contained a little over $4000. There would be no more money drawn down from the reserve account, because that belonged to the Northeast Fiduciary Trust Company and he'd received instructions from the "principals" of the trust to close it. Whittier had severed the final tie between them. Now J.D. and Renovated Data Processing were on their own.

Paul Shawn was the one who came up with the idea. "You own RDP, J.D., so you can sell stock in it. We have a thousand customers. If they average each a thousand dollars' worth of stock, that would be a million!"

When he researched RDP's incorporation at the New York Office of Corporations he found to his surprise that RDP was already a stock company, and that he owned all the stock.

"We'll sell fifteen percent," J.D. said. "If my plan for turning the company profitable works, they'll double the value of their equity in five years.

"We'll take ten percent and distribute it among the employees," he went on. He and the other employees of RDP were meeting at the Bronx warehouse. All of the Illinois employees had voted to stick with RDP, and Prescott had brought them to New York for the meeting. "The rest we'll leave in the company treasury for future use."

"You should have more than the rest of us," Walter said.

"No," J.D. said. "I don't want any more than any employee. If I'm not doing the job, you should get rid of me."

J.D. spent Christmas of 1911 with Madelline and her mother at the Long Island estate of Arnold Yates. Yates had borrowed to the hilt against the property, so this was the last time Madelline and her mother would be using it – creditors were taking it over on January 1.

It was an idyllic Christmas, unlike any J.D. had known. There was a huge Christmas tree in the main living-room and a blazing log fire in the stone fireplace. They sat around the fire and drank egg-nog and exchanged gifts. At midnight a sleigh full of carolers went by outside.

Madelline gave J.D. a gold wristwatch, and he gave her a diamond solitaire engagement ring. She threw herself into his arms.

"I hope," he said to Mrs. Yates, "it's all right with you."

"Of course!" she replied, and gave him a kiss.

"Don't I get asked?" Madelline said.

"Oh, all one has to do is look at your face," her mother said.

January 12, 1912 was a bitter wintry Thursday in New York. The wind scattered icy snowflakes through the lobby of the Federal Building on lower Broadway each time the doors were opened. Upstairs, in District Court No. 3, the trial of the People of the United States vs. Jesse Dinsmore Marvel had been going on for six days. By agreement between the defense and the United States Attorney's office, it had been a trial without a jury. (J.D.'s attorney said this was the best strategy, since there were several points of law that he would use in the defense that a jury might not understand.) The closing arguments had been heard, and final motions made that morning. Now, at three o'clock in the afternoon, the court had reconvened to hear the judge's decision. J.D.'s attorney was optimistic. He thought that the fact that the judge had taken such a short time to reach a verdict could only mean acquittal.

Every New York employee of RDP was in the courtroom, as they had been throughout most of the trial. Madelline sat directly behind J.D., who sat at the defendant's table, and now, when the judge had settled onto the bench with a stack of books in front of him, she put a hand on J.D.'s shoulder and he covered it with his own.

In the past two weeks J.D.'s life couldn't have been better. The RDP sales staff had sold nearly $700,000's worth of stock to RDP customers and a million dollars was going to be easy to reach. He and Madelline had agreed they would be married the week after the trial was over, assuming there was a favorable verdict, which now looked assured. Outside, deadly winter assailed the streets, but inside the stuffy courtroom it was springtime in J.D.'s heart.

The judge droned on, reading from his books. Then J.D. became conscious of a stillness in the room and of his lawyer standing beside him tugging him to his feet. J.D. stood and stared at the judge in a daze.

"Jesse Dinsmore Marvel," the judge declared solemnly. "This court fines you five thousand dollars and sentences you to one year in Federal prison."

FOUR

And from the sky, serene and far,
A voice fell, like a falling star,
                    Excelsior!
                    Longfellow

15

J.D. Strikes a Deal

MADELLINE TOOK J.D. HOME TO HER APARTMENT. The judge had
left him free on the original bail pending the appeal his lawyer had
filed. She sat him on the couch and fixed him a drink. He was dazed.
"I can't understand it," he said. Everyone seemed so sure that it was
an acquittal."

"It won't do any good to worry about it," she said. "Drink this and
I'll fix you some dinner."

"I haven't the time," J.D. replied. "I have to see Walter and Finch
right away."

"You have to eat!"

"I'll eat with them." He gulped his drink and left.

They ate in a café near their hotel. Wanda Agronsky and Paul Shawn
joined them. They voiced their fears. Without J.D. they didn't know if
they could keep RDP going.

"Sure you can," J.D. said. "You're getting the money you need –"

"We need you, Marvel," Wanda said.

"What are we so gloomy about?" Paul Shawn asked. "There's still
the appeal."

"When will you know?" Walter asked.

"My lawyer said ten days."

J.D. was sitting on the bed in his hotel room when the phone rang. It
was Homer Cranston calling from Iolus.

"Marvel, you and I have to talk. Joe Whittier is coming the day
after tomorrow, Sunday. I want you here."

"I guess you didn't get the word, Mr. Cranston. I don't work for
you anymore."

143

"Of course I know that. What the hell's that got to do with anything? You'll stay with me."

"Even if I wanted to come, I couldn't."

"What are you talking about?"

"There are certain authorities here who won't let me leave the state."

"Oh, that. Don't worry about it. I'll get you permission to come."

"Why should I want to?"

"Because I assume, you damn fool, that you don't want to go to jail."

"You assume correctly. But what has one got to do with the other?"

"You come out here and find out."

There was a long silence.

"Did you hear me?" Cranston said.

"I'll be there."

Cranston's assistant met J.D.'s train in Chicago on Sunday afternoon, January 14. "Remember me?" he asked.

"Of course. Jamie Ryan."

"I have a car out front."

During the drive to Iolus J.D. tried to find out why Cranston had summoned him but, if he knew, Jamie Ryan wasn't saying.

"You made quite a name for yourself in Peerless," Ryan said. "Until you came along, Elmhurst was considered a desert. How did you do it?"

J.D. described the ways he had broken sales resistance in Elmhurst.

Jamie enjoyed it enormously. "God, that's rich," he laughed. "No one ever thought of giving away cash registers!"

"Well," J.D. replied, 'the idea was to get them to buy."

"Oh, I see that. But what a coup! It's the first time anyone deviated from the Pitch and got away with it."

"I didn't exactly get away with it," J.D. observed drily. "I was fired."

Jamie gave him a sardonic grin. "Which was maybe the highest compliment."

"How do you figure?"

"Mr. Cranston has fired some of the best salesmen in the country."

"I'm a member of an élite group?" J.D. asked ironically.

"There was Dalton. He's now head of Dalton Motors. And Fletcher, who is Vice-President of Sales for National Cash. Not to mention Armbruster, who's National Sales Director for Easy Sewing Machines and who some consider the best salesman in the country."

144

"All given the Cranston stamp of disapproval?"

Jamie nodded. "But, say – I hope you won't mention our little talk to Mr. Cranston."

"You don't want the mark of Cranston on you?"

Jamie grinned ruefully. "My game is administration. I'm not a super salesman, like you. Jobs are hard to come by."

"Don't worry. I won't mention a thing to Cranston. But maybe you underrate yourself. In the past few months I've come to see that a good administrator can be a hell of an asset. Someone to take care of the details that can nibble away at you like a thousand mosquitoes."

"That's about as good a description of my job as any I've heard – swatting mosquitoes."

"Do you like it?" A vague idea was beginning to form in J.D.'s mind.

"I like the work a lot," Jamie said cautiously, leaving what he didn't like unsaid. J.D. could guess the rest.

The Cranston home was a brick pile in modified Tudor architecture, sprouting a half a dozen chimneys in a park-like setting of rolling lawn, covered now with snow, and box hedges.

A butler met J.D. on the flagstone terrace that fronted the house, took his grip, and led him through a huge entryway and up a curving staircase to his room. Casement windows overlooked the back lawn, a fire blazed cheerfully in a tiled fireplace, and a high four-poster bed stood under a tasseled canopy. The butler deposited J.D.'s grip, informed him that dinner would be at eight with cocktails in the drawing-room at seven-thirty, and asked J.D. if there would be anything else.

"Ah, dinner –"

"Yes, sir."

"We dress for it?"

The butler's eyebrows elevated a fraction of an inch. "Of course, sir. Black tie."

J.D. consulted the gold wristwatch Madelline had given him, and discovered he had nearly three hours until cocktails. He could find nothing to read other than a large Bible on the bedside table. The room was stifling from the fire. He unlatched one of the casement windows and swung it open and stood in the window well and gazed at a stand of denuded white pine on a rise in the distance.

The sound of voices brought his eyes down to the lawn where he saw emerging from behind a hedge three children: two boys and a girl.

They were dressed in winter clothing – mackinaws and bulky trousers that gave them androgenous shapes – but the girl was distinguished by tresses of long, auburn hair that escaped from under the wool cap she was wearing. The children looked to be about twelve and, incongruously for the stark winter landscape, carried croquet mallets.

The voices rose excitedly through the crystalline air, trailing puffs of steam from their rosy mouths.

On an impulse, J.D. threw off his suit and pulled on a pair of old cotton trousers, a plaid wool shirt, some stout shoes, and a sweater. He found his way, without encountering anyone, through halls and elegant wood-paneled rooms with ornately sculpted ceilings, to a set of French doors opening onto a terrace overlooking the back lawn.

The children were playing a kind of field hockey with the mallets and a battered croquet ball. The girl was competing against both boys and, J.D. noted as he drew closer, losing, although what she lacked in numbers on her side she nearly made up for with energy and determination, flying over the frozen ground, emitting little squeals of exertion, as she pursued one and then the other of the boys.

J.D. stood on what he judged to be the sidelines of the game and watched unobserved by the children until, suddenly, the trio whirled to pursue a hard-hit shot that skittered across the snow right at J.D.'s legs. He leaped and the ball passed under him. The children skidded to a stop, startled by the sight of him. They stood panting, regarding him with questioning eyes.

"Are you one of Bixby's men?" the girl asked.

J.D. pointed with his thumb over his shoulder at the house. "I'm a guest."

"Oh." The girl brushed a vagrant lock of hair off her forehead with her wrist.

"Who is Bixby?"

"The grounds-keeper. His men come and go. Can't seem to keep them for long. Sorry I mistook you for one." She took a mitten off her right hand and held it out. "I'm Lucille Cranston. These two hellions are my brothers, Brian and Junior."

The girl's handshake was firm, her eyes direct.

"You seem to be outnumbered," he said, after he had told them his name.

She grinned suddenly. It was a wonderful grin, imparting a devilish gleam to her blue eyes. "Would you like to sign on for my team?"

"I'd be delighted."

"Junior," the girl said. "Run and get Mr. Marvel a mallet."

146

With J.D. on the girl's side it became an even contest that raged back and forth across the lawn between the two hedges that had been chosen for goals. They yelled and slipped and tumbled on the frozen lawn. They crashed into each other and leaped to avoid errant shots and wildly swinging mallets. With the score tied nine to nine a uniformed maid came onto the terrace at the back of the house, and called, "Miss Cranston! It's time."

"Oh, damn," Lucille complained. "Just when J.D. and I were going to win."

This brought hooting disagreement from Brian and Junior.

Lucille put out her hand. "Thanks, J.D.," she said. "We gave them what-for, didn't we?"

"Indeed we did."

"See you at dinner." Then she was off at a run with her brothers accepting the unspoken challenge of a race and dashing after her.

J.D. was surprised to discover that it was six-thirty. He'd been playing for nearly two hours. He made his way to his room weary but happy. The time with the children had renewed him in some fundamental way. The threat of prison didn't weigh as heavily as before and his aspect was more that of his old confident self. While he bathed he found himself whistling.

At seven-thirty J.D., dressed in his tuxedo, made his way downstairs to the drawing-room. Unlike Whittier's custom of segregation, Cranston mingled female and male guests together alike for cocktails. J.D. found a dozen people already assembled with glasses in their hands. He took a champagne cocktail from a tray that a maid offered him.

Cranston and Whittier stood before a huge fireplace in which a log blazed, talking, their heads nearly touching. They looked up when J.D. entered and Cranston raised a finger and waggled it in his direction.

In another group J.D. recognized Mrs. Whittier, who smiled and nodded at him as he passed by on his way to the fireplace.

Cranston's massive body was encased in dinner clothes that seemed ready to burst their seams under the strain. His florid face and military mustache contrasted with the slim elegance of Whittier who looked, beside the bull-like Cranston, almost epicene.

Whittier smiled and held out his hand to J.D. as if nothing untoward had ever passed between them. Cranston did not offer his hand. His intense, close-set eyes bored into J.D.'s face from behind pince-nez that flashed in the firelight.

147

"Well, my boy," Whittier said suavely. "Did you have a good trip out from New York?"

J.D. admitted that he had.

"I want to talk to you," Cranston said abruptly.

"We thought, after dinner," Whittier added.

"That's why I came," J.D. said.

Then Cranston continued the conversation J.D. had interrupted. As J.D. turned to go Whittier flashed him an apologetic smile.

A young woman had entered the room while J.D.'s back had been turned. She was small, red-haired, with a freckled gamine face and large blue eyes, and was wearing a gown that exposed milk-white well-formed shoulders. She was talking to a group across the room but as J.D. walked toward them she detached herself and met him halfway.

He paused, looked down at her, and said, "You must be Lucille's sister. The resemblance is remarkable."

The young woman smiled and said, "I don't have a sister, Mr. Marvel. Just two rather rowdy little brothers who think they're the world champion shinny players."

"Good Lord!" J.D. exclaimed. "I would've sworn you were about twelve."

"Twenty, my last birthday," she replied.

"I'm sorry."

"Don't apologize. I might decide that it's flattering. Tell me – how do you know my parents?"

"I don't know your mother," J.D. said. "I used to work for your father."

"Used to?"

"I – left Peerless last year."

"Let me introduce you."

She led him to a group. Mrs. Cranston was a small, handsome woman in her forties with greying auburn hair, and her daughter's eyes and smile. The others were neighbors of the Cranstons. They were genteel, friendly people and J.D. found himself warmed by their kindness. He stole looks at Lucille Cranston, still not quite believing that this lovely young woman could be the same boisterous tomboy that had been his teammate of the afternoon.

When they went in to dinner, Mrs. Cranston said, "Would you escort Lucille please, Mr. Marvel?"

Her hand on his sleeve was as small as a child's and yet the gown she wore left no doubt that she was a woman.

He was placed at the table next to Lucille Cranston.

"What engages your time now, Mr. Marvel?" Lucille asked. "If you don't mind my asking?"

"I'm connected with a company that sells data-processing equipment. And what engages your time, Miss Cranston?"

"I've been in college."

"Been?"

"I graduated at the end of last term from Vassar."

"What will you do now?"

She wrinkled her nose. "That's a source of debate in our household. My father believes that a woman my age should be married and making a home."

"But you don't?"

"In this day and age, Mr. Marvel, that seems to me a rather old-fashioned view, don't you think?"

"What would you like to do instead?"

"I'm not sure. My education is in history and literature. Hardly the preparation one needs for the business world."

"Would you like a job in the business world?"

"I would. Provided it were something that I felt was significant. Oh, I don't mean I would object to menial tasks. I would just like to think I had the opportunity to go forward to better things. Do you think that's rash of me?"

"Not at all. Perhaps you'll work for Peerless."

Lucille laughed. "That is hardly what I have in mind. I've been interviewing in Chicago."

J.D. remembered the office equipment company that Paul Shawn had worked for and mentioned the name to Lucille. "It seemed like a good company."

"Thank you," Lucille said. "I'll call on them."

After dinner, Whittier came over to J.D. "Ready?"

He bade goodbye to Lucille Cranston and followed Whittier out of the dining-room, down the wide hall, and through a door into a den. There was a fire in the hearth, and a crystal decanter of cognac and glasses on a table. Cranston passed around a teak box of Prince des Galles Perfectos and splashed cognac into three snifters. Whittier and Cranston sat on a thick box-shaped couch and J.D. took an upholstered armchair across from them.

"You've got yourself in a peck of trouble," Cranston began. "The papers are full of it."

"I'm sure you didn't bring me all the way from New York to tell me that," J.D. said.

149

"The fact is, J.D.," Whitter said. "The government is in an ugly mood. The Attorney General, George Wickersham, is out to make a name for himself. He busted up Standard Oil and American Tobacco. That, and all the lurid details of Yates's death blaring forth in the papers, undoubtedly contributed to the judge giving you the maximum sentence. In a way you were a victim of circumstances. A shame, but not much you could've done about it."

"You recommended my lawyer," J.D. said.

"A good man," Cranston added.

"I had the feeling he gave me some bad advice."

"Nonsense!" Cranston exclaimed.

"He advised me not to have a jury trial."

"Then it was the best thing to do," Cranston said placidly.

"You didn't tell me I might go to jail," J.D. said to Whittier.

"I never intended you should."

"But you knew what we were doing was illegal."

"Illegal!" Cranston snorted. "Twenty years ago it would've been considered laudatory. You would've been held up as an example to follow. Politics! It's all politics. Because that bandy-legged demogogue in the White House wants to make himself king, you get keel-hauled!"

"A man died," J.D. said quietly.

"You didn't kill him," Whittier replied.

"Didn't I?"

"He was a coward," Cranston came in. "All his life. Took the coward's way out. He would've sooner or later."

"These government policies are attacking the very thing that made this country great," Whittier continued. "Competition! Without it we're nothing. It's the winnowing that selects out the best men. The most creative and daring. The men who give the country the transportation, food and shelter that it needs, and makes the jobs so every man can have his share. Yates was winnowed out."

J.D. laughed mirthlessly. "Competition killed him."

"That's it."

"Nice. Nobody's responsible that way."

"No," Cranston said. "Yates was responsible. But enough of this caterwauling over Yates. We're here to talk about your future. You don't want to go to jail."

"Of course not."

"We can see to that," Cranston assured him.

150

"I have a feeling it will cost me," J.D. said. "How do you propose to accomplish it?"

"We want the company. RDP."

"What if I tell you it's not mine to give?"

"We know that you've sold stock to customers to raise operating capital. What we want is the rest of the stock."

"It's Treasury stock," J.D. replied. "Not mine."

"I don't care what kind of stock it is," Cranston said. "It's the controlling interest, and you have the say-so over it. I want it."

"What if I say no?"

"You can rot in jail," Cranston said, his eyes glittering like stones.

"You think it's funny?" A smile had spread slowly over J.D.'s face.

"I was wondering what might've happened if I hadn't raised the money to save RDP."

"Pointless speculation!" Cranston growled.

"You would've moved in and taken over the customers," J.D. continued. "After all, they have Peerless equipment. It would've been simple. Then you wouldn't need me."

"Oh, see here," Whittier interjected smoothly. "No sense in going into all that."

"Would I have been winnowed, Mr. Cranston?"

"Yes!" Cranston said. "Because you had gumption and a certain ability, you'll get another chance."

"I'll get more than that," J.D. added quietly.

Cranston stared at him. "What are you talking about?"

"I want to run RDP. I want an iron-clad contract to be President and Chief Executive."

"I'll see you in hell first!" Cranston sputtered. He got to his feet, his face red.

"Wait," Whittier said. "Let's just calm down for a minute, Homer." He turned to J.D. "You'll go to prison, J.D. There isn't any doubt about it."

"So I'll go to prison for a year," J.D. said calmly. "And I'll be twenty-three years old when I get out. But I can't believe that either of you is that poor a businessman to allow it to happen."

"What do you mean?" Whittier asked.

"Just this. What will it gain you? You won't get RDP. In fact, there's a good chance I can come out of prison and run it. The employees are on my team. Even if you can manage a take-over without me, most of them will leave.

"On the other side, I've proved I can run RDP. And I know I can

151

run it on a profit-making basis. You're going to need someone to run it, unless one of you had planned to do it, and I can't imagine either of you has the time or the inclination. So what does it profit you to turn down my offer?"

"He makes sense, Homer," Whittier conceded.

"I don't believe in employment contracts," Cranston said. "Where's a man's incentive, then? Turns good men into lazy parasites. I might go along with your proposal, but no contract."

"It's no deal without it," J.D. said. "You don't have a very good reputation for keeping executives, Mr. Cranston. But look at it this way. I'd be willing to be paid on the basis of the company's performance."

"That would solve the incentive problem," Whittier agreed.

"Employment contract!" Cranston blustered. "It goes against the grain."

"Don't let a prejudice stand in the way of good business," J.D. replied coolly.

Cranston glared at him over the rim of his snifter, then broke into an explosive laugh. "Damn me, if you don't take the blue ribbon for sheer brass, boy! I might go for a six-month contract."

"Three years," J.D. said calmly. "And that's not subject to negotiation. However," he added, "I'd be willing to stipulate that if I don't meet the objectives we set out, I'm fired."

A crafty light came into Cranston's eyes. "That sounds more like it."

"All that's left then," J.D. said, "is to talk about the objectives."

Cranston waved a hand airily. "Joe and I can work them out."

J.D. smiled. "I'm sure you can. But what will be in the contract is this: the performance of RDP will be the same as or greater than that of Peerless, as a percentage against investment, for each of the three years in question."

"What!" Cranston said.

"Surely you don't object to that?" J.D. asked. "That I have to run RDP as well as you run Peerless?"

Whittier grinned. "Looks like he's got you, Homer."

"I'll have my lawyers draw up the contract," Cranston said with a sigh.

"I'll have mine look at it," J.D. replied.

16

The Wizard of De Kalb

CRANSTON AND WHITTIER didn't waste time exercising their influence on J.D.'s behalf. On Wednesday he was summoned to his attorney's office where he found the Assistant United States Attorney who had prosecuted the case. J.D. was subjected to a spate of legal mumbo-jumbo but what it all came down to was that the appeal that his lawyer had filed, having been given priority consideration by the circuit court of appeals, had succeeded and a new trial was ordered, and that the U.S. Attorney's Office had, "in the interest of the taxpayer's moneys," decided not to pursue the case.

J.D. had one question for the Assistant U.S. Attorney. "What if you change your mind?"

"Can't be done," the man replied. "We sign a waiver. But we want something from you in return."

What they wanted was for J.D. to sign a consent decree that would prohibit him and RDP from employing the tactics that had led to his indictment. It was a long and detailed document. When J.D. had finished reading it he signed it. When he left the attorney's office a harsh winter wind was blowing in from the lake, whipping his overcoat around his legs.

On Thursday morning J.D. called a meeting of the New York contingent of RDP, plus Leland Prescott, who happened to be in town. They met in the warehouse in Brooklyn over a catered breakfast and greeted the news of his settlement of the indictment with cheers. Then he read them the salient points of the consent decree.

"Good God!" Walter Hucko exclaimed. "They don't want much. Who's going to make sure the competition plays by those rules?"

This elicited grumbles of agreement. J.D. held up a hand. "If you think about it, there isn't an unfair rule in this whole thing. What they're asking is for us to play fair. That's all. And if we can't play fair and win, I miss my guess, because we've got the best people in the business. And we're going to get better! We're taking over all of the data-processing business of the Peerless Cash Register Company!

"What it means is that we will have our own manufacturing plants," he said. "We'll be an integrated company from top to bottom – sales, service, manufacturing and development. Yes, development, because don't ever forget that we're in a business that won't stand still for anyone.

"Then you'd better light a fire under Ansell Farnsworth!" Leland Prescott interjected.

"I'm going to see him next week," J.D. replied. "In the meantime, we all have jobs to do." He turned to a flip-chart stand. "Tom Finch and I, over the next couple of weeks, will be putting together a sales plan. We need to hire more people if we're going to expand our business. And we need to train them. I envision something along the lines of the Peerless company training school."

"*Not* a canned pitch!" someone groaned.

J.D. grinned. "No. I said 'along the lines of,' not a copy. If you have suggestions for the school, give them to Wanda. She'll be putting together the training plan."

"What does old man Cranston get out of this?" Prescott asked.

"Controlling interest – enough Treasury stock for fifty-one per-cent."

"We're back working for Cranston," Finch said dourly.

"Not quite," J.D. replied. He told them about his contract. "You'll be working for me."

"For three years," Wanda said. "What happens then?"

"Well," J.D. replied. "Look at it this way. In three years, with the core of people we've got, we're going to be the number one data-processing company in the world.

"Then we can always walk out. Start our own company. We'll have the trained people, the know-how to design equipment, the customers. I don't think Cranston or his partners will be dumb enough to let that happen."

"So?" someone asked.

"Then, we take control back." He held up a hand and made a fist. "When we have them where we want them."

Ansell Farnsworth was known as "The Wizard of De Kalb," both for

154

his genius and his eccentricities. He lived four miles outside De Kalb, Illinois, in a rustic farmhouse that had been built fifty years before from hand-hewn logs. The barn had been converted into a shop where he perfected his inventions. Although rural and isolated, the farm had all the modern conveniences. Telephone lines and electricity had been run a good many miles at great expense, an expense borne by the Peerless Cash Register Company in the first honeymoon weeks of the Cranston–Farnsworth association. Farnsworth, who, when he first met Cranston, had been living in a shabby little house in De Kalb and performing his work at the electrical engineering facilities at Northern Illinois University where he had been an adjunct professor, had insisted on the farm as a part of the deal. He'd retired to the place and hadn't left it. His groceries were delivered. He resisted Cranston's blandishments and, later, injunctions, to visit Iolus. Much to Cranston's irritation he had to journey to the farm if he wanted to see the "Wizard," who greeted him ungraciously. Finally, their relationship had deteriorated to the point where they never met, seldom spoke on the telephone, and generally detested each other.

J.D. got off the train in De Kalb on a frosty late-January morning. He'd wired Farnsworth that he was coming and had received no reply. He hired a hack to take him out to the farm. The fields were gone to seed, covered with a frozen yellow stubble. The house stood darkly against the yellow plains. A window had been broken at some time and covered over with weathering-boards. A grey snake of smoke rose lazily from the chimney. A deteriorating harrow slumped beside the path that led from the road to the front door. Behind the house the barn stood, round-shouldered with age.

J.D. had to beat on the front door for several minutes before it was reluctantly opened a crack. A bleary blue eye stared out at him. "What d'you want?" a voice cracking with irritation demanded.

"Doctor Farnsworth?" J.D. asked, peering into the crack.

"What is it?" the voice rasped.

"I'm J.D. Marvel, Doctor Farnsworth. I wired you that I was coming."

"I didn't tell you to come. Who are you?"

"I'm the President of RDP –"

"I don't want to buy anything!"

The door started to close. J.D. put his hand on it. "Wait! I'm the president of the company that's going to sell your equipment."

The door opened a little wider. J.D. could make out a frosty, unkempt beard, a long aquiline nose beneath hazy blue eyes. "What

155

the devil you talking about. *My* equipment?"

"Yes, sir."

A pause. Then, "What happened to Cranston?"

"If you'll allow me to come in, sir, I'll tell you."

Another pause. Then the door was abruptly flung wide. "Get on in, then."

The room J.D. entered had once been intended as the parlor, but was a study in disarray. Spread out on the floor between a couch and a table was a disordered mass of papers covered with finely detailed drawings of machinery. J.D. picked his way carefully through the sheets. When he reached a cleared space in front of the stove he turned to confront his host.

Although Farnsworth was in his mid-fifties, he gave the appearance of being a much older man. He stooped, his white hair was thinning, his long cheeks were furrowed. He wore a yellowing shirt that had once been white, a pair of canvas trousers and leather-thonged sandals. Only his hands were young – long, tapering fingers, smooth, shapely – an artist's hands.

"What's this about Cranston?" Farnsworth demanded.

"Hasn't he told you?"

"Hasn't told me anything."

"My company – RDP – is taking over the data-processing business from Peerless."

"Hmmmp!" Farnsworth snorted. "Not without my say-so."

"Exactly," J.D. replied. "That's why I'm here."

"Get on with it then!"

There was a fire-blackened coffee-pot on the stove. "Couldn't I have a cup of coffee and sit down? I've come a long way."

"If you can find a cup," Farnsworth said ungraciously. "Kitchen." He pointed.

The kitchen was worse than the parlor. Dirty dishes covered nearly every available surface. J.D. found a dirty cup, washed it out at the tap, and carried it back to the parlor. "Can I get you one?" he asked Farnsworth.

"Got my own."

"Doctor Farnsworth," J.D. began. "I'm hoping that we can sell a great many of your machines. I'm hoping that we can make you a very rich man."

"Same thing Cranston said. Didn't happen."

"Well, sir," J.D. went on. "I hope we can do things a bit differently than Homer Cranston."

156

For the next thirty minutes he described the arrangement between RDP and Peerless, the three-year contract he had made – emphasizing that he, and not Cranston, would have complete say-so over what went on in the company – and his plans for his organization. Farnsworth sipped his coffee and listened without comment.

When he was finished, Farnsworth stared at him for such a long time that J.D. wondered if he hadn't gone into some kind of trance. Finally, Farnsworth said, "You're too young!"

"Well, sir," J.D. replied calmly. "I reckon that depends on your point of view."

"What do you mean?" Farnsworth asked irritably.

"Why, from my point of view, I'm just the right age."

Farnsworth stared for a moment and then a fleeting wisp of a smile stretched the thin mouth nestled in his beard. "So," he said. "What do you want of me, besides my patents?"

"Your ideas," J.D. replied simply. "The long-run strength of our company depends on new developments, refinements to the equipment, new inventions entirely. We can't do it without you, sir."

"Or someone like me?"

"Doctor Farnsworth," J.D. said earnestly. "From what I've heard, there *isn't* anyone like you."

Farnsworth helped himself to more coffee, and held the pot out to J.D., who extended his cup. "Expect you'd want me to move to some fancy laboratory in Chicago or New York."

"If you wanted to," J.D. said. "But, as far as I'm concerned, you could stay right here and work on what you wanted to work on."

"Meetings!" Farnsworth exclaimed. "You'd want me at the big meetings where everybody sits around and tells me how to do my job, wouldn't you?"

"No, sir. You could come and visit any time you pleased, you'd be welcome, but as far as I'm concerned it would be a waste of your time when you could be here, doing your rightful work."

"Budgets! Every time I wanted a cotter pin, or a relay, have to submit a budget."

J.D. took a sip of coffee. "Well, sir – we'd have to keep track of costs, that's true –" Farnsworth snorted in a way that said his worst fear had been realized. "But suppose we just make it as easy on you as possible? We'll keep track of what you spend and make up a budget based on that."

"What if I have to buy some big piece of gear I haven't needed before? What about that?"

157

"Why, you just go ahead and buy it. If you think we ought to know about it, fine. Call me up. Or drop me a line. If not, we'll know it when we get the bill, won't we?"

"That's a hell of a way to run a company!"

"Yes, sir," J.D. said, grinning. "Sure wouldn't run any other part of it that way."

Suddenly, Farnsworth grinned and ten years seemed to fall from his face. He pointed a long finger at the papers on the floor. "Want to see what I'm working on?"

"I'd consider it a privilege," J.D. said.

"Later, take you out to the barn and show you my prototypes," Farnsworth added, as he and J.D. got onto their knees among the drawings scattered on the floor. "See this? This is a three-way sorter-counter. As the cards pass through it picks up on, say column eighty — you can set the brushes for any column — and counts the cards with certain punches. You not only sort into pockets, you get counts a different way. Say you want to keep track of certain cross-categories of inventories . . ."

17

Birth of a Legend

J.D. AND MADELLINE were married on a sparkling Sunday in June, 1912. His mother came, his father didn't. But he sent a wedding gift with Elvira: the huge, old family Bible with all the births, deaths and marriages of the Marvel family over the past eighty years recorded in the back. And there, in his father's rotund Spencerian script as the last entry, was recorded the marriage of Jesse Dinsmore Marvel to Madelline Yates.

RDP expanded rapidly. With the infusion of money that came from the sale of controlling interest to a holding company owned jointly by Peerless and Joseph Falk Whittier, J.D. was able to open RDP offices in Washington D.C., Philadelphia, Boston, Cleveland, and upstate New York in the first twelve months. RDP hired a hundred new employees that year and Wanda, who J.D. made Manager of Training, set up a school in an aging estate on the Hudson near Tarrytown that was leased from the heirs of a venerable New York family which had fallen on hard times. Walter Hucko, at his own request, was made an instructor at the school so he and Wanda could be together, and it turned out that he had a natural bent for teaching. He and Wanda were so busy setting up the school that they couldn't find the time to be married until March 1913. J.D. threw them a lavish wedding party at the Waldorf Astoria.

By the end of the first year the warehouse in Brooklyn was no longer adequate either for storing inventory or for offices. J.D. found a large warehouse, only two blocks from the old one, that he leased, and took a suite of offices, half of the fifth floor of a building on Madison Avenue just off 45th, as the corporate headquarters of RDP.

J.D. addressed the first graduating class of twenty men in July of

1912. Wanda had asked him for a photograph of himself to use in the graduation program. He'd gone to a Park Avenue photographer and had a picture taken that he thought made him look like an actor – hands crossed on knee, hair pomaded into a flawless dark shield, eyes half-hooded, with a fuzzy, arty kind of background – altogether a moony kind of look on his face that he didn't care for in the least. But Madelline loved it and ordered an extra print for herself. The meeting room where they held the graduation ceremonies displayed a huge framed print of the portrait over the speaker's podium.

J.D. had spoken to the class members several times during the course of their training, inspirational speeches delivered in his homely Midwestern accent that somehow made them more effective than orotund declamations, and they knew him and greeted him on this occasion with a standing ovation, much to J.D.'s surprise and embarrassed pleasure. Students' hand-lettered signs adorned the walls of the room: "SELL YOURSELF AND THE PRODUCT WILL SELL ITSELF!" "RDP IS THE BEST," "MARVEL'S MACHINES ARE A MARVEL," "HELPING A CUSTOMER IS HELPING YOURSELF," and so on.

After he'd given his speech and been enthusiastically cheered for it, he was delivered another surprise. The class sang him a song under the direction of Walter Hucko. It was sung to the tune of "I've Been Working on the Railroad" and, J.D. found out later, it had been the product of a collaboration by the whole class.

> I've been learning to sell d.p.,'
>   All the live-long day,
> I've been wanting a terr-i-tor-y,
>   To sell for Jay-ay Dee.
> Oh, don't you know he's the best salesman,
>   Best in all this land,
> Yes, you know he's the best salesman,
>   I WANT TO SELL LIKE THAT MAN!

The last line delivered in an unmusical shout. There were several other choruses extolling the school, RDP, and J.D., each as unmetered as the first.

Later, as J.D. was leaving, he asked Wanda to send him copies of the signs that had been on the walls of the meeting room. "You might come into town next week, too," he added. "I'd like to talk to you about the school."

*

160

For the first six months of their marriage, J.D. and Madelline shared Madelline's apartment in Greenwich Village. He left it early in the morning and returned late at night when Madelline would usually have a candle-light supper awaiting him. After dinner they would go immediately to bed and make passionate love. She always greeted him joyously and never complained. When he took time to reflect on their situation, which wasn't often, he concluded that his wife was an exceptional woman, aside from her astonishing beauty, and he was a lucky man. Then, in December, 1912, Madelline told him she had found a wonderful house, and he did not object. It was a three-story brownstone on the corner of 9th Avenue and 57th, only two blocks from the park. It had elegant sculpted plaster ceilings and walls wainscoted in richly aged mahogany, a magnificent crystal chandelier in the dining-room, and a bookshelf-lined study overlooking the street. J.D. thought it far too much house for the two of them, and he also thought the price outrageous. It was owned by a mezzo-soprano who sang secondary roles at the Met and who, apparently, thought her fame added to the value of the house. But J.D. did not voice these thoughts. He could afford the house. His salary was $3000 a month with a provision for bonuses based on the performance of RDP that he expected would yield him an additional $10,000 on the first of the year. However, after Madelline had shown him the house and gazed up at him with eyes sparked with excitement, he feigned a reserve he didn't feel. "I'll think it over," he said, and almost lost his resolve when he saw the disappointment pass over her face like a cloud putting out the sun.

That same night he deposited an envelope on her plate before she served his dinner. "What is it?"

"Open it."

She did and looked at the papers she withdrew from the envelope with perplexity. "I still don't know what it is, darling."

"The papers for your new house."

"My –?"

"I went to the bank this afternoon. We are now proud owners of a brownstone house and a millstone mortgage."

She got up, came round the table, and fell into his arms. They didn't have time to eat their supper that evening.

Madelline threw herself headlong into decorating their new home.

161

The place teemed with drapers, furniture-movers, wallpaper-hangers, and painters.

"I thought it looked pretty good the way it was," J.D. said one night when he came home to the apartment in Greenwich Village and heard Madelline's report of her day's activities.

"J.D.!" she said in a shocked voice. "You can't be serious."

"I suppose not," he replied, and addressed himself to opening the wine. But the truth was that he *was* serious. In fact, he could've as easily continued to live in the apartment. It suited him. It was a cool nest to come to from the heat of his daily life.

When, finally, in March of 1913 they moved into the brownstone, J.D. had to admit that Madelline had worked wonders. The walls above the wainscoting were a soft beige. The dining-room featured a Bugatti table and sideboard of dark mahogany and inlaid brass. The sitting-room was draped in dark-blue velvet with gold brocade stitching, and featured two sweeping Greek-revival Duncan Phyfe couches of mahogany, and gold silk upholstering, with carved lyre ends. The fireplace mantel had been refinished and stained to match the wood in the sofas. There were art-nouveau Guimard tables, Reimerschmid armchairs, and an inlaid antique Portuguese liquor cabinet. The study had an oak roll-top desk. The bookshelves had been stocked by Madelline from second-hand bookshops and J.D. was surprised to find many good contemporary and classical titles among them.

Their bed was a copy of a fifteenth-century English baronial bedstead of carved oak with painted shields and floral motif and a vaulting carved-oak canopy. The baronial motif carried through to the rest of the bedroom furniture. J.D. walked around the bedroom, touching tables, plumping the mattress with his fingers.

"Do you like it, darling?" Madelline asked anxiously. She had refused to let J.D. see the house until it was completed.

He gave her a look. "I like it so well, I think we should try it out immediately." And they did.

In the summer of that year J.D. hired Jamie Ryan as his administrative assistant. Cranston had fumed and called him a damned pirate, told Jamie he would meet J.D.'s offer, but J.D. prevailed.

Jamie did the job that J.D. had hoped he would. He'd taken the administrative details from J.D.'s shoulders, leaving him free for the more productive work of managing RDP's burgeoning field force. Not only was Jamie an invaluable aide, he also became a good friend. J.D.

162

found him to be thoroughly good-natured and unfailingly kind-hearted. While these traits were undoubtedly handicaps for a line executive, as J.D. realized, they suited Jamie perfectly to the job he had.

It was natural for J.D. to fall into the habit of talking to Jamie about his dreams for the company. These discussions usually took place during the evening, long after the rest of the headquarters staff had gone, in J.D.'s office over glasses of sherry from the sideboard bar.

On this particular October evening, the unseasonable warmth of which had caused J.D. to crank one of the casement windows in his office half open, he started the conversation by asking Jamie what kind of razor he shaved with.

"One that was my father's."

"Straight-edge?"

Jamie nodded. "I know it's old-fashioned not to have a safety razor, but I like it because it was my father's."

"I use a Gillette," J.D. said. "And while I was shaving this morning it occurred to me that Mr. King Gillette and I have something in common."

"What's that?"

"He sells razors. Millions of them."

"Everyone has one," Jamie agreed.

"But you know what he makes his money on?"

"Why," Jamie said, hesitating. "I suppose all those razors he sells."

J.D. shook his head. "Think a minute. How long does a Gillette razor last?"

"I don't know. Quite a while, I should think."

"Practically for ever. There are hardly any parts to it. Simply a blade-holder, is what it is."

"Ah!" Jamie said. "The blades!"

J.D. smiled. "Right. The blades. That's where the money is for Mr. King Gillette. And that led me to think of the Kodak Company which sells cameras in order to sell film, where the real money is. And *that* led me to think of RDP –"

"Cards! Punched cards!" Jamie exclaimed.

J.D. grinned. "Now you've got it."

"But," Jamie said slowly, pondering, "we make money on the machines."

"Sure we do. But we don't make a blasted nickel on those cards. Or, hardly a blasted nickel. And do you know why?"

163

"We buy them from Hollerith practically for the same price we sell them."

"Yep." J.D. refilled their glasses. "Hollerith's getting most of the profit on cards from us, and every other data-processing outfit."

"Don't see much that we can do about it," Jamie said. "He's got the patents."

"Actually, the Computing-Tabulating-Recording Company owns the patents. And Hollerith owns a bit of stock and has a job as head scientist." (This new company had been formed out of Hollerith's old one and pieces of other companies in 1911.)

"Were you thinking of buying the patents?"

"It would cost too much, even if they'd sell, which I doubt, because without the card trade CTR wouldn't do very well. They've lost a lot of their equipment business in the past year. Mostly to us. I was thinking of paying a visit to the Wizard of De Kalb."

Farnsworth was in his barn workshop when the station hack deposited J.D. at his front gate. He took J.D. into the cluttered parlor of the house, stirred up the coals in the stove, and made coffee.

J.D. explained what he had in mind. Farnsworth sipped his coffee in silence, eyes vague. J.D. knew him well enough to wait this trance out.

Finally, Farnsworth said, "It would mean changing the feeds on all our machines. Maybe even the sensing brushes. I don't know. It would be a hell of a job."

"But it could be done? You could design a card different enough from Hollerith's to get us a patent?"

"Hell," Farnsworth snorted. "I could not only do that, I could design a better card." He sorted among the papers on the floor until he came up with a blank one, which he spread on a journal on his lap to poise a fountain-pen over. "Look here." He quickly sketched a quandrangle on the paper while J.D. peered over his shoulder. "Hollerith's got eighty columns. Each column's got a row of ten numeric and two zone punches. So you can do all the numbers and the alphabet, right?"

"Right," J.D. agreed.

"But you and I both know that the average data-field length isn't anywhere near eighty columns.

"You can pack the fields."

"Sure! But they still don't come out eighty columns every time. Now, here, just above the zone punches . . ."

164

Farnsworth went on outlining his idea for J.D. It was ingenious. What it amounted to was that Farnsworth wanted to introduce one more zone punch per column, to be called the "data-demarcation punch," which would signal to the machine the end of a piece of data, which could then be packed in rows as well as columns. After some quick calculations, he said, "I figure we could reduce the length of the card by half!"

"That's great!" J.D. exclaimed. "Would it patent?"

"I don't doubt it for a minute."

The forty-column card that was born that day came to be known in the industry not as the "Farnsworth Card," but as the "Marvel Card," because that's what Ansell Farnsworth called it.

In July of 1914 war broke out in Europe but the United States, in the throes of a new prosperity, was hardly affected by squabbling that was a week away by the fastest ocean liners. Woodrow Wilson promised to keep his country out of the war, and the country believed him.

In 1914 the biggest news in J.D.'s life was not war clouds gathering in Europe, but the fact that RDP turned the corner; it became profitable and made, that year, nearly $250,000 on gross income of just over $2 million. The patent on the Marvel Card had been applied for and over half the machines at customers' businesses, and all the new machines in production, had been converted to the forty-column format. At the annual meeting of the board of directors of RDP that took place that November J.D. predicted sales of half a billion Marvel Cards for the first half of 1915. He also made a controversial proposal, that stirred up many old animosities before it was finally resolved.

The RDP board was composed of Homer Cranston, Joseph Whittier, four other men hand-picked by Whittier and Cranston – two of whom were also members of the Peerless board – and J.D. The meeting was held in a rented hall in the Plaza Hotel in New York, as the offices on Madison didn't have a suitable room. Whittier, as Chairman of the Board (Cranston had been dissuaded from taking the post by an uncomfortable interest the Justice Department had in interlocking chairmanships), called the meeting to order. The formalities ran smoothly. The reading and adoption of minutes, then the treasurer's report cast a rosy ambience over the heads of the assembled capitalists. J.D. gave his business forecast which was more good news so that the board was lolling rather like cattle who had been well grazed, when it came time for new business.

"Gentlemen," J.D. said. "We've got the wrong name for our

company, and we should change it before we get so big we can't."

"I don't know," Whittier said mildly. " 'RDP' has a rather nice ring."

"But it stands for 'Renovated Data Processing'," J.D. said, "which is inaccurate."

"Why not just use the letters?" Cranston asked. "Why does it have to stand for anything?"

"Because people – our customers – ask us what it stands for," J.D. replied. "And we don't want to be known as the company that 'stands for nothing,' do we?"

"Good point," someone said.

"What did you have in mind?" Whittier asked.

" 'Marvel Scientific Machines, Incorporated,' " J.D. said levelly.

Suddenly the board's complacency fled. Astonished glances were exchanged. Homer Cranston sat up in his chair, his fat cheeks red, his mustaches quivering with indignation. Only Whittier seemed to retain his former calm. He even smiled a little. "Bold," he murmured.

"*Tommyrot!*" Cranston ejaculated.

Someone muttered something about "upstarts." Whittier rapped the table with his pencil for order. "Let's follow procedure," he said. "We have a proposal before us. Do you want to put it in the form of a motion, J.D.?"

"After I have a chance to discuss it."

"Go right ahead."

"We need a name that is identifiable and unique, one that sticks in the memory. Marvel fills that bill. We need a name that will build confidence, that will allow customers and prospective customers to know we stand behind our product and services, and what does that better than to put a man's name on it? The name of the man who is at the head of the company? And, finally, wouldn't it be grand if our customers, when talking to their colleagues, could say 'I've got a Marvel'?"

There was a tense silence in the room. Everyone was looking at Homer Cranston.

"Peerless was good enough for me," he said heavily. "I didn't feel like I had to glorify my name."

"Peerless is a good name," J.D. admitted. "It means something. And had your name been Homer Peerless it would've been even better."

Whittier grinned.

"What happens when you're gone?" Cranston asked.

"I don't intend to go for a long time," J.D. replied. "But when I do go, I don't see it will present any problem. It certainly hasn't hurt Sears and Roebuck that Mr. Sears and Mr. Roebuck aren't there any longer."

"I don't like it!" Cranston said. "What about you, Joe? You don't like it, do you?"

" 'I've got a Marvel,' " Whittier mused. "Tell me, J.D. – why 'Scientific Machines'?"

"To distinguish us from ordinary business-machine companies – the ones that make typing machines, adding machines, and the like."

"CTR doesn't mean that much." Cranston exclaimed. "I mean, my God! 'Computing-Tabulating-Recording' – what a mouthful. But they haven't seen fit to change it."

"They aren't doing too well, either," J.D. said.

"Don't write them off," Whittier interjected. "They've brought in Tom Watson who used to be Sales Manager of National Cash Registers to head up CTR. That boy is a salesman!"

"You didn't say, Joe," Cranston persisted. "Are you for this tomfool thing, or not?"

"Look at it this way, Homer," Whittier said smoothly. "If we put J.D.'s name on it and he ever leaves, he can't start up a rival company with that name, can he?"

Cranston's eyes widened. "Hadn't thought of that!" He hit the table and let out a bellow of a laugh. "Guess you didn't think of it either, did you, boy?"

"I don't intend to leave," J.D. said stiffly.

"All right!" Cranston said jovially. "All right! Let him have his name!"

By January of 1915 the change in name had been effected throughout the company – letterheads, business cards, machine nameplates – all bore the Marvel name.

Business in 1915 exceeded even J.D.'s forecasts. Marvel machines went into insurance companies, railroad offices, shipyards, factories, and the government, where J.D. personally supervised the preparation of a successful bid to the Census Bureau that displaced CTR machines.

In the meantime, CTR began to provide hot competition in other areas. They bid against Marvel Scientific Machines for a large installation at the Interstate Commerce Commission, and won. Tom

167

Watson was proving to be every bit as good at selling data-processing equipment as he had been at selling National Cash Registers, where he, like Homer Cranston years before him, had been dubbed "The World's Greatest Salesman."

At the board meeting in November J.D. announced that Marvel Scientific Machines would finish the year at just under $3 million in revenue, and $600,000 in profits. The board gaped with pleasure, raised J.D.'s salary to $4000 a month, and voted him a $20,000 bonus. His three-year employment contract was to expire in February and they voted to renew it for three more years. All votes were unanimous. Homer Cranston still considered J.D. a brash upstart with no respect for his betters, but he couldn't argue with success; Marvel Scientific Machines in 1915 outstripped Peerless in terms of return on investment by an almost two-to-one margin, although no one at the board meeting was foolish enough to make that comparison aloud.

In the meantime Madelline Marvel entertained the people in New York that she considered important to J.D. and to her own ambitions as a stellar hostess. She volunteered for charities, supported the arts, joined clubs, and talked J.D. into joining the important men's clubs in order to meet these people. J.D. didn't see what all this activity had to do with running a successful company, but he went along with it because it gave Madelline something to do with her time, something that she obviously enjoyed. He was proud of his wife, of her beauty and of her sophistication; and she was obviously proud of his accomplishments. Everyone who knew them envied them their marriage. They didn't know the problem that had developed over the previous year and a half. It was a problem that loomed large in J.D.'s life interfering with his concentration when he was at work, making him irritable with Madelline: she'd lost interest in sex.

J.D., at twenty-five, had a strong, pulsing sex-drive. Madelline was willing to do her "duty" in the bedroom, but this was so far from the passionate woman greedy for his body that he first knew, that he could only bring himself to accept the offer when the pressure became unbearable. Clumsily he tried to talk to her about it, tried to get some clue as to what the problem might be, had some vague idea about getting her to a doctor, but she cut him off by saying, "Anytime you want me, darling. Anytime at all." As if there were no problem to begin with.

It was from this background of deprivation that he viewed the young woman who walked into his office one crisp, clear spring day in

1916. She was slight, slender as a willow, with a magnificent crown of auburn hair piled high on her head in the latest fashion, and smooth, white skin contrasting with the red of the lips and blue of her large eyes. She came in the office, closed the door, turned and smiled at him. He gaped at her over the papers he'd been studying.

"I asked your secretary not to announce me," she said. "I hope you don't mind."

He seemed to have swallowed his voice. "No –" he croaked. "Not at all."

"You don't recognize me."

Then he did. "Lucille Cranston!" he said. He stood, came around his desk, took the hand she offered. "Lucille! I can't believe it. You look –"

She grinned, the same imp's grin that he remembered so well. "Older?"

"No! So – so beautiful!"

"Why, thank you!" She looked at the papers on his desk. "I've interrupted your work. Don't blame your secretary. I wanted to surprise you."

He laughed. "That you did."

"Perhaps I could make an appointment?"

"Nonsense. Come and have lunch with me."

"At ten o'clock?"

He looked at his watch. "Well, then a late breakfast. There's a place around the corner."

It was a delicatessen with three tables jammed into a small space between the meat counter and rows of hanging cheeses. At that time of day they had the place to themselves. They ordered tea, and bagels and cream cheese.

"What are you doing in New York?"

"Looking for a job."

"You mean you live here?"

"I'm at a women's hostel right now."

She told him that for the past two and a half years she'd worked for the office-supply company in Chicago that he'd recommended to her when she'd been his dinner companion at her father's house. "I finally got fed up with typing and taking dictation and asked to become one of their representatives, but they have a firm rule – no women. The manager explained it vividly to me. 'What would you do, Miss Cranston, if one of our customers became, well, fresh?' 'I'd tell him to stop,' I said. He kind of leered at me, and said, 'And if he didn't?' So I

169

smiled sweetly and said, 'Why, I guess I'd kick him where it would do the most good.' "

"So," Lucille went on. "I knew I'd better quit. The manager was just as relieved to see me go, I think. I don't know if he was offended by what I said, or was afraid I might haul off and kick him."

"What kind of job are you looking for?"

"What I'd really like is to work with machines. I have an aptitude for it, I think. I could take my typewriter apart and fix it as fast as the service man, and I understood their adding machines, and enjoyed working with them. So when I decided to come to New York you were the first person I thought of."

"I'm glad."

"You know, you're famous."

"Oh, I don't know about that."

"Just this year –" she ticked off on her fingers: "An article in the *Wall Street Journal*, featured in *Barron's* with a photograph – quite a dashing picture, I must say –"

J.D. groaned. "I hate that picture."

She grinned at him. "Where was I? Oh, yes – big article in *Chicago Tribune*: 'Local Boy Conquers Business World' was the tone."

"Does your father know you're in New York and were going to see me about a job?"

"Yes to the first, no to the second. Does it matter?"

"Not in the least. I run Marvel Scientific Machines."

"My father and I are, as they say in the pulp magazines, 'estranged.' "

"Thinks you ought to be married?"

"With five kids and a house to clean."

J.D. grinned. "Not your idea of paradise."

"Quite the opposite." She paused to sip her tea. "Well? What do you think?"

"Consider yourself hired."

She put down her cup and eyed him suspiciously. "That's awfully fast."

J.D. shrugged and smiled complacently at her. "What else is there to do?"

"Why, fill out applications, check my references – all that."

"I know who you are. I know who you worked for – I recommended them, remember? I know you have a college education. And I know you've never worked with data-processing equipment."

"*That's* an asset?"

"Definitely. We prefer to hire people with no experience and train them our way."

"Sounds like father."

"Stole the idea from him."

"Just what is this job you're offering me?"

"Well, I haven't figured that out yet. There are several possibilities. None of which includes secretary."

"You aren't thinking of extra-curricular duties, are you? If that offends you, I'm sorry, but I have to ask. I've had a few offers like that in the past –"

"I'm sure you have." He leaned across the table. "And I wouldn't be human, or I'd have to be blind, if I didn't take note of what an ungodly attractive woman you are. But this job has no strings. Got that?"

She smiled sunnily. "Got it! When do I start?"

"How about tomorrow morning?"

18

J.D. Takes Charge

WILSON WAS RE-ELECTED IN 1916 because "he kept us out of war," then declared war in 1917. In July of 1917 Madelline gave birth to a sickly 5lb baby boy. Against J.D.'s objections she named him Jesse Dinsmore Marvel, Junior. It seemed to J.D. that all the juniors he'd known had been a bunch of panty-waists. When little Jesse was two weeks old Madelline hired a nursemaid and turned the baby over to her. The nursemaid brought the household staff to four including a cook and two maids who did not live in. The nursemaid, however, was given a bedroom next to the nursery, and every other Sunday off, days on which Madelline could be reduced to a state of hysterical exhaustion trying to cope with the demands of the baby who was, in turns, colicky, afflicted with heat rash, and, it seemed to his mother, sending out his thin, petulant yowl from the moment the nursemaid left to the moment she returned.

The question of a job for Lucille Cranston was resolved by Wanda Hucko (who still called herself Agronsky). She met Lucille, liked her instantly, and asked J.D. if she could have her at Tarrytown to train as an instructor.

For the year 1918 Marvel Scientific Machines had sales of just over $7 million and profits of nearly $900,000. The board of directors, meeting in January of 1919, declared a dividend of $2 a share, awarded J.D. a bonus of $40,000 and raised his salary to $8000 a month. Madelline celebrated by having the house redecorated.

During 1919 Marvel Scientific Machines opened twenty-six new branch sales offices, extending as far south as Atlanta and as far west as St. Louis. J.D. toured the branch offices at an exhausting pace,

172

leaving the administrative details at headquarters in the capable hands of Jamie Ryan. J.D.'s visits assumed a pattern: first, a banquet at a local hotel where he would deliver a rousing speech to the assembled branch employees. The next morning, a tour of the offices, where his picture looked down paternally upon the ranks of desks, and where the enthusiastic young men would quote back to him parts of his speech of the night before. Then lunch with the branch manager and his senior salesmen, a visit to two or three significant customers in the afternoon, followed by a dinner with some large potential customer upon whom J.D. would try his hand at closing the order with a high percentage of success (which added to his legend, even though it was a poorly kept secret that the local branch managers often presented a customer who was already sold and only lacked putting his name to a contract to close the deal). The following morning, J.D. would board a train for his next stop.

The staff at Tarrytown were straining to keep up with the influx of trainees that the expansion brought on.

One sultry overcast day in June of 1919 J.D. journeyed up the Hudson to visit the school. It had been nearly six months since his last visit.

He wanted to check in on Lucille Cranston, who had become Wanda's assistant and the undisputed top instructor at the school. In the nearly three years that Lucille had worked for the company, her relationship to J.D., despite his best efforts to change it, had remained one of proper and respectful friendship. She had had many suitors but no serious relationships.

J.D. was met at the Tarrytown station by Walter Hucko, whose title was now Chief Instructor.

Hucko had grown prosperous and looked it. His suit was a conservative dark grey, but it had been cut by the finest tailor in New York, the same one J.D. patronized. His face was rounder, his hair had thinned and greyed, but he still had the enthusiastic spring in his step and the gleam of good fellowship in his eye as he greeted J.D. J.D. thought him remarkably fit-looking for a man who would be fifty next year.

"How's the family?" Hucko wanted to know.

"Fine, Walter."

Hucko had deposited J.D.'s suitcase in the trunk of a gleaming new black Buick touring car, and now they were gliding through the streets of Tarrytown toward the Hudson.

"And Junior?" Hucko wanted to know. "Sprouting up like a beanstalk, I suppose?"

"Yes," J.D. replied, not adding that his son was growing more like a sickly weed. "How's Wanda?"

"Working like a mule, but loving it." It was still a wonder to J.D. how two people with such seemingly different personalities and temperaments as Walter and Wanda could have produced such a fine marriage, but there was no doubt that they had.

At the school J.D. was greeted by Wanda in her office. It was late afternoon, and outside, on the well-manicured lawns of the estate, students were strolling, having just been released from their classes, a parade of dark suits, white shirts, and well-barbered heads.

"The future of Marvel Scientific Machines," Wanda said, gesturing at the window. "We're planning on your addressing them at dinner tonight," she added.

"Let's make it a breakfast meeting tomorrow. I like to catch them when they're fresh."

"Very well."

"You've done a great job, Agronsky," he said. "I know how overworked you've been."

"I've had a lot of help. Lucille is a brick. And, of course, Walter. Did I detect a 'but' following what you just said?'

"Not about the job you've done," J.D. replied. "Let's sit down."

They took chairs facing each other. "Now I know I'm in trouble," Wanda said. "When you ask me to sit down before telling me."

"I'm going to ask you to take on more work." Wanda groaned softly. "I'll expect you to staff up for it," J.D. added.

"You've had an idea."

"It's a new sales approach. We've tried it out in the Chicago office. We offer to survey a prospect's entire operation for him. Give him a report on every single function of his business – accounting, sales, inventory – you name it."

"What do we charge for that?"

"That's the beauty. Nothing!"

"Maybe I missed something in Accounting I, Marvel. How do we make money giving away our services?"

"When we're through we know more about the prospect's business than he does. We know where to recommend that he install Marvel machines for maximum profitability."

"And it locks out the competition?"

"Why would he lease equipment from someone who doesn't have

174

the knowledge of his business that we do? The customer benefits, we benefit."

"Where do I fit in?"

"The survey is only half the pie. That gives us knowledge of the customer's business. But he lacks knowledge of our machines."

"*We* train the customers on Marvel equipment."

"Exactly. All of his key employees, from executives right down to the people who will operate the machines. Then, we've really got him locked." J.D. gripped his hands together. "He'll know our equipment so well that he'd never consider going to the expense of re-training on someone else's.

"We train the top people, the decision-makers, in Tarrytown. The others we handle in the field. The executives would be put up here in the mansion. Have at them morning, noon, and night. Inculcate them in the Marvel Way."

"That's free too, I suppose?"

"They pay their way to and from the school, that's all."

"I don't see how they could turn it down. Christ, Marvel – you're going to end up controlling the world!"

All the effects of the war on Marvel Scientific Machines, Inc., were positive – increased business, increased revenues, inroads into the federal government. The manufacture of data-processing equipment was on the government's priority list for the procurement of materials. About the only effect that could in any sense be deemed negative was that the company lost a small percentage of its bright young men to the armed services which, in most cases, was temporary since the great majority of them returned as healthy or even healthier than when they left.

Even the patriotic programs undertaken by the company at its own expense accrued to its benefit. There were war-bond rallies at the plants and sales offices, and patriotic speeches delivered at public gatherings to benefit the Red Cross and various other service groups, at which J.D. was a prominent and in-demand speaker – all of which not only promoted the war effort, but also promoted the Marvel name throughout the country.

As a result, J.D., along with a dozen of his fellow citizens, was summoned to Washington late in August of 1919 to receive a Presidential commendation for his contribution.

Since the end of the war J.D. had been considering ways to expand the business overseas. He'd discussed this only with Jamie Ryan and

175

Thomas Finch. Finch was now a vice-president of the company, and was seen by J.D. as the potential head of a European operation of Marvel Scientific Machines. Finch had an interest in Europe, spoke rudimentary French and Spanish, and had exhibited a talent for organizing the opening of new sales districts. So when he went to Washington, J.D. took Finch and Jamie Ryan with him.

The day after the award ceremonies the three men met with the Assistant Under Secretary of State responsible for liaison between European governments and American industry. He told them that there was a huge demand in Europe for American goods of every description.

The picture he painted was both grim, and ripe with potential for, among other things, data-processing equipment. "Those countries most afflicted by the war must adopt the most advanced business techniques to accelerate recovery, and to be able to compete in world markets . . ."

Thomas Finch raised the central problem. "Where's the money for equipment coming from?"

"I don't know," the Secretary admitted. "But I know this – there will be a market for your equipment, if not immediately, soon. And whoever is there first –" This was the crux for J.D. – to be there first. A recent interview with T.J. Watson printed in *Barron's* had quoted the head of CTR as saying that Europe was going to be a "great untapped market" for data-processing equipment, and J.D. was determined that Marvel Scientific Machines would be there before CTR. "I want you to take charge of this, Tom," he said to Finch. "Get over to Europe. Talk to the governments, the leading business people. Line up employees. I want our European operations staffed by nationals. They're the ones who can sell to their own people, after they're trained in the Marvel Way." J.D.'s eyes gleamed with enthusiasm. "At first we'll ship equipment from here, but eventually we'll have plants there –"

"What about the board, J.D.?" Finch asked.

"What about them?"

"Won't they have to approve a move like this?"

"Let me worry about the board," J.D. said. "I'd like you to leave within the next ten days." J.D. paused. "But for now, let's keep this among the three of us."

The parties that Madelline gave at the brownstone on 57th Avenue became the talk of New York. They were large parties and the guests made an unusual, eclectic group. Madelline had kept her strange collection of friends from her single days – artists, professors and theater people – and had cultivated a new circle from among the Four Hundred: financiers, railroad barons, and the idle rich. Somehow the admixture of these diverse groups worked to produce parties that few guests wanted to leave until the small hours of the morning.

Two nights after J.D.'s return from Washington Madelline gave another party, one of what she termed her "exclusives," by which she meant that instead of seventy-five or so guests serving themselves from buffets, there were twenty to be served at table.

The guests circulated between the sitting-room and the wide hallway where a bar had been set up manned by an efficient young undergraduate at Columbia. J.D. took a position against the wall opposite the bar where he had a view of the hall and part of the sitting-room through the wide doors. He had his customary champagne and cigar and settled in to enjoy the show. Junior, just two that July, was upstairs with his nursemaid. The casement windows in the sitting-room had been cranked open to the balmy September evening. The men were in tuxedos, the women in low-cut evening dresses.

J.D. went to have his glass refilled with champagne and as he turned from the bar was arrested by the sight of his wife. She was standing in animated conversation in the sitting-room, J.D.'s angled view narrowing the doorway so that she was isolated in his vision as though in a picture frame. She was not aware of him. He was struck afresh by her astonishing beauty, the rich gleam of her dark hair, her flashing eyes, the modeled perfection of her shoulders and neck. She would be thirty-seven in a week and yet looked as young as the day he met her, and he was suddenly saddened at the loss and waste in their marriage. The year before he had made a guest bedroom in the house his own. Since then they had had but one sexual encounter, Madelline passive, silent, her lovely body as inert as death; J.D. finally retreating to his own room in limp defeat. The sickening loss that he felt now was heightened by the sexual vitality that seemed to glow from his wife as she talked to her unseeen companion. With a sense of dread J.D. moved so that his view widened until he could see that it was Joseph Falk Whittier who was with Madelline, his narrow face tilted down toward hers, a small smile on his thin, bloodless lips, his slender body poised on the balls of his feet as he leaned near her, an attitude so somehow intimate and possessive that J.D. was struck with the immediate and sure knowledge that Whittier and Madelline were lovers.

*

The board of directors of Marvel Scientific Machines was to conduct its annual meeting in December of 1919. On a blustering fall day in October J.D. went to the office of Goldman, Stern and Kline, investment brokers on Wall Street, where he had an appointment with David Stern, the senior partner of the firm.

A prim, aged secretary ushered him into Stern's office, a wood-paneled room furnished with elderly period furniture and a faded, once-elegant carpet on the floor. David Stern was rather like his office, old and aristocratic, his finely modeled head crowned by a nimbus of white hair.

J.D. introduced himself.

"I've heard of you, Mr. Marvel," Stern said. "Indeed, it would be hard to imagine someone who hadn't. I'm surprised you're so young. Somehow, your newspaper pictures make you look older." Stern summoned his secretary and ordered tea for them.

"Mr. Stern," J.D. began. "I'm here because your firm has the reputation of being the best investment house on Wall Street."

"I'm pleased to hear you say that, Mr. Marvel, but not flattered because, as immodest as it may sound, I must say that I agree." He sipped his tea. The tea service was made of bone china so fine that the cups were nearly transparent. "Allow me to guess why you're here. Your company wants to expand, and you're thinking of floating a bond issue. Perhaps a privately placed bond issue."

"I do want to expand. But I'm not interested in a bond issue. I don't control the company. I would like to change that. I'm interested in finding investors who would buy it for me."

Stern's white eyebrows shot up. "Marvel Scientific Machines is for sale?"

J.D. smiled. "Not quite. The present board would have a mass attack of apoplexy if they knew I was here saying what I've just said."

"Dear me," Mr. Stern said. "I do have a decided weakness for riddles, but I must say I haven't the slightest clue as to the answer to this one. Would you enlighten me?"

And, for nearly two hours, J.D. did. At one point, Stern summoned his secretary and canceled an appointment, but, other than that, he gave his full attention to J.D.

At the end of J.D.'s monolog, Stern sighed deeply, stroked the bridge of his nose while he gazed silently at a Currier and Ives print on his wall, and finally said, "Remarkable. One thing. You would want control of the company?"

178

"That's mandatory."

"With what investment?"

"Minimal investment. I make a good salary, but I'm not a wealthy man."

"You see," Mr. Stern said gently. "When a man invests his money – particularly the millions you're talking about – he expects to have considerable say about how it's spent."

"Mr. Stern," J.D. replied. "You're the financial expert, and I certainly wouldn't presume to tell you your business. But isn't profit what an investor's after?"

"Of course, but –"

"And I can't think of anywhere better than my company for an investor to put his money to make a profit. As for control, I've worked out an idea that I think will answer all but the most timid investor."

Stern smiled. "I will bet that you have."

"It's simply this. A committee of investors would meet once a year and determine my compensation, and the compensation for every vice-president for the coming year."

"If they didn't want you, they could freeze you out."

"And if they froze me out – if I resign – control of the company reverts to the investors."

Stern chuckled. "Mr. Marvel, you have a creative mind."

"Are you interested?"

"Indeed I am. But you don't leave me much time. Your board meets in December, you say."

"I want it resolved at that meeting. It's then, or never."

Stern sighed. "It will have to be then."

"You can do it?"

"It will mean working late evenings and weekends, but we didn't get to be the best by observing normal office hours." He paused. "How would you feel about Goldman, Stern and Kline taking a position in your company?"

"I'd be delighted."

Three days before the board meeting, a small group of men assembled in David Stern's office. Present were Homer Medville Cranston, Joseph Falk Whittier, J.D., a young assistant of Stern's named Fenster, and Stern. Stern offered tea and all accepted but Cranston, who lighted a Prince des Galles Perfecto, glared around the room, and said, "What in the devil is going on? Why did you drag us down here, J.D.?"

179

"Allow me to explain," Stern said. "Mr. Marvel and I have a proposition for you gentlemen. Fenster."

The young man handed Whittier and Cranston each several sheets of paper. Cranston leafed impatiently through them. "What in Hades is this?"

"It is an offer to buy Marvel Scientific Machines," Stern said.

Cranston stared at Stern. "You aren't serious!"

"Mr. Cranston," Stern replied. "I am never facetious when discussing such sums of money."

Cranston got to his feet, his face blazing, and glared down at J.D.

"Is this tomfool idea yours?"

"Yes."

Cranston threw the papers on the floor. "Marvel Scientific Machines is not for sale. C'mon, Joe."

"Mr. Cranston," Stern said. "I would advise you to listen to me. It would be in your best interests to do so."

"Let's hear him out, Homer," Whittier urged. "I'm curious to know what's going on."

Cranston glared around him for a moment like a bull surrounded by baiting dogs and then subsided grumbling into his chair.

"Fenster – if you please," Stern intoned, pointing to the papers Cranston had thrown down. The young man retrieved them and handed them to Cranston.

"Now," Stern began. "On those papers you will see the details of an offer for all the outstanding stock of Marvel Scientific Machines controlled by you two gentlemen. It is a generous offer by any standards. Conservatively I would say it represents one hundred and fifty percent of the present value of the stock. I'm sure you'll agree that that isn't a bad return on investment."

"Mr. Stern," Whittier said. "I know you by reputation. I can't believe that you seriously expect we'd be interested in selling out a company that's growing like ours is."

"See here, Stern," Cranston said. "We're not in this company for a one-time gain. We're in it for the long haul."

Stern looked at J.D. "Perhaps this is a good time to explain."

J.D. cleared his throat, and said, "If you don't sell to Mr. Stern and his investors, I, and every key employee of the company, will take the money and start a rival company."

There was an icy silence in the room. Cranston looked at J.D., removed his pince-nez, and glared at them as though they'd betrayed

180

him. Whittier, who had become very pale, said, "You don't mean that, J.D."

"Why wouldn't I, Joe?" J.D. asked.

"I'll tell you why!" Cranston sputtered. "Because we made you! You owe everything to us!"

"I do owe you," J.D. said quietly. "I owe you, Homer for firing me and for conspiring with Joe to try to steal my company. And you Joe – I owe for nearly ending up in jail."

"Now, see here, J.D." Whittier replied smoothly. "Surely that's water under the bridge. Anything Homer and I may have done in the past, no matter how severely you interpret it, was simply for the protection of our stockholders."

J.D. laughed unpleasantly. "You two own controlling interest. Don't tell me about your charitable concern for stockholders."

"There are the customers who own stock," Whittier pointed out.

"They will still own stock," J.D. said. "The offer is for *your* stock – for the controlling interest."

Cranston thumbed angrily through the papers. "We can get more than that! Assuming we wanted to sell!"

"You'll sell to Mr. Stern and his investors, or you lose most of the employees, and we start another company," J.D. said.

"But this price," Whittier said. "Surely you see it's not fair. At the projected growth rate of the company we stand to make that much in the next couple of years."

"What we're offering you is a chance to get out with a considerable profit," J.D. replied.

"It's robbery!" Cranston shouted. "I won't stand for it!"

"If that's your final word," Stern said. "Then there isn't much point in taking up any more of your time."

"Wait!" Whittier exclaimed. "Listen, Homer – if they're serious about pulling the key people out, we'd better consider this carefully. I'm not in a position to lose what I've got invested."

"By God!" Cranston said. "Try it! We'll give you a run for your money. I'll take over the company myself."

"You're a great salesman, Homer," J.D. admitted. "But you don't know beans about data processing. I also think that you'll find most of our customers are loyal to us."

Whittier nodded. "We'll have to think it over, of course."

"Every day you delay the price goes down ten percent," J.D. said.

Cranston leaped to his feet. "This is an outrage!"

Whittier sighed. "We don't have much choice, Homer."

181

Cranston addressed Stern. "You've got a gun at our heads. Let's get it over with. What do we do?"

"A few papers to sign. Fenster and my secretary will witness . . ."

After Cranston and Whittier had left, J.D. stayed behind to discuss details with Stern and to exchange congratulations. When he emerged from the building he found Joseph Falk Whittier standing beside his black Hispano-Suiza limousine parked at the curb.

"J.D., I need to talk to you. Can I give you a ride?"

"You can drop me at my office," J.D. replied. "I want to talk to you, too."

As the limousine pulled smoothly into Wall Street traffic, Whittier rolled up the partition between his chauffeur and the back seat. "J.D., I don't think you know what you're getting into."

"What do you mean?"

"I'm considerably older than you, and I've been in business for a good number of years." Whittier paused. He was pale, and there was a tremor in his voice. "I like to think of myself as your mentor. After all, it was I who discovered you in that tank town in Illinois. My boy, believe me, I have your best interests at heart. You don't want to get mixed up with those people."

"*Those* people?"

"You know what I mean. Wall Street shylocks. What ever grievances you imagine you have against me, you will look back on our association with a fond eye after the Jew-boys have done with you."

J.D. laughed.

"I fail to see the humor."

"I was telling myself only this morning how refreshing it was, after the conniving and back-stabbing you and Homer Cranston dish out, to be dealing with a real gentleman like David Stern."

"Oh, they're smooth, all right. I don't wonder you think Stern is solid gold. They can make you think that. Just don't turn your back."

"Joe," J.D. said quietly. "I'll take my chances any day with the David Sterns of the world. Why are you telling me all this?"

Whittier extracted a handkerchief from his coat and patted his brow. "I've had a few bad breaks recently, my boy. About the only investment I had that was paying income was our company. I don't mind telling you that, without it, I'm in a spot. A hell of a spot."

"Not that it's my problem," J.D. replied coldly. "But you'll be getting a sizeable chunk of money from the sale of your stock."

"It may look sizeable at first glance, but I've got obligations that

182

I've managed to forestall because I didn't have the cash. When word gets out about this, I'll have to pay off. I tell you frankly that it will leave me in bad shape."

"I still don't see why you're telling me this."

"Look, J.D. – with Homer's stock, and the stock owned by the customers, you'll have controlling interest. You don't need my shares. Let me stay in. I need the income. And if I can hold off the creditors for awhile – not long, a year should do it – why, I can turn my position around. Sell off some things that don't, at the moment, have a market. Consolidate some others. I've done it before – I know how to do it."

"And if I don't agree?"

"It's very probable that I –" Whittier's voice broke. "That I'll be ruined. I'm throwing myself on your mercy, my boy, and asking you to remember all we've been through together."

The limousine glided to a stop at the curb in front of Marvel Scientific Machines' corporate headquarters.

"I do remember, Joe," J.D. said, opening the door. "That's why my answer is no." He stepped out onto the sidewalk.

"J.D.!" With a lunge, Whittier clutched the hem of J.D.'s overcoat. "Don't do this to me!"

J.D. pried the hand from his coat. Then he bent down and looked in at Whittier. "You remember I said I wanted to talk to you? You are no longer welcome in my home. Do you understand?"

Whittier gazed up at J.D. His body seemed to have shrunk. "You – you knew I was in bad shape. You deliberately –"

But J.D. didn't hear the rest because he had closed the door of the limousine.

Three nights later Madelline stormed into the den where J.D. was working late.

"What right do you have to say who comes into this house!" she said furiously.

"It's my house," J.D. replied calmly.

"*Your* house!" She threw an arm around the room. "Who do you think did all this? Who do you think found the house in the first place?"

"Madelline," J.D. said. "You may go on cuckolding me, but you won't do it under my roof."

She stared at him, wide-eyed. "What are you talking about?"

"You know perfectly well what I'm talking about."

"Joe said you were doing it for revenge," she said. "That you ruined

183

him because of some wild idea —"

"*Wild idea!* You and Joe Whittier have played me for the fool for years. But no more, Madelline. No more."

"God damn, you!" she shouted. "You farmer!"

He smiled. "You're right. I've been a farmer, where you're concerned. But I'm getting smarter, Madelline. There's one thing I still don't know, though."

"I'm surprised to hear you admit that you don't know everything."

"What I wonder is, why? Why did you marry me?"

"I refuse to discuss anything with you."

She turned to go. "Very well," J.D. said. "You'll be hearing from my lawyer."

She turned back. "What do you mean?"

"What do you think I mean? I want a divorce."

"You're bluffing! You can't afford to go through another scandal."

"It won't be pleasant, I'll admit that. It will certainly be as unpleasant for you and Joe."

"Joe! You can't mean you'd drag him into it."

"I have no choice. He's grounds for the divorce."

"You'd finish him off. You may already have ruined him beyond repair."

"I can't say that my heart wells with sympathy for Joe."

"I'll never give you a divorce!"

"I don't think you'll have much choice. I expect that I'll be able to get plenty of proof, or, I should say, the investigator who works for my attorney will."

The anger perceptibly drained from Madelline, leaving her pale and shaken. She sat down in a wing chair. "What do you want?"

"I would like a frank discussion of our problems."

"If I – if that happens, you'll forget about divorce?"

"Perhaps. If you're honest with me. After all, Madelline, I've quite a bit to lose, as you pointed out. But believe me, I'll risk it if I have to."

"What do you want to know?"

"Why did you marry me?"

"Didn't you ever wonder why I'd never married?"

"I guess I was foolish enough to flatter myself that the right man hadn't come along until me."

She rested her forehead on her hand. "I was in love with Joe Whittier for years."

"He couldn't divorce his wife?"

"He got started with her money. She owns half of what is his."

184

"She never suspected?"

"She – she's quite naive in some ways."

"She and I have a lot in common. Did Joe deliberately throw us together?"

"It's not like it sounds. Joe cares about me. I was nearly thirty. He wanted me to have security – a nice home, money."

"Why didn't he just give them to you? After all, he was a wealthy man."

"I told you. His wife controls half of everything. Her family accountants audit every move Joe makes."

"If I was the dupe who provided the house for you and Joe to meet in, why did he try to throw me to the wolves after we were engaged?"

"You're exaggerating –"

"Don't tell me you didn't discuss it. Joe is putting the man he's urged you to marry in jail, and you don't mention it? Don't ask questions? Come on, Madelline!"

"He didn't expect anyone would have to go to jail."

"But since it looked like someone might, I was chosen."

"He got you out of it."

"Cranston did."

She sighed. "Is that all?"

"I won't divorce you, Madelline – now. But if I ever suspect you and Whittier are seeing each other, you're finished. I won't even discuss it with you."

"What do you care! You don't love me –"

"I could have. I can't love you now. But I won't be played the fool."

"You and your goddamned pride! You'd ruin my life for it."

"No. You'll ruin it, if it's to be ruined."

"What do you mean?"

"Any time you want a divorce, I'll give it to you. Then you and Joe can be together. It comes down to a simple choice, really." He paused. "All this, or Joe. How strong is your love, Madelline?"

She rose, and ran from the room sobbing. J.D. stared after her, and, for a moment, he looked older even than the photographs of him that hung in every Marvel Scientific Machines office.

19

Lucille

LUCILLE WAS MAKING enough to afford a small apartment of her own only a fifteen-minute walk from the school. Often at night before going to sleep, she would lie staring at the ghostly outline of the French doors in her bedroom and would imagine J.D. there with her.

Those French doors led out to a small, walled garden that was the thing Lucille loved most about her apartment. Roses and trillium grew in brick-bordered beds and beyond the wall a shagbark hickory spread its graceful limbs. In the centre of the garden, resting on a tiny patch of lawn, was an iron bench painted white. She liked to sit there in all seasons – even in winter when the hickory was a skeleton against the leaden sky and the trillium and roses were in hibernation – and sip her morning tea before going to work.

In 1919 Lucille was made Assistant Director of the school. She was given total responsibility while Wanda established the new training program for customer executives. A large new stone building of neo-classical design was built on what had been the east gardens of the mansion to house the executive-training meeting rooms and dining-room. At the same time the rapid expansion of the company brought an increase of nearly fifty percent in the number of employees to be trained in the already overcrowded facilities. In the spring of 1920 J.D. made one of his periodic inspections and took note of the problem. "You need more instructors," he said to Lucille and Wanda.

"We don't have any place to put them," Lucille replied. She was weary from overwork and felt she must look awful.

"See here, Marvel," Wanda said. "Between the mansion and the river we've got three acres. We need to put up classrooms and a dormitory for the employee training."

186

J.D. groaned. "All that rolling lawn down to the river!"

"It's either that, or split the school into two locations," Wanda replied.

"All right," J.D. said. "But let's get a top architect. I want to preserve as much as I can."

Three months later the architect had constructed a model, which stood on a table in the director's office.

J.D. traveled up from New York to see it. He had his mother with him. She was in her fifties, with lovely white hair, large dark eyes, and a proud bearing.

J.D. approved the model. It was a beautiful design, the buildings in low profile, with many windows and skylights, seeming to float on the existing lawn rather like the boats on the Hudson that they overlooked.

Wanda went off with the architect to the site of the new buildings to discuss some details of construction with him, and Lucille found herself alone with J.D. and his mother.

J.D. took out his watch, and said, "Lunch! Will you join us, Miss Cranston?"

Impulsively, Lucille said, "Why don't you come to my place? I can give you tea and sandwiches."

"That would be wonderful, wouldn't it, Mother?"

She'd always wanted to show J.D. her apartment. Now, with his mother along, it seemed perfectly safe to do so. She seated them in her small sitting-room and served them a glass of sherry while she made sandwiches and tea. She put up a card-table in the garden, laid a white linen tablecloth on it, and set it for three. Then she led J.D. and his mother out to the garden, apologizing for having to take them through the bedroom, and seated them on the white bench, with herself across from them on a straight-backed chair she'd brought from the kitchen.

"This is lovely!" Elvira Marvel exclaimed, looking around the garden. It was July, and the roses and trillium were in bloom, and the shagbark hickory's limbs were heavy with leaves. A breeze from the river made the roseblooms nod.

"Where do you live, Mrs. Marvel?" Lucille asked.

"I'm living with J.D. right now," Elvira replied. "Sort of a trial arrangement."

"My father died in April," J.D. explained. "And it's not a trial arrangement, as far as I'm concerned."

187

Elvira patted her son's hand. "I've lived on a farm for so long," she said to Lucille, "I'm not sure I can take the city now."

"You began as a city girl," J.D. said.

"That was long ago. Everything's changed so. I'm afraid I'm terribly old-fashioned and provincial. I've rented the farm to a nice couple – I've known both their parents for years – they say I can have the spare room any time I want to move back."

"I'm sorry to hear about your husband," Lucille said.

"Luther worked hard all his life. The last six months he was helpless, and hated it. He was sixty. Which doesn't seem very old to me. But I know he didn't want to go on, if he couldn't take care of himself."

"He was very independent," J.D. added.

"He was proud of you," Elvira said. "Although he couldn't bring himself to say it."

Lucille saw J.D. again two weeks later. Exhausted by another grueling day, she was in one of the new classrooms putting away her teaching materials after giving a class on the tabulator. The machine stood on a slightly raised platform at the front of the room, the door to its plug-panel open.

"Hi, teacher," J.D. said from the doorway. "May I come in?"

"Of course," she replied. "You are the President, you know."

He walked across the room to stand beside her at the desk. "In the classroom," he said, "the teacher is king. Or, I should say, queen." He knelt beside the plug-panel. "What have we here? No! Don't tell me." He studied the wires for a long moment, then said, "Crossfooting five columns?"

"Right so far."

"Ah, there's more!" He studied the panel a while longer, and finally said, "Printing a sub-total line across on every other group?"

"A-plus," Lucille said. She was impressed. "That model's only been on the market for three months. Where did you learn about it, and how do you find the time?"

He rose to stand beside her. "I make time. I feel I must know our machines. As to how – I read manuals, and practice on the equipment we have at headquarters."

Lucille self-consciously touched her hair. She felt she must look weary and grimy.

"There is a rumor about," J.D. said. "That you're trying to starve yourself."

"If you mean I haven't had anything to eat since lunch, that rumor is true."

"As President, I must protect the health of valued employees."

"It must keep you busy."

"In your case, not nearly as busy as I'd like to be." He took out his hunter watch and snapped open the case. "I know a restaurant that serves excellent steaks until ten. That will give us time for a leisurely meal."

Lucille accepted J.D.'s invitation on condition that she be allowed to go home and bathe and change her clothes. J.D. drove her in a car that he'd borrowed from Walter Hucko and waited in the living-room with a glass of sherry while she got ready. Then they drove to a small chop-house located in an old hotel in town, where they had steaks and a bottle of good burgundy that J.D. had brought with him and persuaded the waiter to pour by slipping the man a bill. The waiter served the wine in amber water glasses, hiding the bottle in the kitchen. Prohibition had begun that January and it was taken very seriously in Tarrytown.

"My mother liked you," J.D. said.

"She's a marvelous lady. Oh!" Lucille's eyes widened. "I didn't mean that as a pun."

J.D. laughed. He covered Lucille's hand with his own. "I told her I was in love with you."

Lucille's heart beat rapidly. "I – I think I've had too much wine."

"You're blushing. It's very attractive. And you haven't had half a glass."

"Your mother must think – I mean, after all, you are married."

"She's met my wife. Mother's living with us, you know."

"What is that supposed to mean?"

J.D. pushed his plate away, took out a cigar, and lit it. "Madelline – my wife and I, she's only that in name, you know."

Lucille felt herself blushing again. For some reason it made her angry. "What makes you think I care to hear the – the details of your marriage?"

"Forgive me. I didn't mean to offend you."

"I'm not a child!"

"I've never thought you were." He smiled. "Only once, when you were my shinny partner."

"I mean, I don't offend that easily. I'm nearly thirty years old. I've been on my own for years." She suddenly felt foolish, defending herself like that. She sighed miserably. "I don't know what I mean."

189

J.D. looked around for the waiter. "Let's get out of here."

The waiter brought the half-finished bottle of burgundy in a paper sack. J.D. put it on the seat of the car between them. They were silent on the short ride to Lucille's apartment. When he parked at the curb in front, J.D. said, "Should I see you to the door?"

"Why shouldn't you?"

"I don't know," he stammered. "The neighbors –"

"Oh, damn the neighbors! Bring your bottle of wine and come in."

They sat on the bench in her little garden. A sliver of moon rode among the branches of the shagbark hickory. Lucille brought wine glasses and J.D. poured. He picked up her hand and pressed his lips to it. She withdrew it.

"I'm sorry," he said. "I thought –"

"I know – it's my fault." She put a hand to her eyes. "I'm confused."

He got to his feet. "I'd better leave." But he remained where he stood, looking down at her hopefully.

"Goodbye, J.D."

He turned, and left without another word. Lucille stayed in the garden for a long time, sipping wine, and staring unseeingly into the inky shadows.

Lucille didn't speak to J.D. again for five months. He came twice to Tarrytown during that time to inspect the new construction, but Lucille didn't see him while he was there.

Then on the Sunday before Christmas of that year, 1920, J.D. appeared at the door of her apartment at eight o'clock in the morning. She had just risen from bed and was in a robe and slippers. J.D. stood on the porch stamping his feet and blowing on his hands. It had been a freezing night and frost covered the ground.

"May I come in?"

She held the door for him. "I have tea on the stove," she said. "Would you like some."

"Love some!" He took off his coat and muffler and put them across the back of the couch.

While Lucille served the tea, J.D. remained silent. Her hand trembled slightly as she poured. When she was finished, she excused herself and went into her bedroom and combed her hair and put on lipstick. When she returned to the living-room, J.D. said, "I've something to say, and I don't know which end of it to begin at."

She was disgusted with herself for the flutter in her heart and the

190

tremor in her hand. "Why not try the beginning."

"My mother went home to Illinois. She left shortly after I brought her up here."

"I'm sorry. I know you wanted her to stay."

"It was best for her. She'd been on that farm so long that she just couldn't get used to city life. It's funny, because I think it had always been kind of a dream of hers to get back to the city some day."

"The reality didn't match the dream."

"Before she left we – she and I – had a talk. I told her about you –" Lucille felt her face burn. "Oh, I didn't say anything about you, really. What could I? Except that you were too much of a lady to have anything to do with a married man. But I told her I loved you. She asked how you felt, and I said I didn't know, which is the truth. I still don't know. She advised me to get a divorce. Not because of how I felt about you, but because of the way Madelline and I lived – like strangers who just happened to be sharing a house." J.D. took a breath. "So I did."

Lucille stared at him. "Did?"

"Got a divorce. It was final last Wednesday. This was the soonest I could get up here. I drove half the night."

"I – I didn't hear –"

"We kept it very quiet. Aside from a few people in New York, you're the first to know. Madelline had always said that she wouldn't give me a divorce without a battle, so that was about half the reason I never tried."

"What changed?"

"She was in love with Joe Whittier."

"Uncle Joe!"

J.D. nodded. "He fell on some hard times, mostly because I bought him and your father out of Marvel Scientific. And he couldn't divorce *his* wife because she controlled the purse-strings of her own money, which was considerable.

"But things changed. Joe is a scrapper, whatever else he is. He battled back. He's in pretty good shape now. And I offered to give Madelline our house and some money, and they figured with that he could afford to divorce *his* wife and –" J.D. held his hands palm-up. "Well – it all worked out."

"What about your son?"

"I'd like to have him. He's not a bad little chap. Small for his age, which is three and a half. I wanted to take him, but Madelline was adamant. Why, I don't know. She hardly ever sees him."

191

"Maybe she'll change her mind."

"That's what I'm hoping."

There was a pause. Finally, Lucille said, "Why are you telling me this?"

J.D. took a sheaf of official-looking papers from his jacket pocket and handed them across to her.

"What's this?" she asked.

"The divorce papers."

She dropped them on a table.

"I wanted you to see the proof," he said.

"I'll take your word," she replied.

J.D. picked up the papers and put them back in his pocket. He cleared his throat. "I – I want you to marry me, Lucille."

"Why?"

"Because I love you. I've loved you from that first day."

"Shinny?"

"Yes."

"You were in love with a twelve-year-old?"

"I only *thought* you were twelve."

"Nevertheless, you married Madelline after that."

"I told myself it was ridiculous to love someone on such short acquaintance."

"If I say no, will you regret the divorce?"

"Never!" He looked stricken. "But, please – don't say no."

She stood. "Come here."

He rose uncertainly. "There?"

"Over here." He did as he was told. She put her arms around him and kissed him on the mouth. His arms slid around her waist. When they finally broke apart, she said, "I love you, J.D. But I can't marry you."

"But – *why*?"

"Because I have a career. I won't give it up."

"Of course you won't have to give it up."

"My career is here, in Tarrytown."

"But you could come to New York. There are responsible jobs – you could name your job."

"I'm a teacher. I love to teach. This is where I belong."

"All right! You can stay here. I'll get up as often as I can. You can come to New York on vacations, some weekends. I'll buy a house here –"

"It won't work."

"You've been talking to Wanda," he said furiously. "She's filled you with all this 'Modern Woman' nonsense! Why the hell can't you be like other women?"

"There are lots of 'other' women," she said coldly. "You won't have any trouble finding one."

"I didn't mean that," he said miserably. "I wouldn't have you any other way. Can't we work it out? You say you love me."

"Yes," she said quietly. "We may work something out."

"What do you mean?"

"I'll be your lover. If you want me."

"But I want you to be my wife!"

"That's the best I can do."

"If that's the only way," he said.

"It is. Now, come to bed."

FIVE

The same heart beats in every human breast.
Matthew Arnold

20

J.D. and the Communist

J.D. WAS IN PARIS ON OCTOBER 24, 1929: Black Tuesday, the day the stockmarket crashed. He'd been in Europe for nearly two months, touring the operations of Marvel International Machines, the foreign subsidiary he had set up in 1919 to bring together under one banner all the company's foreign businesses. Marvel Scientific had sales of just over $20 million in 1928, with earnings of $5.6 million. Of this, foreign operations had contributed $3 million to the gross while breaking even. In the fall of 1929 J.D. decided it was time to push the foreign business over the top in profitability. In 1924 Thomas Watson's Computing-Tabulating-Recording Company had changed its name to International Business Machines, Inc. and, with the name change, took a broader world-view of its business. IBM was beginning to give Marvel International hot competition.

Thomas Finch was the head of Marvel International, and was a vice-president of the parent corporation. He'd done a good job in finding competent nationals to head up the Marvel subsidiaries in each of the four countries in which they operated – England, France, Germany and Italy. But J.D. sensed early on that Finch lacked the creative juices to provide the entrepreneurial flair that would put the business over the top. Finch was not a risk-taker, so J.D. went to Europe in the fall of 1929 to provide what was lacking.

There were manufacturing operations in each of the four countries that made versions of Marvel machines especially adapted to the electrical and business needs of the particular country. Sales forces were trained in a single school, a multi-lingual establishment in a rented villa in the countryside sixty kilometers from Paris. Sales offices resided in Paris, London, Rome and Berlin.

From the day Finch had met J.D.'s ship at Liverpool the two had

197

been working sixteen-hour days, seven days a week. J.D. had reorganized the sales offices into more efficient two-man teams. He had called on the largest customers and prospective customers, and had, personally, sold over $200,000's worth of equipment. He had also given an inspirational speech – that had been translated simultaneously into French, German, and Italian – to a graduating class at the villa. Black Tuesday had seen J.D. and Finch closeted in a small conference room in a hotel in Paris with the respective heads of each of the foreign operations, planning aggressive new sales campaigns, unaware of the calamity taking place in New York. It was after midnight when the men went exhausted to their rooms. J.D. found a cable had been pushed under his door. It was from David Stern, and said: YOUR PRESENCE REQUIRED NEW YORK SOONEST STOP URGENT.

Such was J.D.'s respect for David Stern that he never questioned the summons, nor hesitated in obeying it. The following afternoon he was deposited aboard an ocean liner at Le Havre by Thomas Finch. J.D. sent Stern a cable from the liner, and the grey-haired little man was waiting on the pier when the ship docked six days later. By this time J.D. had caught up with the news and was familiar, through the ship's news service, with the broad outlines of the financial catastrophe that had occurred.

Stern waited until he and J.D. were seated in his comfortable office, with steaming cups of tea in hand, before he began.

"It has been a week like I hope I never see again," Stern said.

"Was Goldman, Stern and Kline hit hard?" J.D. asked.

"No. We survived very well. My partners and I never did believe in this paper fairyland that the market had become over the past few years. We were called old-fashioned, and worse, by competitors, and we lost a bit of business because we refused to be a party to some of the wilder speculations. So we are not only intact, we are healthy."

"It must give you satisfaction to see that you were right."

"Quite the contrary. Some of my best friends have been ruined. It is a tragic time. We're doing what we can to help, but I'm afraid our resources are puny compared to the size of the disaster. But enough of my morbidities." He leaned back in his chair, took off his glasses and rubbed the bridge of his nose. He suddenly looked very old, the skin on his forehead distinctly showed the outlines of the skull beneath.

"Jamie Ryan is a good administrator," Stern began. "But he is not you. More than an administrator is required, as you well know. I'm afraid some things have got out of hand. In particular, the plant in Chicago."

Marvel Scientific Machines had grown to four manufacturing plants. By far the largest was located in Chicago, the only plant that made the full line of equipment: sorters, card punches and the new Model Y tabulator, made exclusively in Chicago, and for which J.D. and the board had great hopes.

"Something gone wrong with Model Y production?"

"That is going as planned – I should say 'was.' A truly fine innovation. Jamie tells me that the backlog of Model Y orders is over a year's production."

"What do you mean, 'was'?"

"You have labor problems at the plant. The signs were there soon after you left for Europe. Jamie tried administrative cures. Citing chapter and verse from the policy-and-procedures manual was his idea of how to address grievances."

"If that didn't work," J.D. said, "you can't blame Jamie. I wrote most of the policy-and-procedures manual."

"And a good job it was. But it was meant as a guideline. As you well know, the human equation must be taken into account. That is where Jamie falls down, I'm afraid."

"What happened?"

"A strike. The plant is shut down."

J.D. tensed. "When?"

"The day I cabled. Since then there has been no progress, some violence. It is hard to know who to talk to. It's a wildcat strike, and there seems to be much agitation and little leadership. I went out there myself after I cabled you, and talked to a delegation of workers. The meeting turned into a shouting match and if the plant guards hadn't been there I'm not sure I wouldn't have been tarred and feathered, or worse. I must say that the word 'kike' flew around my head more than I would've liked."

"I'm sorry, David."

Stern waved a hand. "Name-calling isn't our problem. Focusing on what the workers want is. They are so split in their demands and views it is impossible to negotiate. The only thing I came away sure of was that we have a plant full of dissatisfied people."

"You said there had been violence."

"The day after the strike was called about a quarter of the labor force turned up for work and were met at the gates by the strikers. There was a fight. Fortunately, by the time the police broke it up there were only minor injuries. A headache or two, bloody noses and black eyes. But I'm worried, J.D., that it will become more violent. Jamie, at my suggestion, locked the plant, so we wouldn't have any more such confrontations."

"I'll go to Chicago."

"You should."

"After I talk to Jamie, of course."

"I'm afraid the strike is only part of your problem. This stockmarket fiasco is going to ruin a lot of businesses. I foresee a very rocky time ahead for this country."

"I'll appreciate your counsel on that, David. But first things first. I've got to get that plant up and operating, or we won't have any machines to worry about not selling."

Stern took a sheet of paper from his desk drawer. "There are three people who seem to be the prime agitators of the trouble, if not the leaders of the mob. I've written down their names and addresses."

J.D. took the paper and read it. "Can you tell me anything about them?"

"Less than I would like. First, Frank Joyce. Young, second-generation Irish, hot-headed, bright. Some kind of engineering aide at the plant. Gives the impression that he would rather punch you in the head than talk.

"Gina Marchetti. As you might guess, Italian parents. Even younger than Joyce. Fiery. A Communist, I'd bet on it, and I'm not a betting man. Idealistic and unrealistic. Worst combination you can find. *Very* bright. She'd only been at the plant a year and already she was straw boss of a crew of women in the Model Y electrical assembly section.

"Leo Ward. Mid-thirties. Very large and gives the impression of being slow-thinking, but don't let that fool you. I think he deliberately gives that impression to catch you off-guard. He's the reasonable one. Oh, he's fired-up, like the rest. But I got the impression he might be willing to talk, if you could get him alone. He's a machinist on the Model Y line."

J.D. studied the names. "What set them off?"

"Joyce was fired for insubordination. He is extremely popular at the plant, and, according to what Jamie found out, an excellent worker. He and the assistant plant superintendent, a man called Stan Wylie, got into an altercation on the factory floor, and Wylie fired him."

"I know Wylie. He has a reputation as a fine engineer."

"Well, as I gather, Joyce couldn't have been fired by a worse person for our interests. Wylie is pretty generally disliked at the plant."

200

"I didn't know that," J.D. said, and then added grimly, "Apparently there's plenty I didn't know. But I'm damned sure going to find it out now."

It was a morose Jamie Ryan that delivered J.D. to Grand Central Station to catch the Twentieth Century Limited on the evening of Thursday, November 1, 1929.

"Cheer up, Jamie," J.D. said. "We'll figure a way out of this."

He had nearly thirty minutes before the train was to leave, and J.D. considered going into the station and calling Lucille, but then decided not to. She didn't know he was in the country. He'd only been back two days and the press of business hadn't allowed him a free moment. Now that he had the time, he found himself strangely reluctant to speak to her. For the past nine years they had had a relationship notable more and more by their times apart than by the those together. J.D. had come to see that she had been wise not to marry him, and gave secret thanks that that had been the case. Lucille was very much the woman he thought when his interest had been ardent. What he hadn't known was that the kind of woman she was, coupled with the kind of man he was, would've made for at best a chancey marriage. They were each too strong-willed and single-purposed in the pursuit of their careers. To make for a satisfactory marriage one of them would have had to yield his interests to the other, and now he knew that would've been impossible. He saw, in this light, how ideally suited Wanda and Walter were. The mystery of why their marriage had been such a great success was revealed to him. Walter deferred to Wanda's interests. And, most important, Walter had done it whole-heartedly and out of selfless love. What he'd got in return from Wanda was one who loved him as much as a woman whose first love was her work could ever love any man. And now, after sixteen years, now that Walter was nearing sixty and Wanda was forty-five, their marriage had aged into something mellow and rich, like a fine old wine.

Three years ago, J.D. had created the corporate post of Vice-President of Training and had moved Wanda to New York to fill it. Walter was now Assistant to the President, and performed a variety of tasks which J.D. delegated to him – never anything requiring too much initiative, because Walter could work himself into a near-hysterical state when confronted with complex decisions. Walter was happy. He had what he wanted. Status in the company, colleagues who liked him, a nice office, efficient secretary and, most important to him, Wanda.

201

When Wanda came to New York, Lucille became director at Tarrytown by acclamation. She was so obviously suited for the job that no one else was even considered. And she thrived on it. She'd bought herself an old house on the Hudson and renovated it, only to spend most of her waking hours at the school.

The corporate staff was lean and quick. J.D. did not like top-heavy organizations. Aside from Wanda and Walter, Jamie was now Vice-President of Administration, Leland Prescott Vice-President of Sales, and Ansell Farnsworth Director of Research, although he seldom came to New York. Farnsworth's title was more an award recognizing his years of valuable service than a real responsibility. In truth, J.D. oversaw research, while Farnsworth spent his time on his farm-cum-development lab dreaming up new equipment, and improvements to existing equipment.

When J.D. arrived at the Union depot in Chicago the next morning the sky was clear and an icy sun shone down on the cold winter streets of the city. He rented a Chevrolet from the Hertz Drive-Ur-Self System, which had been founded six years before by the Chicago Yellow Cab Company, and drove directly to the plant.

The factory was located on a city block at 31st and Pulaski. J.D. parked in the deserted parking lot and walked to the main gates where he found his way barred by two burly men in guard uniforms. They were rudely skeptical that he was who he said he was, but after he produced identification they turned deferential and one of them hurried into the guard shack to carry out his request that Stan Wylie, the assistant plant superintendent, be called.

Wylie came hurrying across the plant yard looking at J.D. as if he could scarcely believe his eyes. He was a tall, tubercular-looking man with a thin, pale face surmounted by a head of greying yellow hair. He shook J.D.'s hand and said, "Mr. Marvel! I'd heard you were in Europe."

"I was. Can we go to your office, Stan?"

"Of course!"

Along the way Wylie, who chain-smoked Caporals, lit one and said, "This is a hell of a mess, Mr. Marvel. These people have gone completely nuts."

J.D. said nothing until they were in Wylie's office, a narrow room dominated by a desk and a large drafting table.

After they were seated, Wylie said, "Would you like me to phone for the superintendent?"

202

"I wanted to talk to you," J.D. said, and saw the guard go up in Wylie's eyes. "Tell me what happened."

"A small bunch of hot-heads got the plant riled up. It's only a few bad apples –"

J.D. cut him off. "I mean between you and Frank Joyce."

Wylie's hand trembled as he took a drag on his Caporal. "The bastard was insubordinate in front of half the plant. I couldn't let him get away with that."

"Look. I'm not here to hang anyone. All I want is to try to get this plant operating again. I'm sure you're for that, Stan. I've heard nothing but good things about you. I've been told – and have reason enough to believe from my own experience – that you're a damn fine engineer."

Wylie relaxed perceptibly. "I appreciate your saying that, Mr. Marvel."

"Can I ask you how old you are, Stan?"

"Forty-one."

"You're two years older than I am. Why don't you call me J.D.?"

"Okay, sir. Fine."

"Now – tell me about your run-in with this Joyce fellow."

Frank Joyce was an engineer's aide. He did drafting, computed gear ratios for machinery, and showed a real talent for tool design. Stan Wylie gave him all that. But the fellow was cheeky. Always the flip answer, the thinly veiled sneer when he was given an order. He gave off the impression, Stan Wylie said, that he knew better than you what he should be doing.

On the day in question Wylie went down to the factory floor, to the sorter final-assembly station, to check some production figures with the sorter foreman. There, at final inspection, he found Frank Joyce, up to his elbows in a sorter. Seems that the machine had failed inspection, Joyce had happened by, thought he knew what was wrong and proceeded to fix it, while the foreman and two inspectors stood around and watched. Well, this was just too much for Stan Wylie. The man's job was in engineering, not sorter inspection. And engineering had a backlog of work to be done. *And* here were three employees watching, out of action, while someone else did their job. Not only that, but the foreman's presence seemed to Stan to be a silent collusion against the rules of the plant. Stan admitted that he blew up, but he felt he did so with reason. He ordered Joyce back to engineering. Joyce didn't even look up from the machine, muttering that he would have it fixed in a minute. This, Stan said, was out-and-out insubordination.

He told Joyce he was fired.

Joyce lost his temper. There ensued a shouting match. The foreman and another man had to pull them apart as blows were about to be struck. By this time a crowd of workers had gathered to witness the spectacle. Joyce was escorted off the premises by security guards. Wylie ordered everyone back to work and returned to his office.

"The next day," he concluded, "they went out."

"What are their demands? Hiring Joyce back?"

"That's just an excuse. Sure, they say they want Joyce back. But they're so hopped up they don't rightly know what they want. First one group wants this, then another group wants just the opposite."

"Things must have been pretty bad for some time, to have them blow up like this."

"*Bad?*" I don't have to tell you, Mr. – J.D. – that we pay the highest wages in the industry. Among the highest in the Chicago area. Production bonuses! Paid vacations after they've been here three years! Unheard of! What the hell have they got to beef about?"

"Then why did they blow up?"

"I'll tell you why. We're too soft on them. Give them all those benefits, and they start to think they're better'n anyone else. Just like kids. You can't be too soft on 'em. Ruins 'em."

"All those 'benefits' were my idea," J.D. said softly.

"Oh, see here, Mr. Marvel. I don't mean they weren't well-intended. Lord knows your heart is in the right place. But you can't change human nature, and that's a fact."

Frank Joyce lived on the south side, not far from the plant, in a flaking three-story frame rooming-house. The fat, Irish landlady directed J.D. to a small, greasy café on the corner where three men, the only customers, occupied a table at the window.

"Frank Joyce?" J.D. asked the men, and a short, fair man nodded. He was strongly built through the shoulders and neck, with a flushed face and a wide, expressive mouth. The men had coffee cups in front of them, but it wasn't coffee that was in the cups.

"Could I speak to you in private?" J.D. asked.

Joyce stood, picked up his cup, and walked to a table at the back of the room.

"I suppose you know why I'm here," J.D. began.

"I suppose I could guess, though I must say I'm surprised."

"Surprised?"

"That a big man like yourself would be here in person. I thought you big-shots always sent some minion to do your dirty work."

"I really would like to talk to you, Frank. If you think you could get off."

"Get off?"

"Of that high horse you're riding."

Joyce put his head back and laughed. "I guess you are good for a laugh. What is it you want to know?"

"For starters, why were you fired?"

"I was fired because Old Sly'd been achin' to ever since him and me first crossed paths."

"Wiley is Old Sly?"

"S'what we call 'im, and worse."

"Then you weren't fired for cause?"

Joyce grinned wickedly. "Now, just what is 'cause,' Mr. Big-Shot? It's whatever you and your flunkies dream up. Ain't that so?"

"No, it's not. Not in this company. I asked you a serious question, Frank. Do you think Stan Wylie had reasonable cause to fire you?"

"You might say so, if you took that one incident out of context, so to speak. But if you put it in the big frame around all the provokin' that Wiley did of me over the years, why it was just the final touch, you might say, to his tar job."

"Care to fill me in on what you mean?"

"To what purpose?"

"If what you say is true, I'll see that the right thing is done."

"The 'right thing,' is it? And what might that be?"

"For instance, I could give you your job back."

"You couldn't."

"I run the company, Frank."

"Oh, I don't mean you don't have the authority. I just mean that if you did that, Stan Wiley would go beserk. He's a bastard now. But if you put me back he'd turn into a bloody monster."

"This is all speculation, because I haven't heard these circumstances you were talking about. But if I do decide to put you back to work, you let me worry about Stan Wiley."

"Okay. I'll tell you my story."

When he had finished, J.D. was silent for a while, thinking. Frank Joyce's story wasn't original. J.D. had heard it often enough in the past. The good technical man, Stan Wylie, elevated to management where it was discovered that technical skill had nothing to do with skill in handling subordinates. If Joyce was telling the truth then Stan Wiley had been a very poor manager indeed. And, apparently, he'd

205

taken a particular dislike to the irrepressible Frank Joyce.

According to Joyce the plant superintendent had, unfortunately, delegated many of his supervisory duties to Wiley, so that Wiley had been in a powerful position to carry out what Joyce characterized as his petty vendettas against workers he felt had slighted him in some way.

"Assuming all you say is true," J.D. said, "it's no wonder the workers were unhappy."

"Old Sly was a part – a big part – but that ain't all there is to it, J.D."

"What else?"

Joyce rubbed his chin with his palm. "Well, now, I tell you. I'm not much on politics, and that's what the rest is about."

"Politics?"

"You need to talk to Gina."

"Gina Marchetti?"

"Be careful there, sport. She ain't easy-goin', like me. She'll chew you up and spit you out and forget you ever existed two minutes later."

"What about Leo Ward?"

Joyce shrugged. "A professional nice boy. Wants everyone to love him. Succeeds pretty well, at that. But he doesn't have the spine to lead this strike. Gina's your woman for that. We all listen to her." He grinned. "We'd better."

"Gina it is."

Gina Marchetti lived in a neat white frame cottage with a picket fence that had a trellis bowed over its front gate. A large, swarthy hawk-faced old man was sitting on the front stoop smoking a pipe. His head was bald and his dark eyes were surrounded by laugh-lines. He was dressed in overalls, a heavy mackinaw coat, and gloves.

J.D. came up the walk and said, "I'm looking for Gina Marchetti."

"What for?" The man looked to be several inches over six feet, with a barrel chest and log-like arms that bulged under the mackinaw.

"I have a business matter to discuss with her. Are you her father?"

"That's me. She's not interested in buyin' nothin'."

"That's good, because I'm not selling anything."

The man stared at J.D. for a moment, and then threw his head back and bawled, "Gina!"

The door to the house opened, a woman's face peered around the doorpost at J.D., said, "Oh, my God!" And disappeared. J.D. waited. The man stared at him. Finally the face reappeared, this time

206

attached to a body clad in a wool coat. She had a scarf tied around her head. She rushed out the door, down the steps, took J.D.'s elbow in a grip any man would've been proud to own, called over her shoulder, "I'll be out for a while, Pops," and propelled J.D. down the sidewalk and out the gate onto the street.

She stopped by the rental Chevrolet at the curb. "That your car?"

"Yes."

"Get in. I know a place we can talk."

She directed him to a small park by the lake. J.D. stopped the car and they got out.

"Nice view," J.D. said, shivering in his coat.

"What do you want, J.D. Marvel?"

"It's about the strike."

"You must be concerned, to come here yourself."

"Of course I'm concerned," J.D. replied. "I wouldn't be much of a president if I weren't."

"*President!*" she snorted.

"You don't like presidents?"

"I don't like the whole capitalistic tyranny that gives to the few royal titles, and lets the rest of us support them."

"I'd heard you were – political."

"I'm not political. I'm *politicized*."

"I don't know the distinction."

"When one is politicized, one *becomes* an instrument of the masses."

"Why did you come with me?"

"Morbid curiosity. I suppose if you'd fought disease all your life you wouldn't be able to resist that first look in the microscope at the enemy."

"You're putting me under the miscroscope?"

"That was a metaphor."

"Look, I'm freezing. I haven't had my lunch. What would you say to going into town for something to eat and a talk."

"Do you think you can buy a sympathetic ear with a lunch?"

"As a matter of fact, I was planning on you paying for your own."

She gave him a sharp look, and then a grudging smile. "I guess even presidents can have brains. All right, J.D. Marvel, where is this café?"

"Downtown. It's called Jiggs Muldoon's."

She'd been there before, once. "Couldn't afford it even then," she said. They were seated at a table with glasses of beer. Jiggs Muldoon's had converted to speakeasy style early in Prohibition, which meant

207

you had to be a "member" to get in. If you weren't a member, you paid the doorman a dollar, and he made you a member on the spot.

"I suppose you realize that, from the moment you walked in here, every man in the place has been staring."

She ignored the comment. "You wanted to talk."

"What do you want, aside from re-hiring Frank Joyce?"

"Why are you asking me?"

"Because I've been told you're one of the leaders."

"Have you seen Leo Ward?"

"No. I intend to."

"Did you send that little grey-haired Wall Street shark out here?"

"How anyone could describe David Stern as – as –"

"Okay, okay," she said. "So he's a buddy of yours. As Wall Street sharks go, I admit he wasn't too bad. But I couldn't figure out why he was here. And then when he left, he locked us out."

"He was here to try to find out the same thing I'm trying to find out. What you want. And he didn't lock you out. He suggested that the plant be locked to avoid any more violence."

"A regular saint."

"You know, although you have many attractive traits, sneering is not one of them."

"There you go again. Why is it you can't talk to me for five minutes without bringing sex into it."

J.D. stared in astonishment. "*Sex!* How the hell do you imagine I brought that up?"

"My 'many attractive traits.' And, a while ago, that comment about all the men staring. Don't look so shocked. 'Sex' is a perfectly good word, right there in Webster's along with 'sanctimonious.' "

"*Sanctimonious!*"

She startled him by laughing merrily. "You are a rare case, J.D. Marvel. You don't seem to mind being called a capitalist exploiter, but 'sanctimonious' makes you go all blue in the face."

J.D. took a deep breath, a large gulp of beer, and forced a smile to his lips.

"Tell me what the J.D. stands for."

"Jesse Dinsmore. It's no secret."

"Let's see. Should I call you 'Din'? 'Jesse'? I have it! 'Jess.' "

"I'd rather you didn't."

"Well, then it's definitely Jess, Jess." She cupped her face sweetly in her hands, and said, "Now. What was it you wanted to speak to me about, Jess?"

208

J.D. sighed, and said, "I wanted to hear your demands. The demands of the strikers."

"My demands are my own. I may speak for the others, I may not. I don't know, and I don't care."

"Then let's hear yours."

"Turn the plant over to the workers."

"Would this afternoon be soon enough?"

"Now who's sneering?"

"I wanted a serious discussion."

"Okay, Jess. I know I'm dreaming. But some day, you'll see –"

"I know. We'll be another Russia. But until then?"

"The conditions are lousy."

"The *conditions?* That's one of the most modern plants in the country. The cleanest, best lighted –"

"I'm not talking about physical conditions. I'm talking psychological."

"Tell me."

"No one gives a damn about the worker. All they care about is production, production, production. That last straw was the Model Y line. The bosses treat it like the Holy Grail, and they're the knights sent out by King Jess to get it, no matter how many of us infidels they have to walk over on the way."

"You do have a colorful way of putting things. But could we leave the Theodore Dreiser imagery for a while, and get down to some facts?"

"I'll give you facts. We're ordered from one job to another with no rhyme or reason. Just when you've learned to do something well, you're uprooted and shifted somewhere else, and given impossible quotas to meet."

"Stan Wylie doesn't seem to have made many friends."

"Stan Wylie should be in charge of the Union Stockyards. He's ideally suited for ordering cattle around."

There was more. But all the stories had the same message: the plant management, driven by high quotas from New York, had grown callous to the feelings of the workers. By the time their lunch ended J.D. felt as though he'd shared a nightmare.

He stopped the Chevrolet at the front gate of the Marchetti house. Mr. Marchetti was on the porch, smoking his pipe. He stared suspiciously at the car.

"Look," J.D. said. "I'm going to try to straighten this thing out. I think you have legitimate grievances. I wish it hadn't come to this, but

209

now that it has, I need your help."

"Don't expect me to come over to your side."

"Would you be willing to be part of a worker's committee to see what we could do?"

"Who else would be on it?"

"You tell me."

She thought for a moment. "Frank Joyce. Leo Ward."

"Done."

"Whatever we agreed to would have to be put to a vote."

"All right."

"Many of us think we need a union."

"Give me a chance first. I hate the thought of having to talk to my employees through a third party."

She shook her head sadly. "You've got some pretty naive notions, Jess."

"You're not the first to say so. And maybe I do. But will you give me a chance?"

"It's your funeral." She started to get out of the car.

"Will you have dinner with me tonight?"

"I already have a large Italian boyfriend." She got out of the car, and looked back. "Let me know when you get the rest of the committee together."

J.D. saw the amiable Leo Ward that afternoon and got his agreement to serve on the committee.

J.D. called the first meeting of the committee the following morning. He rented a small conference room at the Blackstone Hotel and had it stocked with coffee and pastries.

By noon he'd made every member of the committee understand what he had in mind. They had lunch in the hotel dining-room. Ward talked about his children, the eldest of whom was in his senior year in high school. Frank Joyce told a funny story about his parish priest and a widow who wanted the priest to help her find a good Catholic man to marry. Gina Marchetti was silent throughout the meal. Several times J.D. felt her eyes coolly appraising him.

After lunch they went back to the conference room and the questions and objections rained down on J.D. He met each one. At four o'clock a silence fell on the room.

"By God, J.D.," Frank Joyce said. "I think we may have somethin' here."

"The workers will have to vote on it," Gina warned.

"The question now," J.D. said, "is are *you* for it?"

"Sounds like just the ticket to me," Leo Ward replied.

"I'm in," Joyce added, and then, "Gina?"

Her eyes met J.D.'s. She nodded. "I just hope you're not planning some kind of double-cross."

"Give the man a chance!" Ward exclaimed.

"No," Joyce said slowly. "Gina's right to doubt. We've been stabbed in the back more than once by management."

"Well," J.D. said. "It doesn't cost a nickel to find out."

Wanda and Jamie Ryan came to Chicago on the train that same evening. J.D. had booked them rooms at the Blackstone. After they had registered, J.D. took them into the dining-room where they had dinner while they reported to him.

"I've outlined a training program," Wanda began. "But I don't know where we're going to get instructors and facilities."

"Jamie?" J.D. asked.

"I phoned around Chicago and have three possibilities for sites. I've got appointments to see them in the morning. Do you want to come along?"

"Whatever you decide is fine. But I want first-class facilities. Now. What about instructors?"

"The best we could do on this kind of notice is a skeleton staff stolen from the training centers," Wanda said.

"Let's try training permanent instructors chosen from among the plant workers. Now, Jamie, we come to Stan Wylie. What have you come up with?"

Jamie consulted a notebook. "Before he was promoted to management, he was an engineer with plant development. He devised solutions to sticky problems, and has a reputation as a sound engineer. I recommend we transfer him to our Atlanta plant. They have an opening for a senior development engineer."

"Offer him the job. With a ten percent raise, or else he leaves."

Jamie made a record in his notebook.

"What about the superintendent?" J.D. asked.

Jamie replied, "The man is a good manager who has been ignoring personnel problems to work on pet projects."

"Talk to him," J.D. said. "Give him a choice: start being a manager again, adopt our new policies, or accept a transfer out to an engineering department in some other plant."

211

"With a raise?"

J.D. shook his head. "A cut to whatever the going rate is where he transfers. We're giving him a choice."

*

Two days later a meeting of all the employees was held in the plant parking lot. A speaker's stand was erected against one wall.

On the stand with J.D. were Gina Marchetti, Frank Joyce, Leo Ward and a chastened plant superintendent, who wanted to stay, and who had whole-heartedly endorsed the new policies. Stan Wylie had accepted the transfer to Atlanta and was at that moment at his home helping his wife pack their belongings. In the parking lot were the 300 plant workers, quiet, somber, a sea of doubting and resentful faces staring up at J.D. as he stepped forward to address them.

He began by telling them his dream for Marvel Scientific Machines: a company of individuals drawn together by a common purpose, a shared business ideal. " 'Respect For The Individual,' " J.D. said. "That is the motto on our banner. But here in Chicago we let the dream get away from us. Through neglect, poor personnel policies and, above all, by letting production quotas become more important than individual workers." All that was now past, he said. The future would be different. First, every manager at the plant, from the superintendent down, knew that Respect For The Individual would be his guiding principle. Second, every worker at the plant would be trained in a new school that was at that very moment being set up in Chicago. "You will, each and every one of you, be taught the workings of the company; what we're trying to do, here and in Europe. What our plans and goals are. After this indoctrination, you'll be taught the functions of every machine that is assembled at this plant, so you'll be able to see how your part fits into the whole of producing data-processing systems that solve real business and scientific problems for our thousands of customers. Instructors will be trained from workers chosen from among you. If you're interested in applying for an instructor's job, let your foreman know. It is now a company-wide policy that every job opening, be it in a branch sales office, or in a laboratory, or a factory, will be made available to every person in the company. What this means to you is that you will be notified of every opening anywhere in the company, and you can apply for it. We will always try to choose the best person for each job from *within* the company. Finally, as of the day you return to work, you will each be on a monthly salary like everyone else in the company. And what were formerly production bonuses will now be a part of your salary. Never

212

again will you have to depend upon production for your pay. If we can't make good equipment in the quantities our customers demand by working together as a team, we won't make any equipment . . ."

When J.D. finished there weren't any cheers, but there was a murmur of astonished approval tinged with an undercurrent of skepticism. Each of the three members of the committee gave a brief speech, endorsing J.D.'s plan and advising the workers to come back to work and give it a chance. The vote accepting the proposal was by acclamation. There was not one 'nay.'

As the meeting broke up, J.D. shook the hand of each member of the committee and thanked them for their help. He came to Gina last. She looked him levelly in the eye, and said, "That was quite a speech, Jess. I can't decide whether you're sincere, or a devil, out to play us for fools."

"You could gather more information on that at dinner tonight."

"Did you forget my large boyfriend?"

"Bring him along. I might need a bodyguard."

"Are you serious?"

"Deadly."

She looked at him appraisingly for a moment. "Okay. Where do we meet you?"

"I'll pick you up. How about your house at seven?"

"We'll be ready."

When he returned to the Blackstone there was a message to call David Stern.

"I understand Jamie is with you," Stern said.

"He and Wanda are out right now signing a lease for a building to use for a training center. We've stopped the strike."

"Congratulations. I'm afraid there are serious problems that require you back in New York, J.D."

"What kind of problems?"

"Cancellations of Marvel equipment are pouring into the office. The financial situation in the country is getting worse, and I see no end in sight."

"I'll be back tomorrow afternoon," J.D. replied.

After he hung up, J.D. poured himself a glass of bootleg Scotch and sat in a chair in his room staring out at a leaden Chicago sky. He had saved his factory, only to face the new threat of not having customers enough to keep it operating.

*

213

This time Gina's father was not on the porch. The door was opened by a very large, very handsome young man. "Gina'll be along in a minute," he said. "Want a beer?" There was no one else in the sitting-room.

J.D. accepted a beer and studied the young man. He was ruggedly handsome and had the build of a cruiserweight boxer in peak condition. "Where'd you plan to eat?" the young man asked.

"I thought Jiggs Muldoon's," J.D. replied. "Unless there's someplace you think would be better."

"Me?" The young man shrugged. "Don't matter to me. I hear Muldoon's is pretty fancy. Never been there myself, though. I eat over at Leone's when I eat out."

"Leone's?"

"Spaghetti joint over on 47th. Plenty of food, cheap. Muldoon's a speak?"

"Yes."

"How do you like the beer?"

"Very well."

"The old man makes it in washtubs." The young man winked.

"Gina's father?"

"Yeah – here she is now."

Gina came into the room. She was wearing a white dress that bared one shoulder and high-heeled white shoes. Her hair had been brushed until it gleamed. Over her arm she carried a beige wool coat. The sight of her fairly took the breath from J.D.

"You've already met Roberto?"

"Not formally," J.D. replied. He held out a hand and the young man took it. "I'm J.D."

"Hell, I know that," Roberto said. "The big cheese from New York."

"Should we go?" Gina asked.

J.D. put his overcoat on and stood waiting.

Gina was at the door. "What're you waiting for?"

"Don't you want to get a coat?" he asked Roberto. "It's freezing out there."

Roberto looked perplexed. "What?" Gina broke into laughter.

"I'm sorry," she gasped. "Roberto is my brother."

She was still chuckling when she got in the car. "Very funny," J.D. said. "Where do we go to pick up the real boyfriend."

"He couldn't make it."

J.D.'s heart leaped. He started the car. "Too bad. I hope it was something serious."

214

21

Love and Marx

JUNIOR MARVEL was a gangling, painfully shy boy of twelve when his mother announced to J.D. that their son could no longer live with her.

They were sitting in the den of the brownstone on 57th that J.D. had given Madelline when they divorced. Joseph Falk Whittier was not in evidence and Madelline didn't explain where he was, nor did J.D. ask. Madelline and Whittier had been quietly married the day after Whittier's divorce became final.

"The boy is a problem," Madelline said. "The only solution is to send him to a special school. There's one in Virginia, a military school, that handles problem boys."

"What kind of a problem?" J.D. was having difficulty focusing his attention on what Madelline was saying. He'd arrived back from Chicago the afternoon before and had spent half the night and all the day immersed in the crisis facing Marvel Scientific. Madelline had called him that afternoon and asked him to come over. It was eight o'clock before he could get away and J.D. hadn't eaten since morning. The Scotch that Madelline had given him rested uneasily on his empty stomach.

"He's listless. Not interested in anything. His grades are atrocious, although his teachers say he's bright enough when he tries, which isn't often." She sighed dramatically. "I've done all I could."

Which, J.D. said to himself, isn't much. Whittier's fortunes had steadily risen since his near ruin and, J.D. had heard from David Stern had taken a dramatic leap in the crash: Whittier had been selling short and had apparently reaped millions. Madelline had launched herself back into society with a vengeance. A pubescent boy would hardly fit into her plans to become the social queen of New York.

"I don't want Junior to go to military school," J.D. said.

"Well, my dear, you hardly have any say in it, do you? After all, I'm his guardian."

"Give him to me," J.D. suggested.

"You aren't serious!"

"I am."

"How in the world would you care for him?"

"I'll do a better job than a military school, I guarantee it."

"You *are* serious."

"Very."

"When would you want him to come?"

"As soon as I can find a suitable house." J.D. had rented a one-bedroom apartment after he'd moved out of the brownstone. "It won't take long, I'm sure. And if that's not soon enough, he can sleep on the couch."

"Of course, we can keep him until you find a suitable place." She stood. "Well," she said brightly. "I'm certainly glad we had this talk."

J.D. did not stand. "There's another opinion I'd like to have."

"Which?"

"Junior's."

Junior's eyes wouldn't meet his father's. J.D. was surprised at how thin he was. The boy perched on the edge of a chair.

"It's good to see you," J.D. began. Junior didn't reply. He stared at a spot just above J.D.'s head. "How have you been?"

"Okay, I guess."

"How is school?"

"Okay."

"Do you like it?"

"It's okay."

"Your mother and I have been talking about your future."

"Military school, you mean."

"I'm opposed to your going."

For the first time the boy looked at his father.

"I'd like you to come and live with me."

Junior's eyes shifted back to the spot above J.D.'s head. "I like it here."

"Well," J.D. said. "I'd like to say you have a lot of choice, but you don't. What it boils down to is military school, or me. I'd very much like you with me."

"Why?"

216

"*Why?*" J.D. exclaimed. "You're my *son*."

"Oh."

J.D. bought a penthouse apartment atop a stately twenty-story building on 5th Avenue across from Central Park. It had seven spacious rooms, including three bedrooms and a den. Its broad terrace had a sweeping view of the park and the buildings of lower Manhattan beyond. He hired a live-in cook and housekeeper; a young, sturdy, rosy-cheeked Irish girl named Kathleen O'Hare.

Junior moved in the week before Christmas and J.D., determined to start things off right, took time away from business to try to arrange a memorable Christmas for the boy. He bought a tall, thick Noble Fir and on Christmas Eve he and Junior decorated it. Junior's participation was desultory, but J.D. pretended not to notice.

At ten o'clock Wanda, Walter, and Jamie Ryan and his fiancée came by. J.D. allowed Junior to stay up. Perhaps 'allowed' wasn't the right word – with gentle urging he dissuaded Junior from hiding in his room with a book, and was rewarded to see him brought a little out of his shell by the attentions of the friendly guests. They drank Tom and Jerrys, sang carols, exchanged gifts, and generally enjoyed a warm and companionable evening that only old friends can produce when they come together on such occasions. Everyone was very attentive to Junior and, by the time he went off to bed at twelve-thirty, he actually had some color in his cheeks and a small if slightly wan smile on his lips. J.D. considered the evening a minor victory.

It wasn't until March of 1930 that J.D. felt he could make the time to visit Chicago again. He wanted to see for himself the effect of the programs he had instituted at the plant.

The superintendent met him at the station and drove him to the factory for a tour. The changes were remarkable. Everywhere they went on the plant floor, J.D. was greeted by cheerful, friendly workers. He paused in the engineering department to chat for a few minutes with Frank Joyce, who he found bent over a drafting table.

Joyce displayed his infectious grin. "I have to hand it to you. You haven't given us the shiv in the back – yet."

"You think there's still a chance I will, Frank?"

"Gettin' dimmer and dimmer."

J.D. shooed the superintendent off, saying he could find his way around by himself. It was a different version of Gina Marchetti than he had ever seen that he encountered in the Model Y tabulator

217

assembly area. Her hair was wrapped tightly in a white scarf, she wore a white smock, and had an air of confident authority. She was in charge of twenty women who had the delicate task of assembling reading mechanisms, tiny brushes that fell through the holes in the punched cards to make contact with a copper alloy plate, thereby completing an electrical circuit.

He drew her out of earshot of her fellow workers and said, "I'd like your ideas about how things are going at the plant." When she started to speak, J.D. said, "Not here. I was thinking of dinner."

"A business dinner?"

"Exactly."

"I suppose that means I couldn't bring my large boyfriend."

"He would be bored."

"This is the same table they put us at last time," Gina said at Jiggs Muldoon's.

"I asked for it. I thought we could talk better here."

The waiter brought an ice bucket with a bottle of champagne. Gina eyed the bottle suspiciously. "Champagne for talking?"

"Loosens the tongue. Tell me something – your father – is he really still an anarchist?"

"Oh, yes!"

"How did he get that way?"

"He worked in the stockyards and experienced capitalist exploitation at first-hand. He's an intelligent man, well-educated in Italy. But since his English is not good, the stockyards was the only place that would hire him.

"You should see him on May Day. It's the big event of the year for him. His old cronies, the ones that are still alive, come around and they drink *vino* that Pop makes himself, and swap stories. Then they raise a toast to all the fallen comrades."

Over coffee, J.D. said, "This fellow of yours – has he asked you to marry him?"

She stared at him. "You've had too much champagne, Jess."

"No, I haven't. I've thought a lot about you – about us. I've hardly thought about anything else."

"Drink your coffee."

"I don't think there is a boyfriend."

She flushed. "Why? Just because I don't get you two together?"

"That's part of it."

218

"I don't want to see you get your face pounded. I might lose my job."

"This 'boyfriend' makes a good suit of armor."

"I don't know what you're talking about."

"I think you do. You can use the mythical, big, handsome Italian as a shield."

"Listen here, Jess. You really don't know what you're saying. *I'm* not sure what you're saying, as far as that goes."

"This. Marry me."

She hit her forehead with her palm. "*Buono Deo!*"

He smiled. "I hope that means yes."

"Think, Jess! You, a big capitalist, the big cheese from New York, with a Communist around the house. What would you do when your friends came over? Lock me in the cellar?"

"I don't have a cellar. I'd be proud to have my friends meet you."

"I'm not penetrating, Jess. Think of it this way: your capitalist friends drop by for a little food and drink –"

"Yes?"

"And before you know it, darling wife is quoting chapter and verse from the *Manifesto*."

"Sounds wonderful. Especially that part about darling wife."

She blew out her cheeks and cast her eyes about. Finally, she said, "This is too fast. Too fast."

"I don't have much time. I can't keep running out to Chicago. I have a business to manage."

"We haven't done the things you're supposed to do. You know, courted."

"You mean a hard-headed Communist like yourself believes in sentimental ritual?"

"You've never even kissed me."

"We can amend that." He put his arm around her shoulders.

"You probably won't like it," she warned.

"Shut up," he replied, and kissed her. Then they stared into each other's eyes. "You were wrong," he said.

J.D. was wrong about the boyfriend; he existed. All six feet three inches and 225 lb of him. His name was Guido and he was a conductor on the Elevated. Gina had met him at a cell meeting. He was handsome, not very bright, and wore tight black suits that showed off his bulging muscles when he took Gina on dates or to Party rallies. She had known him for a year, had been to bed with him once (where his

219

grunting, thrusting insensitivity appalled her), everyone said they were a stunning couple, and she was bored to death with him.

Gina had been born in 1905 when her father was forty-three, her mother thirty-six. Every Sunday afternoon the Marchetti house became a gathering place for all the old Italian radicals in the neighbourhood where the name of the Unione Sindacale Italiane was honored and the name of Benito Mussolini spat upon. These men were violently anti-clerical and anti-Communist. Lenin and the Pope were just two manifestations of the same evil: bureaucratic organization. Gina had never been inside a church.

She was a radical the same way she was a Marchetti – by the inevitability of her genes, it seemed. By the time she was at high school her intelligence was manifest. Her brother, a year older, was an average student of average abilities, but Gina was exceptional. In her senior year she won the Valedictorian. She wanted to go to college, but her father pondered what to do with her, how she could best be fitted out to serve The Cause.

Thus he ordered her to go out and get a job and to see at first-hand how the masses were enslaved by bureaucracies. Her first job was as a seam-ripper in a garment sweatshop, tearing out seams from garments that had been incorrectly sewn. She worked twelve hours a day for $1.50 and came home at night with her fingers stiff and bleeding. Out of her weekly paycheck her father gave her 50c and, as a lesson to Gina, donated the rest to a tiny Syndicalist union that was trying to form then in Chicago.

The physical aspects of the job were bad enough, but what infuriated Gina was the mind-numbing boredom. She put up with it for a year, and then quit without telling her father. By the time the weekly pay envelope was due she had a job in a factory that made furniture polish. She presented this fact to her father and told him that from then on, with the exception of what she would give her mother for room and board, she would be keeping her pay.

At the polish factory Gina was, at first, assigned to the clean-up crew, a group of ten women who mopped floors, scrubbed out processing vats, and swept and dusted offices. The work seemed a vacation to Gina after her life at the garment factory. She only worked ten hours a day, she had the companionship of her fellow workers while she toiled, and the pay was twenty-five cents more than the garment-factory job.

It wasn't long before her quick mind and hard work were noticed by the management. Five months after she began work there was an opening the lab for a sample-runner, and Gina got the job.

During this time she became, through reading and discussion with friends, a Communist. She thought Communism more effective and positive than the nihilistic beliefs of her father, while, at the same time, addressing the same social problems. She joined a cell near her neighborhood, avidly studied the literature and read the *Daily Worker*.

The sample-runner job gave her her first experience with data processing. The lab had a Marvel sorter and tabulator for keeping inventories of chemicals, calculating costs of the various polishes, and doing the plant payroll. The operator was a spindly little man in his thirties with a pencil-line mustache and black hair pomaded flat against his head. He was very shy but took a kindly, avuncular interest in Gina and began to teach her how the equipment worked. Soon she had mastered the sorter, and could wire the tabulator plug-board to do simple jobs. Wiring the plug-board fascinated her. It was like a complex game.

Gina had been a sample-runner for two years when the data-processing operator told her he was leaving for a better job, and that he'd recommended her for his position. It paid a dollar a week more, but she would've taken a cut to have it. The joy she felt when she anticipated days filled with wiring plug-boards and running calculations was nearly boundless, for it never occurred to her that she wouldn't get the job. Never occurred to her, that is, until she walked into the lab one morning and found a stranger running the tabulator.

Gina went to the supervisor of the lab and demanded an explanation.

"You're a good worker, Gina," the supervisor said. "But data-processing operator is a man's job."

"A *man's* job!" Gina gasped. "How do you figure that?"

"It needs a logical mind, Gina," the supervisor explained patiently. "A mathematical bent."

"I've wired the plug-board!" Gina said.

"Besides, you aren't married –"

"You have to be married to do that job?"

"No. But when you do marry, you'll be raising a family, I expect, and where would we be then? Without an operator, that's where."

"Who told you I was getting married? And that I was going to raise a family, if I did?"

"You're an attractive girl, Gina. No one has to tell me. Besides, the fellow we hired *has* a family he supports. You wouldn't want to take income away from his wife and children, would you?"

"My God!" Gina said. "I came in here to ask why I didn't get a job I deserved, and you make me out to be some kind of monster who wants to starve children!"

"Now, Gina. Let's keep our voices down."

"You keep *your* voice down!" Gina shouted. "And keep your job, too! *I quit!*"

Several people in her neighborhood worked at the Marvel plant. She went there that afternoon and found they were hiring. They needed assemblers and hired women because they had small hands. Her hands were long and broad, but they needed workers, so she was hired, anyway.

It took her hardly a week to learn the job she was assigned, which was the assembly of master gear drives for tabulators. Her foreman marked her as a comer right away.

Then one day her foreman sent her downtown to the post office to pick up a parcel containing important drawings of a new tabulator part. She took the trolley. The conductor was big, handsome, and amusing, and before she quite knew what was happening she had agreed to a date. Guido *was* amusing and charming, but, as she'd come to know, that was about as deep as he got. He had no political consciousness, had hardly read a book, and felt there was no greater joy than a beer and a hot dog during a game at Wrigley Field.

Gina was made a straw boss and given a raise a year after she began work at the plant. All of the regular supervisors were men. Straw boss was as high as a woman could go.

Being straw boss of twenty or so women was more interesting than assembling master gear drives.

It was Frank Joyce who gave Wylie the nickname "Old Sly." Joyce helped keep them all from cracking. His quick wit and irreverent jokes relieved the pressure. Wylie, as a consequence, hated Joyce.

Gina thought conditions at the plant were typical of those that must prevail in any capitalistic enterprise, and never missed an opportunity to say so to her fellow workers. She exhorted then to organize, but they were split by factionalism. Some believed in traditional unions, others thought unions would only make things worse. There were a few anarchists who were all for burning the plant down. There were Communists, like Gina. And then there were those like Frank Joyce, who didn't seem to give a damn one way or another.

If Stan Wylie had set out to bring all these factions together against the plant he couldn't have done a better thing than fire Frank Joyce.

J.D. Marvel's portrait hung high over the main floor of the factory. Gina, when she imagined the man behind the portrait, saw a kind of human machine, whose purpose was the production of money no matter what the means. It was inconceivable to her that such a man could have any of the nobler human emotions.

J.D. in the flesh confused her. He seemed so gentle. Oh, he was hard-minded, all right. But it was his talk about the welfare of his workers that had blunted her attack. Her own words seemed like quotes from mindless tracts in the face of his reasonableness.

He was magnificent – there was no other word for it – when he had spoken to the workers in the parking lot. His words seemed to elevate them, to invest them with dignity. And he'd kept all his promises. The plant had suddenly become a pleasant place to work in. Even the superintendent turned out to be a reasonable man who carried out J.D. Marvel's humane policies to the letter in good spirit.

She'd gone to dinner with him once more against her better judgment. Then he'd proposed. And she'd allowed herself to be kissed.

It was impossible, of course. Such a marriage would be a battleground. She imagined the arguments. The long discussions. Marx versus Jay Gould. Hegel versus Henry Ford. So she sent him back to New York. But he wouldn't allow her to say no and insisted she think about it.

She didn't see him for three weeks. He didn't call, didn't write. Then one steamy Friday morning in early April the superintendent sent for Gina.

"The New York office has come up with a solution to the second read brush problem on the Model Y," he said. And New York wanted someone to go there to learn the new procedure for installing the brushes. Since Gina was in charge of the crew that did the assembly, she was a natural choice. He handed her a ticket and said that the train was leaving that evening. She would be expected back at work on Tuesday. An engineer she didn't know would meet her train.

She arrived at Grand Central at eight o'clock on Saturday morning. There were hundreds of people thronging the main concourse when she emerged into it. She decided the best thing to do was to stand near the tunnel from her train and hope the engineer would somehow recognize her.

"Gina!"

She turned to find J.D. hurrying toward her. He stopped in front of her and took her in his arms. She averted her head from his attempted kiss.

223

"This is a cheap trick!" she said, surprised at the depth of her anger.

He released her, and said, "Give me a chance to explain." He looked around. "Let's go in the coffee shop over there."

They sat at a table and ordered coffee. "Gina," J.D. began. "This isn't a trick. I found out quite by accident that you were coming, and asked the engineering department if I could meet your train."

"I suppose if you hadn't found out I would never have seen you again."

"I'd intended to come to Chicago the week after next. This was a lucky accident."

"Unless my memory is going, didn't you propose to me?"

"I did."

"You certainly don't seem anxious for an answer."

"You'll never know how anxious I was. I didn't write or phone because I didn't want to rush you. Then, too, I was afraid the answer would be no.

"While you're here will you stay at my apartment? Before you jump to conclusions, I have a perfectly adequate guest room, and a maid and a son as chaperons."

"A son?"

"Junior. I suppose I should've told you about him before this, but it seemed I was throwing plenty at you as it was."

"How old is he?"

"Thirteen." She stared across the room. "What are you thinking?"

"That I was twelve when he was born." She pushed her cup away. "Well, let's go meet this offspring."

"I was planning on taking you to dinner first."

"Not until I know where I'm staying. I want to meet this son and see this guest room before I'll agree to stay there."

In the elevator Gina asked, "How high is your apartment?"

"It's on the top. Thirty stories. Junior and Kathleen aren't expecting us until later, so I can't tell you what kind of shape the place will be in."

J.D. opened the door into a dark room. "Funny," he said. "Maybe they went out to a picture –" He flipped a light switch and two lamps sprang to life. The room was large and beautifully furnished. There was a fireplace and, to each side of it, a Louis XV couch. On one of the couches was a tall, thin boy with a handsome head and face. He was lying face down, his head averted from the door. He was naked. Under him was a stocky, fair young woman, who was also naked and who had her legs wrapped around the boy's thin flanks.

J.D. let out a curse. "Meet your chaperons, Gina . . ."

22

J.D. Meets the Differential Analyzer

THROUGH HIS SHOCK J.D. took note of two things: how thin and pale his son's body was, and the magnificent thighs of Kathleen O'Hare.

"Get dressed," he said, and the boy and the woman disentangled themselves and ran from the room.

J.D. turned to Gina after they'd gone and found her trying unsuccessfully to suppress laughter. "Oh, I'm sorry, Jess," she gasped. "But – it was so like a French farce."

A tentative grin spread itself on his face, and then he too was gasping for air as he laughed until tears stood in his eyes.

"What will you do?" Gina asked.

"What do you suggest?"

"You shouldn't be too hard on the boy. You can bet it wasn't his idea initially, as young as he is."

"Damn it, Gina – now that this thing has happened, I guess marrying me is about the last thing you'd want to do."

"I'm still thinking."

"Then you'll stay?"

"Show me my room," Gina said.

In the summer of 1930 Lucille Cranston came to New York on what she considered a mission of great moment. She had just spent four days at a seminar at the Massachusetts Institute of Technology. The seminar had been entitled "Modern Data-Processing Practices" and Lucille had gone as a part of the Continual Training Program that J.D. had instigated in the company whereby every employee was afforded the opportunity to take time off for the improvement of his education in fields related to his work, all at the company's expense.

226

The seminar, as well-presented as it was, offered little that Lucille didn't already know. She was prepared to skip the last presentation in order to catch an early train for Tarrytown, when a fellow participant urged her to stay. "You'll be missing the best thing here," he said. "Worth the whole seminar."

So she stayed, and as a result heard and saw Dr. Vannevar Bush, who was the sole reason that she had taken the late train for New York instead of Tarrytown.

When Lucille arrived at corporate headquarters the next morning, she was told that J.D. was in conference until noon. She went to Jamie Ryan's office and found him dictating to his secretary. He dismissed the secretary and Lucille told him just enough about Vannevar Bush to galvanize Jamie into action.

Jamie spoke into his intercom. "Tell Mr. Marvel's secretary that Miss Cranston and I must have lunch with him. It's urgent." Jamie knew this would not fail. He seldom used the word 'urgent,' so that when he did J.D. heeded.

They lunched at the Plaza. "I had to break a date with David Stern," J.D. said.

"You won't regret it," Lucille replied.

They ordered lunch and J.D. said, "So tell me what all the excitement is about."

Lucille told him about the seminar. "The last presentation on the last day was by Dr. Vannevar Bush. He's a scientist at MIT. He presented a machine he and his colleagues have developed called the 'differential analyzer.' It is designed to solve ordinary differential equations –"

"Whoa!" J.D. said. "They may be ordinary to you, but I haven't the faintest."

"I'm no mathematician, either," Lucille replied. "But Bush gave a fine explanation of what the equations are about. They are to measure infinite things. Slopes of curves, by approximations of the slope whose error becomes so small as to be negligible, for example."

"Ah." J.D. nodded. "Differential calculus."

"You know what she's talking about?" Jamie asked.

"Vaguely. I've done a little reading – popular stuff written for the unwashed masses – on calculus, and Newton and Leibniz who came up with it."

"The exciting thing about this machine is that it operates by steps," Lucille continued.

"Well, so do our tabulators."

"Yes. But the differential-analyzer steps can be changed while the machine is in operation."

"You mean to perform different functions?" J.D. asked incredulously.

"Let's say that you set up the machine to add on step ten. But on step nine you discover some condition – say, a register had overflowed. Then the machine can change step ten to subtract, or whatever's appropriate, *before* it does the step."

"My God," J.D. exclaimed. "Think what you could do with a tabulator like that. The best we can do now is skip steps."

J.D. had to see this amazing machine for himself. He phoned Dr. Bush at MIT and got an appointment to see him in two days. He told his secretary to make him a reservation on the train, then, on a sudden inspiration, called her back into his office and told her to make it two.

He phoned the plant at Chicago and had Gina called off the floor. The connection wasn't good and he had to shout to be heard. "I want you to go to Cambridge, Massachusetts, with me to look at an amazing new machine."

"Why?" Gina asked.

"I want your opinion. Besides, I want to see you. You owe me an answer."

It had been nearly three weeks since Gina had been in New York. There was a pause. Finally, she said, "I'll see if I can get on a train tonight."

He met her at Grand Central the next morning, and took her to the penthouse. Junior seemed glad to see her. J.D. introduced her to the new housekeeper and cook he'd hired – a round, middle-aged motherly woman with grey hair and half-moon glasses – and took Gina's suitcase up to her room. When they were alone he took her in his arms and kissed her. She kissed him back with a passion. Finally, J.D. said, "God, I've missed you."

"Me too."

"I wish you'd say yes."

"All right."

"What!"

"I said, all right. Yes."

He stared at her. "You'll marry me?"

"Yes." She smiled at the astonishment on his face.

"Gina!" He kissed her again. "You won't regret it. Wait here."

228

When he returned he had a box in his hand. In it was a diamond engagement ring.

"It's lovely, Jess. How long have you had it?"

"I bought it when I got back from Chicago the first time I asked you to marry me."

"You must've been awfully confident."

"Awfully hopeful."

She put on the ring, and held her hand out to admire it. "Step One," she said.

"What do you mean?"

"To becoming a capitalist."

He laughed. "That will be the day!"

Dr. Vannevar Bush was an intense, terse man of forty. He was an electrical engineer who loved nothing better than to construct esoteric, involved machines. He'd been working on the differential analyzer since 1925. Although it was powered by electrical motors, it was a mechanical device. The quantities it calculated were represented by the number of degrees through which gears rotated.

"This is an analog machine," Bush explained. He and J.D. and Gina were standing around a table in Bush's laboratory at MIT. On the table rested the differential analyzer, a seemingly hodge-podge array of gears, levers and electrical motors. "By that, it is meant that there is a physical representation of numbers. In this case, the angle of rotation of certain gears corresponds to numerical quantities. Hence, an analog for numbers. Would you like to see it work?"

"Very much," J.D. said.

Bush pointed to a blackboard upon which was chalked an equation:

$$\frac{dy}{dx} = 2 \sin(1 - 2x), \, y = \cos(1 - 2x)$$

"The machine is set up now to solve this derivative of a simple curve, computing for a range of values."

Bush flipped a switch and the machine whirred, gears turned, levers jumped. "There!" Bush said after a few minutes. "You can read the solution directly from these gears." He stepped to the blackboard and wrote a series of numbers on it.

"How long would it take a man to do the same computation?" J.D. asked.

"An hour or two," Bush replied.

"Wouldn't it be simpler if you had numerical registers to read the answers into?"

"My work is experimental. I've neither the time nor the money to design and install registers."

"Of course. Could you give me an idea of what you might use this machine for?"

"Perhaps the most interesting would be the calculation of trajectories for very large guns."

"You mean you might aim such a gun with this machine?"

"Yes. Of course, you'd have to do some work with it. Have a bank of gears to factor in wind velocities. Make it easier to read out. The best thing would be to have this machine in communication with the gun-aiming mechanism itself, through a series of linking gears."

"Then it would be automatic!" J.D. exclaimed.

"Virtually."

After the demonstration, Bush took them to his office where he served them coffee from a battered coffee-pot on a hot-plate.

"Dr. Bush," J.D. asked. "Who else is working on a machine similar to yours?"

"No one that I know of. That's one of the problems in this field, if you could call it a field. We only find out about other work accidentally. There is no society, no journal, that links us together. I wish there were."

"Do you think the automatic step modification in your machine could be adapted to tabulating machines?"

"I'm not sure. I know little about tabulators. We have several around the campus. But I'm afraid I haven't made a study of them."

"If I could arrange for you to have one of our new Model Ys, would you be interested in tackling the problem?"

"No, I'm sorry, Mr. Marvel. My interest's in the differential analyzer."

"Well, then – what would you say to a grant from Marvel Scientific Machines to further your studies?"

"I would say that it would be very welcome indeed, provided there were no strings attached."

"Only that the money should go toward research on the differential analyzer. If you're interested, could you submit a proposal to my assistant in New York?"

"Very well."

J.D. gave him Jamie's name and the address of the New York office.

"May I ask, Mr. Marvel, what your interest is in funding work on the analyzer?"

"I'm not sure, Dr. Bush. I know, but couldn't prove, that somehow, somewhere down the road, our interests are going to intersect."

"You know, perhaps you'd be interested in talking to a colleague of mine who has done some theoretical work on similar problems."

"Very much. Is he at MIT?"

"No. At Princeton. He's Hungarian, and he arrived in this country only this year. I've known him long enough to realize he is a remarkable man. He's a chemical engineer, but that hardly defines him. His interests are protean, his abilities amazing."

"What's his name?"

"John von Neumann."

Over dinner back at their hotel in Boston, J.D. asked Gina, "Have you ever seen New Jersey?"

"Jess, before I met you I'd hardly seen Chicago."

"It's a nice train ride from here."

"You're determined to see von Neumann?"

"Yes."

"What if he's not there, or busy?"

"I'll try to phone him in the morning. What do you say?"

"I say it's about time I saw New Jersey."

He took her hand across the table. "It seems a shame to use two rooms tonight. Hardly the Communist way, all that consumption, causing maids extra work."

"It may not be the Communist way, but it's going to be my way until we're married."

They caught a train for New Jersey the next morning. J.D. had tried to phone von Neumann, found he was on campus, but teaching a class, and decided to take the chance that he would see them.

On the train, Gina said, "You're really excited by all this."

"And I'm not sure why. I have the sense, really an instinct I suppose, that what Bush is doing, and people like him, if there are any, will be exceedingly important to our business."

John von Neumann was a rumpled, stocky, friendly young man in his late twenties. His slight accent simply served to underline his articulate use of English.

When J.D. and Gina arrived in Princeton on that hot Tuesday afternoon in July, 1930, they tracked von Neumann to his tiny office in the Sciences Building. The office was so small that von Neumann was obliged to take them to a vacant classroom to talk. During their talk he constantly fiddled with an old briar pipe, tapping out the ashes in a waste basket, reloading and tamping the tobacco, relighting it.

J.D. told von Neumann of their visit to Bush.

"Vannevar is doing interesting work. His differential analyzer may be a step along the way toward solving some problems that interest those of us who work in formal mathematics."

"He said that you had some ideas about such devices."

"Just ideas. You see, I don't agree entirely with Vannevar's approach, as ingenious as it is. He knows this. I've discussed it with him."

"How don't you agree?"

"The differential analyzer is an analog machine. To solve some of the problems I'm interested in, I believe you need a discrete system, that is one that works directly with digits."

"You mean like a calculator does?"

"Well, no. Calculators are simply analog machines that have digital registers to make reading the results more convenient. I mean a machine that would do its calculations directly on discrete numerical quantities."

"But is such a machine possible!"

Von Neumann smiled. "Who knows, Mr. Marvel? Theoretically, I think I could show it was feasible. If I cared to take the time."

"What sort of problems could you solve if you had such a machine, Dr. von Neumann?"

"Oh, many interesting ones. For example, I've taken an interest recently in turbulence in the field of hydrodynamics. Our present analytical methods are simply not powerful enough to give us closed solutions to problems. Another field is that of meteorology, world-wide weather models. It's been known for some time that the entire climate of the globe is an interdependent system. A low-pressure system in Europe, for example, can set up a chain of climatological events that will affect the weather over the United States. We know those connections exist, but we can't analyze them with the present methods.

"My philosophy is to solve problems in the physical world with the quickest method you can devise. My mathematical colleagues look on me as a bit of a low-brow as a consequence. They would rather devise elegant formal systems of mathematics. I don't object to that. I do a lot of it myself. But when you want to calculate turbulence around a

232

ship's propeller, and the elegant methods aren't there to do it, I say build a machine that will grind away on the numbers and produce a solution."

"Then why don't you?" J.D. asked. "If it's a question of money, my company might arrange a grant."

Von Neumann laughed. "Yes, that would be fun, no doubt. The problem is, Mr. Marvel, I have other things I'm working on that are more fun; things in mathematical logic, and an area I call Game Theory."

J.D. and Gina caught a train that night for New York. J.D. was simultaneously disappointed and excited; disappointed that von Neumann wouldn't be applying his genius to the concoction of machines of the type he'd so eloquently described, and excited by what he'd learned from von Neumann and Bush.

"Do you really think that your company would want to make machines for mathematicians like Bush and von Neumann?" Gina asked.

"Yes, I do. Oh, I know that the market might not be very large. After all, how many people are even capable of understanding the problems von Neumann was talking about, much less tackling their solutions? But what I think is this, Gina: somehow those machines, if they could be devised, will lead to new advances in the kind of data processing we're engaged in. I might be wrong. But I know this: I'm going to stay in touch with von Neumann and Bush."

SIX

Revolutions are not to be evaded.
Disraeli

23

The Beginning

ELVIRA MARVEL DIED IN MAY OF 1933. Unlike her husband she died suddenly and painlessly in her sleep at the farm where she had lived for so many years. She was sixty-eight years old.

Gina and J.D. had been married in September of 1930 and so far few of Gina's fears about the marriage had been realized. Rather than the fat, greedy capitalists Gina had anticipated having to entertain, she found that J.D.'s circle was confined to the people he worked with. They thought her political views strange but rather charming. To her surprise, she found that most of them were almost apolitical. Their entire interests focused on Marvel Scientific. The exception was David Stern, who was a zealous Roosevelt Democrat. David confided to Gina that, in his youth, he'd been an anarchist, but that age had banked the fires of his political ardor, and now "I find Roosevelt quite radical enough for me."

J.D. was also a Democrat and backed Roosevelt with campaign contributions. He thought he'd been a good Governor, and, in his first days in office, was proving to be the President the country needed. But his political interests and convictions didn't go much deeper than that and when, shortly after F.D.R. was elected, he had been offered a job as Presidential Advisor for Industry, he'd turned it down with a kind of private horror. The last thing he wanted to do, he told Gina, was to become a bureaucrat.

J.D., Gina and Junior journeyed to Johnson County for the funeral. After the burial in the church cemetery the funeral party convened at the farmhouse for food and drink. J.D. wandered down to the pig pens and perched on a fence there staring off down the road, the same road that he'd first seen Walter Hucko's old truck approach on. Gina found him there.

237

"You want to be alone," she said.

He hopped off the fence and took her in his arms. "With you."

"What were you thinking about?"

"Did I tell you I began my business life selling organs?"

She looked up into his face. "No. Where?"

"All over Illinois. The farm country, anyway. Walter Hucko and I. He came driving up that road one day, in an old chain-driven truck, and sold my mother an organ. I think Walter was in love with my mother for a while."

He gazed at the pigs rooting in their trough. "It was my job to feed the pigs. Oh, I was a raw country galoot, Gina. And my daddy wanted me to be a preacher, and my mother, probably out of pity for the congregation that would be saddled with me, got me out of it."

Junior Marvel, at sixteen, had filled out. He was tall, and resembled his father but also had his mother's large, smoldering eyes and rich black hair. He was still a quiet boy, quieter than J.D. would've liked, but he had, for the past three years, done better in school, maintaining a C-average and in the past year joining the track team as a fairly good high-jumper. He had a friend or two that he brought to the penthouse occasionally, so, overall, things had improved for Junior.

Junior adored Gina. Mixed with a kind of protectiveness he exhibited toward her was an admiration for her intelligence and grace that led him to emulate her in many things. He was an ardent Communist, or believed he was. J.D. took this in good humor, figuring that it wouldn't do Junior any harm to have a cause and that most boys of sixteen needed something to make them feel less of a child and more of a man. And if Communism did that for Junior, then it was all right with J.D., provided he outgrew it, as J.D. expected he would.

J.D., at forty-three, was a tall, lean figure. His sharp features had grown even sharper, the chin and nose more pronounced, the eyes deeper set. Gina said that when he was angry he looked like a hawk when it was circling a rabbit.

His strategy of helping customers cut their costs and streamline their practices had paid off. In the distressed economic times few firms of any size could compete without data processing. Now, with Roosevelt's many proposed government programs to aid recovery, a huge new market seemed about to open up.

"They're going to need lots more machines down in Washington," J.D. told his board. "We're doubling the size of our Washington office."

238

The overseas business had shrunk – Europe was in its own severe depression – but J.D. still saw it as a huge market of the future and made sure that Thomas Finch had good equipment to sell, and good people to sell it, so that Marvel Scientific would be ready when that market came.

In 1933 the company grossed $18.5 million and earned $4 million. In 1934 the gross was nearly $20 million and earnings over $5 million. The board voted J.D. a raise. They figured he had brought them through the depression. Their particular view of the economy was that if Marvel Scientific Machines was turning around, then the depression was on its way out. The *Wall Street Journal* reported accurately that J.D.'s new salary was $1 million a year, and resurrected the old sobriquet "World's Greatest Salesman" for him.

The day the *New York Times* reported the same item, Gina greeted J.D. when he arrived home with a somber face. It didn't take him long to find out what was bothering her – Gina was not one to hide her feelings.

"It is immoral!"she said, "to make that kind of money with people starving!"

J.D. sighed. "I wish they hadn't voted me the raise. Today we had pickets around headquarters, carrying signs saying I was a blood-sucker, and worse."

"What are you going to do about it?"

"Let me think about it."

It was a chilly atmosphere at dinner, with Gina scowling, Junior his usual quiet self, and J.D. lost in thought.

When they had married, Gina had insisted on two things: she didn't want a maid and cook, seeing those jobs as symbols of the worst in the capitalist system, and she wanted to go on working. J.D. finally convinced her that if she let Mrs. Fletcher go in those severe times, the poor woman would undoubtedly be unable to get another job. So Gina let her stay – the contest between her convictions and her compassion easily won by the latter. J.D. wanted to make her his personal assistant, but Gina would have nothing to do with anything that smacked of nepotism. On her own she applied for a job in the lab, and got one as an engineering aide in the tabulator-development section.

Mrs. Fletcher's job, in the meantime, became much easier because Gina simply couldn't let the woman wait on her. She helped with the dishes, the cooking, even the housework. Mrs. Fletcher's protests, never strong to begin with, eventually faded away and she went about the house with the benign expression of a woman who couldn't believe her luck.

After dinner J.D. went into the kitchen where Gina and Mrs. Fletcher were doing the dishes. J.D. took the dishtowel from Mrs. Fletcher and shooed her out of the room.

"I've come up with something."

"Yes?"

"I'll give the money away."

"Give it away!"

"Oh, I don't mean all of it. We need something to support this apartment, and so on. But I sure as hell don't need a million a year. I figure I can give half of it away, anyway."

"Who would you give it to?" Gina asked, her voice softer, the dishes forgotten for the moment.

"That's where you come in."

"Me!"

"I suppose we'd have to set up some kind of foundation or something. I'll have to ask David about it. But, whatever – I'd want you to head it, be the one who decides who the money goes to."

"J.D.!" She threw her arms around his neck.

"You're getting soap on my shirt," he laughed. "There's one condition –"

She drew back to look up at him. "Yes?"

"None of the money can go to political organizations."

"I wouldn't give it to any political organizations. I'd give it to the people."

"Mmmm. That's not as simple as it sounds."

"What do you mean?"

"I mean, what do you do? Stand on a street corner with the money in bushel baskets and hand it out?"

David Stern laughed. "Hardly," he said. "You'd be mobbed, and lucky to come out alive."

Gina and J.D. were sitting in Stern's office. It was late in the afternoon of the day following their discussion in the kitchen. "How do we go about it, then?"

"Let me see if I understand the situation," Stern said. "You want to give half your salary to worthy causes."

"The poor!" Gina exclaimed. "The starving mothers and babies –"

"The poor, then," David replied. "And you will put in half a million immediately –"

240

"Provided you can raise it for me," J.D. said.

"You have enough liquid to raise that easily. Then you'll put up half a million a year."

"Make that half my salary, whatever it is."

"And Gina is to administer it?"

"Yes."

"Shouldn't be any problem. We set up a trust. You and Gina can be two of the trustees. I'd be willing to serve. We could get one or two others. And Gina would be president of the organization. The trustees will serve without pay, of course. What about Gina?"

"No pay for me. What would be the point of the whole thing if we take salaries out of it?"

"Very well," David said. "I'll set up the trust, free of charge, of course." He pulled a yellow legal pad to him and poised a pen over it.

"What would you like to call it?"

"The J.D. Marvel Foundation," Gina suggested.

"No," J.D. said.

"It's not a bad idea, J.D.," David pointed out. "It would offset some of this hostile reaction to the *Wall Street Journal* article."

"No," J.D. repeated. "I don't want any publicity out of this. I want my part kept secret."

"But, Jess –" Gina began to protest.

"I won't argue about it, Gina."

"Then what *would* you like to call it?" Stern asked.

"If it's all right with Gina, I'd like to call it the Elvira Dinsmore Foundation. That was my mother's maiden name."

In the beginning the Elvira Dinsmore Foundation didn't rival the Rockefeller or Carnegie Foundations, with their millions. J.D. was well off, but wasn't among the wealthiest men in the nation, as was commonly believed of him. He had taken only as much stock in Marvel Scientific as had been given to other employees and, in any case, since it wasn't a publicly held corporation, his shares weren't liquid. He'd saved some so that when David Stern, who managed J.D.'s personal finances, said J.D. could raise half a million, he was right – what he failed to say was that, aside from the penthouse and his and Gina's personal possessions, that left J.D. with a little less than $100,000. A position that would've been envied by many, certainly, but hardly a position that would rank him with the Rockefellers, the Cranstons or the Whittiers.

At first Gina thought she would find some way to funnel the money directly to the poor and needy. But on reflection, and re-reading her Marx and Lenin, she decided that the best use of the money was for scholarships for the children of the poor. The education of the masses was the way to eliminate poverty once and for all, she believed. She established scholarships at MIT, Yale, Columbia and Vassar in the first year of the Foundation. She continued to work at the lab, because the Foundation job wasn't enough to keep her occupied full-time.

In 1935 the Social Security Act passed Congress. In that same year President Roosevelt reorganized the Federal Reserve System, giving it more authority, and establishing an open-market committee to buy and sell government securities and thereby regulate the money supply. Both these events opened up enormous new markets for data processing. J.D. went to Washington to personally oversee Marvel Scientific's bids for the government business. IBM won the Social Security contract, and Marvel won the Federal Reserve. The new Model Z alphabetic tabulator, that had just been developed at the lab in New York, was the machine chosen by the Federal Reserve. It was a remarkable advance in technology. The Model Z could read and print alphabetic data, it had twice the number of arithmetic registers of the old Model Y, and was nearly three times faster.

Through all of this J.D. found time to maintain his interests in what Bush at MIT and von Neumann at Princeton were doing. Bush had received a grant from Marvel Scientific that had been renewed each year and as a result the differential analyzer had grown from a primitive research toy to a sophisticated machine. In 1935 Bush won a small grant from the War Department to develop a gun-aiming device based on the differential analyzer.

Von Neumann, having written the definitive work on Game Theory, turned part of his protean mind to the contemplation of calculating machines. In 1935 he had, along with Albert Einstein, become one of the first permanent members of the Institute for Advanced Study at Princeton. This gave him and his colleagues more time to work in pure research. Von Neumann realized at a very early time that many of the problems in applied mathematics that interested him would only be solved when calculating devices of sufficient size and sophistication were created.

In the fall of 1936 J.D. flew to Princeton with Junior. The airplane was a new type that had just been put into commercial service that year, the Douglas DC-3. It only flew as far as Philadelphia, where they would take a train on to Princeton.

After they had taken off and were on their course the cabin attendant, a slight girl who didn't look any older than Junior, came back from the cockpit to announce that their air speed was now 180 miles an hour, which brought a murmur of awe from the twenty passengers.

"They used to think," Junior announced to his father, "that a man would die if he went over a hundred miles an hour."

"Apparently they were wrong," J.D. replied.

The weather was clear the entire trip. J.D. and Junior stared out the small window by their seats in a reverie of awe at the view.

They arrived at Princeton in time to take von Neumann, who was expecting them, to lunch. He was full of questions about their flight. He had flown for the last five years in various aircraft as a passenger, but had yet to fly on a DC-3.

They went to lunch at a small inn on the outskirts of Princeton. J.D. and von Neumann ordered cocktails, Junior a beer. Prohibition had ended nearly three years before, but it was still something of a wonder to J.D. to be able to order a drink openly in an ordinary restaurant.

"Well, J.D.," von Neumann said. "I see you won the Federal Reserve contract."

"We wanted the Social Security business, too. That will be larger by far."

"Tom Watson beat you on that one, did he?"

"IBM's a good company, and a tough competitor. But I'd rather have them around, than not. It keeps our people on their toes."

"Ah, yes," von Neumann said. "The theory of competitive excellence. You know it reduces to a zero-sum game, don't you?"

"No, I didn't know that," J.D. said with a grin. "And I still don't know anymore now than I did before."

Von Neumann laughed. "Simply put, there is a winner and there is a loser in a zero-sum game."

"Then that's the game we're in, all right."

"Have you thought anymore about our last talk?" J.D. asked.

"I can't take a grant from your company, J.D.," von Neumann replied.

"Why not?"

"Because I want to be free to work on what interests me. And I never know, sometimes, from one day to the next what that will be. If I tied myself down to research on machines I'd be miserable."

"I can understand that. What if Marvel Scientific gave the Institute some money?"

"That would be a different thing. I don't get involved in administration, so you'd have to talk to someone else."

"I'd also like to give the Institute some of our equipment. We have a new tabulator – the Model Z – that is the most advanced around."

"Interesting," von Neumann said politely. "I looked over your equipment that the University has in its business office one day. I think it wouldn't be too difficult to wire the tabulator to run integral tables."

"And that's the old Model Y!" J.D. exclaimed. "Think what you could do with twice as many registers and three times the speed."

"Yes. But registers and speed aren't advances, J.D. They are improvements on the same technology, no?"

"What *would* be an advance?"

"Stored instruction sets."

J.D. frowned. "I don't understand."

"The way the present equipment works is that you wire in instructions for a job, and while the job is running those instructions are immutable, right?"

"Yes, that's true. Although we can change panels for different jobs, so you don't have to re-wire every time you get a new job."

Von Neumann waved his pipe. "Not the point. You asked about an advance in technology. You would take a quantum leap if, during the running of a problem, you could alter the instructions."

"Ah, you mean the way Bush's differential analyzer alters steps?"

"The same principle, yes. But Vannevar's machine is mechanical. What is needed is a new medium. Not wires and plugs. Perhaps electrons flowing in a chemical bath. Or varying the impedance of a radio tube."

"And what would that do for us?"

"It would raise the technology to a new level. You could then change instruction n-plus-one according to the conditions discovered at n, and do it fast enough so that the computation time would hardly be affected."

"That's very exciting! I wish you'd change your mind. You might find it more interesting than you think to work on that problem."

"Oh, I grant you it's interesting, and I may indeed work on it. But only at *my* pace."

*

J.D. and Junior took the train back to New York – the plane only

244

made the Philadelphia–New York flight once a week. Junior was now six feet tall, a handsome boy, but J.D. was concerned that he seemed to have no direction in his life. In his first year at Columbia he had just managed to pass all his courses, but he had yet to settle on a major.

"What did you think of von Neumann?" J.D. asked.

"Does he always talk that way?"

"I suspect when he's talking to me he tries to simplify what he's saying."

Junior shook his head. "I couldn't make out half of what he said as it was."

"He is truly a genius. Anything he say catch your interest?"

"How do you mean?"

"Oh, I thought you might want to study science of some kind. You could even go to Princeton if you thought you wanted to be around people like him."

"My grades aren't good enough."

"I could maybe arrange something. One of the trustees at Princeton is on our board. It would probably be on a probation basis. You'd have to bring the grades up."

"I don't think I'd be interested."

"Then what *would* you be interested in, if you don't mind telling me?"

"I think maybe I'd like to go to Spain."

"*What!* Why in hell would you want to go to Spain? There's a war going on over there."

"Exactly. A group of Americans are organizing a volunteer brigade."

J.D. stared unbelievingly at his son. "A volunteer brigade?"

"It's a war with international implications, Dad. It's not just the Loyalists and the army. It's Facism against Communism."

J.D. opened his mouth to make an angry retort and then checked himself. "Junior," he said patiently. "That's not your concern, surely."

"It's the concern of every member of the Party."

J.D. sighed. "I was hoping you'd outgrown all that by now."

"It's not the measles, Dad. It's – it's my *belief.*"

"Junior," J.D. said levelly. "You are nineteen years old. To get a passport you need my permission. Get Spain out of your head, because you're not going."

They rode the rest of the way in strained silence.

*

245

"Spain!" Gina exclaimed.

"He wants to join some wild volunteer brigade," J.D. said. They were alone in their bedroom the night that J.D. and Junior had returned from Princeton.

"Oh, no!"

"He wants to go fight someone else's fight, and in the process probably get his head blown off."

"What did you say?"

"I forbade him to go, of course."

"That's why he was so quiet."

"Gina, this Communism thing has gone too far when it makes Junior want to throw his life away in some crackpot war."

"I don't want him to go any more than you do, Jess. But it is not a crackpot war. It has international implications –"

"Now I know where Junior got that claptrap!"

"You think I want him to go?"

"You don't deny you've talked to him about it, do you?"

"We may have discussed it, but I never imagined –"

"That's the trouble with you fuzzy-headed idealists. You never imagine the consequence of all that talk! Well, let me tell you – you'd better start being responsible for what you say!"

"I won't listen to this! You are being your usual bull-headed, self-righteous self!" Gina stormed from the room.

At the board meeting in November one of the members brought up the matter of the time J.D. spent visiting universities. "These – ah – people you speak to, J.D.," the board member, a wizened little monkey of a man who was one of Wall Street's richest, said. "What possible value could they have to us that would recompense the valuable time of our chief executive?"

J.D. gazed down the table at the little man. "Do you realize when the tabulator was invented?"

"Some years ago, I believe."

"In 1890. That's forty-six years ago. And since that time we've made no advance in the technology."

"Oh, see here, J.D.," the little man retorted, "you've told us yourself that the Model Z is the most advanced tabulator ever."

"That's my point. The Model Z *is* the most advanced tabulator, but it's still a tabulator."

"So, we've done very well with it, and all those that preceded it."

246

"That we have. But let me tell you, gentlemen, that unless we guard against smugly sitting back on our past profits, our future profits are in danger."

"How do we avoid that, J.D.?" David Stern asked.

"By asking ourselves what business we're in."

The little man smiled superciliously. "*I* thought we were in the data-processing business all this time. Are you telling me I've been wrong?"

"No. But data processing is a narrow way of looking at it. The business we're in is that of data *transformation*. I know that might seem to be splitting hairs, but data processing is associated with sorters, key punches and tabulators. We need to look beyond that technology. I've recently talked to John von Neumann at Princeton. He thinks the next great step in the technology will occur when we create the ability to store instructions."

"Don't we do that now?" David Stern asked. "With the plug-boards?"

"Not in the way he means. Those instructions in a plug-board are wired in and can't be changed for the duration of the job. If we could change an instruction to an entirely new one during the course of a job, then think of the power we would have!"

"I can't see what difference it would make," the little man said. "Sounds like just the thing some university professor would dream up."

"Whether you can see the significance or not is hardly the point," J.D. replied. "It is the direction of the future. And I don't intend to see Marvel Scientific left in the dust of advancing technology. If you gentlemen don't like the way I'm doing it, you're always free to find yourselves another president."

"Now, J.D.," David Stern said. "No one is suggesting anything like that. I for one believe you should do what you think is best. If the work von Neumann and Dr. Bush are doing is, in your opinion, that important, then I think you should pursue it and I'd like a unanimous vote from the board to that effect."

24

The Blonde Doctor

WITHOUT HIS KNOWING exactly how it happened, Gina became Junior's friend. He had thought he could never be in her presence without experiencing anew the shame he'd felt the first time she'd seen him. But gradually her good cheer, and kind, intelligent interest wore away the shame, which was replaced by love for Gina.

She spoke to him like an equal. She shared her beliefs and fears. Eventually he did the same with her. She was the most beautiful woman he'd ever known, but he felt no sexual stirrings toward her, only the kind of love that he guessed a brother might have for an older sister.

He'd never thought much about politics because, until then, his interests had been self-centered. But Gina made him aware that there were other people in the world, some of whom were deprived of even the means to provide themselves with the needs necessary to human existence. It was a romantic cause for a young boy, the cause of the downtrodden masses.

She also made him see his father in a new way. For the first time he felt a stirring of interest in his father's business. Gina made it sound exciting and glamorous, on the leading edge of science and technology. Fired by Gina's enthusiasm for the machines she worked with, he began secretly to read books that, a year before, he would've done anything to avoid. He didn't understand all that he read, but gradually some of the dark spaces in his scientific education became illuminated. He haunted the public library. His favorite find was a book entitled *The Machinery of Numbers: A History of Calculating Machines* by a professor at Harvard. In it he discovered that the first adding machine had been invented and built in 1642 by a Frenchman named Blaise Pascal. Then Leibniz invented a machine that could multiply as well as add. But the most fascinating chapter of the book, one that Junior read over and over, dealt with an Englishman named Charles Babbage. In 1822 Babbage completed construction of a machine he called the "Difference Engine." It consisted of a series of gears and levers that would compute algebraic expressions, such as $x^2 + 3x - 6$, to an accuracy of six decimal places. Enough of Junior's algebra class had rubbed off to allow him to be amazed that such a machine existed over a hundred years earlier. Babbage's next creation, the Analytical Engine, accepted its data from punched cards similar to the ones used by his father's machines. The use of punched cards wasn't original with Babbage. A French inventor named Jacquard had devised a loom that operated from punched cards, capable of weaving intricate patterns from the absence or presence of holes it sensed mechanically in the cards. An illustration of a rug so woven was included in the book. The rug's pattern was a portrait of a man, believed to be Jacquard himself, and it was as detailed as a fine painting.

The finest descriptions of his Analytical Engine were not written by Babbage, but by his friend, Ada Augusta, Countess of Lovelace, the only daughter of the poet Byron. She saw great beauty in the machine. She wrote of the Analytical Engine: "We may say most aptly that the Analytical Engine weaves algebraic patterns just as the Jacquard loom weaves flowers and leaves." She went on to write, "This engine surpasses its predecessors, both in the extent of the calculations which it can perform, in the facility, certainty and accuracy with which it can effect them, and in the absence of all necessity for the intervention of human intelligence during the performance of its calculations."

Junior came to understand that nothing like the Analytical Engine had existed before or since Babbage. Tragically for Babbage, it never really existed in his time either, although various attempts were made, under a variety of grants, private and public, to build it. But, as the book's author stated, "sufficient knowledge in the skills of machining parts fine enough to meet the exacting standards of the Analytical Engine did not exist, so that, although the machine was feasible in every way *logically*, it could never be *physically* attained."

He told no one, not even Gina, about his explorations in the library. He knew if he told her, she would tell his father, and he didn't want to bear the responsibilities that his father's undoubted pleasure would bring. He wasn't sure what, if anything, he wanted to do with this interest, but he wanted to be free to choose, even to forget it. It never occurred to him that his father might not know about Babbage and his wonderful engine. Surely his father knew about everything that had to do with his business.

In the fall of 1936, the beginning of his sophomore year at Columbia, Junior signed up for a business course because he needed a non-elective to fill out his schedule. Gina approved. "The better you know the enemy," she said, "the easier he is to defeat."

But he found himself liking the course above all his others. It was taught by an energetic and articulate young professor whose enthusiasm for his subject infected his students. Balance sheets, stock structures, and the Law of Diminishing Returns all assumed a kind of magical aura under his inspired instruction. There was something about the translation of abstract power and wealth into concrete principles and methods that appealed to something very deep in Junior. It was like being in possession of a lever that could move enormous objects. He wondered why he'd not known about this before, why the existence of these principles weren't shouted from headlines and weren't on the lips of everyone. It was as if the wizards of business had sworn each other to secrecy. And here was Junior Marvel, sitting in a class that any sophomore could've taken, learning those secrets. It was a magical event, a kind of gift of the arcane.

By the third week of the class, he had made up his mind – he would be a business major.

Gina surprised him by taking the news gladly.

"I was worried," she confessed. "When your father said you wanted to go to Spain – I never intended that you would risk your life."

"I only said that to get back at him for thinking I didn't have any commitments."

He told J.D. that same night at dinner.

"Why, that's wonderful, Junior!" J.D. exclaimed.

"Another thing," he said. "I'd like to be called Jesse."

In January of 1937 John von Neumann phoned J.D. to tell him about an assistant of his, a young woman who had received her Ph.D. from Radcliffe. Her name was Clarise Duncan.

"She's very bright," von Neumann said. "Dr. Duncan has worked with me for a year. She is current on my thinking . . ."

J.D. rearranged his schedule and went to Princeton the next day. Von Neumann and Dr. Clarise Duncan met him at the station in Princeton.

She was a slight girl of twenty-four. Very large blue eyes were accented by horn-rimmed glasses. She had wheat-colored hair, very fine white skin, and a serious mien. She was the daughter of a Kansas farmer and had exhibited at an early age a prodigy's talent in mathematics. Her father had been a progressive man who worshipped his daughter, and he had made sure her talents were nurtured. It was he who had read an article in *Barron's* about the work of John von Neumann and had suggested she apply to him for an assistantship after she had taken her Ph.D. at Radcliffe.

They talked in von Neumann's office at the Institute for Advanced Study. Clarise Duncan's academic background was impressive. She'd done her dissertation on the application of mathematical analysis to the solution of some arcane problem in fluid dynamics that J.D. didn't pretend to understand.

Later, von Neumann and J.D. talked alone.

"Clarise is ambitious," von Neumann said.

"What does she want?"

"To be president of your company – or any large company."

"Nothing wrong with that. I prefer ambitious people."

"Just so. I wanted to make sure you understood."

"How well would she do in research?"

"I predict very well. She is extremely bright. She understands the ideas I've had about large calculating machines and has contributed some original ideas of her own."

"Johnny, if I took her on, could I expect you to keep in touch with what she's doing?"

"Sort of a consulting arrangement?"

"Exactly."

"Provided it didn't interfere too much with my work here."

"I'd make sure it didn't."

"Then we have a deal."

Ansell Farnsworth was eighty-one years old and for some time had been head of Marvel Scientific's research department in name only. Technology in data processing had advanced and passed him by. But J.D. kept him on, letting him putter away at his farm-cum-lab in De Kalb, as a reward for all the contributions he'd made early in the history of the company, and because J.D. couldn't bear to let anyone go, even though in Farnsworth's case it would be to retirement.

The main research work of the company was performed at the corporate headquarters on Madison Avenue. The corporate staff had grown so that they now occupied all thirty floors of the building that had, when they'd started, satisfied their needs with half the fifth floor.

The research lab occupied the twentieth and twenty-first floors. The twenty-first was given over to offices and the twentieth to the lab – a small machine shop, an area for the assembly of experimental equipment, an electrical testing shop. (It was in the assembly lab that Gina worked.)

The head of this activity, with the title of Assistant to the Director of Research, was a mechanical engineer named Leonard Franks. Franks was the real head of research at Marvel Scientific.

For some time J.D. had been dissatisfied with Franks' work. Not that the man didn't work hard; he was the first at the lab, the last to leave. And he was fiercely loyal. The problem was that he was limited in education and intelligence. J.D. had many talks with him about the things he'd find out from Bush and von Neumann, and gave him technical papers written by the two, only to discover that Franks hadn't the least notion what to do with the information. He simply didn't understand it.

Clarise Duncan arrived at the corporate offices for her first day dressed in a tweed suit without jewelry, a pair of sensible-looking oxfords, and very little make-up.

The first project that J.D. gave her was a survey of the advanced work in computational machinery. Clarise traveled to MIT to speak to Bush. Then she went to Harvard where, it was reported, a young professor had some revolutionary ideas in the field. And she checked in with von Neumann frequently.

When she was finished she presented her findings to J.D. and Franks in J.D.'s office.

"This Ph.D. candidate at Pennsylvania?" J.D. said.

"Howard Aiken," Clarise replied.

"His idea is that all machines are alike?"

"Not quite. He's been working on a machine that will solve non-linear ordinary differential equations. These can be done only by means of numerical approximations, and the calculations required are very lengthy. In the course of thinking about his own machine, he looked at Dr. Bush's differential analyzer, as well as other machines. Aiken began to think that all these machines have basic things in common. This led him to think that a single machine might be constructed to solve all these problems, as well as many others. He's only at the thinking stage, but I discussed his ideas with Dr. von Neumann, and he was excited by them."

252

"Did Johnny think we could profitably pursue that line?"

"Yes, he did."

"And that's what you'd like, Dr. Duncan?"

"Very much."

At that moment the Universal Machine Project at Marvel Scientific was born.

Franks began taking up a lot of J.D.'s time with complaints about Clarise. J.D. grew impatient at his whining. Most of his complaints were petty: Dr. Duncan didn't follow department policy in requisitioning supplies; she worked odd hours, arriving at the lab late and staying late (Franks claimed this was bad for morale); and on and on until J.D. would find his mind wandering to other, more pressing matters.

It was Gina who came up with a possible solution. He'd told her about the Franks–Duncan situation and all the trouble it was causing him, and she said, "Why not have them to dinner? Perhaps if they got to know each other in a more relaxed setting . . ."

J.D. nearly didn't recognize Clarise when she arrived. He'd only seen her in masculine-cut suits and lab smocks, but now she wore a white off-the-shoulder gown, gold hoop earrings, a pearl necklace at her throat and golden strap sandals on her well-shaped feet. Her hair had been brushed to a golden shimmer and then piled high on her head.

Franks arrived shortly after Clarise, with Mrs. Franks, a small, dark woman with a quick wit and a friendly disposition. J.D. liked her immediately, and wished that her husband had some of his wife's saving humor.

The dinner party didn't work out the way Gina and J.D. had hoped. Franks maintained a frosty politeness to Clarise throughout, and Jesse managed to dominate so much of her time anyway that there was little chance to work on improving the relationship between the two scientists.

Afterwards, when J.D. and Gina were getting ready for bed, Gina said, "Dr. Duncan has made a conquest."

"Adolescent infatuation," J.D. replied grumpily. He was disappointed that the evening hadn't come off the way he'd hoped. "Jesse's puppy-dog behavior ruined the chance to get Clarise and Franks together."

"Don't blame Jesse. He wasn't a part of our scheme."

*

253

The echo of jackboots on the *Strasse* of Germany forced J.D. to close the Berlin office in early 1938. Until then he had largely ignored the politics of Europe – he figured it wasn't his business, or the business of Marvel Scientific. But when his Berlin manager, a man named Abraham Weiner, was arrested, he could no longer maintain his indifference.

Weiner was a competent man who had doubled the business in Germany from the time he'd taken over in 1936. But he was also a Jew. And on Christmas Day of 1937 he was arrested in a massive roundup by the Berlin police, along with over a hundred other Jews, on trumped-up charges of subversion and desecrating a holy holiday.

When he received the cable from Thomas Finch about the Berlin manager's arrest J.D. decided on the spot to go to Germany. He took Jamie Ryan with him. They sailed in early March, arriving in Bremerhaven on March 12, the day Hitler invaded Austria. The city was a turmoil of military activity.

They managed to get a train to Berlin the following morning and arrived to great excitement in the city. Crowds thronged the streets cheering the news of the Austrian *Anschluss*.

A somber Thomas Finch met them at the hotel. "Things are very bad, I'm afraid," he reported. "They've taken Abe's family into custody, too." J.D. had met Weiner's wife and two small daughters on his last visit to Germany two years before.

"What possible excuse could they have for this outrage?" J.D. asked.

"They're Jews," Finch replied. "That's all the excuse they seem to need."

They took a cab to the Gestapo prison, a huge, stone, square edifice built around a central courtyard. Gestapo Oberleutnant Helmut Hoffer was a small, dark man with an unctious air. He spoke excellent English with a slightly British accent.

"Now," he said, the amenities out of the way. "You are here on –" he pulled a file to him and read the label on it, "the Weiner matter?"

"Yes," J.D. replied.

The Oberleutnant folded his hands on the file and smiled. "How may I help you?"

"Herr Weiner is my employee," J.D. began. "He is the manager of our company in Germany. I'd like an explanation."

The officer raised an eyebrow. "Explanation?"

"For this outrage," J.D. said.

"Ah, *outrage*! Let me ask you, Herr Marvel – if I were to come to

America and demand from you an explanation for why your police had in custody one of your own citizens for subverting the constitutional government of your land, how would you answer me?"

"Abe Weiner has never subverted anything."

"You are perhaps better informed than our professional police, whose job it is to investigate such things?"

"About Herr Weiner, apparently so. And your professional police can't seriously expect anyone to believe that two young girls, not even in their teens, are spies."

"No one is talking about spies here. But you must understand that there is a certain class of people in Germany today who would like nothing better than to defeat the purposes of the Third Reich."

"You mean Jews."

Hoffer shrugged. "Subversives come in many packages, Herr Marvel. I must say, though, that I've yet to see one in an Aryan package." He smiled.

"Oberleutnant Hoffer," J.D. said quietly. "I demand to see the commander of this prison."

"Demand?"

"Let me explain my position, Oberleutnant. My company has installed, at your Ministry of Economics, nearly two hundred of our machines. Herr Bremer, the Minister, is a personal friend of mine. I haven't contacted him on this matter since I got here, because it was my belief that there was no reason to cause trouble for the Gestapo authorities who have made this mistake. After all, perhaps it was an honest mistake . . ."

Hoffer rose. "One moment, please," he said. He hurried from the room.

When Hoffer returned he was accompanied by an officer in the uniform of a Gestapo Oberst. He did not introduce himself. "You are Herr Marvel?" he asked J.D. in thickly accented English. J.D. said that he was. The Oberst pointed to the telephone on Hoffer's desk. "Call Minister Bremer, please. Hoffer, give him the number."

The Oberleutnant looked up the number in a small book with a swastika on its cover, and read it off.

The Oberst stared at J.D. "Well, Herr Marvel – what are you waiting for? Perhaps you were – what is the word, Hoffer?"

"Bluffing."

J.D. rose, went to the phone, and dialed the number. When he finally got through the batteries of secretaries and aides to Bremer, he explained the situation.

255

"I can't become involved in a Gestapo matter, Herr Marvel," Bremer said in his bombastic voice. J.D. could imagine him sitting at his huge oiled walnut desk, a bloated pig of a man, with shrewd little eyes.

"Herr Bremer," J.D. said. "You have one hundred and eighty-seven Marvel machines installed in your ministry. Herr Weiner is our manager in Germany. With him incarcerated, I cannot guarantee the reliability of those machines."

"Are you trying to coerce me, Herr Marvel!"

"Of course not. I'm merely trying to protect the interests of a valued customer. Herr Weiner is the constructive force behind our Berlin office. Without him to run it, I'm afraid I'm helpless to assure you the excellent service to which you're accustomed."

"We could get other machines. IBM –"

"Surely you've heard, Herr Bremer – IBM has discontinued operations in Germany?"

"There are other machines in Europe. I won't be intimidated –"

"You're right. I understand the French are developing machines."

"The French!" Bremer spluttered. "We don't do business with the French!"

Two hours later J.D., Jamie and Finch greeted the Weiner family at an exit from the prison.

J.D. took them to his hotel. "We have to get you out of Germany," he told Weiner.

"It's no use," Weiner replied. He took his passport from his belongings and showed it to J.D. Stamped across the first page in red ink was "JUDE."

"We'll find a way," J.D. said. "Give us a little time."

Weiner shook his head sadly. "My parents, my wife's parents, are in Germany. We can't leave them. But perhaps you could take the girls. I have a cousin in Chicago –"

It turned out to be easier than any of them had thought. Weiner had had time to plan it while he was in prison. An American technician on loan to the Berlin office from the Marvel lab in New York had brought his family, including two daughters near the ages of Weiner's. He readily donated their passports. In the turmoil at Bremerhaven where hundreds of Jewish families were trying to get exit visas the customs officials barely glanced at the passports of two little American girls accompanied by two American men. After J.D., Jamie and the girls were safely in New York the American technician reported his

256

daughters' passports stolen to the American embassy in Berlin and was issued new ones.

In New York J.D. turned the problem of the girls over to David Stern, who called a highly placed friend of his in the State Department who, in turn, arranged to have the Weiner girls officially admitted to the United States under the immigration quota. J.D. and Gina saw the girls off on a train to Chicago where they were joyfully met by Weiner's cousin and his family.

The Weiners never saw their daughters again. In 1942 they were put in a cattle car and sent to Auschwitz. They didn't come back. J.D. returned from Germany with the conviction that there would be war in Europe. He instructed Finch to begin to pull Marvel Scientific out of the Continent, and to do what he could for the employees and their families in helping them find new jobs or to relocate to America, if that could be arranged. He was especially concerned, after the Weiner example, about Jewish employees in Germany. But there was little he or anyone could do. They managed to get a few Jewish families out intact, through a combination of intrigue, deception and out-and-out coercion, and they got out even more children of Jewish employees, but, in the end, J.D. felt that the effect of their efforts, compared to the need, had been puny indeed.

Clarise Duncan greeted him upon his return with the news that Howard Aiken, at the University of Pennsylvania, had accepted a grant from IBM to work on his Universal Machine.

"Damn!" J.D. exclaimed. "Watson beat us. Why didn't we offer him a grant?" It turned out that Clarise had suggested that very thing to Aiken, but by that time he was already committed to IBM.

One day, after a meeting of several of the top lab people with J.D., Clarise lingered in J.D.'s office.

"Your son has been asking me out," she said.

"What did you say?"

"Oh, he's far too young for me. Besides, I was sure you would object."

"Why would I object?"

"I just thought –"

"Dr. Duncan, your personal life is your own. As long as it doesn't interfere with your work, or bring discredit to the company."

In July of 1938 Gina had a twenty-first birthday party for Jesse. The only guest Jesse requested was Clarise Duncan. Gina asked if he minded if she invited a few old family friends. After he found out Clarise was coming, who else was there hardly mattered to him.

The Sterns, Walter and Wanda, and Jamie Ryan and a young woman he'd recently been seeing, comprised the rest of the guests. J.D. secretly observed Jesse and Clarise during dinner. The boy was truly smitten. He couldn't stop gazing at Clarise with an expression that J.D. thought resembled that of a Cocker Spaniel with digestion problems.

Jesse and Clarise had been dating for three months, and it was apparent to J.D. that she viewed the whole thing with the slightly amused condescension of an older, sophisticated woman for the flattering attentions of a callow boy.

The Universal Machine Project threw J.D. and Clarise together more and more as J.D.'s initial enthusiasm for it grew. Aiken's thesis was that the specialized computational devices built by him, Bush, and others, all had fundamental principles in common that, if defined and incorporated in a general machine, would allow for the solution of all those problems on the one machine. These problems were scientific and rather abstract in nature. J.D. was interested in a machine that could solve all such problems, but what interested him more was the idea of a machine that could be generalized even further – one that could do an accounting problem as well as it might calculate a differential equation. Neither he nor Clarise were sure that such a machine was possible, but they proceeded with the research as if it were. What J.D. imagined when he thought of their objective was a kind of super tabulator.

In the spring of 1939, after months of exhausting work, Clarise made the first breakthrough. J.D., after hearing a report from Clarise at a meeting in the boardroom attended by Jamie Ryan and the top executives of the lab, was so impressed and excited that he felt the occasion called for a celebration and sent his secretary out for champagne. It was after hours, and J.D. did not feel that he was breaking the company policy that forbade employees to drink during business hours.

Later, J.D. and Clarise were left alone in the boardroom, in animated conversation over her discovery. At one point, J.D. went to his office to retrieve a journal in which he'd read an article he thought pertained. He was light-headed from wine and the excitement of the afternoon. When he returned he found the lights out in the boardroom and for a moment thought that Clarise had gone home. As his eyes adjusted he made out a white form leaning against the board table. His breath caught in his throat. Clarise stood before him, leaning back on the table on her hands, her breasts thrust up, and, with the exception of the brown, sensible oxfords she favored when at work, she was completely naked.

25

The Advance of Clarise Duncan

THE BREAKTHROUGH that Clarise made originated from an idea von Neumann had suggested. The machines of Bush, Aiken and others, he pointed out, were *analog* machines; that is, numerical quantities were represented analogously through the movement of machine parts – the angle of rotation of gears, for example – while the functions the machines performed were carried out through the motion of other machines' parts – the movement of levers to rotate the gears, and so on. Von Neumann suggested that there was no essential difference between the functions and the numbers, as represented by the machines. In other words, he said, they were information. Wouldn't it be wonderful, he asked, if a machine could be devised that treated both the functions and the numerical quantities as data?

The potential of such a machine was enormous. The functions could be modified just like data, as the machine ran, so that different functions could be performed independently of those originally set up according to the numerical results and the nature of the data as they were encountered.

The Bush and Aiken machines did this in a very limited way. There were different paths of functions that the machine could take, depending upon the numerical results. But these paths had to be pre-determined before the machine started.

The breakthrough that Clarise made was in recognizing that a new type of machine was needed to perform these wonders. Whereas the Bush, Aiken *et al.* machines were analog, what was needed was a machine that was digital – that is, a machine that represented numerical quantities *directly*, rather than through the movement of machine parts.

She went back to von Neumann with this idea and he suggested that such a machine could operate with a binary number system. This would simplify the construction of the machine because each digit could be represented by an on or off condition. This, in turn, suggested an electrical circuit, where the absence or presence of current could represent either a zero or a one, the two digits of the binary number system.

This was as far as Clarise had got when she gave her report. But it was far enough for J.D. to see that such a machine would be universal. There would be no reason to limit it to scientific calculations – it could as easily compute a payroll as an integral equation. He authorized the immediate funding of a project to attempt to build a prototype of such a machine.

In his astonishment the report he was carrying slipped unnoticed from J.D.'s fingers. Clarise raised her arms to him. Her firm young breasts shimmered in the moonlight.

"What –" he cleared his throat. "What the hell are you doing?"

"J.D.," she breathed. "Take me –"

J.D. turned his back on her. "Get your clothes on!"

"But, I want you!"

"Well, you can't have me! Put your clothes on."

He heard the rustle of cloth. "I didn't figure you for a prude –"

"Are you dressed?"

"Enough."

He turned. "Listen to me, Dr. Clarise Duncan. You are very important to me, and to this company. I'm going to forget this happened. Mark it down to the excitement and the champagne. I want that prototype!"

"But I don't understand. Why couldn't we have both? We're so much alike –"

"*We can't have both!*" J.D. roared. "Get that through your head!"

She nodded. "Okay. I'll take your word for it."

"Listen," J.D. said. "I want that prototype. And I love my wife. I won't jeopardize either the project or my marriage."

"Oh," she said in a small voice. "I should have known."

J.D. turned and left the room.

In September Germany invaded Poland, and Britain and France declared war. Russia and Germany signed a non-aggression pact. Gina was shaken, but still faithful to the cause. But it was the headlines in the *New York Times* of September 18 that finally broke her

261

faith. They reported that the day before Russia had invaded Poland from the east, and von Ribbentrop and Molotov had met and agreed to divide Poland between their two motherlands.

"How could they!" Gina raged. "The hypocritical *bastards*!" Gina, overnight, became avidly anti-Soviet.

"I still believe in Communism, as an ideal," she told J.D. "Perhaps someday it will be put into practice somewhere where it will work. Stalin is *not* practicing it. Instead of a dictatorship of the proletariat, he has instituted the dictatorship of Joseph Stalin."

Jesse graduated from Columbia in June of 1939, with a bachelor's degree in Business Studies. His last two years had been outstanding and he was offered a fellowship at Columbia to attend graduate school.

By October Jesse still hadn't enrolled in graduate school, and J.D. asked to see him. Jesse came by his office.

"I thought it might be good to talk about your future," J.D. said. "If you'd like."

"I don't mind," Jesse replied mildly.

"Do you think you'll be going to graduate school?"

"Actually, Dad, I was thinking of the RCAF."

J.D. tried to remember what the RCAF was. Finally, he got it. "You mean the Canadian Air Force."

"That's the one."

"Why would you do that?"

"I know you're busy, Dad," Jesse said with a gentle smile, "but surely you've heard there's a war on."

"But it's not *our* war."

"You mean because we aren't being attacked. That will come soon enough, you'll see."

"Why not wait until it does? I mean, I'm all for patriotism, Jesse, but *this* is your country."

Jesse gave his father a pitying look. "This isn't the nineteenth century. What happens in Europe affects us. And I want to do my part."

"I know it sounds glamorous, flying off into the wild blue yonder, and all that, but when the bullets start I'm sure the glamor wears a bit thin."

Jesse gave him a strange look. "You're not an America Firster, are you?"

"Good God, no! You should know me better than that. I support

262

F.D.R. right down the line. We have to be prepared, and we have to help our friends."

"The RCAF is forming an American squadron. If I pass the physical, and I don't see why I shouldn't, I'll begin training next month at Downsview Aerodrome outside Toronto."

"You mean you've already looked into this?"

"I've done more than that, Dad – I've signed up."

"Good Lord, Jesse! I wish you'd talked to me first."

"So you could've talked me out of it?"

"Frankly, yes. This sounds dangerous as hell. When you became interested in business, I must admit that I had hoped that you might want to join Marvel Scientific at some point. I'm putting it clumsily, Jesse – but you're the only son I've got."

"I'll take care of myself. The training is first-rate. We'll have new Spitfires."

"If they give you new planes they must be intending to use you."

"We aren't being trained to fly the mail, Dad."

There was a silence while J.D. stared morosely at the October sun streaming through a window.

Finally, Jesse said, "I've asked Clarise to wait for me."

"And?"

"She said she would."

"Well," J.D. managed, clearing his throat. "Congratulations."

"We aren't engaged," Jesse said. "Nothing that formal. With the uncertainties involved – well, I thought it better if we simply had an understanding."

Clarise and Jesse had been seeing each other whenever Clarise could spare the time from the Universal Machine Project, which wasn't often. She was working long hours with a staff of four, attempting to find the right technology for creating a digital-machine prototype. They had tested and discarded resisters as being too slow. For awhile they thought they had a solution in iron rods that could be magnetized directionally – fluxed first clockwise around their diameters, and then counter-clockwise for a binary representation – but they finally had to abandon the idea because they couldn't find a way to make the rods maintain their charges over a long enough time to serve the purpose.

J.D. kept close track of the project. The business was better than ever. Revenues in 1938 had been $38 million with a profit of $9 million. That year the half of J.D.'s earnings that he'd given to the

263

Elvira Dinsmore Foundation had been three-quarters of a million dollars.

Gina still worked at the lab in the tabulator-assembly department, but she'd cut her hours back to half time because the Foundation required more and more work. She'd established scholarships for children of the indigent at Yale, Columbia, Princeton, Harvard, Vassar and MIT. She'd also established a special preparatory school in an old warehouse in the Bowery where those candidates for scholarships who needed it were given special tutoring to bring their skills up to the admission standards of the various universities. The prep school included a boys' and a girls' dorm, a new kitchen and dining-room. In the fall of 1939 the prep school had twelve students, and Gina had plans to double that in 1940.

Jesse was sworn into the Royal Canadian Air Force on November 6, 1939. The ceremony took place at the Canadian Embassy in New York and the oath was administered by the chargé d'affaires himself. Clarise, J.D. and Gina attended. Two other New York men were sworn in with Jesse. The next morning they were all flown to Downsview Aerodrome to begin training.

Jesse spent his last evening after the swearing-in with Clarise. J.D. knew it was unreasonable of him, but he couldn't help resenting it. He had a feeling bordering on superstition that if he didn't spend every moment with Jesse up until he left that he would never see him again. He did see him off at North Beach airport which had opened just that fall.

That night Gina took a depressed J.D. out to dinner.

"He'll be fine," she told J.D. over cocktails. "Jesse is a bright young man."

"Brains may not be enough," J.D. said. "He needs a good dose of luck to go along with it. What I can't understand is how in the world they'll ever teach him to fly an airplane."

Gina laughed. Jesse was a notoriously poor driver, distracted, driving too fast, charging through yellow lights. As a consequence he'd had a number of minor scrapes in the 1936 Olds convertible his father had bought him on his nineteenth birthday.

"Perhaps," she said, "an airplane is just what he needs. He can go fast enough to suit even him, and there aren't as many things to run into up there."

Later, over coffee and brandy, J.D. commented, "I haven't heard much from Jesse about Communism in the past couple of years."

"He was a *business* major, remember?"

"I know, I know. But he could've been finding out about the enemy. In fact, I think you or he said something like that about his studies, once."

"He was never as committed as I was."

"Then why –?"

"To have something of his own. Something that wasn't yours."

J.D. stared at his wife. "Are you certain?"

"He never said as much. But I'm as certain as I can be."

"Oh, God," J.D. groaned. "It just occurred to me that maybe he's doing this RCAF business for the same reason."

"No. He really believes in what he's doing. Oh, he may have romantic notions about it, but he believes."

J.D. flew to Toronto in December to attend Jesse's graduation from flight training. He'd wanted Gina to come along, but she said, "You be with your son. I'll see him later." Jesse had a week's leave and was going to fly home with his father for the Christmas holiday.

An RCAF car took J.D. out to the aerodrome, a collection of weather-worn buildings surrounding a tarmac airstrip.

It was a blustering day and the wind was charged with particles of snow. The ceremony was held on the tarmac in front of a rank of Spitfires. Each new pilot received his wings from the base commandant. J.D. thought Jesse looked very dashing in his blue-grey dress uniform.

After the ceremony the pilots gathered in a knot to congratulate each other and then drifted across the field to find their relatives in the small crowd of spectators.

Jesse gripped his father's hand in a manly handshake. His gaze seemed somehow more direct, more assured, than it had been eight weeks before. "Would you like to see my plane, Dad?"

"I sure would."

It was a sleek-looking machine, its spindly landing gear pointing its nose at the steel-grey sky. It was painted in grey and blue camouflage colors. On the fuselage under the cockpit were lettered the words: "Sgt. J.D. Marvel."

"Sergeant?" J.D. queried.

Jesse smiled. "The Canadians and British take rank very seriously; they don't throw around officer's pips indiscriminately. Don't worry, Dad, I didn't do poorly. Every one of us was made sergeant when we finished training."

"Well," J.D. said, "it's a beautiful machine."

"Want to sit in the cockpit?"

"Of course!"

Jesse stood on the wing and pointed out the instruments and controls over J.D.'s shoulder. "That throttle controls a thousand-horsepower Rolls-Royce engine. It's the best aircraft engine in the world," Jesse announced proudly. "In fact, this is the best fighter plane in the world."

"How fast will it go?"

"I'm afraid that's classified," Jesse said, and then winked. "Let's just say it will top four hundred."

J.D. whistled. "Gina predicted that these planes would go fast enough even for you."

On the plane to New York, Jesse said, "You must be working Clarise awfully hard."

"She works herself hard."

"I asked her up to see me get my wings, but she said she had too much to do." He said it casually, but J.D. could sense the hurt.

"She wanted to get caught up so she could spend more time with you in New York."

"She said that?" Jesse brightened visibly.

"Yes," J.D. lied.

That Christmas was a period of foreboding for J.D. Jesse was a living reminder of the turmoil in the world that seemed to be creeping like a noxious gas across the Atlantic toward the United States. Not that Jesse was about that much. He spent every moment he could with Clarise.

J.D. and Gina gave a party at the penthouse on Christmas Eve. Walter, Wanda, the Sterns, Jamie Ryan and Jesse and Clarise were there. David Stern was fascinated by Jesse's experiences in Canada. For years Stern had followed aviation and had invested his clients in some fledgling companies, like Pan American, which just that year had inaugurated a transatlantic flight. J.D. was surprised at how much technical detail Stern knew about flying.

"You trained in Spitfires?" he asked Jesse. "Isn't that unusual? I thought most of it was being done in older planes."

"Our first four weeks were in Stearman trainers, that's true. But the RAF sent us Spitfires for the last four. They want us combat-ready when we get over there."

"Combat-ready," Stern echoed. "After eight weeks of training?"

Jesse laughed, and J.D. was struck by his off-handed, careless attitude about what could be a question of his life or death.

"Well," Jesse conceded. "As ready as we could be."

"But the German pilots have hundreds, even thousands of hours of combat experience," Stern said.

J.D. was startled. "How could that be?"

"Spain," Jesse said. "The Luftwaffe cut its teeth there. What David says is true – they've had a lot of combat experience."

In January of 1940, Jesse's squadron was sent to England. J.D. thought it ironic that they went on a ship with their planes lashed to a cargo deck. On February 12 Clarise asked to see J.D. He assumed it was about the project.

"I'm pregnant," she said.

"Are you sure?"

She laughed. "Sometimes you are so naive," she replied, which was the first personal thing she'd said to him since that spring, "Of course I'm sure."

"Ah – I assume –"

"It's Jesse."

"Well," J.D. said. "That could be good news."

"Not for me it isn't. I need your help."

"Of course." J.D.'s mind raced ahead. They would have to somehow arrange a wedding. He wondered if Jesse could get emergency leave. Or perhaps Clarise could go to England – he almost missed what she was saying. "A doctor?" he repeated.

"I don't want some quack who will endanger my life."

"Good God, Clarise, you can't be serious."

"Why not?"

"You're asking me to participate in the killing of my grandchild?"

"It's nothing right now. Barely seven weeks, a lump of pink flesh with no features you'd call human. Think of it as a growth, like a tumor."

"Don't!" J.D. said.

"You won't help me?"

"I didn't say that. Will you give me some time to think?"

"All right. But don't take long. The longer I wait, the greater the danger."

The following day J.D. took Clarise to lunch.

267

"You've found a doctor?" she asked.

"Listen to me for a moment, won't you, Clarise? Indulge me just for a moment."

She eyed him suspiciously. "All right."

"I'll be fifty this year. I'd hoped that Jesse would want to come into Marvel Scientific when he graduated. But now – even assuming he comes out of this thing all right – I don't know that he will. I don't have much family, Clarise. I didn't have brothers or sisters, so I don't have nieces and nephews. My parents are dead. I'm too old to have any more children. I'm physically capable, I imagine, but too old, nevertheless, to be a new father. I'm not trying to elicit your sympathy. I'm simply trying to make you understand that that child you're carrying is important to me."

"Fetus," she replied.

"What?"

"It's not a child. It's a fetus."

"Good God, Clarise! How can you be so cold. I mean, it's yours –"

"That's right," she said in a harsh whisper. "It *is* mine. I'm glad you finally remembered."

J.D. massaged his forehead wearily. "Look. I'd see to it that things were easy. You and Jesse could be married right away. If he can't come here, you could go to England. You'd have a good place to live, one large enough for you and the child. I can promise you you'd have help. A maid, a nurse – whatever you wanted."

"Is the project that unimportant to you, J.D.?"

"The project!"

"It will die without me."

"We're talking about the life of my grandchild!"

"I can see you're serious. Let me tell you a few things about myself. I will not give up my career for a child. That project is going to succeed, despite the best efforts of Leonard Franks to undermine it. Why you haven't got rid of that incompetent jerk a long time ago – but that's another subject. I am not going to turn myself from a princess into Cinderella."

"There has to be *some* way, Clarise."

"There is. I thought about this for a long time last night. I'll have the child –"

"Clarise!"

"Before you order champagne, you'd better hear the conditions."

"Conditions?"

"Franks has to go. The lab is split between the two of us, and just

268

isn't operating efficiently. I want to be in charge of research."

"You know Ansell Farnsworth is Director of Research."

"That's why I should be Vice-President of Research and Development. Then Farnsworth can keep his title. That's all the value he is to us anyway – just a title."

He stared at her in silence for a long moment. Finally, he said, "Johnny told me you were ambitious. I didn't fully understand what he meant until just this moment."

"I'm more than ambitious," she said fiercely. "I also produce."

"Yes, you do. If I go along with all you've proposed –?"

"I'll have the baby. But I want to work as long as I can, and I want to come back to work as soon as I can. I figure not more than three months."

"You'd marry Jesse?"

"Oh, sure. We can't have our vice-presidents having children out of wedlock."

"And if I don't go along?"

She made a jabbing motion toward her stomach with her thumb. "I'll find a doctor."

"All right. You'll have it your way."

"You'll make the announcement this afternoon?"

"That doesn't give me enough time. What do you think I'm going to do about Franks?"

"I suggest making him some kind of adviser emeritus, if you can't bring yourself to fire him. Give him an office and a secretary and some papers to shuffle."

"The board must approve the appointment of corporate officers."

She smiled, "J.D., you can do anything with that board you want to, and you know it, everybody knows it. What are you stalling about?"

He sighed. "All right. I'll do it."

"Don't worry, J.D. I can handle the job."

"I'm not worried about that."

"What are you worried about?"

"What are you, Clarise – twenty-six?"

"That's right."

"What I'm worried about is what it will take to satisfy you."

Clarise laughed. "Now you can order that champagne, J.D."

Clarise flew to England a week later. But first J.D. sent her to his personal doctor who confirmed that she was pregnant. Clarise and

269

Jesse were married on February 23 at a small chapel on the base where his squadron was stationed. She returned to New York on March 1 and immediately assumed her new duties.

26

Birth and Death

ON AUGUST 8, 1940, the German Luftwaffe launched Operation Sea Lion and the Battle of Britain began. News of Jesse was hard to come by. His infrequent letters to his father and Gina gave no information about what he was doing, but J.D. could deduce from news accounts that he must have been in the thick of the battle in the skies over Britain. On August 15 Spitfire squadrons shot down 180 German planes, taking heavy casualties themselves. On August 23 the Luftwaffe began the Blitz, pounding London night after night with 1000 lb bombs, just three days after Churchill had made his "Never . . . was so much owed by so many to so few" speech, praising the Spitfire pilots for their stalwart defense of Britain.

On the evening of August 22, Clarise was delivered of a 6lb 7oz healthy baby girl. Gina and J.D. had taken Clarise to the hospital that morning – for the past week she'd been staying with them. She'd taken leave from her job a month before, and then only reluctantly after the doctor had warned her that she was endangering the life of the child, and J.D. had reminded her that she was Vice-President of Research and Development because of the child.

When she was released from the hospital after eight days, Gina collected Clarise and brought her and the baby back to the penthouse, where the guest room had been prepared for them.

J.D. was shocked to find that the child had yet to be named. Clarise seemed indifferent to the question – she said she'd written to Jesse, asking what he wanted to name his daughter.

Clarise was an efficient mother, if nothing else. She cared for her daughter's needs scrupulously, but J.D. wished she'd show some pleasure in the infant.

271

Jesse wrote an ecstatic letter to Clarise, which she let J.D. and Gina read. Jesse said he wanted to name the child Jessica, if that was OK with Clarise. Since Clarise cared not at all, and since J.D. and Gina thought that it was an excellent name, Jessica she became.

Clarise was with them a month. She found a three-bedroom apartment in Greenwich Village and hired a live-in nursemaid. Two days after she'd moved out of the penthouse, she showed up for work at the lab. Within a week she was working as hard and as long as ever. She'd been gone only two and a half months.

Research on the project was hampered by the shortage of electrical materials Clarise needed to build a prototype. She came to J.D. with a solution.

"We should work with the government. That's what Bush and von Neumann are doing."

J.D. agreed, and Clarise flew to Washington for a week and came back with a government contract to develop the prototype Universal Machine. The Army was interested in applying the machine to calculating ballistics equations for large guns. With the contract came priority access to materials.

In November of 1940 more than 4500 Britons were killed in air raids. J.D. expected any moment to hear that Germany had invaded England.

Without Jessica, Christmas that year could've been a grim affair. David Stern had suffered a stroke in November and was confined to bed. He was in his eighties, and J.D. worried that his old friend would never recover. Walter and Wanda had gone to Chicago to spend the holidays with her family, and Jamie Ryan, who had finally married the girl he'd been courting for several years, went with her to her home town in upstate New York.

Jessica was a beautiful four-month-old child. She had her father's dark hair and eyes, her mother's fair, perfect complexion. She was a quiet child. She seldom cried, but then she seldom laughed either.

J.D. loved to hold her and feed her. She would gaze soberly up at him around the bottle with a wondering, wise expression that made J.D. feel as though she could see into his very soul.

That fall Gina had finally quit her job at the lab. Besides running the Foundation, she had taken on a volunteer job. She had organized a coterie of their friends' wives into an aid group who gathered relief

272

materials for Britain. At thirty-five she was, it seemed to J.D., more beautiful than ever. Their sexual life was still exciting, and there had grown up between them over the years a deep understanding and friendship.

In June of 1941, Germany invaded Russia and, that same month, Jesse returned from a mission supporting British Lancaster bombers on a raid over Germany with his plane so badly shot up that he barely made an emergency field at Dover where he was hurt in the crash-landing. His injuries weren't life-threatening, but they were severe enough to take him out of action for three months in the hospital and then a recuperation period, during which he got leave to come home.

Clarise, J.D. and Gina met him when his ship docked. Jessica was at the apartment in Greenwich Village with her nurse.

Jesse hobbled down the gangplank on crutches. His most serious injury had been a compound fracture of his left leg which was now in a walking cast. He gathered Clarise into his arms for a long embrace, and then hugged Gina and shook hands with his father.

Gina had a dinner party for the family at the penthouse the second night Jesse was in New York. After dinner J.D. and Jesse retired to the study. It was the first time since he'd come back that J.D. had had a chance to be alone with his son. He was eager to hear about what Jesse had been doing in the war.

"Not much to tell," Jesse said. "Our squadron has been on escort duty for the past couple of months."

"What about the German fighters? Are they good?"

"Sometimes too good. Especially the Messerschmitt 109s. There are some things over there that would interest you, Dad."

"What sort of things?"

"New technologies being developed. Be right up your alley. If this war lasts long enough, it's going to change a lot of things for ever. It has already changed flying."

"I'd forgo the advances to have it over with tomorrow," J.D. replied.

When Jesse left two weeks later the cast had been removed from his leg and he walked with hardly a trace of a limp. J.D. thought he detected trouble in Jesse and Clarise's relationship. However, it was hard to pin down, because Jesse was so infatuated with his daughter that his happiness as a father tended to gloss over any rift between him and Clarise, if, indeed there was one. By the time her father left, Jessica was just as smitten with him as he was with her. Jesse was the only person who could make Jessica laugh anytime he wanted to.

When the attack on Pearl Habor came J.D. and Gina were in Los Angeles where Marvel Scientific had just opened a new regional office. With the increase in the aircraft- and boat-building industries, Marvel Scientific had expanded to eight branch offices on the West Coast and J.D. thought it time to consolidate them all under a regional manager. Even though the company now had thirty-six branch offices organized under three regions, J.D. still made it a point to be on hand every time a new office opened.

On Saturday night, December 6, J.D. gave a dinner party at the Ambassador Hotel for the employees of the new regional office. On Sunday morning he and Gina, who were staying at the Ambassador, slept late and breakfasted in their room. When they came down to the lobby they found it in a turmoil of excitement, and it was then that they heard of the attack on Pearl Harbor.

The war changed Marvel Scientific. The Universal Machine Project became the Automatic Gun-Sighting Project, and was put under a tight lid of secrecy by the Army.

J.D. joined the advisory board of the Office of Production Management at the invitation of William Knudsen, the Director-General. He spent one week a month in Washington helping to formulate plans to gear United States industry to all-out war production.

In June of 1941, President Roosevelt created the Office of Scientific Research and Development, and made Vannevar Bush its director. Clarise recognized that her project and the things Bush was attempting to do at OSRD were parallel, so she lobbied the War Department to have her project transferred to Bush's office. In January of 1942 this was done, and Clarise began working closely with her former mentor.

In July of 1942 David Stern died. J.D. mourned the loss of his old friend. Without him J.D. knew that he couldn't have developed Marvel Scientific into the company it had become.

The next month Joseph Falk Whittier died at the age of seventy-seven. Madelline gave him an elaborate funeral which J.D. attended, he didn't know quite why. He supposed it was out of appreciation for the start Whittier had given him and out of a kind of nostalgia for his own youthful naiveté which Whittier had had a large role in dispelling.

*

In the summer of 1944 J.D. met John von Neumann at the Aberdeen Proving Grounds, forty miles north of Baltimore. Vannevar Bush and Clarise were working at Aberdeen on their joint contracts to perfect artillery trajectory machines. J.D. was there to check on the progress of the project. The Army was using the Bush analog machine and a hundred girls to do hand calculations, all under the direction of Lt. Herman Goldstine. The results and speed were not satisfactory, and Clarise was working long hours at Aberdeen and back at the Marvel labs in New York, trying to come up with a better machine design. Von Neumann, who was a consultant to a very secret project in Los Alamos, New Mexico, was also consulting at Aberdeen.

J.D. had lunch with von Neumann in the cafeteria at Aberdeen. Because of the pressure of their jobs they hadn't seen each other for months.

"How are you, Johnny?" J.D. asked.

"Okay," von Neumann replied in a distracted manner. He never had been one for small talk. "I want to tell you about something. Do you know Herman Goldstine?"

"The young lieutenant heading the calculations? Brilliant fellow."

"I ran into him at the railroad station the other day. He told me some exciting news. They're developing a new machine at the Moore School at the University of Pennsylvania. It's electronic and they expect it will be a thousand times faster than anything that exists today."

"A thousand times!" J.D. pushed his tray away. Eating suddenly seemed unimportant.

"It uses vacuum tubes instead of electromechanical relays. This allows the use of the binary number system. I know you are working on a universal machine," von Neumann continued. "You should get over to the University of Pennsylvania and see these fellows who are developing this monster. I certainly intend to."

J.D. knew that von Neumann's job at Los Alamos was to find new ways to perform huge calculations, but what those might be used for he had no idea. He only knew that it was so secret von Neumann would say nothing.

Von Neumann told him that the names of the two professors who were developing the new machine were J. Presper Eckert and John Mauchly. Eckert was an electrical engineer and Mauchly a physicist. "Perfect combination of talents for the job," von Neumann added.

*

275

J.D. took Clarise with him to the University of Pennsylvania to talk to Eckert and Mauchly. The Aberdeen Proving Grounds were backing their project. Eckert was a sharp-witted young man of twenty-six, acerbic in speech, impatient with questions. Mauchly, on the other hand, was a rumpled man in his late thirties, who was quiet and had the professorial air of abstraction – his conversation was discursive, but came from a man of much erudition and brilliance.

They called the machine they were developing the Electronic Numerical Integrator and Calculator, shortened to ENIAC. J.D. and Clarise spent a day at their labs, and would've spent longer had it not been apparent that their questions were interfering with the project.

At that time the machine consisted of various electronic assemblies scattered across the lab floors and benches. J.D. couldn't conceive how all the complicated equipment would eventually come together into one machine. On the train back to New York, he voiced his doubts to Clarise.

"Can't do it any other way, J.D.," she replied. "Each unit has to be bench-tested individually, then sub-assemblies put together and tested, and so on, until you lash the whole shebang together."

J.D. sighed. "They've stolen the march on us," he said.

"Not by a long shot," Clarise replied, her eyes sparkling with enthusiasm. "They've given me a lot of good ideas, but they've missed the most essential point."

"Which is?"

"The ENIAC stores data, but it doesn't store instructions."

It was on the visit to the University of Pennsylvania that J.D. and Clarise first began to call the machine they wanted to develop a "computer," using Mauchly and Eckert's name.

Clarise urged that Marvel Scientific begin its own computer project. The Universal Machine Project had been subsumed under the work being done by Bush at Aberdeen, and the Bush machine was electromechanical and too slow for what Clarise had in mind. Besides, it also lacked stored instructions.

In September of 1944 the board of directors rubber-stamped J.D.'s proposal for a computer research effort. He rejected the notion advanced by the more timid members of the board that they seek War Department financing for the project.

"First, we wouldn't own the rights – the Army would. And, second, we couldn't develop the machine according to our own desires."

The last point had bothered J.D. for some time. Most of Marvel

Scientific's customers were commercial users – businesses and government agencies who used the Marvel tabulators and sorters to do accounting and inventory applications. The small percentage of scientific users of Marvel equipment represented an even smaller percentage of revenue. J.D. wanted a computer that would do commercial work. The War Department's needs were for machines that could perform complex mathematical calculations.

J.D. came up with a name for the machine they would try to develop: the Automatic Tabulating and Computing Machine, or ATAC.

Gina and J.D. saw little of each other. J.D. was consumed with trying to keep the company going under wartime restrictions and overseeing the research project in the lab. Gina, aside from her work for the Foundation, which had grown until the preparatory school now had forty-five boarding students, was caught up in war-bond drives. She traveled the country putting together shows and giving speeches to promote the sale of bonds. She had been coaxing J.D. for some time to join one of the tours and finally, in December of 1944, he agreed, primarily because he thought it would be an opportunity for him to spend some time with his wife.

The tour encompassed the South, beginning in Miami and working its way north through Georgia, Alabama and the Carolinas. It was a whirlwind tour, the whole thing scheduled to take ten days. J.D. joined them in Atlanta – he'd been detained by a crisis at one of Marvel Scientific's largest customers.

When J.D. arrived in Atlanta he discovered that he'd just missed Thomas Watson, head of IBM, who'd given a speech that same day from a platform that had been erected on the steps of the courthouse.

"You know," J.D. said to Gina that evening over cocktails in the hotel restaurant where they'd gone for dinner, "Watson and I have never met. We've both been in the same business for over thirty years, and we've never crossed paths."

"He mentioned that," Gina replied. "He said he was beginning to think you were, like the unicorn, a mythical character."

J.D.'s schedule called for him to leave the tour in Raleigh. The night before he was to leave there was an enormous rally at an armaments plant outside the town, at which J.D. spoke. When it was over he and Gina slipped away from the local dignitaries pressing them to join them for a party, by pleading vague appointments.

They bought sandwiches and a bottle of white wine at a deli-catessen and went to a small park that boasted a statue of a mounted Civil War hero. They sat on the grass, ate their sandwiches and drank the wine. The only light was provided by a yellow half moon – Raleigh, as with other cities, was under wartime blackout.

It was chilly, and J.D. put his coat around Gina's shoulders and held her.

"Your speech was great," she said. "I especially liked the part about how those of us who had to stay behind while our boys fought had the good luck to be able to participate in the war effort through bonds."

J.D. gazed up at the monument shimmering whitely in the moon-light. "Do you think we'll erect statues to the heroes of this war? Like old Beauregard what's-his-name there?"

"Beauregard's his *last* name," Gina said. "And I don't care if we erect monuments or not. I just want it over with."

"When it is, let's go away – just you and me."

"For ever?"

"Well, maybe a little less than that. I was thinking of a month."

"At the rate we've seen each other lately, that sounds like for ever."

"Would you like it?"

"You know I would. But where?"

"Not Europe. It will be a mess over there. Somewhere where we can be alone, and have the sun and the wind in our faces."

She laughed. "You're becoming a poet, Jess."

"I've always wanted to learn to sail. Suppose we go somewhere in Mexico, like Baja, and get us a little boat, and some wise old señor to teach us to sail it?"

"I'd love that! When can we go?"

"Let's make a pact right now. How about one month after the war's over?"

"It's a deal! How do we seal it?"

"A handshake won't do it."

She kissed him. "How's that?"

"Better. But I'm afraid it won't stand up in court."

She looked at him with large eyes. "What did you have in mind?"

"We appear to have this park to ourselves."

"It's cold, don't you think?"

"It won't be for long, knowing us."

J.D. had asked Gina not to fly. The war had made commercial

aviation a risky business. Beacons were blacked out, and the skies were dominated by military planes with priority access to the most direct, safest routes. Gina had readily agreed. She wasn't a good flier anyway, becoming greenly airsick the one time J.D. had taken her on a DC-3.

Thus it was that Gina was one of the passengers on a train that stopped ten miles east of Winston-Salem because a faulty signal falsely informed the engineer that another train was headed his way on the same track. He was backing the train to a siding when it was struck from behind by a freight loaded with Jeeps and half-tracks. All forty-three passengers in the last three cars were killed instantly, and eighty-five passengers in the other cars were injured, some fatally. Gina was in the next to last car, a coach, talking to a young soldier who was on his way to his parents' home in Winston-Salem on leave, when she died.

A lethal, sickening fog seemed to descend on J.D.'s mind. It was Jamie Ryan who broke the news to him, and it was Jamie who sent for J.D.'s doctor.

They were seated in the living-room of the penthouse on 5th Avenue. It was late, almost one in the morning, but Jamie had found J.D. up, working in his study. The Marvel Scientific branch manager in Winston-Salem had phoned Jamie with the dreadful news. "The press has got ahold of it," the branch manager told Jamie in his soft southern accent that Jamie, in one corner of his mind, recognized as contrasting so sharply with the words he'd just heard. "I thought maybe you'd want to get to Mr. Marvel before they did."

"You're *sure* –?" Jamie asked.

"Yes, sir. Some of her party were further up in the train. They – they identified her remains."

Jamie failed to thank the man who, after all, was only doing a kindness. But, at that moment, Jamie felt a fury for the branch manager that he was sure, on later reflection, must have showed. Two days later he called him back, apologized, and thanked him properly.

Jamie broke the news as quickly as he could. He didn't believe in stretching out bad news, but when he saw J.D.'s reaction, he wondered if he'd done the right thing.

J.D. turned as pale as a corpse. He said nothing. He stared at Jamie in deathly silence. It was some minutes before Jamie recognized that J.D. was catatonic with shock, and it was then that he summoned the doctor who gave J.D. a sedative and, with Jamie's help, got him to bed.

Jamie phoned his wife and spent the night with J.D. He slept in Jesse's old room, and set the alarm to be up before J.D. awoke.

When J.D. opened his eyes the following morning, thinking that perhaps it all had been a ghastly nightmare, the first thing he saw was Jamie Ryan's concerned face, and he knew it was no dream. To Jamie's relief, he broke down and cried for an hour, while Jamie held his head in his arms, and rocked him like a baby.

For the next ten days no one saw J.D. He sent Jamie home and holed up in the penthouse. He didn't answer the phone or the doorbell.

Walter Hucko was seventy-four years old in 1944. He was still assistant to J.D., still handled the details associated with the office of the President of the corporation: greeting visiting dignitaries, arranging transportation and lodging for J.D., seeing to the various little things that made J.D.'s life run more smoothly. There had been no talk of his retiring. He was in good health, he enjoyed his work, and J.D. wanted him around.

Wanda was fifty-nine. She was Vice-President of Training for Marvel Scientific, as she had been for a number of years. She was an invaluable employee, making the training functions of the company run smoothly and to a standard of excellence surpassed by no other. Both Wanda and Walter were devoted to J.D. and Gina and they took the news of her death with shocked grief.

They heard about it, the morning after it happened, from Jamie Ryan. He came dragging into the office after his night at J.D.'s apartment. After the initial shock had passed, Walter tried to call J.D. For ten days he, Jamie and Wanda alternately tried to call and went by the penthouse, to no avail.

Finally, Wanda said to Walter, "We're going to have to blast him out of there. This can't go on."

"At least we know he hasn't done anything foolish," Walter said. The doorman at J.D.'s apartment building had reported groceries and alcohol being regularly delivered to the penthouse.

Wanda and Walter went to the apartment building and roused the superintendent.

"I don't know," the superintendent said. "I could get in trouble."

"You have a choice," Wanda replied. "Us or the police."

The superintendent capitulated. He took Wanda and Walter up to

280

the penthouse, unlocked the front door with his master key, and then scurried back down the stairs.

The apartment was closed up and stale-smelling. It hadn't been cleaned in days, because J.D. had sent the housekeeper home when she'd tried to get in. They found J.D. in his study in a bathrobe, unshaven and hollow-eyed, a glass of Scotch in one hand and a much-handled letter in the other.

He looked up when Walter and Wanda entered the room. "Hello," he said, as though their presence was entirely natural and expected.

Wanda pulled back the drapes and cranked open the casement window. "You need some air in here, Marvel," she said.

J.D. nodded vaguely. "I've been reading a letter from Gina."

For a moment Walter and Wanda wondered if J.D. were in his right mind. Then, seeing the looks on their faces, he added, "I got it years before she died. You know she only wrote me this one letter. I guess we weren't apart enough to do much letter writing. She was in Chicago visiting her folks. We'd been married two years. I was busy and couldn't go with her. So she wrote me this letter." He held it up.

The look in his eyes was almost more than Wanda could bear. She rushed to him and held his head against her breast. "Oh, Marvel," she sobbed.

Wanda and Walter managed to get J.D. cleaned up, fed and out of the penthouse. The next morning he was back at work acting as if nothing had happened. The only evidence of his grief was hollowed eyes and a body that was gaunter and more angular than ever.

He threw himself into the ATAC project, turned his routine administrative duties over to Jamie Ryan and only emerged from the lab when there was a problem that no one else could solve.

Clarise had an office prepared for him next to hers. She worked closely with him on the project. Had J.D. been aware of anything but the project he would've noticed a change in Clarise's attitude toward him. She was quieter, somehow more watchful, when he was around.

During the ten days in his penthouse, at his more rational moments, of which there weren't many, J.D. had decided that Gina's death was the punishment of a jealous God. He'd made machines his gods, particularly the ATAC, and a more ephemeral, less mechanistic God had lashed out in a jealous passion. Now he went back to his true gods – machines. He became over the next months a priest of the machine. He was celibate. He didn't denounce worldly goods, he ignored them. He hardly ate or slept.

The funeral for Gina had been according to her wishes. Her remains were cremated and then a simple memorial service was held in a samll chapel in Greenwich Village a month after her death. She had written all this out in a will. She stated that she felt that a month's time was long enough to view her and what she'd been with an unmaudlin perspective. Being an atheist, she ordered that the service be non-religious, and that it include only a few close friends and family.

Her father and mother had long since died. Her large brother came from Chicago. Jamie and his wife, Wanda and Walter, and Clarise came.

It worked the way J.D. imagined Gina had hoped it would. The mourners could laugh at some remembered witticism of Gina's. They could recall her good works without breaking down. At least it seemed so. To J.D. it simply made him realize anew the yawning abyss that her death had left in his life, an abyss which he seemed precariously perched upon the edge of.

After the service, which was held on a raw March day, Clarise approached J.D. on the sidewalk outside the chapel, and said, "Can you give me a ride?"

J.D. held the door to his La Salle for her and then started through slow traffic toward the corporate offices.

"I don't know about you," Clarise said, "but I could use a drink."

"It's still working hours."

"To hell with it! Let's take the day off."

It so surprised J.D. to have the ever-working Clarise suggest such a thing that he agreed to it.

"We're near my apartment," she said. "You can see Jessica."

Suddenly, seeing his granddaughter became the most important thing in the world to J.D. He had seen her only once, and then briefly, since Gina was killed.

J.D. held her on his lap while he had his drink. At four and a half she had a very mature vocabulary and few child-like attributes. Even her toys seemed somehow adult. She had a doll, but she displayed it in her room, dressed in finery of crinoline and lace ribbons, rather than played with it. Her favorite playthings were a set of illustrated books of the Grimms' fairy tales and a jigsaw puzzle of large pieces that formed, when properly assembled, a knight on a white charger, and that she could put together in no time in a blur of chubby hands.

Clarise had Jessica's nursemaid take her away much too soon to suit J.D.

"I want to talk to you," Clarise said when they were alone and she had fixed them a second drink. J.D. noticed that she seemed oddly nervous – he was accustomed to her almost glacial self-assurance.

"You and I have a great deal in common," Clarise began. "We are interested in the same things – you might even say obsessed, when it comes to developing the ATAC. You're alone, now. And that's not good for you, J.D. It hasn't been good for me."

"This war won't last much longer, Clarise," J.D. said. "And then your husband will be with you."

"That's what worries me," she replied.

"What do you mean?"

She leaned earnestly toward him. "You know why I married Jesse."

"Well, yes. But I thought that your love would grow from there. Jesse loves you a great deal."

"He doesn't know me. When he does, I think he'll find we have little in common."

"What are you saying?"

"You and I are a perfect match, J.D. We always have been. I'm thirty-one years old. I don't think I'm unattractive. I have lots of energy and drive. We could be a team like the world's seldom seen."

"Sort of an Antony and Cleopatra?"

"Precisely."

He put his glass down and stood. "I won't listen to any more of this, Clarise. You are my son's wife."

"Oh, don't be such a prig! You know you find me desirable."

"That doesn't mean I would ruin my son's happiness for my own selfish reasons."

"You can't be serious. You *don't* want me?" She stared disbelievingly up at him.

"That's right."

"But we have so much in common!"

He shook his head. "Only our interest in ATAC. And believe me, that's not enough."

That same week he received a letter from Jesse. He wrote to say how much he would've liked to have been at the memorial service. In 1942 Jesse and his squadron had been taken into the United States Army Air Corps. Jesse had risen to squadron commander and the rank of Major. In the letter he reported that he had been assigned to a ground job, without giving a reason. He said that he'd been working with the

283

British on things that he knew would interest his father very much. "If you could ever make it over here, I think you'd find it rewarding."

Coming in such close conjunction with his talk with Clarise, Jesse's letter acted as a catalyst on J.D. He took a train down to Washington and talked to people he knew at the War Production Board. The chairman said that, coincidentally, they had a delegation of scientists going to England within two weeks to look into a new scientific method of scheduling production that had been developed by the British. If J.D. would like to go along as their industrial representative, he thought it could be arranged.

J.D. arrived in England in April of 1945, to be greeted by the news that Roosevelt had died at Warm Springs, Georgia, while J.D.'s plane was in flight. He and the group of three scientists had flown over on a C-54 carrying replacement parts for P-51s. They landed at a military field outside of London and caught a military bus from there to Cambridge where the British scientists were located who were working on the methods they'd come to study.

J.D. had managed to get a cable through to Jesse that he was coming. Jesse was attached to SHAEF in London and J.D. got through on the telephone to him from Cambridge after a four-hour wait and made an appointment to see him in London in three days. Jesse said he would see about getting his father a place to stay.

The group working at Cambridge were mostly university dons and their assistants. Churchill had early on in the war put them to work applying the tools of science to the requirements of the war – figuring out the optimum use of manufacturing facilities and the most effective deployment of war resources.

The group at Cambridge called their investigations "Operational Research" and J.D. was surprised to learn that an imitative effort, although smaller, and not as advanced in technique, had begun in the United States, where the discipline's name had been shortened to "Operations Research."

By the time J.D. arrived in London his imagination was fired by his time at Cambridge. He was shocked to see the devastation that had been wrought by the Blitz and by the subsequent V-1 and V-2 rockets. V-2s still fell sporadically.

There were signs of mourning for Roosevelt: black wreaths on the doors of the hotel, long paeans to him in the *The Times*.

Jesse arrived an hour late at the hotel lobby where they'd arranged to meet, apologetic for being held up in a meeting at SHAEF. After

284

they'd greeted each other, they adjourned to the crowded hotel bar. They managed to squeeze into one corner and Jesse ordered two large whiskies. J.D. thought Jesse looked very smart in his uniform. Since the war J.D. had become more familiar with military insignia, and he noticed the silver oak leaves on Jesse's shoulders.

"You're a colonel!" he exclaimed.

"Lieutenant-colonel," Jesse replied.

"Congratulations!"

"At SHAEF a lieutenant-colonel is one grade above janitor."

"You're not flying, then?" J.D. asked.

"Grounded," Jesse said tersely. J.D. noticed a tracery of fine lines in his face that hadn't been there before. "The flight surgeon thought I should step down for awhile."

"What's that all about? Nothing serious . . ."

"A bit of high blood pressure, touch of nerves. That sort of thing."

"Do you miss it?"

"Not really. I've had nearly six years of it. That's plenty. And my health, although not serious, could've caused problems for my squadron. I certainly didn't want that."

"What kind of problems?"

"Oh, errors in judgment. Blackouts at the wrong time. That sort of thing."

"Now you have me worried."

"Don't be." Jesse smiled reassuringly. "I'm almost twenty-eight years old, Dad. And I've been at this business a lot longer than the average time. It's bound to take its toll. But it's nothing I won't get over."

Jesse had managed to find J.D. a small apartment near Knightsbridge. "It belongs to a brigadier-general on the staff. He's on TDY for a few days."

"TDY?"

"Temporary detached duty," Jesse said. "Military talk for spending a few days at the front."

"Do you have to do that?"

Jesse shook his head. "I go along as observer on a '29 now and again. Ike is big on his staff seeing first-hand how their plans are working. Tends to make you pay attention to the job."

"I shouldn't wonder," J.D. said.

They had dinner at a small restaurant located in what appeared to have been at one time a shop.

"This place was bombed out of its old location," Jesse said. "I think you'll like the food."

They had roast beef and Yorkshire pudding. "Since you're in England," Jesse remarked, "you should have some English cooking." The food was excellent. They shared a bottle of burgundy, and had brandy with their coffee afterward. J.D. told him something of what he'd discovered at Cambridge. "They're doing amazing things, Jesse. Many of which can be adapted to peace-time industry."

"What kind of things?"

"They have a way of calculating – they call it an 'algorithm' – the best way to run a factory to get the most effective output, taking into consideration various levels of priorities of need. That particular technique, which is called 'Linear Programming,' could be adapted to a peace-time factory where the objective was maximizing profit."

"And they're doing this on machines?"

"Not really. They have rooms full of clerks, each room with its specialized computations, and each communicating results to another room for further computations."

"Sounds like they're imitating a machine."

"Indeed they are. And we are working on a computer at the lab in New York that I believe could perform such calculations automatically. Can you imagine the potential! Every factory in the country would want one."

"The computer Clarise is working on?"

"Yes."

"How is Clarise? And Jessica?"

"They're fine. I saw both of them not ten days ago. Jessica has the vocabulary of at least a seven-year-old. She loves books, and I swear she can read them, although her nurse claims she's simply memorized the words."

It was strange to J.D. that they'd both waited this long to bring up Clarise and Jessica. J.D. understood his own reluctance – Clarise's shocking proposition was too fresh in his memory. But why Jesse had been reticent he couldn't figure out. Then, Jesse hinted at the reason.

"Clarise isn't a very good correspondent. When she does write, which isn't often, she says little about anything."

"Well, she's a scientist, Jesse."

"How does that explain anything?" Jesse asked hotly.

"Just that they think differently from other people," J.D. said. "She's caught up in her work."

Jesse sighed. "I wonder sometimes if there's any room in her life for me, or, for that matter, Jessica."

Jesse changed the subject, but it wasn't a fortunate choice. "I – I can't tell you how shattered I was about Gina . . ."

"I'd prefer not to talk about it," J.D. said brusquely.

"Of course," Jesse replied.

"Look, son," J.D. said. "I appreciate what Gina meant to you. But she was everything to me, and I just can't talk about it yet."

Jesse changed the subject again. "Let me tell you of the work I wrote to you about . . ."

It was being conducted at a place called Bletchley Park. "I've done some liaison between there and SHAEF. I can't tell you much about it until we get you clearance. They have a machine there that I think will interest you."

Bletchley was fifty miles north of London. The following day Jesse drove his father there in a SHAEF staff car. He'd managed to get J.D. a limited clearance. "Can't tell you what they're using the machine for," he told J.D. "But one of the staff will give us a look at it."

The machine was called COLOSSUS. Bletchley Park was a mansion of Tudor design set in a rolling green lawn. Beside it several huts had been built. It was in one of these huts that the COLOSSUS resided.

The staff member assigned to show them the machine was Alan Turing, a mathematician who had been a Fellow at Cambridge before the war. He was a slight, intense man.

The COLOSSUS was like no other machine J.D. had seen. It was composed of rack after rack of input jacks, electro-mechanical counters, power supplies and thousands of vacuum tubes which Turing referred to as "valves."

Turing had a habit of punctuating the pauses in his speech with "Ah-ah-ah . . ." effectively preventing anyone else from speaking while he organized his next thought. They weren't together for more than five minutes before J.D. knew he was in the presence of genius.

Turing explained how the instructions were wired into the COLOSSUS – "programmed," he called it, the first time J.D. had heard the term. He explained the Boolean functions of the various "valves," how the counters could interact with one another, to spill quantities from one to the other, but never did he let it slip what the machine was used for.

At one point, Turing said, "This is really rather a primitive machine, you know."

J.D. remembered this curious statement when, later, they were having tea at Turing's invitation in the hut that served as the Bletchley Park commissary, and asked him about it.

"Well, you know, it is primitive, compared to what, given the time and the resources, could be built."

"And what would that be?" J.D. asked.

"What I call a 'thinking machine.' One that replicates the human thought processes. For example – ah-ah-ah – looking ahead in the thought process. As I speak, I am organizing what I'll be saying, 'looking ahead' at data, as it were. Now, a machine that had stored instructions, instead of wired, could be made to do that – ah-ah-ah – look ahead to other instructions to determine the logical choice for the present instruction. Then there is backing up, as I'm about to do. That is, picking up an idea that occurs to me based on what I just said, but that, in logical sequence, precedes it. Re-use, as it were, logic I've just used, but in a different form. A machine could back up to former instructions based on some test, such as mini-max criteria – ah-ah-ah – that will minimize processing time while maximizing effectiveness, that sort of thing. This, quite naturally, suggests a tree of logic, a look-ahead tree, for example, that, based on an evaluation function to assign strategic values to the terminal nodes of the tree, could drive the logic along the branches."

J.D. understood little of what Turing said, but he had the sense that it was enormously important. He described the work on the ATAC.

Turing nodded. "Quite conceivable. Sounds rather like some ideas I discussed with an American chap when I was in the States in '42 – von Neumann."

"Why, Johnny's been consulting with us on the ATAC!"

Turing smiled. "Not in the least surprised. Quick fellow, von Neumann."

Driving back to London, J.D.'s mind was a whirl. "You know, Jesse," he said. "I've only met one other person that was as brilliant as that fellow Turing, and that's John von Neumann."

"I remember when you took me with you to see von Neumann."

"That's right! We flew on a DC-3 – first time for both of us."

"I also remember thinking that what you and von Neumann were talking about reminded me of something I'd read about a man named

288

Babbage. In fact, I was reminded again when we were talking to Turing at tea."

"Babbage?" J.D. drew a blank.

Jesse laughed. "I assumed you knew all about him, when I heard you and von Neumann talking." Jesse told his father what he could remember about Babbage.

"You don't mean that was 1820!"

"Or thereabouts," Jesse said.

"But what you've described – this Analytical Engine – sounds very much like what Bush spent ten years of his life developing! And I'd bet everything I've got that he hadn't heard of Babbage – at least not when he was working on the differential analyzer . . ."

And that turned out to be true. One of the first things J.D. did when he got back to the United States was to look up Bush at OSRD and put the question to him. Bush gave him a rueful smile. "I first learned of Babbage in '42. I wish I'd known about him earlier. He'd worked out, without the benefit of electricity mind you, most of the logic that I needed for the differential analyzer. If he'd lived seventy-five years later, I would've been out of a job, because he would've had the technology to build his machine."

By 1944 Howard Aiken, with support from IBM, had completed the construction of the Automatic Sequenced Controlled Calculator, Mark I. It was put into operation at Harvard University. It was paper-tape fed, stored data in electro-mechanical registers, used numerically coded instructions, and telephone relays as its main logic switching devices. It took 4.5 seconds to multiply 23-digit numbers.

At about the time the war ended J.D. decided that celibacy was idiotic. At fifty-five the juices of life seemed to flow as strongly as ever in him. Also about this time he noticed a young woman from the stenographer's pool at his offices who seemed to go out of her way to run into him. The Friday of the week that J.D. noticed the young woman's attentions, he summoned her from the steno pool.

"Miss Agatha Bennett," he said when she stood before him in his office nervously clutching her steno pad. "I don't intend ever to marry again. And I'm not looking for long-term entanglements. Would you like to have dinner with me at my apartment tonight?"

After she'd caught her breath enough to speak, Miss Bennett said that, indeed, she would.

*

J.D. discovered that the steno and typing pools were veritable harems. They were populated with eager young women with firm and quick bodies. One day, several weeks after he'd made this discovery and had been acting on it almost every weekend, Jamie Ryan came to his office to see him. He'd never seen Jamie so nervous. "Er – J.D. – there are – ah – rumors floating about."

"What kind of rumors?"

"Regarding – regarding you and the secretarial pools."

J.D. grinned wickedly. "All true, I'm sure."

"But damnit, J.D. – is that wise?"

"I don't know about wise," J.D. replied, "but it sure as hell is relaxing."

Jesse came home in December of 1945, just in time to celebrate Christmas. J.D. wanted to have an old-fashioned Christmas at the penthouse, with Jesse and his family, and Wanda and Walter, and Jamie and his wife, but Jesse demurred. "I've only been back a week. I'd like to be alone with my family. I hope you understand, Dad."

"Of course," J.D. said, swallowing his disappointment.

In February of 1946 Eckert and Mauchly completed work on the ENIAC. The *Wall Street Journal* hailed it as "the electronic brain." It was a thousand times faster than Aiken's machine. J.D. journeyed down to the University of Pennsylvania to see it. He took Clarise with him, and, at the last minute, Jesse asked to come along. J.D. was delighted to have him.

The ENIAC took up 1800 square feet in a room that was elaborately air-conditioned for the sake of the heat-sensitive electronic components. They saw a demonstration of the machine. It did in seconds an involved calculation that would've taken a man-year to do by hand. Lights on consoles flashed and operators rushed about changing wires, servicing punched-card readers, and toggling switches. It was all very impressive.

"It doesn't have stored instructions," Clarise said on the train back to New York.

Stored instructions or not, the ENIAC marked the beginning of a revolution.

SEVEN

You're not a man, you're a machine.
G.B. Shaw

27

Jesse and Clarise

THE SEEDS OF THE COMPUTER REVOLUTION were scattered across some 120 years, from the development of Babbage's Analytical Engine to the end of World War II, and the completion of the ENIAC at the University of Pennsylvania, although Babbage's work was a seed that didn't germinate.

Herman Hollerith made a large contribution along the way. Although his tabulating machines lacked the essential capabilities of the computer, they provided two circumstances important to its development: they started people thinking about the automatic manipulation of data, and they brought together some of the most effective salesmen in the world to sell them. Out of the tabulator experience rose up sales organizations whose philosophy was ideally suited to the marketing of computers. The first wave were recruited from cash-register salesmen, organ salesmen, hawkers of tinware and bicycles; men who thought in terms of volume, and in effect said: Give us the product, we'll find uses for it. The entrepreneurs of this new industry were cut from the same cloth as the men who started the railroads and founded the steel mills – the latter-day prophets of the Industrial Revolution. They thought big, and they operated with an arrant self-assurance that more often than not ripened into arrogance. As advanced for its time as Hollerith's tabulator was, the men who saw its potential as a profit generator regarded it no more romantically than they did pots and pans, organs or cash registers. The potential unit profit was large, the market enormous. It is little wonder that data processing early on attracted the best and the worst from the American free-enterprise system. And little wonder, indeed, that brilliant, eccentric Herman Hollerith was eventually squeezed out of the industry he founded. He had missed the point entirely. He thought that if his product was good, the customers would come to him. He abhorred – as a scientist, inventor, and self-designated intellectual – the antics of the hucksters who turned his precious business into what he must have thought of as a carnival.

The computer revolution first stirred when the Bush Differential Analyzer came to the attention of the War Department. At the time artillery trajectory tables, used to aim large guns, were done by hand and were, as a consequence, slowly produced and filled with inaccuracies. The differential analyzer, after years of development, was perfected to quickly and accurately compute these tables. So profound was this advance in the aiming and firing of large guns, that the American government circulated the rumor that the effort had failed in order to keep the Axis from knowing of the advance and, perhaps, to discourage their own efforts to develop a similar machine.

Meanwhile, in England, at Bletchley in Buckinghamshire, the British government had established the Code and Cypher School. This organization was devoted to analyzing and attempting to break the Germans' secret codes. A motley band of mathematicians, physicists, linguists, and chess wizards were brought together at Bletchley early in the war. Among them were Hugh Alexander, the U.K. chess champion; I.J. Good, a mathematician; and Alan Turing, another mathematician, who was to make some of the most significant contributions to computer technology. (It was not until the war was over that it was revealed that Turing was a homosexual. So significant were his contributions to breaking German codes that it was said by I.J. Good that, had British security known of Turing's sexual preferences, he might have been denied clearance, and Britain, as a result, might've lost the war.)

The first machine developed at Bletchley was code-named BOMBE. It was an electromagnetic relay machine designed for the special purpose of cryptanalysis. As such, it had little in common with the general-purpose computers developed later. But BOMBE led to the development of COLOSSUS, a truly remarkable machine, still with the special purpose of cryptanalysis, but with many similarities to the computer that followed. It was operational in December of 1943 and was enormously successful in its specialized function. A later version of COLOSSUS read data at 25,000 bits per second, and could carry out sextillion Boolean operations in a row without error. It used 2500 vacuum tubes to perform its switching logic and storage of digits. This remarkable machine, which was undoubtedly the world's first computer, did not contribute to the computer revolution because the

British government, under the Official Secrets Act, kept it a complete secret until 1975, and then only released a partial description.

If anyone were to be given paternity for the birth of the modern computer, it would have to be Alan Turing. In the astonishingly early year of 1937, when he was only twenty-five, Turing published what was to be the seminal work on computers. It, in effect, proved that it was possible to construct a family of automata, of which the computer was a member. Later, during the war, he was the first to posit the concept of instruction sets that could be stored in the same way as data. Von Neumann had earlier toyed with this idea, but in his construct the instructions and the data were physically separated. Turing's proposal treated them the same, and it was this one feature that finally lifted computers to a new level that left super calculators and analog analyzers far behind.

Early in the war the British government organized scientists from universities and industry to tackle problems attendant to the conduct of the conflict. The idea was to apply mathematical techniques to the solution of wartime logistics problems – problems such as how many of the scarce British gunships to send to protect convoys to get the highest number of cargo ships through while using the fewest escorts, or how to allocate scarce factory production among the many war needs to produce the most effective war machine. This new scientific discipline was given the name Operational Research. Some of the calculations involved were so enormous and complex that they had to be performed by rooms of clerks who (it was later recognized) were organized in a way that paralleled the various logic components of the yet-to-be-born computer.

Out of this hodge-podge of demand arose the need for computational devices of unprecedented power. Turing's 1937 paper had proved that there was such a thing as universal automation. But outside the specialized world of mathematics little notice was taken. Then, as the demands of the war intensified, there was an explosive growth of machine-automaton technology, generally uncoordinated between countries, and often even within countries. When the war ended, the revolution advanced on several fronts at once.

In March of 1946 Jesse invited his father to lunch. They ate at a delicatessen around the corner from J.D.'s offices.

When they were seated over pastrami sandwiches and glasses of beer, Jesse said, "I'd like to go to work for Marvel Scientific."

J.D. nearly dropped his sandwich.

"That's wonderful, Jesse," J.D. replied.

"I'd like to start as soon as possible."

"Have you thought what you'd like to do?"

Jesse grinned wryly. "I suppose the Hollywood answer is that I'd like to start at the bottom, without special favor, and work my way up."

"But that's not your answer?"

"I'm twenty-eight. I don't feel like wasting time. I want to start at the top, or as near as I can. I thought maybe an accelerated training program to learn the business, leading, in a few years, to an executive position." He paused. "Of course, you could insist I start at the bottom and work my way up, and I would."

"I don't believe in Hollywood," J.D. said. He grinned. "I like your plan."

J.D. needed two weeks to work out the details. In the meantime he loaded Jesse down with policy and equipment manuals. He also gave him the latest reports on the development of the ATAC to read.

Jesse went through the training program at Tarrytown. Lucille was in New York the week he graduated, and went to see J.D.

"Your son ate up the course," she reported. "I've never seen anyone work harder."

"You think he'll make an executive, then?"

"I shouldn't be surprised. But he hasn't been tested."

"How do you suggest we do that?"

"Make him a salesman – see how he does."

Jesse began his job as salesman in the New York branch office on January 2, 1947. His sales quota was the largest in the office. He had fulfilled it by March 1. When J.D. heard this he went to the New York branch and spoke privately with the manager.

"Yes, sir," the branch manager said. "Your son is a truly gifted salesman."

"It appears so," J.D. replied. "But appearances can be deceptive. It seems to me that he was given the plum territory."

"It's true that the territory was a good one," the branch manager admitted. "But Jesse handled it in an outstanding manner. I would've expected one of my better salesman to fulfill quota on that territory before the end of the year, but not in three months."

296

It remained to try Jesse's managerial abilities. Included in a postwar expansion program was the establishment of a new branch office in Schenectady. J.D. named Jesse the branch manager.

By the summer of 1947 the ATAC project had stumbled on a sizeable snag. Subassemblies of the prototype machine had been built and were being tested in the lab in New York. The vacuum-tube assembly was not reliable enough to pass the standards – tubes would break down or lose their charge, which made the whole machine useless.

Clarise was working long hours trying to solve the problem. She drove the scientists under her mercilessly. J.D. began once again to spend the greater portion of his long work days in the lab. Although he couldn't contribute technical knowledge, he lent his organizational skills, relieving Clarise of many management tasks and freeing her to work on the problem.

Jesse had been in Schenectady for three months when, late one night, Clarise came into J.D.'s lab office. Her white smock was smudged with machine oil, and there were dark circles under her eyes. She threw herself wearily into a chair and lit a cigarette.

"I didn't know you smoked," J.D. said.

"I didn't until we hit this tube problem."

"Any progress?"

She shook her head wearily. "Damn it! I sense that we're just missing it. That there is one little thing, that if we looked at it correctly, would clear it all up. Does that make sense?"

"Very much. You need a fresh perspective. Why don't you take Jessica and go up to Schenectady for a few days?"

"That's the *last* thing I want to do."

J.D. sighed. "Since you've brought up Jesse, what are you planning for him?" asked Clarise.

"He hasn't discussed it with you?"

"Some kind of training program, he said. Where does it end?"

"In an executive position, if he can cut it."

"Grooming the heir to the throne?"

"Something like that."

She stubbed out her cigarette in an ashtray angrily. "Do you think that's fair?"

"It won't be if Jesse is handed something he can't handle."

"Whatever happened to earning what you get? Do you have any idea how many hours I put in here?"

"A very good idea."

297

"I don't have to tell you how important ATAC is to the company."

"You don't."

"I'm responsible for developing it. Have you thought how you might reward me for that, assuming I can bring it off?"

"What would you like?"

"Your job. I don't mean tomorrow, or next year – but, when you decide to step down, I want that job."

"I see."

"I know what you're thinking. There are no women presidents of large corporations. That doesn't mean I couldn't be the first."

"I wasn't thinking that."

"Then why don't I have the chance that Jesse has!"

"I don't intend to step down for a long time. I won't be sixty-five for another eight years. And even then, I'm not the kind to dodder around town with a carnation in my buttonhole, trying to find a checker game."

"All right," she said. "But get one thing clear – I won't work for Jesse!"

After the war, von Neumann had gone back to the Institute for Advanced Study at Princeton. J.D. went to see him about the vacuum-tube problem. "Can't help you," von Neumann said. "Don't have the time, and, besides, electronics is not my field. Why don't you see what you can learn from Eckert and Mauchly? They're building a machine for the Remington Rand Corporation called UNIVAC."

J.D. journeyed to the University of Pennsylvania, but Eckert and Mauchly were reluctant to help him. J.D. couldn't blame them. Remington Rand, after they got their hands on the machine they were designing, would be a formidable competitor in the computer field.

Schenectady was a new branch office. The first thing Jesse needed was staff. After spending a week in the town looking over the situation, Jesse journeyed by train down to the school at Tarrytown to interview trainees for sales positions. He hired three. One of them, a young man named Duane Hopper, he especially liked. He was a brash young man. Lucille told Jesse that Duane had been the maverick of his class, that, at times, she wondered if he would ever fit into the Marvel mold, although his aptitude and intelligence were exceptional. Jesse thought a maverick is just what he wanted working for him – an intelligent maverick, who would have original ideas. A recent *Wall Street Journal* article on the company had called the executives of Marvel Scientific

298

"grey old men." Jesse hoped some day to have the chance to change that image. He and a few Duane Hoppers, he thought to himself, would, when the time came, do the trick.

Jesse timed his Tarrytown trip so that he could spend the weekend in New York. Although he'd only been gone a couple of weeks, he'd missed Jessica desperately. He'd missed Clarise too, but he couldn't reasonably say why. Since he'd come back from Europe their relationship had been one of strained cordiality.

He loved Clarise, loved the way her quick mind worked, the ready access to humor she had at strange and wonderful times. She didn't laugh at the same things ordinary humans did.

He could not get it through his head why she didn't love him, when she must know how he adored her. He thought of himself as presentable enough. He'd been told he was even handsome and, in England, more than one young woman had made it plain that she would welcome his advances. But he'd been faithful to Clarise. That was another reason she should love him, he told himself, although she seemed without curiosity about his experiences in England and, if he had indulged in affairs, he couldn't imagine it arousing jealousy in her. He wasn't as bright as she was, but how many men were?

He took the train to New York and a cab from Grand Central Station. They still had the apartment in Greenwich Village and Jessica went to school at St. Agnes, two blocks from the apartment. This summer she was in an advanced program there.

When he arrived at the apartment late on a Friday afternoon in early August he found Jessica and her nurse at home. As he had anticipated, Clarise was working and wasn't expected until late. Jessica greeted him with what, for her, was enthusiasm. They spent a happy couple of hours in the sitting-room, Jesse with a drink, while Jessica showed him her school work.

The nurse prepared Jessica's dinner and Jesse had coffee and talked to her while she ate it. After her dinner, they listened to the radio, and, even though the nurse said Mrs. Marvel forbade her, Jesse allowed Jessica to stay up and listen to "I Love A Mystery." After that she went willingly to bed. Jesse tucked her in, kissed her, and turned out the light.

The nurse retired to her room, and Jesse sat up in the living-room with a drink and the *Saturday Evening Post*. He resisted an impulse to try to get Clarise on the phone. She resented being disturbed at work, and he didn't want to do anything to start this weekend off on the wrong foot. Finally, at a little after nine o'clock, he heard her key in the lock and stood and went into the hall to greet her.

She stared at him in surprise. It had been raining and her hair was covered with a waterproof scarf. She looked tired and distracted. "What are you doing here?" she demanded, her coat dripping on the floor.

"I was in Tarrytown and thought I'd drop in for the weekend."

"I do wish you'd let me know," she said, taking off her coat. He took it from her and hung it in the hall closet.

"It was a last-minute thing," he lied. He realized now that he had neglected to call her because he had been afraid she would've asked him not to come.

He'd hoped they could have a late supper together at a small Italian restaurant in the neighborhood, but she'd had sandwiches at the office and was exhausted. He prepared them both a drink.

"You go ahead and get something to eat," she said. "You're probably starved."

"I'd rather talk to you."

"I won't last much beyond this one drink. I've had a long day, and I've got another one tomorrow."

He swallowed his disappointment. He'd had some idyllic dream of the three of them spending Saturday in the park with a picnic lunch.

She collapsed in a large, overstuffed chair, and as he handed her a drink he bent down and kissed her. Her lips were cold from the rain, and unresponsive.

He tried to tell her about his job, but she was too tired to pay attention. The one thing he could always get her to talk about was her work, and now he resorted, in desperation, to that.

She sighed heavily. "We simply don't have the resources we need. We should have a new lab, new testing equipment, the latest components for the ATAC . . ."

"Why haven't you? I know Dad believes in your project."

"We don't have the money, compared to the UNIVAC development, for example. The Army funded initial research on that, and now they've got Remington Rand."

"But we're as large as Remington – larger, I think."

"Remington's a public company."

"They have money from stock sales."

"That's right. So does IBM. We've got cash reserves, but J.D. and the board are old-fashioned about cash. They think having a lot of cash around is the sign of a healthy company."

300

Jesse hadn't realized that. He was beginning to see how little he knew about the inner workings of the company.

"Surely Dad doesn't hold with old-fashioned ideas. He's always been the leader in the company getting research started, in exploring new technologies . . ."

"He's a mixture. When it comes to technology, no one is more forward-thinking than J.D. But when it comes to fiscal management, he's still back in the nineteen twenties with nightmares of another depression dancing in his head."

They talked about the project until nearly midnight. Then, looking at her watch, Clarise said, "My God! I have to be up at seven!"

She was too tired for sex. She worked late on Saturday. Jesse spent the day with Jessica. The two of them had their picnic in the park. Then, that evening he took her to the little Italian restaurant. She was good company, and he loved being with her, but there was a hollowness in his heart.

Saturday evening was a reprise of Friday. Jesse got Clarise talking about her work simply because he wanted her company for as long as he could have it. Again, she was too tired for love-making. Jesse lay awake in bed beside his sleeping wife and tried to remember the last time they'd had sex. He couldn't.

He left for Schenectady on Sunday morning in a despondent mood. The only bright spot in his weekend had been Jessica.

The costs of developing the ATAC were stunning. And they'd yet to solve the fundamental problem. The vacuum-tube component was faulty – the tubes weren't holding the proper charges consistently, giving off false signals.

On December 10, 1947, at the annual meeting, J.D. reported on ATAC. George Fenster had replaced David Stern as the representative of what was now Goldman, Stern, Kline and Fenster.

The board was in rebellion. "We've spent a million dollars on this project," Fenster told J.D., as if he didn't know to the penny what they'd spent. "And what do we have? A machine that doesn't work, and shows no signs of working."

"And if we do get it working," said one stockholder, a wizened little old lady who was the widow of an early investor, "what is the market? I see in the *Wall Street Journal* that T.J. Watson at IBM predicts that a half a dozen machines the size of their Mark I will meet all the computing requirements of the United States."

"I don't agree," J.D. replied. "He's only talking of scientific applications at a few research facilities, our machine has a much wider application."

It was a battle – they wrangled all afternoon – but, in the end, J.D. got them to agree to a compromise: they would put another quarter of a million into ATAC. But the board insisted that, if by the time that money was gone, the vacuum-tube problem hadn't been solved, the project would be scrapped.

J.D. went back to his office, accepted a cup of coffee from his understanding secretary who could see the kind of mood he was in, and brooded on the short-sightedness of his board.

From the outset of the company J.D. had insisted that he was to receive no more stock than what he considered fitting for a top employee of the company. As a consequence he owned a little more than five percent. He kept his job simply on the basis that the board, until now, had felt that no one else could do it nearly so well. But he could see cracks beginning to develop in their confidence in him over the ATAC project. The irony was that he felt deeply that they must develop the ATAC or the company would die. Computers, he believed, were the machines of the future, and the data-processing company that didn't develop one would be left in the dust of those who did.

It was odd that Remington Rand was on the verge of producing the first production computer. J.D. had always assumed that it would be either Marvel Scientific or IBM who would achieve that honor. Strangely, T.J. Watson, historically the most visionary of men, was dragging his heels on computer development. J.D. could understand his caution, in the light of the millions it took to develop a computer, but he didn't agree in the least with Watson's prediction. He knew from experience with tabulators and sorters that applications for computers would likely spring up where none had existed before. Having the power of machines set men's minds free to think grander thoughts, to want more sophisticated computations. He'd seen it happen time and again. Install a tab and sorter in a company to do payroll and inventory, and pretty soon the accounting department would want to run balance sheets on them, and the engineering department would start fooling with them to see if they couldn't be made to calculate a cut-and-fill, or stress tables.

It was true that they'd cut heavily into the company's cash reserves to finance the ATAC project. But now, with the war over and the limit on profits lifted, money was beginning to pour in from the rental of equipment once again. The Model Z tabulator, with alphabetic capabilities and automatic sequencing of instructions was, along with

IBM's Model 405 tabulator, the standard for the industry.

But both machines were outdated. They'd been designed in the early and the mid thirties, and there hadn't been a major advance in a commercial machine since.

J.D. had no idea what they could rent or sell the ATAC for, assuming they could build it. This was another problem he had with the board. He couldn't forecast sales or profits since he had no cost basis or demand upon which to base them.

The *Wall Street Journal* claimed that IBM was in the forefront of technology and remained far ahead of its competitors. All this was predicated upon a strange lash-up of several tabulator machines (which were now being called "electronic accounting machines") with a device that stored data. This machine was called a "Card-Programmed Calculator," CPC for short, and J.D. viewed it with mild scorn as simply bastardizing the old technology. However, he had been severely criticized by several members of the board for not developing a machine to compete with the CPC. The irony of this was that developing a competitive machine would cost even more of the precious dollars that the board was hoarding so carefully and would be, in J.D.'s opinion, nothing more than a stop-gap. The real technological advance, the way of the future, lay in computers. He only wished the board was capable of seeing that.

Jesse forgot his depression over his marriage by hard work and threw himself into making Schenectady a model branch office. Duane Hopper proved to be an able salesman and, as Jesse had hoped, a source of fresh ideas. By the time Christmas of 1947 approached, the Schenectady branch had indeed become a model office. It had exceeded its quota, had established itself as a force in the business life of Schenectady, and Jesse and all his employees had become well-liked additions to the community. Jesse decided he deserved a Christmas vacation. He put Duane Hopper in charge of the office and took a few days off.

When he arrived in New York not even Clarise's luke-warm greeting could quell the holiday mood he felt. He bought a tree, and he and Jessica decorated it.

Then, on the Saturday night before Christmas, Clarise, who had worked all day and part of the night, came dragging home. Jesse prepared her a drink. He could tell by her expression that something was wrong. He asked her.

"The board has given me an ultimatum," she said angrily.

He handed her a drink and sat across from her. "What ultimatum?"

"We've been given enough money for the next six months. If we haven't got a prototype of the ATAC running by then, they'll scrub the project."

"No wonder you're worried!"

"It will be the end of my career."

"Nonsense. You have too much talent to talk like that, Clarise."

"I meant the end of my career at Marvel Scientific. I'll have to go somewhere else and start over."

"Don't talk like that, darling. Dad would never let you get away. He knows how valuable you are."

"You are so naive, Jesse. Do you think I could stay after a failure of this dimension? J.D. might keep me on, against all the advice of the old fogies on the board, but my effectiveness would be shot. I'd be forever tagged as the woman who ran the ATAC aground."

"Where would you go?"

"I don't know. The number of openings for female vice-presidents of corporations is zero, as far as I know. There aren't any other executives like J.D., who don't give a damn if you're female, male or orang-utang, just so long as you can do the job. I'll probably end up teaching," she concluded bitterly.

That night they made love for the first time in months. Clarise seemed to have a need, an emptiness, and she used Jesse to fill it. Her passion and need were the greatest Jesse had ever experienced from her. They made love, slept, awoke at Clarise's insistence, made love again, and this pattern repeated through the night until Jesse lost count, and fell, exhausted finally, into a deep near-catatonic sleep at dawn from which he did not awaken until early afternoon.

Clarise had gone to the lab. Jessica's nurse made Jesse coffee and he drank it at the kitchen table in a kind of reverie of sated peace. He hadn't felt so well in months.

He spent the rest of the day with Jessica, until it was time to leave to catch his train. He was disappointed that Clarise didn't return, or at least call, before he left. But he didn't dwell on it because he didn't want to poison his memories of the night.

More and more Jesse found himself using Duane Hopper as a confidant on problems with the Schenectady branch office. Duane's quick mind and wit were ever ready to attack the issues.

These discussions took place after the work of the day was done, which, for both of them, was usually beyond seven o'clock. They formed the habit of having a late dinner together at a café on Edison Street that catered to the shift workers at the nearby General Electric plant.

Hopper was a bachelor and, as far as having any reason to be home at any particular hour was concerned Jesse might as well have been. They would linger long into the night over coffee and cigarettes.

Hopper had been assigned a territory that was made up of small businesses – machine shops, sheet-metal fabricators, hardware wholesalers, and the like. In this territory the companies were too small to be able to justify their own data-processing machines, so Duane Hopper organized two or three firms, each of which had similar data-processing needs, and then sold each group an installation whose cost they shared. The machines were installed on the premises of the company that had the most room, or was the most centrally located, and a messenger would deliver results to the other locations, and pick up the raw data to be processed and take it back to the machine center. Even with the cost of the messenger, this plan reduced the cost to each partner in the arrangement to a level they could afford.

The scheme was so successful and innovative that it had spread to other branch offices. And when Lucille Cranston heard of it she invited Duane to Tarrytown to speak to her students about it.

On a Friday evening in early April of 1948 Jesse and Duane Hopper sat in Jesse's office. They had just returned from entertaining one of Duane's prospects and his wife at a restaurant that evening. It was an unseasonably warm night. The windows in the office were up and a faint whiff of honeysuckle blended with the usual daily smells.

The two men had their coats off and held cups of strong coffee that had come from a pot behind a screen of filing cabinets.

Jesse said, "I'm going to New York tomorrow."

"Oh?"

"I'll be gone about a week. You're in charge."

"Okay. A little vacation?"

"No. I received a telegram this morning."

"Summoned to Valhalla?"

"No. My mother died last night."

305

28

Jesse's Trials

IN RECENT YEARS Jesse had hardly seen his mother – at Christmas he would drive out to Long Island and deliver a present. Sometimes she'd receive him, sometimes not. She had grown strange. She lived alone in the big house, keeping up the pretense of the social queen when, in truth, she had hardly any friends left, having estranged most of them with her pretensions and delusions.

At the news of her death Jesse felt only a kind of numbness. His father had sent him the telegram; the funeral was to be in two days. Jesse flew down to New York in an Eastern Airlines DC-4. He'd phoned Clarise that he was coming, but it was J.D. who met him, and he had brought Jessica. The little girl ran into her father's arms and Jesse held her tightly. She was eight years old, tall for her age, with a beauty that stopped his heart when he looked at her.

On the drive into the city, J.D. said, "Clarise was tied up at the lab."

Jesse nodded glumly. He realized he hadn't really expected Clarise to meet him, and a sudden anger at his wife surged in him so strongly that he trembled for a moment causing Jessica, who was snuggled up at his side, to look searchingly up at him.

J.D. dropped them at the apartment in Greenwich Village. "I'll pick you up at noon," he said. "That'll give us an hour to drive out to the funeral."

The nurse put Jessica to bed at nine o'clock – past her usual time, but Jesse had insisted she be allowed to stay up with him. The nurse retired to her room. Jesse fixed himself a drink and sat brooding in the dark living-room. A familiar ache settled in his chest and he recognized it as the old companion of all the times he'd spent waiting for Clarise. The anger he'd felt in the car returned. He took a light

306

topcoat from the hall closet and went out. He walked to a bar where he got gloomily and quietly drunk, not leaving until one o'clock. At the apartment, he was fishing clumsily through his pockets for his keys, when the door was thrown open to reveal Clarise in a wooly white bathrobe. "Where have you been!"

"Went out for a drink."

"You're drunk!"

"Gloriously."

She took his arm to help him but he shook off her hand. "I'm not that drunk," he said.

He flopped down in a chair in the living-room with his coat still on and noticed that all the lights were blazing.

"I called your father," Clarise said, standing across from him and hugging her arms.

Jesse looked up in surprise. "What for?"

"What for! I was worried sick. I had no idea where you were. Couldn't you have left a note?"

"Worried *sick!*" Jesse said, and began to laugh. He laughed until a fit of coughing stopped him.

Clarise brought him a glass of water. After his coughing subsided, she asked, "Was it that hard?"

"Hard?" He looked at her, puzzled.

"Your mother's death."

He shook his head sadly. "What's hard is the death of our marriage."

"What are you saying?"

"No, I guess it wasn't really a death, was it? It was still-born. I kept trying to breathe life into a corpse." He chuckled drunkenly. "Must've been pretty ludicrous, huh, Clarise?"

She helped him undress. When he was in bed, she said, "Would you like me to go to the funeral?"

He shook his head. "Pretty grim business. No fun. You stay with ATAC . . ." And then he fell asleep. Just before he dropped off he heard someone sob once, and wondered if it had been him or Clarise.

"I wasn't sure you'd want to go," Jesse said to his father. It was the next day, a little past noon, and J.D. was weaving his Cadillac through the heavy traffic, making for the Triborough Bridge.

"She was my wife," J.D. replied. "And your mother."

"It seems I hardly knew her."

"None of us did. Madelline was an enigma. I never did understand her. But when she was young, she was a magnificent woman, and that enigmatic quality added to her charm."

Jesse massaged his forehead with his fingers. His father gave him a knowing look. "Clarise phoned me last night."

"I hope you weren't worried."

"I told her you probably wanted to be alone. Losing a mother can do that to you."

"I had a few drinks at a bar."

"Good."

"In fact, I had a lot of drinks."

"Even better."

Jesse studied his father's profile for a moment. "Was it hard? The divorce, I mean?"

"Hard enough."

"Was it mutual?"

"The divorce was my idea. But your mother didn't care about me."

"Ever?"

"I don't know, Jesse. I think maybe, in the beginning –" he made an impatient gesture with his hand. "I was always very good at kidding myself about Madelline."

"I know the feeling," Jesse said, and drew a sharp look from his father.

"Anything you want to talk about?" J.D. asked.

"No," Jesse replied.

Madelline would've loved her own funeral. All the old friends that she'd alienated showed up dressed in their furs and jewels and it was the social event of the season. J.D. and Jesse hardly knew anyone. They left as soon as they decently could after the service.

On the drive back, J.D. said, "I want you to come to New York."

"What do you mean?"

"I mean I want you to come and work at headquarters. You've been away from your family long enough. It's not healthy, Jesse, to be apart from them."

"I don't want charity," Jesse said hotly. "Just because I'm the son of the President –"

"It's not charity!" J.D. replied quickly. "I put it clumsily. I guess the funeral got me thinking about all the time I missed with Gina because I was too busy. I've been thinking for some weeks now about putting you in the New York Office. You've done very well with

Schenectady. You've turned a moribund office into one with plenty of potential."

"The job's not done."

"Someone else can carry it through. The truth is, Jesse – I need you."

"If I really thought that, it would be different."

"It's the truth. The board is giving me fits."

"I thought they were a rubber stamp."

"I'm sure everyone thinks that. And at one time, we were certainly more compatible. When David Stern was alive, the board and I were a smoothly working team. But rubber stamp? Never. You knew David. Do you think he could've been anyone's puppet?"

"I hadn't thought about it that way. Why don't you have the same relationship with this board?"

"Natural selection, I guess you might call it. The first board was composed of the original investors – men who were businessmen, who had made their own money, and who knew what had to be done to make a successful company. As they died off, they were replaced by their heirs. And I'm afraid most of them wouldn't know how to run a company if you drew them a picture. They are first and foremost interested in protecting the money that they never earned in the first place. Funny, isn't it – how money that is hard-earned doesn't seem nearly so important as money you're given on a silver platter?"

"How do you think I could help with the board?"

"I don't. That's my problem. I would want you to take some of the administrative chores off my hands so I could concentrate on appeasing the board and getting ATAC off the ground while, at the same time, trying to protect our revenue base from the competition."

"I thought Walter and Jamie did that for you!"

"They do. But Walter is seventy-eight years old. He wants to retire, and I don't blame him. Jamie is in his sixties. We need some new blood, some young energy. I'd want you to train under Walter's wing to take his place."

They rode in silence for several miles. Finally, J.D. asked, "What do you think?"

"I think I'd like to try it."

"Wonderful."

"There's a young salesman at Schenectady – Duane Hopper – that I'd like to bring with me."

J.D. frowned. "What for?"

"I'm not sure. But you have promising young men come into the

309

corporate offices to train for field management."

"You see Hopper doing that?"

"Something of the sort. I'm just not sure where he'd eventually fit, but he's a brilliant guy. I'd like him to work with me."

J.D. shrugged. "If that's what you want."

Jesse said he needed a month to wrap things up at Schenectady. J.D. agreed.

"In this file," Walter Hucko said, "are all the train and plane schedules. You see, if you want a train on Friday, you look under 'Friday' " – he pulled forth a card – "and here we have all the trains leaving Grand Central on a Friday. Under each line here is listed the connections to various destinations."

Jesse was sitting at the corner of Walter's desk. Duane Hopper was seated next to him. Jesse and Duane exchanged a look. "But, Walter," Jesse said. "Do you spend all your time arranging my father's travel schedules?"

Hucko chuckled. "Lordy, no! I am also the official greeter. When we have a stockholder coming to town, or one of our big customers, it's my job to get out to the airport, or down to the station, to give him the official greeting. Now, we have two company limos. There's the Lincoln and the Cad. The stockholders like the Lincoln, except for Taggart. He always likes the Cad."

"Schedules and greeting," Duane said.

"Then there's employee relations," Walter continued. "Your dad likes to find bright young fellers out in the branch offices and bring 'em up to New York for a few months. You have to see to their housing – the Caldwell Men's Hotel is my favorite – and get them outfitted with proper clothes, and the like. Sort of hold their hands while they're here. Some of these lads never been out of their home towns. Though, with the war, more and more of them have been over half the world and back. Vets . . ."

"Well, friend," Duane Hopper began. "I don't see that you're going to be needing an assistant. After all, how much work is there to buying train tickets and renting rooms for barefoot boys?" Duane and Jesse were sitting in the bar at the Plaza Hotel having a drink after their first day at work in the New York office.

"This isn't what I had in mind."

"You know," Duane said. "That office looks like an old folk's home. Is there anyone there under fifty?"

310

"Dad is the youngster, aside from Clarise."

"Ah, yes – your wife. I caught a glimpse of her today, rushing by in a white smock. A beautiful woman."

"I'm sorry I haven't had a chance to introduce you."

"No problem. You've been busy learning which limo which board member likes."

Jesse grinned. "You found a place to live?"

"Not yet. Apartments in my price bracket are a rare species. But the Y is okay for now."

"I have a meeting in fifteen minutes," J.D. said. He was busily sorting through papers on his desk.

Jesse was sitting across from his father. He glanced around at the office. Even the furnishings of the executive offices were outdated – heavy, dark desks; leather couches; faded oriental rugs; wainscoting of dark-stained oak.

"It's about this job of mine," Jesse said.

"What about it?" J.D. asked without looking up from his papers.

"It's a waste of time."

J.D. looked up now, his hands frozen on the papers. "A waste of time! You mind telling me whose?"

"Mine. I've tried to prepare myself to be an executive in the data-processing industry. I think I've done a good job of it. Being a high-priced lackey is a waste of that preparation."

J.D. put down the papers and leaned back in his chair. "Is that what Walter Hucko is – a high-priced lackey?" he asked in a dangerous voice.

"The job he does could be handled by one competent secretary for a tenth the salary."

"I see. Would it make a difference if I told you that the job Walter does helps me immeasurably?"

"It doesn't change my opinion that a secretary could do it."

"You've been here less than two days, and you already know more than I do about how to run the office – is that it?"

"No, it's not. But about one very minor function in the office I do have a strong opinion."

"That's the job you agreed to."

Jesse shook his head. "You said you needed me. You don't need *me* for a job that any fairly bright and conscientious person could handle."

"Well, Jesse, the fact remains that that is the job I have for you."

311

"In that case, I want to go back in the field."

"That's the only job I have for you in Marvel Scientific."

"All right. Consider my resignation effective as of now."

"You don't mean that."

"Of course I do."

"What would you do? Where would you go?"

"I'd go to another company. I'm reasonably certain I could get a job."

"You'd do that to me? Go to work for a competitor?"

"If the only alternative is to waste my time scheduling train trips."

J.D. stared at his son. Jesse did not avert his gaze – he stared back. Finally, J.D. sighed, and said, "I have to leave for that meeting. Couldn't we talk about this later?"

"If you understand my position. Otherwise, why waste time?"

"Goddamn it! I understand your position. I'd have to be a moron not to. Now, could we talk about it later?" J.D. rose to leave.

"When?"

"I don't know when, Jesse. When I have the time. Right now, I'm late for a meeting."

"Not good enough, Dad," Jesse said calmly. "I want to get this thing resolved."

"All right! Seven o'clock tonight. Be in my office!" And J.D. stormed out.

"Jesse why don't you just take the job for a few months? It will give you a chance to see how the office operates. Then we'll see."

It was seven-thirty that evening. Jesse had been prompt, J.D. nearly thirty minutes late.

"I'm sorry, Dad, but I'm not going to have that job even for a few months."

"Damn it! Why are you so stubborn? Don't you see that what Walter does is important to me? I don't want to have to deal with a secretary on those matters."

"I'll be responsible for what Walter does. I'll deal with the secretary. And I'll guarantee you it will be as good a job as Walter's been doing. But I want something else I can get my teeth into."

"And what might that be?"

"I was hoping you'd have something in mind."

"I don't."

"I guess we're back at the same impasse. Sorry to have taken up your time."

"Wait, wait, wait. Look – why not do this? Make yourself a job. Look around and see what's not getting done that should be done. I'm sure there are things that are lost between the sheets. How does that sound?"

"What about authority?"

"You make your own. I'm not going to hand it to you on a silver platter."

"But will you pull the rug out from under me?"

"What do you mean?"

"If I find some of these things that are lost between the sheets, will you let me handle them?"

"Of course I will! For God's sake, that's what I just said, wasn't it?"

"Okay," Jesse said. "You've got a deal."

In 1948 two events occurred that were to profoundly affect the data-processing industry and the broader world within which it existed although, at the time, only a few university professors and research scientists had any idea of their importance.

In early 1948 three scientists at the Bell Telephone Laboratories – John Bardeen, Walter Brattain, and William Shockley – developed the transistor, one of the greatest inventions in the history of electronics, ranking in importance with the vacuum tube, and for which, in 1956, the three were to win the Nobel Prize.

Then in July and October of 1948 Claude Shannon, a thirty-two-year-old scientist, also at Bell Labs, published two papers which consisted in part of a set of theorems dealing with the problems attendant to sending a message from one place to another, giving birth to a new science called Information Theory.

At Marvel Scientific only Clarise and a couple of her colleagues were vaguely aware of the work that had been accomplished by Bardeen, Brattain and Shockley; and weren't at all aware of Shannon's papers. Clarise was capable of understanding the import of the works, especially the invention of the transistor, but she was too caught up in trying to save the ATAC to notice much else.

Jesse and Duane Hopper had set out, early in June of 1948, to try to define significant roles for themselves at Marvel Scientific. Jesse hired a sharp, presentable young woman to learn Walter Hucko's job, and she learned it so well and so quickly that Hucko was able to retire in June. J.D. threw a banquet at the Waldorf Astoria in honor of his old friend, where Walter was toasted and celebrated and lavished with gifts. His favorite present, and one that brought a tear to his eye, was a solid gold miniature of an old-time organ that J.D. had had made specially.

As the banquet ended and the guests were filtering out, Wanda took J.D.'s arm and pulled him aside. "Marvel," she said. "This will be my last year, too."

J.D. was shocked. "Surely not!"

"I'm sixty-four years old. And Walter and I want to do a bit of traveling while we're still able."

"What will I do without you, Agronsky?"

She grinned up at him. "D'you remember the times we had when we first met?"

"Are you serious! Of course I do! You were the prettiest thing I ever saw."

"Did you ever imagine we'd wind up where we are?"

"Not in my wildest dreams. I was a hayseed organ salesman, and you were about the most sophisticated woman ever. If it hadn't been for you introducing me to Hollerith, none of it would've happened."

"I don't believe that, Marvel. Maybe I speeded things up a bit, but you would've got there, all the same." She looked up at him appraisingly. "I'm real proud of you, Marvel. But you're pushing sixty yourself."

He looked at her suspiciously. "So? You aren't trying to put me out to pasture, are you? That'd be just like you, Agronsky. If you think retirement's a good thing, then it must be good for everybody."

She laughed. "I would never try to talk you into retiring. But I think it's about time you got some young blood in. Remember what the *Wall Street Journal* called us . . ."

J.D. snorted. " 'Grey old men' my rear."

"They counted me as one of the fellows, I guess," she said. "But they had a point."

"Jesse is here now."

"That's a good start, provided you listen to him."

"Have you been talking to him?"

"Not about this. I just know you."

"What's that supposed to mean?"

"That you like to run the show yourself. Nothing wrong with that up till now – you've done a good job. But you have to make room for the next generation, or Marvel Scientific will get decrepit."

"Thanks for the advice," J.D. said. What he didn't tell her was that while he was alive no one was going to tell him how to run his company – not Wanda, not the board, and most of all not his own son.

Jesse and Duane were working from early morning until late at night, carefully documenting what they discovered in a growing notebook that they'd taken to calling between themselves the "Book of the Dead."

"It's hard to believe, chum," Duane Hopper said one night when they were finishing up a fourteen-hour day. "Here is a company that's supposed to be on the forefront of technology, and it's being run like a whale-bone corset factory."

By the time Jesse arrived that night at the apartment in Greenwich Village, it was after eleven, but he found Clarise waiting for him. She was dressed in her wooly robe, and had a drink in her hand. Jesse could tell that it was the successor to several.

He fixed himself a drink and sank wearily into a chair across from Clarise who was sitting tensely on the couch.

"If I ask you something, will you answer me honestly?" she said.

"Of course."

"Do you have another woman?"

Jesse laughed. "Good lord! What made you ask that?"

"You didn't answer."

"No, I don't have another woman."

"Since you came back from Schenectady I've hardly seen you."

"This is a switch," he said. "Usually I'm the one complaining about your late hours. But I never accused you of having another man. Maybe I should have."

"You know better than that. I don't – *need* it the way you do."

"*It?* You mean sex?"

"Yes. I won't take it if you have a woman, Jesse."

He shrugged wearily. "Even if I had, which I don't – what difference would it make?"

"I have my pride."

"Jesus, Clarise! Is that all I mean to you? Pride? A possession?"

Her head was bowed as she stared into the glass she held between her hands. "I haven't been a very good wife."

"No," Jesse said quietly, "you haven't."

She looked up with a struck expression. Then, with a sob, she flung herself from the couch, ran into their bedroom, and slammed the door.

315

29

The Grey Old Men

"I've mapped out some areas I'd like to be responsible for," Jesse said.

J.D. looked up from the floor of his living-room where he was playing a game of Monopoly with Jessica. It was a steaming Sunday afternoon in July, 1948, but the penthouse was agreeably cool; J.D. had had air-conditioning installed that year. Clarise was in the kitchen helping the cook prepare their dinner.

"I've got more important matters at hand," J.D. said. "I've just landed on Boardwalk."

"One thousand dollars!" Jessica said gleefully.

"I'd like to see you about it tomorrow," Jesse persisted.

"Go ahead and do whatever you think's necessary."

"It's not quite that simple, Dad. I need a budget –"

"Very well!" J.D. said impatiently. "See my secretary in the morning and tell her I said to make an appointment. Now, young lady – suppose we negotiate for that rent. I'm afraid I'm a little short . . .''

J.D.'s proclivity for young women from the typing pool had expanded to include his personal secretaries. He'd hired a succession of young, attractive women, ''promoting'' them to other duties when he tired of them. Jamie Ryan, when J.D. had rid himself of the last girl, had taken matters into his own hands. One Monday morning in the spring of 1948 J.D. had arrived at his office to find a prim, large-boned woman with her hair done in a brown bun sitting at his secretary's desk. "And who might you be?" J.D. asked.

"I'm your new secretary, Mr. Marvel," the woman replied in a no-nonsense voice. "Eleanor Pribash."

"Who says?" J.D. asked, eyeing her ample figure.

"Mr. Ryan."

"Ask him to step into my office."

"Now, J.D.," Jamie said soothingly. "Try her for awhile. Your files are a mess, your correspondence has to be done over by my secretary half the time, and when's the last time you could depend on your appointment book?"

"Christ, Jamie! The woman is elderly."

"She's thirty-eight, J.D. – which makes her considerably younger than you."

In the end, J.D. agreed to give Miss Pribash a try. He figured in a month or two Jamie's concern would blow over, he could "promote" Miss Pribash, and hire a young woman more suited to his needs.

Miss Pribash flipped open the appointment book on her desk, consulted it, and looked up at Jesse. "Mr. Marvel could see you at one-thirty for an hour, Mr. Marvel."

"That would be fine," Jesse said, admiring the neatness of the appointment-book entries. Miss Pribash bent over the page to enter his name in a fine Spencerian hand.

"In the past two years our customer base has shrunk ten percent," Jesse said.

"Revenue is steadily up," J.D. replied testily.

"True. But the demand built up during the war among the customers that survived gives a false market picture."

Jesse and Duane Hopper had placed a flip-chart stand in front of J.D.'s desk. Jesse stood beside the stand with a pointer, referring to the first of a thick set of charts.

"As soon as that demand is satisfied," Jesse said, "revenues will decline. We estimate the decline could be as much as twenty percent. Already, in this quarter, total revenue is down three percent from last year."

"Do you think I don't know that?" J.D. asked.

"No, sir. I am pointing it out as a preface to what follows."

J.D. waved an impatient hand. "Get on with it, then."

Jesse turned over a new chart. "There are three areas that need attention if we're to reverse the trend." He tapped the chart with the pointer. "Public relations, research, and executive policy." We have an image as a company run by grey old men –"

"Good Lord!" J.D. exploded. "How long is that going to be thrown up at me?"

317

"The fact is that the average age of headquarters executives in Marvel Scientific is 57.2 years. If you exclude Clarise it's 61.6."

"You don't get the wisdom to run a company without experience," J.D. countered.

"Perhaps. But the question here is how the public, or more to the point, how our customers and prospective customers, perceive us." Jesse turned to another chart. "Over the same two-year period IBM's customer base has grown nearly fifteen percent. The average age of their headquarters executives is a little over forty-six years."

"Forty-six! Why, Tom Watson is older than I am!"

"That's true. Mr. Watson is seventy-four now. But he and Tom Watson, Junior have pulled in a lot of young executives to help them run the company. And Tom Junior is only thirty-four, himself."

"Don't try to tell me that the difference in our customer base over the past two years is caused by the difference in the ages of our executive staff!"

"Not entirely. But I do suggest that's part of it. I think we need to hire a specialist to help us improve the face we present to the public."

"We have an advertising firm."

"And they aren't doing the job. Our ads lack punch. We need to get off the back pages of the *Wall Street Journal* and *Barron's* and into *Time*, *Life* and the *Saturday Evening Post*, and on radio . . ."

"Do you have any idea what that would cost?"

"We've prepared an estimated budget for everything we're going to present today. If you could hold off on that until I'm done . . .?"

"All right, all right –"

"Another public relations area that is being neglected is the Foundation –"

"That was Gina's baby –"

"It is doing hardly anything. And it has accumulated a sizeable amount of money."

"I lost interest in it after Gina died."

"There is enough money to hire a full-time executive director. I think Gina's scholarship idea was an excellent one. We should pursue that. It wouldn't cost the company a thing. The money is there."

"You may be right," J.D. said. "I've been meaning to do something about that, but somehow I just didn't have the heart to get into it. Why don't you take care of it, Jesse?"

"All right. To summarize, we recommend hiring a full-time public relations man, and revamping our advertising."

"I'll bet Tom Watson doesn't have a full-time public relations man."

"Oh, but he does. Hired just this year by Tom Junior."

"Ah," J.D. said. "The kids want to take over, is that it?"

"No, sir. But I feel I have a job to do, and I'm trying to do it."

"Oh, don't get starch in your underwear. Go ahead, go ahead."

"All right." Jesse turned to a new chart. "Research. Our main product now is the Model Z tabulator, which was designed over ten years ago. We have to develop new products to compete, and the product we need most to develop is a computer."

"We're working on it," J.D. said.

"Not the way we should be. The budget for the ATAC isn't enough to do the job, and it's just enough to make sure we have a resounding failure. We'd have been better off never to have begun, considering the adverse publicity we're going to have when it goes down the drain. We'll be known as a company that can't cope with new technology."

"You know the board's giving me hell over the ATAC!"

"I think we've come up with solutions to that. But let's go on. We need a new research facility. Two floors of this building aren't enough for the company to compete in development. If we did develop the ATAC, where are we going to build it? We can't do it in our old plants. They aren't designed for a computer-assembly operation. We need new test equipment. We need more engineers and physicists . . ."

J.D. held up a hand. "Hold it! Do you have any idea of the kind of money you're talking?"

"I'm talking about the survival of the company. If we don't do it, Remington Rand and IBM will wipe us out."

"IBM! Old Tom Watson doesn't believe there's a market for computers."

"Young Tom does. And he'll win that battle, if my guess is right. And when IBM gets rolling, we'd better be sure we aren't one of the companies it rolls over."

"Look, Jesse – don't think I haven't thought all of this myself. But we just don't have the resources to compete. In that the board is right."

"We have cash surpluses in the millions –"

"Damn right we do! I made sure of that. If we ever fall on hard times, if there's another depression, you'll see which company is in the best fix. And that company will be Marvel Scientific."

"Dad – we can't run the business defensively. That isn't the way you started it. We have to go forward on the assumption that our

319

economy is in good health. And it's not a bad assumption to make, when you look at the figures."

"Nobody touches those surpluses!"

"Somebody might, without your permission. This company is ripe for a takeover. Plenty of cash. A scared board, that would probably look favorably on an offer that would let them get their money out and get rid of the worry."

"I've thought of that."

"And what have you done about it?"

"What do you suggest?"

"Go public."

"Never!"

"Why not?"

"I'm not turning my company over to a bunch of idiots who wouldn't know a balance sheet from a laundry list."

"It doesn't have to be that way. The broader the base of stock, the more control you'd have. What's giving you fits now is that the power is held by a few, and those few pretty much meet your description about balance sheets and laundry lists. The little guy with a hundred shares of IBM is content to let the people who know how run the company. Do you think Tom Watson doesn't have control?"

J.D. looked at his watch. "Your time's up."

"But we haven't finished."

"Sorry. I have another appointment."

Jesse and Duane Hopper trudged wearily back to Jesse's office, where they deposited the flip-chart stand, the charts and the pointer, and flopped into chairs.

"By golly," Hopper said. "That is a tough old man."

"Tell me about it," Jesse said, trying to massage away a headache.

"Do you know how many points you won?"

"Precisely one – I can hire an executive director for the Elvira Marvel Foundation."

Jesse went to see Jamie Ryan in his office. He told him he wanted to hire a public relations man.

"I've thought for some time that we should do something about our stodgy advertising," Jamie said. "But your father didn't believe public relations was a valid occupation for a grown man."

"Maybe if you tried again –" He told Jamie about the presentation he and Duane had made to his father.

320

"Whew!" Jamie said. "You hit him with a lot, all at once."

"But, damn it, Jamie – every point we made needs doing."

"I think you're right. But you have to remember that attitudes change slowly."

"If we *don't* change, the company will wither and die."

Two days later Jamie called Jesse. "You can hire your PR man."

"How did you do it?"

"Let's just say that after the softening-up you and Duane gave him, J.D. was easy pickins. He wants you to be responsible for the PR stuff, so the new man is to work for you."

"What about my other points – research, younger executives, considering going public?"

"You have to learn patience, Jesse. You've won one – let that hold you for awhile."

Before the war Earl Baxter had been a reporter for the Detroit Free Press, and then a member of the news department for the Mutual Radio Network. During the war he'd risen to the rank of Major as a press relations officer for the Air Corps. Since the war he'd been working in the public relations department of General Motors. In 1948 he was thirty-seven years old, married, with two daughters.

Jesse heard of him from an executive recruiting firm he'd gone to seeking applicants for the public relations job in Marvel Scientific.

Baxter was a short, compact, sandy-haired man with twinkling blue eyes, and an incisive mind. Jesse liked him immediately. In September of 1948 he came to work at the New York office as Director of Public Relations. The first thing he did was fire the old ad agency. He then organized a speaker's roster from the executives of the company, and began to book them across the country.

After he'd been on the job for four weeks, Earl Baxter came to Jesse with a new idea.

"This computer we're building, it's about the most exciting thing in the company."

"Agreed," Jesse said.

"We aren't doing much of a job promoting it."

"What did you have in mind?"

"First, a series of ads in top-circulation mags. The ads would be little essays about computers, and specifically ATAC. You know, tutorials in a kind of *Reader's Digest* scientific article style."

"I think that's a great idea," Jesse said. "Let's do it right away."

*

321

On a bitterly cold day in February of 1949 J.D. summoned Jesse to his office. The radiators were hissing and popping and the whole building smelled of damp wool.

J.D. was sitting behind his desk with the *Saturday Evening Post, Time, Life* and *Newsweek* spread open before him.

"These ads," he said. "Whose idea were they?"

"Earl Baxter's. They're excellent, aren't they?"

"Do you have any idea what kind of position this puts me in? I'm battling the board to keep the damned project alive, and here you are announcing to the world that we're developing a computer. What do you think will happen when we have to scrub it?"

"Don't scrub it."

"Would you mind telling me where we'll get the money to keep it going?"

"Go public."

"Jesse –" J.D. said wearily.

"Did you know that science teachers are collecting those ads for their classes? A publisher in Chicago has asked to put the whole series together in a booklet to be sold to schools and the public."

"I don't dispute that the ads are effective. But for God's sake, Jesse – what kind of effect will this have on our public relations if we have to discontinue the ATAC research?"

"What does the board think?"

"They're furious. They think it's a trick on my part to keep ATAC alive. I can't very well tell them that I had no idea these ads were coming out, can I?"

"Well, I don't see that the board can scrub the project now."

"Jesse, did you do this deliberately, knowing it would back us into a corner?"

"I only hoped, Dad."

J.D. glared at his son for a long silent moment. Then he said, slowly, "I'm torn between admiration for your deviousness and a strong urge to take you to the woodshed."

"Look at it this way, Dad. I have no power. But I do believe as strongly as I've believed anything, that we have to develop that computer. So, wouldn't I be derelict if I didn't do everything I could to see that it goes forward?"

"Damn it! Don't compound the sin by giving me that line of sophistry. Tell me what we're going to do now that you've painted us into this corner."

Jesse shrugged, and grinned. "You're the President. I'm just –
come to think of it, I don't have a title, do I?"

"Mud!" J.D. said. "That'll be your title if you keep this up." He
swiveled his chair and stared out the window at the grey day.

After several moments of silence, Jesse cleared his throat, and said,
"If that's all –"

"No, it's not all," J.D. said in a low voice. "What – what would it
entail, this going public?"

Jesse tried not to show elation. "I don't know all the details, but I
can get them."

"How soon?"

"Would two days be soon enough?"

"Yes. Keep this secret – I don't want a word leaked anywhere,
inside the company or out. Do you understand?"

"Yes, sir."

"Now get out of here before I change my mind about the woodshed."

Duane and Jesse hardly slept for the next two days. They haunted the
public library and the Columbia University library. They learned
about the Securities and Exchange Commission regulations on public
offerings of stock. They gathered together over a dozen prospectuses
from companies that had offered stock to the public, to use as
examples. Finally, late in the afternoon of the second day they made
up a draft prospectus of Marvel Scientific stock.

On the third day they presented their findings to J.D.

Toward the end of the meeting, Jesse said, "The only fly in the
ointment is that each of the present shareholders has the right to buy
new stock up to his proportionate present interest."

"That won't be a problem," J.D. said. "I don't think many of
them'll want to put up new money."

"One thing you might consider, Dad, is to have someone else make
an offer for the shareholders' stock before the company goes public.
Then you'd have them out –"

"And they'd have their money. But who?"

"There's a firm on Wall Street – Bracken and White. I went to
Columbia with George White."

"I've heard of them. A hot-shot brokerage."

"Nevertheless, very successful. George is an extremely bright guy.
Bracken, his partner, is older. A good combination."

"Can this friend of yours keep his mouth shut?"

323

"I would think so."

"Feel him out, then – but no commitments!"

Jesse had dinner with George White the next evening. They talked until late into the night.

The next morning Jesse reported to his father. "George is definitely interested. He thinks he'd have no problem putting together a group of private investors to take over the present shareholders' interests. One thing – he said that we should, at the earliest opportunity, hire a top-notch securities attorney so that it all gets handled in an above-board manner and we don't inadvertently stub our toe on some Securities and Exchange Commission regulation."

"All right," J.D. agreed. "Find us a lawyer . . ."

In the fall of 1949, Marvel Scientific Machines, Inc., went public. A group of investors, headed by Bracken and White, bought out over eighty percent of the existing stockholders. In 1948 Marvel Scientific had had revenues of nearly $120 million with earnings of $18 million. For the first quarter of 1949 – the last quarter reported in the prospectus – earnings had been down to $4 million on revenues of $27 million. The prospectus said that the proceeds from the sale of stock would be used to build a new research facility on the company property at Tarrytown, to complete development of the ATAC computer, to build a computer-manufacturing facility at Tarrytown on property adjacent to the company property that was in option, and to launch an aggressive sales program to market the ATAC and a new, improved version of the Model Z tabulator being developed in the New York labs. The prospectus frankly admitted that the company had been hurt by its conservative attitudes, which the money from the stock offerings would correct. It said that most of the old shareholders had been bought out, and that a program of bringing younger executives into the corporate offices had been inaugurated under the direction of Jesse D. Marvel, Jr., recently named Vice-President of Corporate Development, who was to be in charge of management development, corporate training, corporate public relations, and research and development. Clarise was now working for her husband.

"I think I should resign," Clarise said.

"We need you!" Jesse replied. "You're the heart and soul of the ATAC project." They were sitting in a booth at Ciro's where they'd just finished dinner. Jesse couldn't remember the last time they'd

324

been out to dinner alone. Clarise had surprised him by asking. It was two days after Jesse's promotion had been officially announced, and just a week before the stock offering.

"I don't know that I can work for you, Jesse."

"Think of it this way, Clarise – you won't be working for me. How you run that project is up to you. But I'll be there to take some of the details off your shoulders, and to run interference for you with the rest of the company."

"I doubt that it would work."

"Look – you have what you've always wanted. The money to complete the ATAC. You can have a first-class lab now, with all the latest equipment. You can have the best components for the prototype. You can hire more people."

She gave him a strange look. "How do you know what I've always wanted?"

"Am I wrong?"

She passed a hand across her eyes. "No. You're right. It's what I've worked for." Jesse thought she was very beautiful. She was more rested than he'd seen her look in a long time. He covered her hand with his own.

"Clarise, I know what I wish you wanted. I wish you wanted me."

She stared at him silently for a long moment, and then said, "You've changed so much since I first met you."

"I was a kid."

"You've grown up, that's true. But you've also gained a kind of *core*, an integrity. If I hadn't been so self-involved, I think I could've admired you. Your father told me that it was you who engineered the changes in the company, single-handed, and without any real authority. I think he admires you quite a lot. He's also scared of you."

"*Scared!* Dad?"

"He feels his throne teetering."

"I don't think an atom bomb could blast Dad out of his throne."

She looked away again. "What do we do now, Jesse?"

"Now?"

"Do we get a divorce?"

"Listen, Clarise! If I thought you could ever love me, I'd do anything – anything! Do you hear?"

She put her hand on his cheek. "Oh, Jesse. I don't know. I just don't know. I'm thirty-six. Maybe it's too late for me."

"It's not! You said if you could love anyone, it would be me. So will you give it a chance? One good chance?"

"All right." She leaned forward and gently placed her lips on his.

EIGHT

Thinking is very far from knowing.
Proverb

30

The Flying Squads

In 1949 MARVEL SCIENTIFIC MACHINES had gross revenues of $98 million, and profits of $9 million. Compared with 1948, revenues were down nearly twenty percent and profits were cut in half. In the meantime IBM's revenues had grown to $183 million and profits to $33 million. The new Marvel board of directors decided something drastic must be done to stem the tide.

The research facility at Tarrytown was built in stages. Stage one was completed in early 1950 and Clarise and her staff moved in. They had fifty percent more floor space than at their old facilities in New York and, more important, the labs were equipped with the latest in testing equipment. Even with the infusion of cash, added staff, and better components and lab equipment, Clarise and her senior research staff estimated that the prototype of the ATAC couldn't be completed before the summer of 1952. In February of 1950 a crash program was initiated at Tarrytown to create a new machine, a card-programmed calculator capable of competing with the IBM machines of similar design known as the 600 series, or the CPCs. In the meantime, IBM was just on the point of announcing the 701, a machine intended to compete with the UNIVAC, but inferior to it in both technology and performance, although an advance over the 600 series.

The strategy devised by the board, with the advice and consultation of a management team composed of J.D., Jesse, Clarise, and Jamie Ryan, was to produce a CPC of their own that would allow Marvel Scientific to compete with IBM for the 600 business, and then leap-frog their 701 series with the ATAC which would be superior to it and, Clarise promised, a worthy competitor to the UNIVAC.

The target date for the completion of the prototype of the Marvel

CPC was September of 1950. This was such an ambitious schedule and the possibility of it slipping was so great, that J.D. decided it would be kept secret from the public at large, since a publicized failure to meet the date would be disastrous for stock prices. Jesse went to Tarrytown to personally take charge of the project. He took Duane Hopper with him.

Tarrytown was like the honeymoon that Jesse and Clarise had never had. And a strange honeymoon it was. They took a furnished bungalow half a mile from the lab. Jessica stayed in New York with her nurse to attend school. They worked long and exhausting hours, but when they came together at night for what was usually a cold supper and a glass of wine, their flagging energies were magically revived and they would spend long, languorous nights of love-making. Clarise's sexuality was suddenly and miraculously awakened. It was as though once she committed herself to the marriage all the barriers, psychological as well as physical, fell away.

The card-programmed calculator that was being developed was called, among the research staff, the Model Omega. Duane Hopper came up with the name, because, he said, the machine would be the absolute end of what could be done with electronic accounting-machine technology.

The Model Omega was a strange lash-up of two Model Z tabulators communicating through a vacuum-tube storage device. Intermediate computational results were stored in the vacuum-tube component to be passed back and forth between the two tabulators.

The prototype machine was ready in July of 1950. A problem in integral calculus had been selected for the initial test of the machine. On a rainy July Friday, the Omega staff gathered together in the large room where they had assembled the machine for the test. The Omega was programmed by punched cards fed into its card-reader, each card containing an instruction. Jesse placed the program deck of cards in the feed hopper and pressed the "Read" button on the central console. The card deck began to melt away as the reader swept the cards under its sensor brushes and deposited them in an output stack at the opposite end. Above the whir of the belts and pulleys that ran the feed mechanism, the passage of the cards made a rhythmical *click–swish–click–swish*. Then, a breathless thirty seconds after the cards had all been read, the two tabulators did their computations. Finally, with a *chunk–chunk–chunk* the printer began to pass paper through its feed sprockets.

Duane Hopper stepped to the printer and read off the results as they appeared. The correct result had been chalked by one of the technicians on a blackboard that hung above the machine. When the last result had been read by Duane, a cheer went up in the room and echoed around the bare walls. The Model Omega had passed its first test.

During the succeeding weeks the machine was put through an exhaustive series of tests. Problems were encountered, but none took more than a day or two to correct, so that by August 15, two weeks ahead of schedule, Jesse was able to phone his father and report that they were ready to begin production of the machine.

The announcement of the Marvel Stored Data Calculator (a name chosen by J.D. himself to distinguish the machine from IBM's), caused a public stir. The *Wall Street Journal* made it a front-page item. *Newsweek* did a feature story. *Barron's* not only did a feature, they included a profile of J.D. and the new management philosophy at Marvel Scientific. During the week of the announcement Marvel stock shot up from $17 to $28 on the New York Stock Exchange.

With the Stored Data Calculator in production, J.D. pulled Jesse back to New York. Jesse had lost weight, and fatigue had put dark smudges under his eyes. Not all of these changes, as J.D. thought, were wrought by long hours on the project. J.D. didn't know about the nights of Jesse and Clarise, but he saw that his son was in remarkably high spirits, and put it down to his success with the Stored Data Calculator.

They met in J.D.'s office with Jamie Ryan the morning after Jesse's return.

"We have the machine," J.D. said. "What we need now are orders."

"How many do we have?" Jesse asked.

Jamie consulted a sheet of paper. "As of this morning, thirty-six."

"Break-even is three hundred," Jesse commented.

"The problem is," Jamie said, "the Stored Data Calculator is a special-purpose machine. Our commercial accounts really haven't the applications for it, although nearly half of our orders are up-grades of existing accounts."

"Why would they order machines they can't justify?" Jesse asked.

"Prestige," J.D. replied. "They want to own the latest. Ego is a big selling aid in this business, Jesse. Tell him about Kingman Manufacturing."

"They're our largest account in Atlanta," Jamie explained. "They're building a new headquarters, and including a glass-walled room to house their Stored Data Calculator."

"Everyone walking into the lobby will see the machine," J.D. added. "Although they could do all their work on a bunch of Model Zs for half the cost."

"How do we get another two hundred and sixty orders?" Jesse asked.

"From businesses who have IBM equipment and UNIVACs on order," J.D. replied. "We know they're already sold on a machine the size of the Stored Data Calculator. All we have to do is convince them that our machine is the one they really want."

"How do we do that?"

J.D. grinned "Salesmanship. After the technical people are through building machines, the thing that gets them sold is plain old-fashioned salesmanship, Jesse."

"I realize that. But it seems to me we'll have a tough time talking them out of the UNIVAC and IBM machines."

"We have one large advantage – we can deliver. The assembly plant at Tarrytown will put out, what? Forty machines a month?"

"Once it gets rolling, which should be within the next two months."

"So," J.D. said. "We can fill three hundred orders over the next eight or nine months. The initial customers can have a machine within two or three months. The UNIVAC isn't going to have production models for years. The IBM CPC has a wait of at least a year. We have a machine every bit as good as the CPC, competitively priced, and available a lot sooner. And who's to say that the UNIVAC will even work when it goes into production, or how much it will cost?"

Later, Jesse and Duane were discussing the problem in Jesse's office.

"An idea," Duane began.

"Shoot," Jesse said.

"Flying squads of salesmen, especially trained, coordinated by us out of the New York office. We find out where Remington Rand and IBM have machines on order. We learn all we can about the companies in question – who the decision-makers are, the politics – then the squad moves in. We point out that the UNIVAC is unproven, the

CPC has long delivery. We assemble a dossier of horror stories about companies that have had bad experiences with both. We offer to move a Stored Data Calculator on the premises, and let them prove for themselves that it works."

"Is it ethical?" Jesse asked.

"What's unethical? If it's not against the law, it's okay."

"I won't debate the finer points of that statement," Jesse replied drily.

"We need to sell nearly three hundred machines! We aren't going to do that by politely knocking on doors."

"We could do it by unpolitely knocking the competition?"

"Only the truth."

"Partial truth?"

"Call it what you like. I'll bet we'd lease three hundred machines inside a year."

Jesse paused, then smiled. "I like the idea."

J.D. more than liked the idea. He adored it. "By God!" he said. "We could blitz the country with – what did you call them?"

"Flying squads," Duane replied. They had found J.D. alone in his office, working late over a stack of papers.

"Flying squads," J.D. repeated, savoring the phrase. "How soon can we begin?"

"We figured we'd bring top salesmen from the field into the office here for special training. Then Duane and I would supervise their forays."

"Attacks!" J.D. said, laughing. "That's what they'll be."

"And the beauty is that these same prospects that we sell to will be A-one prospects for ATAC when it's ready."

"You know," J.D. said to Duane. "I wondered, when Jesse wanted to bring you from Schenectady, if it was wise to advance someone so young so rapidly. I just stopped wondering!"

The salesmen they brought to headquarters were already well trained in the Marvel Way. All that remained was to give them a crash course in the Stored Data Calculator and, more important, inculcate them with the principles of the Flying Squad. They were taught how to approach key employees of prospective customers to learn the internal politics of the organizations and were armed with tales of failures of their competitors' equipment which had been gathered from Marvel branch offices throughout the country. Finally, the same branch

333

offices provided lists of firms in their territories which had UNIVAC or CPC equipment on order. Within six weeks of getting the go-ahead from J.D., eight flying squads of three men each set off from New York in different directions. Duane and Jesse hop-scotched around the country, using every mode of transportation that would get them there the fastest, supervising the flying squads.

They began in December of 1950 and by the following March had orders for ninety-three Stored Data Calculators.

In June of 1951 the Korean War had been going on for a year. The day after it broke out, J.D. had sent a telegram to President Truman offering the full resources of Marvel Scientific to the cause. But, other than a slight increase in government business, the war changed little at Marvel Scientific. For a while it looked as if Jesse's inactive reserve unit might be called up, but they were passed over for active units who had training in jet fighters.

By June of 1951 the flying squads had garnered just over two hundred orders for Stored Data Calculators. What delighted J.D. the most about these orders was that more than 150 of them came from companies that had been "un-hooked" from Remington Rand or IBM.

Then, in September, when they were in New York for a weekend, Duane and Jesse met in Jesse's office to plan their activities for the coming week. Duane told Jesse that he was engaged to a girl from Schenectady named Linda Larkins.

"That's great, Duane!" Jesse said. "But when the hell did you have time to court her?"

Duane grinned. "Didn't you notice that I always managed to take the flying squads working the northeastern part of the country? Well, if you ever want to know how to get to Schenectady from anywhere in the northeast, ask me – I'm an expert."

Remington Rand delivered its first computer, the UNIVAC I, to the Census Bureau on June 14, 1951. By that time it was a well-known story around the data-processing industry that Tom Watson, Senior had had a chance to have the UNIVAC for IBM but that instead he'd offered Mauchly and Eckert low-echelon jobs in his research organization, causing Mauchly and Eckert to take their machine to Remington Rand where they were treated to money, royalties and prestige.

Oddly, the potential objection that Jamie Ryan had foreseen about the Stored Data Calculator – that it was primarily a scientific

334

machine, containing too much high-priced computational power to be economical for commercial accounts – never really came into play. Only about a fifth of the total eventual sales of the machines were for purely scientific purposes. For the rest, the ingenuity of the flying squads in thinking up ways to apply the Stored Data Calculator to commercial applications, and the egos of company executives who wanted to own an "electronic brain," combined to bury any objections.

Marvel Scientific Machines, Inc., finished 1951 with sales of $185 million and profits of $11 million. The profit was deceptive. Most of the card-programmed calculators were leased to customers, so that their research and development costs wouldn't be recovered for some time. Even though these costs were amortized forward, J.D. had decided, conservatively, to enter as direct expense the costs of the machines themselves, thus lowering the profit margin considerably. The effect that this had in 1952 was startling. 1952 total revenues were $196 million, a small increase over 1951, but profits shot up to $34 million, because most of the Stored Data Calculators that were on lease had been paid for the previous year.

The schedule for the ATAC prototype slipped by six months – it wasn't finished until January of 1953. J.D. came to the conclusion that it had been worth waiting for. It was as fast as the UNIVAC, featured both punched-card and paper-tape input, and was the first computer to store its programs like data.

A private demonstration of the ATAC prototype was put on for company executives. Clarise, as beautiful as anyone could remember seeing her, conducted the demonstration herself. It was a marvelous show of lights flashing on various instrument panels, switches being toggled, cards being gulped up by the reader, paper tapes spinning, and printers clattering. The same demonstration was given to the press the following day. The prototype had been shipped to New York weeks before the demonstrations. Months before, J.D., bitten by the same bug that had afflicted Kingman Manufacturing and others, had ordered a room on the ground floor of the Marvel building prepared to house the first ATAC. The room featured a glass wall between it and the lobby, so that all who passed through the portals of headquarters would see the machine. The press wrote glowing articles about the demonstration. National publications ran features about how the company had shaken off the "grey old men" image and was now on the leading edge of computer technology.

In the same year IBM came out with a machine it had informally called "The Defense Calculator," but re-christened the 701. It was clearly a scientific machine, with relatively high computing capacity and very little input-output capacity. As such it was much inferior to the Stored Data Calculator which at least had a card-reader and a printer that operated at decent speeds.

Tom Watson, Sr., seeing the hole in his product line, immediately ordered the development of a new, commercial computer to compete with the UNIVAC and the ATAC. He put in charge of this development Vincent Learson, one of the IBM genuises of computer manufacturing and marketing. The new machine was called the 705 and was the first machine to use a revolutionary development produced by engineers at MIT, core storage – the storage of data and programs in tiny, doughnut-shaped metal cores that could be bi-directionally magnetized to represent the two states of the binary number system. Learson and his team announced the 705 as a new IBM product ninety days after he'd been given the task by Watson, Sr., an unbelievable feat of engineering.

So, within months of the triumphant introduction of the ATAC into the commercial world, IBM was once again baying on the heels of its competition, threatening to run them to the ground. J.D. saw immediately that core storage made the vacuum-tube relay system of the ATAC obsolete, and he ordered the research facility at Tarrytown to turn its attention to, first, modifying the ATAC to use core storage and, second, to developing an entirely new computer that would incorporate every advance in the technology, including core storage. He was determined to win the race against his competition. What he couldn't foresee was that the technology would develop faster than it was possible to create computers to incorporate it.

31

Jessica

THE UNIVAC that was delivered to the Census Bureau in 1951 arrived in time to make a profound difference in the tabulation of the 1950 census. Just as Hollerith's machines had displaced scores of clerks in the Bureau in 1890, so the UNIVAC displaced numerous electronic accounting machines, many of them IBM and Marvel. By the time Mauchly and Eckert joined forces with Remington Rand in 1951, they had orders for six more UNIVACs at over $1 million apiece.

The ATAC was an even larger success. From the prototype installed in the Marvel corporate headquarters grew orders that, by the summer of 1954, numbered twelve machines. Executives were brought to New York, at Marvel Scientific's expense, where the ATAC was demonstrated. J.D. took delight in running these demonstrations himself, under the watchful eyes of a clutch of technicians ready to rush in if anything went wrong.

Immediately after the completion of the first ATAC J.D. formed a pricing committee for the machine. He was the chairman, and the committee comprised Jesse, Duane Hopper, Clarise, and Jamie Ryan. They decided that, rather than sell the ATAC, as Remington Rand was doing with the UNIVAC, they would lease it. After all, this had proven to be an eminently successful strategy for their electronic accounting machines. Not only did it generate a steady, monthly cash flow, but the leases locked Marvel Scientific and the customer together in an ongoing legal obligation, and made it easier, when the time came, to upgrade the customer to other Marvel equipment.

The ATAC had cost nearly $20 million to develop. The engineers at Tarrytown, who had designed the line that would turn out production models of the computer, estimated that each unit would cost $640,000 to manufacture. At best, the potential market for the machine was

337

nothing more than an educated guess. J.D. set it at fifty machines, which meant, at the projected lease life of each machine of four years (another guess), they would have to rent at $35,000 a month to return something like $30 million in profit to the company.

J.D. was convinced that research must press on, developing better machines. This would take money, and since the nature of the leases meant that over $600,000 would have to be invested in each computer before the first monthly lease check could be taken in, there would be at the outset, and for some time, a negative cash flow from the computer side of the business. Jamie Ryan prepared a series of charts showing all of these effects, and J.D. reluctantly agreed to put the company in debt by issuing bonds. This was done in the summer of 1954, and the subscription was sold out before its official release, yielding, after underwriting expenses, a little under $50 million.

In 1952 Thomas Watson, Jr. had been named President of IBM, his father stepping up to Chairman of the Board. Tom Watson, Jr. was only three years older than Jesse, a point not lost on Jesse. He made it a private goal to become President of Marvel Scientific Machines by 1955 when he would be, at thirty-eight, the same age as Tom Watson, Jr. when he became President of his father's company. But 1955 was to come and go, and J.D. not only showed no signs of relinquishing his control of the company, he actually increased it. He took a more active role in the marketing of the ATAC. He became a frequent visitor at Tarrytown, wandering around the labs and the ATAC manufacturing line, asking questions, offering suggestions, and generally making his presence felt. At sixty-five he seemed as energetic as ever, though in recent years his sexual fires seemed to have cooled somewhat. He no longer raided the typing pool in New York as though it were his personal harem. He still had his occasional fling with a secretary from a branch office that he might be visiting, or with a particularly willing woman that he might meet at the occasional social functions his position required him to attend, but his energies were concentrated on the business more and more.

In the summer of 1954, when the ATAC production line was functioning properly, Clarise asked for and received from J.D. a leave of absence. She was determined to make a home for Jesse and Jessica. To that end she convinced Jesse that they should sell the Greenwich Village apartment and buy a three-bedroom brownstone in the East 50s. Clarise threw herself into decorating their new home. She also drew up plans for getting to know Jessica, organizing outings to the theater for the two of them and cozy dinners in front of the fireplace when Jesse worked late, which he often did. Jessica, who was nearly fourteen when her mother took her leave, suffered these impositions on her active life with kindness. But she couldn't return the warmth that her mother offered. She'd been on her own too long. She'd created a world that suited her, and her mother's overtures were an intrusion on that world.

Jessica went to St. Anne's Episcopal School for Girls in Manhattan and had been president of the first-form class. She was also Vice-Chairman of the Science Club which she'd co-founded with a senior girl, and had made straight As in science and math, and Bs and As in languages, history and English. She'd gathered about her a coterie of girls who were as serious-minded as she, and of whom she was the undisputed leader. They met together often at one girl's house or another to drink milk, eat cookies, and discuss their lives. They attended the dances jointly sponsored by St. Anne's and St. Mark's – the Episcopal Boys' School – but they did so with the superiority of those who had more serious things on their minds than the posturings of callow boys. Jessica led by example. She had her mother's creamy, limpid complexion, and her father's dark hair and eyes. Although she was very slender at thirteen, the long legs and the lithe body showed the unmistakable promise of a beautifully formed woman-to-be. The boys of St. Mark's were intimidated by her beauty and her haughty air. As a consequence the plainer, more accessible girls got more dances than Jessica, which seemed to suit her fine.

Jessica knew something about computers – being around Jesse and Clarise and her grandfather, some facts couldn't help but stick to her acquisitive mind – but her knowledge was frustratingly shallow. She proposed to her mother that she should tutor her in computers. Clarise was delighted. Clarise stocked the den with a flip-chart stand and a stack of ATAC manuals, gave Jessica a primer in Boolean logic and took her through the construction of the computer. They worked past midnight, absorbed – Jessica with the exciting new world that was opening up before her, and Clarise with the fascination born of discovering that her daughter had a mind as fine as her own.

The next day Clarise visited the Marvel offices for the first time in months to borrow programming materials. That night, when Jessica entered the den, she found it rearranged like a classroom. A blackboard had been hung against one wall, from which tables had been cleared and pictures taken down. A table stood a few feet in front of the

339

blackboard, with a chair pulled up to it, to serve as a desk for Jessica. On the table were carefully laid out manuals and blank coding sheets, the forms upon which programs for the ATAC could be written.

The ATAC was a thirty-two-bit word machine. That is, the machine operated on data and instructions which it organized into "words" of thirty-two binary bits, each bit capable of representing a binary digit of 1 or 0. The coding sheets were printed with rows that had been marked off into thirty-two divisions to represent words in the ATAC. Each of the rows was divided into two sections; the first on the left consisting of eight bits, the last, twenty-four.

Clarise explained that the first section was meant to contain the codes for the ATAC instruction set, and the other section to contain the address for data. Thus, an instruction could cause the machine to operate on data found at the address in the storage unit.

"For example," Clarise said, filling in a blank on one line of coding words that she'd drawn on the blackboard, "the binary number 8, represented by 1 in the fourth position, will cause the data found at the address represented by the other portion of the word to be transferred to the arithmetic register of the computer. Let's say we've stored the number 15 at address 1038, and we wish to add to it the number 65, which we've stored at the address 1792. Now, the instruction code for "add" is binary 12. We need two instructions to perform the operation –" When she'd finished writing, the coding words on the blackboard looked like this:

/ / / / /1/ / / / // / / / / / / / / / / / /1/ / / / / / / /1/1/1/ /

/ / / / /1/1/ / // / / / / / / / / / / / / /1/1/1/ / / / / / / / / /

"The arithmetic register," Clarise went on, "consists of two words, or sixty-four bits, and has a floating point function, so that you can keep track of decimals . . ."

By the time they finished, just before midnight, Jessica was writing simple programs, which Clarise promised to take down to the Marvel offices the next day and run on the ATAC.

Jessica was excited to see the output of her programs, a series of printed numbers on lined, continuous, track-fed paper, but a sense of frustration tainted her pleasure.

"Why can't I run my own program?" she asked.

Clarise thought for a moment. "I don't see why you can't. I'll tell you what – I'll reserve us an hour on Saturday."

Jessica wrote five simple programs to try on Saturday, stealing time away from her other studies to do it. Clarise had reserved time at six o'clock in the evening, when the regular production work of the computer would be done.

Clarise gave Jessica a brief lesson on the keypunch, which, since she already knew how to type, was all she needed, and then left her to keypunch her programs while she went to the small room behind the computer where a percolator was kept, to have a cup of coffee. The room was occupied by a young man, sitting at the only table, hunched over a set of coding sheets with a cup of coffee at his elbow. Clarise poured herself a cup and silently sat across the table from him. There was a protocol among computer programmers that said that when one was debugging a program one's privacy was inviolate. Clarise didn't recognize the young man, and concluded that he must have been hired since she'd left, as she'd known every programmer at headquarters, as well as Tarrytown. She picked up a month-old copy of *Time* magazine that was on the table and leafed through it.

Finally, the young man looked up with that bleary-eyed stare that Clarise knew so well, a look that indicated a reluctant return from the world of logic problems to the imprecise world of people. Now that she saw him full face she saw that he looked younger than she'd imagined, about seventeen or eighteen, although she knew it was impossible for him to be that young and an employee of the programming department of Marvel Scientific.

"I know you," he said. "You're Clarise Marvel."

"I don't think we've met."

"I've seen your picture. I'm Tom Ryder." He had coarse, straight blond hair that had been cut short so that it formed cropped shocks above his high forehead. His face was broad and flat, with a short nose and large staring blue eyes that added to his look of youth. His skin was very pale in the fluorescent light of the coffee room.

"You're a programmer?"

He nodded. "In the business department."

She glanced at the coding sheets. "An accounting problem?"

He shook his head slowly. "A project of my own," he replied.

Jessica chose that moment to burst into the room, a printout and coding sheets in her hand, and a look of utter frustration clouding her face. "Mother!" she exclaimed, ignoring the presence of the stranger.

341

"I keep getting the most outrageous drivel. Can the printer be on the blink?"

Tom Ryder laughed. "Typical programmer reaction," he said.

"What does he mean?" Jessica demanded hotly of her mother.

Clarise couldn't help smiling. "He means that the first impulse is to blame the equipment."

"Well, couldn't it be on the blink?"

"Unlikely," Tom Ryder answered. "I just ran a rather long output on that printer not an hour ago."

"Jessica, this is Mr. Ryder. My daughter, Jessica. Mr. Ryder is a programmer."

Jessica gave the young man a baleful stare. Clarise had come to know her well enough in the past few months to know that there was nothing that could arouse her anger more quickly than to have her intellectual abilities questioned. "I have checked my program thoroughly," she said icily.

"Not thoroughly enough, evidently," Ryder replied placidly.

Jessica turned to her mother, turning her back on Ryder. She held out the coding sheets. "Here, mother – see for yourself. I've checked the program several times."

For motives she didn't fully understand, Clarise said, "Perhaps Mr. Ryder would look at it for you."

"Happy to," Ryder replied in that same placid voice that was infuriating Jessica.

Jessica didn't exactly throw the coding sheets at Ryder, but she didn't hand them over politely either. Calmly, he collected them together, leafed through them for not more than five seconds, and looked up with a weary little smile. "Index registers," he said.

"What about them," Jessica asked stonily.

"You're branching on register value zero."

"That's right."

"How many times do you want to loop through the main program?"

"Three." Clarise could see that Jessica, in spite of herself, was becoming interested in what Ryder was saying.

"So what are you initializing the register with?"

"A three, of course."

"Of course," Ryder said with his little smile. "The problem is you're branching on register zero *after* the loop, so what you get is *four* times through the loop." He held up four fingers of his left hand and

342

tolled them off with the index finger of his right. "Three, two, one, zero – four loops."

"Oh," Jessica said, in a small voice. "I see." She gathered up the coding sheets, looked at them for a moment, and then looked up at Ryder. "How did you find it so fast?"

"Everyone makes that mistake when they start," he said.

"It'll only take me a jiff to fix the instructions," Jessica said to her mother. "I'll run it again."

"Do you need the computer right now, Mr. Ryder?" Clarise asked.

Ryder looked at his wristwatch. "I'd better get out of here. I've been at it since last night." He began to gather up his things.

When he was gone, Jessica said, "Do you suppose he meant it, that he'd been here all last night and all today?"

"I'm sure he did. When you're debugging, time seems to melt away. I've done quite a few all-nighters myself."

Two weeks passed before Jessica saw Tom Ryder again. During those weeks she hurried through her homework each afternoon in order to spend the rest of her evenings writing programs. During that first week Clarise showed her a technique, called flow-charting, for planning and organizing her programs before she began to write them. Using a metal template Jessica was able to draw diagrams of the program logic. The template contained various cut-outs. One could trace the cut-out shapes onto paper. There was a diamond for branching – lines terminating with arrows could be drawn from each point of the diamond to indicate the possible branches from a group of computer instructions. In fact, each figure on the template corresponded to one or more instructions for the computer. There were rectangles with the base a wavy line, to represent printing, ordinary rectangles in which to write computations, and so on. This provided an enormous breakthrough in Jessica's competency as a programmer. By constructing a flow-chart first, she found she could debug most of the logic before writing a single line of computer code.

By the end of the second week she had flow-charted and written a program to solve second-order algebraic equations using the quadratic formula, something that she'd recently learned in her algebra class at St. Anne's, and she was eager to take it to the ATAC for a trial run.

Saturday evenings were the only times that Clarise could get computer time on the ATAC and when Jessica did not have to be in bed early for school the next day. It so happened that the Saturday after Jessica had finished coding the quadratic equation, her father

343

and mother had to go to a party at Earl Baxter's apartment. He was the public relations man for Marvel Scientific, and the party had been arranged to mingle Marvel executives with certain influential members of the press and television. Jessica was sorely disappointed.

"Listen, darling," Clarise said. "I don't see why you couldn't go down to the computer center tonight. You don't need me."

"Could I!" Jessica brightened like a wilting flower that had received water.

"I can call Frank to let you in." Frank was the night guard at Marvel headquarters. "But you'll have to promise to be home no later than eleven, and to take a cab both ways. I'll give you the fare. Frank can call you one from the lobby, when you're ready to go."

Jessica arrived at the lobby entrance of Marvel headquarters at seven-thirty. Frank was waiting for her on the other side of the glass door, and opened it with a welcoming smile.

Jessica had her program and flow-charts in her school satchel. Eagerly she went across the lobby and, as she did, could see, with a stab of disappointment, that someone was using the ATAC – a slender form was sitting at the console, hunched over the toggle switches, back to her. She tugged the door open, the vacuum created by the air-conditioning sucking against her, and stepped onto the tiled false-floor under which, she knew, having been shown once by her mother, ran a spaghetti-like network of cables connecting the components of the ATAC to one another. She stood behind the man at the console, whom she recognized as the young programmer she'd met two weeks before. She struggled to remember his name, couldn't, and ended by saying, "Er –"

He spun around, startled, his large, slightly exopthalmic eyes leveling their blue gaze on her face. "The apprentice programmer," he said, in that casual, slightly mocking tone of his that she remembered so well.

"Will you be long?" she asked briskly.

"Have you a program to run?" he replied.

"Yes."

"No problem." He toggled switches. The printer started to chutter out several sheets of printout, then stopped. He stood, stepped to the printer, gripped the paper with one hand, flicked it with the fingers of the other to burst the perforated seam, and turned with it, rather like a conjurer at a magic show. "All yours."

"I didn't mean to chase you off." She felt suddenly embarrassed.

344

"I was just noodling," he said. "I've got plenty of debugging I can do in the back."

"Noodling?"

"Improvising. Fooling around. Running the harrow over the old fallow ground." He pointed to his temple.

She followed his retreating form with her eyes for several seconds, thinking what a strange man he was – or, *boy*, she amended. He didn't look much older than she. Then she turned to her task, and for the next two hours she thought of nothing else. When, finally, she had, with an exultant rush of triumph, managed to get the quadratic-formula problem to run on the ATAC, she looked up at the big, white-faced clock on the wall and was astonished to discover that it was nearly ten o'clock. It seemed to her that she'd only been there half an hour.

She gathered her materials together in her satchel, walked to the door of the back room, and opened it. The young man was there alone, bathed in the fluorescent light, bent over a disorderly pile of coding sheets, his head propped on the palm of one hand and a stub of a pencil in the other hovering over lines of code.

"Excuse me," Jessica said. "I'm through. If you want –"

He looked up with the abstracted gaze of a sleep-walker, and she had the sudden intuition that here was someone else for whom the last hours had gone like minutes.

His eyes focussed, and he smiled – the first time she'd seen him smile, and it was rather dazzling. He had small, even white teeth, and a generous mouth. "Got it to run?" he asked.

"Yes!" Suddenly Jessica wanted very much to share her triumph with someone.

"What were you programming? A chess game? Strategies for the Cold War?"

"The quadratic formula." She flopped her satchel on the desk and opened the buckle. "Here, I'll show you –" then, suddenly shy, her hand froze with the papers half out of the satchel, "I mean, you're probably busy –"

He leaned back in his chair, smiled, and held his hands wide, in a gesture that conveyed that he had absolutely nothing better to do than to hear about Jessica's program.

For the next ten minutes she explained it to him. He was terribly quick. He admired a little technique she'd come up with for resetting index registers, a kind of nested iteration, that she was very proud of, and that he found without her showing him. Then he suggested that

345

three routines could be combined into one set of instructions, with only the variables changing each time, since the computations were almost identical for the three, and she immediately saw the point.

When she was finished and was putting her papers into her satchel, he stretched mightily, looked at his wristwatch, and said, "You know, I should really buy you a drink to celebrate."

Once again she froze, staring at him. "Celebrate?"

"Your program. It's the first –"

"Oh no! I've written others."

He shook his head. "None like this, I'll wager. This is a *real* program, not just some learning exercise. You know, 'Sort twelve numbers and print them in inverse order.' "

Jessica laughed. She was amazed at how good she felt. She couldn't remember ever feeling quite so good, in a kind of through-and-through way that seemed to permeate every fiber of her being. "You're right," she said. "But I couldn't have a drink with you, I'm afraid."

"Why not?"

"I'm – I'm not old enough, you see."

He shrugged. "How old are you?"

"Sixteen," she replied. She wouldn't be fourteen for another two months, and she'd never lied to anyone about her age before.

"Look," he said in a reasonable voice. "I don't want to talk you into something you don't want to do. But this place we go is just around the corner, and no one has ever questioned me, even though I'm told I don't look like I'm out of high school. Besides which, I am one of the lowliest of the low around here, and, as such, I would be the last to do anything improper with J.D. Marvel's granddaughter."

"I have to be home at eleven," she said.

"Where do you live?"

"The East Fifties." For some reason she found herself holding her breath. She let it out slowly.

"I promise I'll have you in a cab by ten to eleven. It's no more than ten minutes this time of night. There's an old custom, you know."

"What's that?"

"When a new programmer, like you, has his first big success, an old-timer, like me, buys the drinks."

"Well," she said, with a quavering smile. "If it's customary . . ."

The bar was across the street and half a block down from Marvel

346

headquarters. It was called "Donkey's," why Jessica didn't know, and was too shy to ask.

When he'd stood to leave, the young man had pulled a shapeless corduroy coat with leather elbow patches from a coat rack and put it on. He was wearing wrinkled but clean cotton pants, a maroon shirt with a button missing at the collar under a white sweater, and saddle shoes with white, wooly looking socks. Jessica suddenly remembered, in a hot flush of embarrassment, that she still had on her school clothes. They weren't quite a uniform, but the dress code at St. Anne's was so specific that it might as well have been. Her dress was of red and black plaid wool, with a jumper, under which she wore the prescribed white blouse buttoned to the chin. Her beige socks were knee-length. Her shoes were tan loafers. Over all this she wore a cumbersome lined coat of tan cotton that had been treated with a water-repellent finish and sported a floppy hood, which she hated. As she walked down the street beside the tall young man with her satchel under her arm she felt as though she must look like all the other knobby-kneed, red-nosed and gawky little girls that one saw all over the city in the mornings and afternoons.

The bar was dim, and strange smells wafted through its heated air like tropical zephyrs – a mixture of old leather, floor polish, wet wood, and alcohol. She felt a delicious thrill of adventure course through her as the young man (she still couldn't think of his name) guided her to a padded booth along one side of the narrow room. The mahogany bar that ran the length of the room was thronged with patrons, most of whom the young man seemed to know, which solved at least part of the name problem for Jessica, as several of them addressed him as "Tom."

The waiter was a thin man with an insipid mustache who was wearing a dirty white apron.

"A champagne cocktail for the lady," Tom said. "And my usual."

The waiter, hardly giving her a glance, slithered off to get the drinks.

Jessica sat with her back straight, her knees together, and her fingers laced on the table in front of her. Tom, who was lounging with his back to the wall, one leg cocked up on the bench, said, "What's it like being J.D. Marvel's granddaughter?"

"How do you mean?"

"You know! The man's a legend. 'World's best salesman.' 'Father of data processing.' "

She shrugged. "He's just my grandfather, to me. He treats me very well."

He seemed to consider this as he gravely took a pack of Chesterfields from his jacket pocket and offered one to her. She shook her head; he took a cigarette and lit it with a chrome Zippo lighter.

The waiter brought the drinks. Jessica's glass had a dark cube on the bottom and was delicious. Tom's drink consisted of a glass of beer and a shot glass full of amber liquid. He lifted the shot glass and dropped it into the beer glass. They both watched the little glass sink to the bottom of the larger glass. Tom raised the beer glass, touched her glass with it, and said, "To programming."

"To programming."

She watched fascinated as he tilted the beer glass to his lips. The little glass stayed on the bottom, seemingly defying gravity. He noticed her look. "Ever see one of these before?"

She shook her head.

"It's called a boilermaker, don't ask me why."

"What's in the little glass?"

"Bushmills – Irish whiskey."

She suppressed a shudder. "Sounds ghastly."

He laughed. "I can see you're not Irish."

"You are?"

"Oh yes! Even though Ryder may not sound it. My father was half Irish, my mother was a thoroughbred, from the Auld Sod."

"Was?"

"Both dead," he said matter-of-factly.

"I'm sorry."

"It happened a long time ago. I was five. My father loved to get roaring drunk and then drive his Model A flivver as fast as it would go. Mother usually went along. She certainly did the last time."

"Oh."

Tom Ryder held up two fingers to the waiter. Jessica noticed his glass was empty, and then was surprised to find hers was too.

"So what happened?" she asked.

"Happened?"

"You were five, with no parents."

"Oh. My sister and I were 'taken in,' as the phrase goes, by my mother's brother."

"Where?"

"In Philadelphia – same town. We just had to move three blocks, as a matter of fact. All the Irish live in the same section there, y'know.

348

The shanty Irish, anyway."

The waiter deposited their drinks and Jessica watched Tom sink his shot glass of whiskey in the beer. He made it seem a ritual of some kind.

"How long have you been programming?" Tom asked.

"A couple of weeks."

"Not bad. Did your mother teach you?"

"Yes."

"You had the best."

"You know her?"

"Of her. She's the mother of the ATAC."

Jessica stared at him. "I never thought of her that way."

He laughed. "I'm sure you didn't."

"How long have you been programming?"

"I don't know – a couple of years."

"Did you learn at the company?"

He shook his head. "I used to hang around the lab at the University. Mauchly and Eckert were there from time to time, though you didn't see much of them."

"The University?"

"Of Pennsylvania. Moore School of Engineering. It's where they built the ENIAC."

Jessica felt as though she were a stranger in a foreign land where she didn't speak the language. "I'm sorry. Is that a computer?"

"Yes! I've been rambling on like you're an old hand. Somehow it's easy to think of you that way." Jessica was enormously pleased by this remark. "You know of Mauchly and Eckert?"

She shook her head.

"Professors at the Moore School. They've since moved on to Remington Rand, where they built the UNIVAC –" he smiled, "Short for Universal Automatic Computer."

"And ENIAC?"

"Electronic Numerical Integrator and Calculator. It's pretty primitive by today's standards, but when it was completed around '46 it was the most complex device of its kind in the world."

"So you went to the University of Pennsylvania?"

"For a year. Then I was thrown out."

"Thrown out!"

He grinned, and held up two fingers to the waiter. "Spent too much time hanging around the ENIAC, and not enough time cracking my books."

349

A full glass was put in front of Jessica, and the other whisked away. Solemnly, Tom launched his shot glass into his beer.

"Y'know," he said, "it's strange. At Pennsylvania, you have to major in electrical engineering to get to study computers."

Jessica nodded sagely. She had the momentary sensation that her head was trying to float up to the ceiling like a balloon. "Well, a computer is all electrical parts, and so on, isn't it?"

"Of course. But how much do you know about electrical engineering?"

"Not much, I'm afraid."

"Nor do I, but we're able to program that beast across the street, aren't we?"

Jessica felt a surge of pride that he used the collective pronoun. She nodded gravely. "I see your point."

"It's like –" Tom looked around the bar, as though he would spot what it was like. "It's like saying Barney Oldfield should've had a degree in automotive engineering."

"Barney Oldfield?"

He waved a hand. "Old time race-driver." He lit a cigarette and brooded over his drink, the cigarette hanging from his lip.

"I wanted to work in the labs at Tarrytown, y'know."

"No," Jessica said. "No, I didn't know that. What prevented you?"

"They want degrees at Tarrytown. Preferably several per researcher. Someone else has my allotment of degrees. So I program accounts receivable and inventories."

"Is that what you were working on tonight?"

"Do you think I'd work on the crap in my own time!"

"N-no. I suppose not."

He leaned across the table and took her hand in his. "Listen," he said. "Would you like me to tell you what I'm working on in my spare time?"

"Well, yes – if it's not top secret or something."

"I'm working on a compiler." He released her hand, sat back, and looked at her expectantly.

"Oh!" she said. "I see."

"You only have one question," he said.

She nodded. Then, not quite in unison, they said, "What's a compiler?" And broke down in helpless laughter.

When he'd regained control of himself, he reached under his sweater and took out a pen. He took a napkin from the chrome container on the table, and poised the pen over it.

350

"First, I should explain an assembler to you. Right now you program the ATAC in machine language, right?"

"Well, yes. Is there another way?"

"When you want to add two numbers, how do you do it?"

"I write a binary 8 to transfer the first quantity to the register, and a binary 12 to add the second quantity."

"And both addresses are binary, too, aren't they?"

Jessica nodded.

"Suppose you could write, for transfer, 'TR'?" He wrote the letters on the napkin. "And for the first address, instead of binary, decimal – like, say, 1029." He wrote "1029" next to the "TR." "Then for the add, suppose you could simply write 'A.' " He wrote an "A" on another line. "And then say the second quantity was at address 840?" He wrote "840" next to the "A," and shoved the napkin over to Jessica.

She stared at the lines he'd written. "You mean that's all you have to do?"

"That's all."

"But – but how does it work?"

"Another program, written in machine language, takes the symbols there like input data, and translates them into the proper binary codes. Then it causes them to execute, so that you get your two numbers added together."

"Is this possible? I mean, can I do it now?"

He laughed. "You're a true programming nut, Jessica. Show a programming nut a new toy, and he wants it right away. No, you can't do it on the ATAC, but the new computer they're developing up at Tarrytown will have an assembler.

"But that's old stuff." He flicked the napkin with a fingernail. "The exciting work is in compilers." He turned the napkin over. "Suppose, for your quadratic-formula program, you could write minus b, plus or minus the square root of b squared, minus $4ac$, and so on . . ." He wrote on the napkin as he spoke. "Of course, since we don't have radicals and multiplication signs, and so forth, in the Hollerith code, we'd have to make up other signs for them – say two asterisks for radicals, and fractions for the surd." He rewrote the equation using the new symbols, and then passed it to Jessica.

As she gaped down at the symbols on the napkin, she had the feeling that she was being transported to some place she'd never been before. A distant door seemed to open somewhere down a long corridor in her brain. "That's wonderful," she gasped.

351

He patted her hand. "You are a quick one, my girl."

"How – how does it work?"

"It doesn't, right now. No one has a compiler worthy of the name. Oh, a few of us, here and there, have put together a bit of syntax that runs. And there's a rumor – no, more than a rumor, it's a fact – that IBM has started a large project to develop a formula-manipulating compiler."

"But are we doing one?"

"We?"

"You know – Marvel . . ."

"Ah. *That* we. No, we aren't."

"But why not! We must!"

He smiled his lazy smile, and signaled to the waiter.

"None for me, thanks," Jessica said, covering her glass.

"Fact is," Tom said. "There's a debate raging in the higher stratospheres of the computer biz. It seems no one knows if a compiler is possible."

"But you have it all figured out!"

He laughed with delight. "Oh, a lot of folks – or, at least, quite a few – could write a compiler. The problem is to get it code-efficient." Then, seeing her questioning look, he continued. "Which means getting a problem to run in near the time and storage requirements of the same problem coded in machine language by a competent programmer."

"Ah."

"Ah, indeed. A couple of pseudo-brains at MIT wrote a compiler last year. Trouble was it ground away for hours to perform a test problem that could be, and was, coded in machine language to run in fifteen minutes."

"Oh," Jessica said gloomily.

"Never fear, little one. I believe there's a solution to the whole mess."

"What?" she asked eagerly.

"An intermediate step in the translation using string language – the so-called Polish notation. Look," he said, hunching across the table toward her. "Suppose you take the formula symbols and, before you translate direct to machine language, you translate the computational parts, the parts that take time and storage, into Polish notation."

"Suppose you do," Jessica said giddily, not having the least idea what Polish notation was.

"Well, when you have it in Polish notation, you can perform

operations on the formulas to minimize running time. *Then* you go into machine language."

"Gorgeous," Jessica breathed.

"I wish I could take credit for the idea," Tom said, submerging another shot of Bushmills into a glass of beer. "I read about it in an American Mathematical Association journal. And I'm sure the lads at IBM must know about it."

"Then all the more reason why we *must* do the same."

"I wish you were your grandfather saying that. And, of course, inviting me to be a part of it."

"Oh, you will be, Tom! You know so much!"

He looked at his watch, and started. "My God! It's a quarter past eleven. I've got to get you in a cab, or I won't have any job at all . . ."

Outside, on the sidewalk in front of the bar, the cold air cleared her head a bit. Tom ran up the street and brought back a cab. As he was helping her in, he gave her cheek a chaste peck. "Happy New Year," he said.

She turned toward him on the seat, the door open. "Happy New Year?"

"In a few months it will be 1955," he said solemnly. "That was in case I don't see you before."

"Oh, but surely . . ." she began. But he'd closed the door, and the impatient cabbie was already pulling the taxi away from the curb. She stared out the back window at his receding figure on the sidewalk, swaying a bit as she did, and not entirely from the motion of the cab, and wondered how he could stand so straight and steady with all those boilermakers inside him.

32

Fortran

IN DECEMBER OF 1954 John von Neumann was in New York City for a meeting of a scientific society. J.D. met him for dinner at the Waldorf Astoria. Von Neumann was uncharacteristically depressed. It didn't take J.D. long to find out why.

"Alan Turing is dead," von Neumann said.

"I'd heard. He was so young!"

"Forty-one. We've lost one of the most brilliant minds of the century."

"Heart-attack?"

"No." Von Neumann took a mournful sip of his wine. "Suicide. I've just been told the circumstances."

"Good Lord, why?"

"In a sense, a very real sense, he was killed by his own government."

"How do you mean, Johnny?"

Von Neumann told him. A couple of years before someone had broken into Turing's house and stolen various valuables. Turing knew who had done it – a young man who had been his lover. When the police questioned him, Turing frankly admitted his homosexuality.

"The British have laws against it," von Neumann said. "They put Turing under the care of a clinic instead of in jail – they think of themselves as achieving enlightenment since Oscar Wilde's day. They gave Alan hormones to 'cure' him. He grew breasts, became impotent. They drove the poor man crazy. One day he injected an apple with strychnine and ate it. The witch and Snow White, all in one."

They ate in gloomy silence. Finally, von Neumann said, "There's

354

another matter I wanted to talk to you about. IBM is developing a formula-manipulating language."

"We looked into developing one at Tarrytown," J.D. replied. "They tell me it's too inefficient, that programs would run many times longer than in machine-language code."

Von Neumann shook his head. "There are ways around that, I'm convinced. You'd better get into it, J.D., or you'll be left at the post."

"But we have a very good symbolic processor we're developing. Surely that's all you need . . ."

"No. With a symbolic processor, the programmer is still machine-dependent. He needs to know the computer in detail. With a compiler – a formula manipulator – he just learns syntactical rules, and then concentrates on the problem in the terms of the *problem*, rather than in the terms of the computer. It will open up the computer to many scientists and engineers."

Two nights later Jesse and Clarise had J.D. to their home for dinner. Over cocktails in the sitting-room before dinner, J.D. reported what von Neumann had said about the formula-manipulating language. "IBM is calling it 'Fortran,' " he said. "For 'Formula Translation.' "

Jessica chimed in, "I've heard of that." The adults turned their surprised attention to her. "You have an employee, Grandfather, who is working on a formula-translation program."

"I do? Who?"

"His name is Tom Ryder."

J.D. looked at Jesse and then Clarise. "Who in blazes is Tom Ryder?"

Jesse looked blank.

Clarise said, "He's in the business department at headquarters."

"What in hell is the business department doing developing compilers?" J.D. said.

"Oh, it's not the business department," Jessica replied. "Tom is doing it in his own time."

"And how do you know so much about this Ryder fellow?" J.D. asked.

"I was debugging at the center the other night, and got to talking to him."

"Debugging?" J.D. said.

"I've been teaching Jessica programming," Clarise explained.

"You were down there alone?" Jesse asked.

"It was the night we went to the Baxters," Clarise interjected. "I let

355

her take a cab. She had written her first significant program . . ."

"The quadratic formula," Jessica interrupted.

J.D. laughed. "She's caught the fever, I can see."

"It's very exciting, Grandfather," Jessica said, her eyes shining. "I made up an iterative loop for setting the index registers. You modify the reset instruction on a negative result –"

J.D. held up a hand. "You've lost me. I only run the company, Jessica, I don't program the computers."

"I'm not sure I like having you down there alone at night," Jesse said.

J.D. snorted. "What's going to happen to her at headquarters, for God's sake, Jesse?"

During dinner, J.D. said to Jesse, "What do you think about this Fortran business?"

"The research department said it wouldn't work. That the code was too inefficient. But if what von Neumann says is true – if the eggheads at IBM think they can lick the problem – then we shouldn't let them run away with the idea."

"My thoughts exactly," J.D. replied. "You're in charge of research and development. See what you can get started . . ."

The next morning Jesse asked to see Duane Hopper in his office. Duane and Linda Larkin had been married quietly the month before, and the occasion had reminded Jesse that he'd been meaning for some time to reward Duane for his excellent work, so he had arranged to have him promoted to the title of Vice-President of Administration and Corporate Development, a job created especially for Duane, and in which he still reported to Jesse.

After Jesse had repeated what his father had told him the night before, Duane said, "We'd better get cracking on a project. It sounds like IBM is already several lengths in front of us."

"Who do we have at Tarrytown we can put on it?"

"The most experienced compiler people are the two fellows who did the report that said a formula manipulator wasn't feasible. I don't think they're the ones."

"I agree."

"We may have to start with people who know nothing about compilers. There probably aren't half a dozen people in the country, outside of IBM, who are what you would call experts."

"Apparently there's a fellow right here in the building who's been doing work in his own time on a compiler. Name's Tom Ryder. Do you know him?"

"Is he the young fellow in the business department?"

"That's the one. I don't know how good he is, but it might be worth looking into."

Tom Ryder had never been above the sixth floor, where the business department resided, and had to restrain himself from gawking at the tasteful elegance of the executive suite as he was ushered by a secretary through the reception area to Duane Hopper's office.

Hopper stood to shake hands as Tom entered his office, and motioned him to a chair.

"I hear rumors that you're working on a compiler," Hopper said curtly.

"Yes."

"How old are you?"

"Twenty-three."

"You look younger."

"So I've been told," Tom replied.

"How would you like to work on a compiler for Jesse Marvel and me?"

"When do I begin?"

"Report here tomorrow morning."

They gave him the title of Senior Development Programmer, and for the first week he was the only one working on the compiler project. They found him a tiny office on the second floor so he'd be close to the computer. During the second week three design programmers arrived from Tarrytown to work for him.

It wasn't until the middle of February of 1955 that Tom saw Jessica Marvel again.

She came to his office one wintry evening, stuck her head in the door, and said, "Is this an office, or a cloakroom?"

Tom looked up from his desk. "Hello, Jessica."

"May I come in?"

He motioned to the only other chair in the room.

"I haven't seen you in the computer center," she said.

"I'm working on a project that doesn't require computer time at the moment."

"The Fortran compiler?"

"Yes. Although that's really IBM's name for its own version."

"What do you call yours?"

"We haven't decided on a name. I was thinking of recommending Marveltran."

"Are you still sinking Irish whiskey in you beer?"

"When I have the time."

"I owe you a drink."

"Well –" he hesitated.

"It's an old custom, you know," she said.

He grinned. "Let me get my coat."

Von Neumann visited Tom's project in April of 1955. He had been hired as a consultant for one day by J.D. Tom and his crew had finished the preliminary design of the compiler, now officially named MathTran, and they were at the point where the company had to decide whether to continue or not. Continuing meant, by Tom's estimates, putting ten more programmers on the project for at least two years. Before this commitment was made J.D. wanted von Neumann to give his opinion.

Tom was awed at the prospect of meeting von Neumann, who towered over everyone in the design of computers and computer languages.

Tom and his crew spent two days putting together a presentation for von Neumann. They had flip-charts, flow-charts, and handouts, and had practiced the presentation on each other until late the night before von Neumann arrived. They figured it would take most of the day. As it turned out, they were finished before lunch. Von Neumann had the uncanny ability to not only quickly grasp what he was being told, but also to jump several steps ahead to the conclusion of each point. When they were done, Tom felt as if it were von Neumann who had given the presentation and he who had received it. They all trooped up to J.D.'s office to hear von Neumann's conclusions.

Jesse and Duane Hopper were hastily summoned, and von Neumann said, "Well, I think you have a project." He went into detail as to why he thought what Tom had proposed would work. When he was finished, J.D. said, "I don't see any reason to delay things, do you Jesse? Duane? In that case –" he turned to Tom. "You have yourself a project, young fellow."

Tom couldn't suppress a big, Irish grin. "Thank you, sir."

"One thing," J.D. said. "Let's beat IBM!"

In 1954 Remington Rand had delivered to the General Electric plant at Louisville the first business-application computer. Two months later Marvel Scientific delivered its first ATAC computer to General Electric in Schenectady. It replaced four Marvel Stored Data Calculators.

The Justice Department filed an anti-trust suit against IBM in 1955. At the same time it filed a memorandum of intent for a similar suit against Marvel Scientific Machines, Inc. Tom Watson, Jr., in defiance of his father, signed a consent decree with the federal courts in the fall of 1955. A debate began to rage inside Marvel Scientific about whether they should do the same. J.D. wouldn't hear of it; Jesse and Duane wanted to sign.

"I will not have the government telling me how to run my business!" J.D. raged. "That's out-and-out socialism."

"While we're spending a considerable portion of our resources fighting this thing for years and years, IBM will have all of its resources available to run away with the market," Jesse told his father. But J.D. was obdurate. The issue touched deep-seated beliefs in the old man. It also raised the specter of his humiliating conviction in 1912. This time, by God, he intended to fight and win! No deals!

Tom Watson, Jr. had been able to sign the consent decree for IBM because he was President of the company. Jesse had no such power. His father was not only President and Chief Executive, he was also Chairman of the Board. So Jesse had to rely on persuasion and strategy if he was to get his way.

Jesse spent long hours arguing the point with his father. "Look, Dad – all they want is for us to agree to business practices that make sense anyway. No knocking the competition. No discounting our prices to freeze out the competition. No unhooking. It's simply good business and would give us the reputation of being an honest company."

"We *are* an honest company," J.D. fumed. "Are you saying we aren't?"

"Of course not." Jesse sighed. "This would simply make it explicit."

"No government lawyer in a tight suit is going to tell me how to run my business!"

In early 1956 the board of directors of Marvel Scientific met and authorized the final stage of research to begin on the development of the new computer, to be called ATAC-2. It would incorporate core storage and use transistors instead of vacuum tubes. The commitment was the largest in money and manpower that the company had ever made. Preliminary estimates were that the ATAC-2 would take two more years and an additional $25 million to complete development.

Jesse was anguished at the thought of trying to develop such an advanced computer while fighting an anti-trust suit. He came to a decision. The first person he shared it with was Duane Hopper.

"You can't mean it!" Duane said, deeply alarmed. "You'd quit?"

"I simply can't stay and watch the company ground down. Did you see the discovery the Justice Department filed? It will take hundreds of man hours to dig out all those files. And think of the days and days of testimony for you, me, Dad – all the top people here. How the hell are we going to do that and launch the second generation of computers at the same time? IBM will eat us alive."

"But, my God, Jesse! What will you do if you quit? This company has been your life."

"I suppose I might teach at some business school."

"Teach!" Duane said. "You should be President of the company!"

"I'll share a secret with you. When Tom Watson, Jr. was made President of IBM he was thirty-eight. That was in '52. Watson is three years older than I am. So I set myself a private goal – to be President of Marvel Scientific no later than '55, when I'd be thirty-eight. As you can see, I missed it. And the way Dad is going, not only do I doubt that he will give up any of his authority, he'll probably outlive me."

"But, damn it, Jesse – surely the board –"

"No," Jesse interrupted. "The last thing I want is to start a fight in the company."

It was Clarise who told J.D. For months she'd known that Jesse was distracted, working too hard, and subject to fits of depression. She thought that once the ATAC-2 project was launched the pressure would ease off a bit. She was completely unprepared when he told her of his intention to resign from the company.

The next day without telling Jesse what she was doing, Clarise got an appointment to see J.D. She told him what she'd come to tell him without preamble. He was visibly shocked. "You can't be serious!"

"I wish I weren't. But I know Jesse. He means every word of it."

"I had no idea –"

"Another thing," Clarisse went on. "I know Jesse well enough to know that once he submits his resignation, there will be no talking him out of it, no deals."

"I had no idea he felt so strongly about this goddamned Justice Department business. Oh, I knew he felt *strongly* – but not *that* strongly. So, he'd lay down his job over it, would he?"

"You sound rather pleased by the whole thing."

"Not pleased. I admit I'm a bit proud of him, that's all. What does he imagine he'd do if he left?"

"He thinks he might teach at a business school."

"Teach!" J.D. said with disgust. "Jesse is too fine an executive to be wasted that way."

"But haven't you been doing just that?"

"Now see here, Clarise!" J.D. retorted angrily. "I've given Jesse more and more responsibility. He's in charge of our whole research and development effort."

"But have you given him all the responsibility he's capable of handling? Every time there's a big decision, one that effects the very nature of the company, who makes it?"

"Jesse knows his opinions are valued," J.D. said stiffly.

"Does that answer my question?"

"Damn it, Clarise, you don't have to be so goddamned bright all the time, do you?" J.D. stared broodingly out the window for a long moment. Clarise remained silent. Finally, he sighed. "I guess I'll have to cave in. I'm not prepared to lose Jesse."

She smiled. "You may be stubborn, J.D., but you're not dumb."

"It is not easy for me to say that I'm wrong," J.D. said stiffly. He and Jesse were at a table in the L'Escargot Restaurant, where J.D. had invited Jesse for lunch. It was the day after Clarise's interview with him. "I guess it's because I've had so little practice saying it."

"What do you mean, Dad?"

"I'm going to give in on this Justice Department consent decree."

Jesse was startled. "Do you mean it?"

"Every word."

"But – what changed your mind?"

"You did. By attrition. All those months of arguing. It's like drops of water wearing away a rock." He pointed to his head and smiled. "And I got to looking around the office the past few days, and I could see that this goddamned thing is causing us to spin our wheels, to go off in two different directions, when we need to be concentrating on whipping IBM." He held up a hand as Jesse started to speak. "Don't say it. I know this is what you've been telling me all along. It has finally sunk in."

"That's great, Dad. I'll call the U.S. Attorney and set up an appointment for you."

361

"No, Jesse. I want *you* to sign the damned thing. Spare me that, at least."

"I'll need a power of attorney from you."

"No, you won't." J.D. paused. "I polled the board this morning by phone. As of ten o'clock, you were President of Marvel Scientific."

J.D. was still Chairman of the Board and Chief Executive Officer. Jesse was made Chief Operating Officer.

In May of that same year, 1956, Tom Watson, Sr. gave his son the added title of Chief Executive Officer. Then, on June 19, Thomas Watson, Sr. died. He was eighty-two. Tom Watson, Jr. was now in complete control of IBM.

Watson's death depressed J.D. He'd never met Watson. So it wasn't a sense of personal loss, of losing a friend, that depressed J.D. It was the intimations of his own mortality that he saw in Watson's passing. J.D. was sixty-six, and in excellent health. But he was still at an age when most men were retired, and he resented the indications of elderliness – the little deferences from young waitresses at restaurants that weren't so different than the same attentions they paid to very young children; having younger men from the company rush to help him out of cars, or to hold doors for him (he couldn't deceive himself that this was a deference afforded rank – they didn't do those things for Jesse); the little aches and pains that made him walk stiff-legged, and the tendency of his body to try to permanently assume the shape of whatever chair he was sitting in. Most of the time he ignored ageing. He looked forward to seeing the development of all the new and exciting products at Marvel Scientific come to fruition, and beyond that, the evolving of other, yet to be dreamed, advances. The very nature of the business, the rush of technology, gave him a feeling of endlessness that Watson's death somehow tainted. He didn't like it. He resented Watson for having died.

In 1956 Marvel Scientific passed the half billion dollar mark in revenues. The company made a profit of $55 million. In December, Jamie Ryan announced his retirement. J.D. was shocked, and tried to talk him out of it.

"Damn it, man – I need you."

Jamie smiled. "I appreciate your saying that, J.D. But I'm seventy years old –"

"You're only four years older than I am."

"I'm tired, J.D. I want to move to Florida and sit in the sun and maybe do a bit of fishing."

"You'll go nuts."

Jamie shook his head. "No. *You'd* go nuts. I won't. I'm an administrator, J.D. A good second banana. I never had your creativity or drive. And now I'm ready to bow out. I'm the last of the grey old men."

J.D. snorted. "That damned *Wall Street Journal* reporter. He didn't know what the hell he was talking about. It's the men of our generation who made the data-processing industry, Jamie. Without us, it wouldn't exist."

"Without men like you," Jamie amended. "I don't kid myself. J.D., that there weren't plenty of men who could've done my job."

"You underrate yourself. I knew from practically the first time I met you – do you remember? – that you were quality stuff."

"I remember very well. I was old Homer Cranston's whipping boy. And I thought you were about the brashest young man I'd ever come across. But the talent stuck out all over you."

J.D. couldn't dissuade Jamie. Jamie also wouldn't let J.D. make a fuss about his going. He didn't want parties or speeches. He just wanted, as he put it, to "slip away without fanfare, without notice." And, in the end, that's what he did. One day he was in his office at his desk, the next he wasn't, and his desk was bare, his chair empty. J.D. ordered the office redone. He couldn't bear to look at it with Jamie's old furniture in it.

Jessica and Tom Ryder had an arrangement for seeing each other. Jessica had agreed to her parents' demand that she spend only one night a week at the computer center. On the chosen night she would arrive by cab at around seven o'clock, be let in by the guard, spend two hours debugging, and then Tom would arrive at their appointed hour of nine, and they would go to Donkey's.

She had learned to nurse one champagne cocktail through the evening. Tom drank many boilermakers. Occasionally she would smoke one of Tom's Chesterfields, which he said she smoked like a girl. They would talk, hold hands, and once in a while Tom would lean across the table and kiss her gently on the lips. Then, promptly at ten to eleven, Tom would go out on the street and find her a cab and she would go home.

In 1957 Lucille Cranston retired. She was sixty-five, but J.D.'d not thought of her as being of retirement age. Her energies seemed to him undiminished from since when he'd first known her, and her administration of the training school at Tarrytown was beyond compare. But he could see her mind was made up. J.D. brought her to New York, put her up at the Waldorf, and threw a banquet for her. Several hundred people attended, many of whom had been through the Tarrytown school under Lucille's guidance. J.D. presented her with a Cartier diamond wristwatch, and Lucille smiled through her tears during the many toasts after the dinner.

A month later John von Neumann died. J.D. had always thought him a youngster, and his death shocked him, partly because he was so unprepared for it. Von Neumann was only fifty-four. J.D. mourned him as a friend and genius who had contributed as much as any man to the development of computers.

1957 was also the year that IBM announced the completion of its first Fortran compiler, to be available on the IBM 704 computer. Jesse and J.D. had been hoping to beat IBM to the punch with MathTran, but it wasn't to be. Tom and his staff had worked long hours, and they had worked intelligently, but IBM had had a six months' head start.

In announcing their compiler, IBM also announced that they would forbear applying for a copyright on the name Fortran, since they wanted to encourage the universal use of the language. Tom immediately suggested to the MathTran management committee, consisting of Jesse, Duane Hopper, and J.D., that they change the name of their compiler to Fortran and make it as compatible with IBM's version as possible. J.D. was furious at the suggestion, while Jesse and Duane thought it made eminent sense.

"I won't have IBM dictating to me what I call my software," J.D. raged. "Next thing, you'll want to change the name of the ATAC-2 to 704."

"It's not the same thing at all, Dad," Jesse said patiently. "The computers are quite different. But if we're going to try to have a universal formula-translating language, we need to standardize it as far as possible."

"We'll develop a better language," J.D. persisted. "And make them conform to *our* standards."

"What do you say to that, Tom?" Jesse asked.

"With the jump they have on us, I don't think we could ever catch up, much less pass them."

In the end, they convinced J.D. – MathTran became Fortran.

Marvel Fortran was announced in the summer of 1958, at the same time the ATAC-2 was announced. The ATAC-2 caused a sensation. It was the first all-transistorized computer. It used core storage, and had, in its main memory, 32,000 binary words of 32 bits each, which required 1,024,000 individual magnetic cores. It used over forty thousand transistors and was hailed as the first of the second generation of computers.

But IBM was not to be left at the starting post in the race for second-generation computers. A month after Marvel Scientific began taking orders for the ATAC-2, IBM announced its own line of solid-state computers, the 7070 and 7090, and, within weeks of that announcement, came out with the smaller 1401 and the 1620.

Although Fortran was the acknowledged leader, a number of other, more specialized, scientific languages were being developed by computer manufacturers and universities. At the same time a clamor went up from the commercial users for a language that they could call their own, and that would incorporate a lexicon natural to their applications.

The U.S. Department of Defense, the largest user of computers in the world, became alarmed at this tower of Babel and, using its clout as the industry's biggest customer, called a conference of all the computer manufacturers in Washington to discuss a standardized commercial language. Marvel sent Tom Ryder to the conference, where preliminary specifications for such a language were presented by Defense Department computer experts, who named it Common Business Oriented Language, or, COBOL for short. The Defense Department had stated that, henceforth, any computer they ordered must include COBOL as one of its languages. About twenty-five percent of Marvel business was with the government, so they had no choice but to authorize research on a COBAL compiler for ATAC-2 and its successors that were being developed at Tarrytown. Tom was put in charge of the project.

Jessica began her second year of college in the fall of 1958. Her mother had wanted her to go to MIT, but Jessica balked, and Clarise relented. Jessica was at Columbia. The reason she'd wanted to stay in New York had occurred one night over drinks with Tom at Donkey's.

He had handed her a present wrapped in silver paper. It was an engagement ring.

"I wanted to get a larger diamond, but that's the best I could afford."

"It's beautiful."

"Would you like me to put it on for you?"

365

"I – I can't, Tom. My parents wouldn't allow it. I can wear it on a chain around my neck, though."

"Hide it, you mean."

"*We'd* know. That's what counts."

"Am I so unsatisfactory as a son-in-law?"

"Of course not. They just don't think I'm old enough to be engaged."

She stared at the table for a moment, and then looked up. "I lied to you about my age. You thought last August, when you bought me that beautiful bracelet, that it was for my twentieth birthday. But it was really my seventeenth."

He laughed with relief. "Is that all!"

"All! I hated lying to you – having our relationship built on a lie."

"I thought you were going to tell me you had signed on with a nunnery, or something." He took her hand, leaned across the table, and kissed her gently on the nose. "Darling, it doesn't matter how old you are."

"Tom," she whispered. "You know what I'd like, to celebrate our engagement?"

"Anything you want, darling."

"I'd like to see your new apartment."

Tom was very proud of his apartment. It was the first place of his own he'd ever had. It was on the second floor of an ancient brick building that had once, long ago, been a warehouse, but that had been renovated into light, airy apartments. His had three rooms. He'd furnished them carefully, with items that he'd picked up at auctions and used-furniture stores. Jessica wandered around inspecting the apartment. In the bedroom they paused before a brass four-poster bed, which Tom had covered with a white fluffy down comforter. He took her into his arms. Her body moulded to his.

He undressed her, folding each garment carefully and putting it on a chair, until she stood revealed before him, her eyes closed, her face flushed with excitement.

He held her gently until her trembling, which had started the moment he touched her naked body, abated. Then he led her to the bed. Then he undressed.

Her skin was fine silk. Her young breasts were small and firm, the nipples erect. Her thighs were firm and eager. And yet he was impotent. Never before had this happened. He lay trembling with shame and anger, while Jessica stroked his chest and kissed him gently.

366

"It's all right, darling," she murmured.

"I can't understand it," he said thickly. "Not a bit of it."

In August of 1959 Jesse went into his father's office, took a deep breath, and said, "I think we've got to reorganize the company."

"What does that mean?"

"I mean the field sales force."

"What's the matter with it?"

Jesse could almost see his father's hackles rising. J.D. had been responsible for creating the field sales force in his own image.

"It has been the best of its kind. But the times have changed, Dad. We can no longer afford to sell the way we did."

"Now you're the sales expert," J.D. said.

"I'm the President, and I expect that, as long as I am, I will feel a concern for every aspect of the business."

"Even if you don't know anything about it."

"Dad!" Jesse was hurt, and surprised.

"Well, I have to speak my mind," J.D. said. "You wouldn't want me to pussyfoot around, would you?"

"If you think I'm incompetent, I'd like to hear it. I'd also like to hear why you picked me for President in the first place."

"Oh, come off your high horse, for God's sake, Jesse. I think you do a whale of a job."

"In the areas I know something about."

"Right."

Jesse sighed. "I know quite a bit about marketing. Not as much as you, granted – but enough to know when we're going in the wrong direction."

"You'd better spit it out. I reckon you're going to sooner or later, and I'd like to get it over with."

"The average age of our branch managers in cities over one million population is forty-nine, Dad. Their average income is seventy thousand a year. Most presidents of companies don't make that. And, with the system of delegated responsibility we have in marketing, these fellows are like feudal lords with their own fiefs, dispensing favors, punishing and rewarding – in short, running their own business."

"To my specifications."

"Granted. The trouble is they operate under a sales philosophy that was great for selling electronic accounting machines, but is wholly inadequate for selling computers."

"These computers are the eighth wonder of the world to you, I know, but to me they're not much more than glorified tab machines."

"But they are more, Dad," Jesse said. "A lot more. They have changed the marketing imperative for data processing, and if we don't acknowledge it, and adjust accordingly, we'll be left in the dust of the companies that do."

"Like IBM."

"Like IBM."

"Jesse, why don't you let well enough alone? You don't have to come up with an idea a minute to justify your title."

"Do you really think that's what motivates me?"

"Oh, hell, J.D. said. "Tell me about this imperative thing."

And Jesse did. For nearly an hour they sat while Jesse talked. When he was through, J.D. gave a sigh.

"You want to weed out these old-timers."

"That's right."

"And put in younger fellows who understand this technological imperative thing."

"It's the only way, Dad. IBM's already doing it."

"You know it is an unshakable policy – my policy – that there will be no lay-offs at Marvel Scientific?"

"I don't propose to lay them off."

"What then?"

"Offer them re-training, and if they can come up to the mark, they can stay. Also offer them the choice of early retirement, with a bonus based on the number of years they've been with us."

J.D. pondered that for a moment. "Yes," he said, finally. "That would be the way to do it, providing I agreed to such a scheme."

Jesse felt a glimmer of hope. "Will you at least think if over, Dad?"

J.D. nodded. "I'll think it over. Now, let's both get back to work."

NINE

Men have become the tools of their tools.
Thoreau

33

The Third Generation

IN THE END, J.D. relented and let Jesse and Duane reorganize the company. In April of 1960, Jesse hosted a meeting of the company executives at a resort hotel in Southampton, Long Island. He wanted them away from the day-to-day pressures to consider the new organization. It soon became apparent that the whole organization needed changing. Simply modernizing the sales force would be like having a Model T Ford with only one fender streamlined. Jesse didn't flinch at what he saw as his duty. By the fifth day of the conference they had evolved a completely new corporate structure.

The new organization was headed by five group vice-presidents and a staff vice-president for administration and public relations, all reporting to Jesse. Duane Hopper was named Group Vice-President for Research and Development. Leslie Parks, a brilliant salesman and administrator who had been Director of Field Marketing in the old scheme, was named Group Vice-President of Marketing. Parks' first job was to be the implementation of a new, streamlined field sales organization. The "grey old men" image was once and for all dispelled. Duane Hopper, at thirty-eight was the youngest of the new executives, and Earl Baxter, at fifty, the eldest. The average age of the seven, including Jesse, was forty-four.

One of Leslie Parks' first acts in his new position was to bring Joe Weston to New York as his assistant. Joe, who had just turned thirty, had joined the company in 1952 after graduating from Harvard with a degree in business, as a salesman trainee. His eight-year career had been distinguished. When Parks tapped him for his assistant, he was branch manager of the Marvel office in Bethlehem, Pennsylvania.

Joe hadn't married. He liked dating and he loved his work. His life,

371

it seemed to him, was ideal, and he couldn't see any reason to change any part of it.

In 1961 Jessica graduated from Columbia with a degree in General Science. After the graduation ceremonies, Jesse and Clarise took her to Twenty-One for a celebration dinner. Over cocktails, and after Jesse had made his toast to the new graduate, Jessica said, "How would you feel if I hit you up for a job, Dad?"

"I'd love to have you work for the company. But, there is a condition, Jessica."

"Yes?"

"Our business is based on sales. I'd want you to learn marketing."

In 1961 Marvel Scientific introduced a new line of computers. The ATAC-C was an immediate success, providing worthy competition for the IBM 1401 which, up to that point, had been sweeping the small-computer commercial market virtually unchallenged. The ATAC-2.5 and the ATAC-S were more qualified successes. It appeared that Marvel's large commercial market had been adequately met with the ATAC-2, and the small scientific market – at which ATAC-S was aimed – wasn't nearly so large as had been anticipated. Nevertheless, 1961 was a great year. Revenues reached $820 million, and profits broke the $100 million mark for the first time in the history of the company.

A few years earlier, scientists at Bell Labs and Texas Instruments had invented integrated circuitry – the etching of several circuit elements onto one silicon chip no bigger than a man's thumbnail – in effect, combining the work of several transistors into a tenth the space and a fraction of the cost, and providing for speeds of computation several times greater than before. It has taken the intervening years to perfect this advance so that integrated circuits could be reliably mass-produced at an attractive cost, but that work had nearly been accomplished, and now, in the summer of 1961, rumors reached the ears of the data-processing industry that IBM was at work on a whole new line of computers incorporating integrated circuitry. The rest of the industry reacted, and the race for the third generation of computers was on, barely two years after the second generation had been born.

Jessica began work at the New York offices in July, 1961. She had struck a compromise with her father – she would spend half of each day programming, and the other half learning marketing. For her

372

programming assignments she was delighted to learn that she would be working for Tom Ryder who was in charge of projects developing COBOL and a new Fortran compiler, to be known as Fortran II. In the mornings Jesse had assigned her, after consultation with Leslie Parks, to Parks' new young assistant, Joe Weston.

Jessica and Tom had seen each other as much as their busy schedules would permit. Neither of them had mentioned again the disastrous night at Tom's apartment, nor had they ever since attempted to repeat it.

Jessica loved her job. Even, she was surprised to discover, the marketing training. She had a heretofore unrealized curiosity about that aspect of the business, and Joe Weston was a good teacher. Jessica found him articulate and witty. They were fast becoming friends.

Two weeks after she began work, Tom dropped a bombshell. He announced that he was being transferred to Huntsville, Alabama, to be project leader on the research and development of a new programming concept known as 'time-sharing.' Time-sharing was the very latest in programming thought, an exciting concept of chopping the resources of a computer up into microscopic time slices, and parceling these slices out to multiple users, who communicated with the computer through terminals, so that each user would have the effect of the entire computer dedicated to his needs. The reason that Tom was going to Huntsville was that Marvel Scientific had a contract with NASA to develop a particular and very esoteric use of time-sharing, called 'real-time,' wherein a computer on the ground would monitor all the many sophisticated devices on board manned rockets, and adjust them through the use of servo-mechanisms.

Jessica was pleased for Tom. But the thought of his going left a raw ache in the pit of her stomach. He was leaving immediately, the following morning. They went out for a farewell dinner during which Jessica cried, and they promised to write to each other daily. Tom said he would be back on business and vacations, and that he still wanted to marry her, if she felt the same. She said, of course she did. They kissed. Jessica fervently wished he would take her to his apartment and make love to her. Instead, he put her in a cab.

The week before Thanksgiving Tom called to tell Jessica that he was taking the whole four-day vacation in New York and wanted to spend it all with her.

"Oh, yes!" she said. "I'll have to have dinner on Thanksgiving with

373

the family, but the rest of the time – yes! You can have dinner with us!"

"No," Tom said. "I've got my old aunt in Philadelphia. Thought I'd run over there. I've taken a room in the Ritz Carleton . . ."

" 'Marketing is King; Engineering, Prime Minister; and Programming, Court Jester,' " Jessica said.

Joe Weston laughed. "Where did you come up with that?"

They were having lunch at a small, Italian restaurant three blocks from the office.

"It's a saying in the programming department."

"I might've known."

"From what I've seen, there's more than a grain of truth in it."

"I suppose so. We must sell the computers, or there wouldn't be anyone around to work on them. And Engineering does have to come up with competitive designs – hardware that is state-of-the-art, and yet priced right. I suppose Programming could feel that they're at the bottom of that particular pile."

"I suppose we like the image, too," Jessica said. "You know – the romance of the oppressed, but talented. 'Do your worst by us, we'll come up with fantastic programs.' "

"We?"

"I consider myself a programmer."

"I was hoping I might make you a born-again marketeer."

"You are a good evangelist, Joe – but my apostasy is unshaken, assuming I ever *was* a member of the marketing religion."

"Oh, we're all born into it," Joe said with an easy smile. "Selling our way in the world, as best we can." He paused and pushed the pasta around on his plate. "Holiday's coming up," he commented.

"Yes."

"I suppose you'll be having Thanksgiving with your family."

"Yes. And you?"

"Up to Boston for a day of relatives and food and drink. See here, Jessica – I'd like to ask you out, but I don't quite know how to go about it."

"Seems like you just have."

"Yes, but in a clumsy, roundabout way. Dammit, why do you make me feel like a tongue-tied schoolboy?"

"Joe," she said. "I think it would be better if we kept our relationship the way it is. I like you. I like working with you. Why spoil it?"

374

"Who said it had to be spoiled?"

"I'm not available."

"Someone else?"

"Yes."

"Ah, well – in that case. If your status ever changes, I'd love to know."

On Thanksgiving evening Jessica met Tom at Donkey's. It was a snowy, blustering night. Tom had just come in on the train from Philadelphia. They ordered drinks. Tom seemed troubled and wouldn't meet her eye. Finally, he said, "Listen, Jessica. You know that – that *problem* I had – you know, that time –?"

She nodded quickly, trying to help him over his embarrassment. "I know, Tom."

"Well – I've solved it. I think I've, ah, got it licked."

"Oh, Tom! That's wonderful! Did you get help?"

"Help? Oh, yes – yes, that's right . . ."

They had dinner at Tom's hotel. Afterward they went up to his room. His hand trembled so that Jessica thought for a moment that she would have to unlock the door. He ordered a bottle of Bushmills from room service. Jessica wanted only coffee. After the bellhop had left, Tom poured a large drink, gulped it, and poured another. Then, abruptly, he went to the closet, rummaged about in it for a moment, and came back with a box that he placed on the bed. The box had the name of a Huntsville department store printed on the lid. He took the lid from the box, removed a garment, and held it up. "How do you like it?"

It was a *peignoir* of cerise nylon with white lace at the neck and sleeves. She stared at it. "Is that supposed to be for me?"

"That's not all," he said eagerly. He reached into the box and began to lay out items on the bed. There was a lipstick of the reddest shade Jessica had ever seen, rouge, eyebrow pencil, and a bottle of perfume. Finally, he brought forth a pair of panties. They were black.

"You expect me to – to what? Make up in this stuff?" Jessica asked.

"Sure! Oh, you'll see, Jessica. It will work. I can tell already!" His eyes were feverish.

"Where did you get this 'help'? At a brothel?"

"I thought you wanted to beat this problem as much as I do. I want to marry you, Jessica."

"Do you call this a solution, Tom? To make me into something I'm not?"

"It would only be for a bit."

375

"How do you know that?"

"After the ice is broken, so to speak, I'll be okay."

"Is that what the doctor said?"

"Doctor?" He looked blank.

"You haven't seen anyone. This is all your idea, isn't it?"

"I didn't need to see anyone. It's a systems problem, really. My body's a system –"

"Well, mine's not!" she retorted. "You can't flow-chart every problem in the world, Tom!"

"You see, it's this thing called the Madonna and the Whore complex," he went on feverishly. "All it takes is for you to dress up a bit, a time or two, and then I'm through it, don't you see?"

"Oh, Tom," she whispered. "You really are sick."

He hit her so suddenly she hadn't time even to flinch. She was thrown to the floor, where she lay slumped against the wall, her mind reeling in that twilight between consciousness and unconsciousness.

Her first coherent impression was of Tom sobbing over her, and the touch of something wet. Tom was on his knees beside her, gently sponging her face with a wash cloth. She pushed his hand away and struggled to her feet.

"Darling, I'm so sorry," Tom said with a sob. "Please try to forgive me –"

"Stay away from me," she replied in a voice she hardly recognized as her own. She found her coat and put it on.

"You can't go like this," Tom pleaded desperately. "You should lie down."

"Don't ever come near me again," she said. She opened the door, went out, and closed it behind her.

In the chill of the night air she began to think clearly. She couldn't go home as she was. She could feel swelling in her jaw and she'd torn a seam in her skirt when she'd fallen.

Then an idea struck: Joe Weston. She found a phone stanchion down the block, praying Joe didn't have an unlisted number, and that he wasn't still in Boston for the holiday. Her first prayer was answered when she found a Joseph M. Weston listed on West 54th. His unmistakable Boston accent came across the line after the third ring.

"Well, Jessica!" he said. "What's up? Did the ATAC throw a shoe?"

"I need some help, Joe," she said.

Immediately his voice became serious. "Of course."

"Could I come to your place for a little while?"

"Where are you?"

She told him.

"I'll be there in ten minutes."

He came in a cab. He leaped out, took one look at her face, put his arm around her shoulders, and bundled her inside.

At his apartment he sat her on a couch and gently took her chin in his hand and turned her head to the light. "Do you want me to send for a doctor? I know a superb fellow right here in the building, if he's in."

"Not now. Please – might I have a drink?"

"I've some very old brandy."

"That sounds good."

He prepared two snifters and brought them to the couch and sat beside her. "Do you want to tell me about it?"

She shook her head.

"Because if it was a mugging, or something, the police should be notified."

"It wasn't."

"Was it this wretched fellow of yours?"

"I don't want to talk about it, Joe."

"Very well. But when you've finished that brandy, I insist we have the doctor up."

The doctor was at home and came right up. He was a large, hearty man, who examined Jessica's face with stubby, sensitive fingers. "Nothing broken out here. Let's have a look at those teeth." Jessica opened her mouth and he probed about for a moment. "Nothing that won't heal," he said. "I'll leave some pills for the pain."

The doctor spoke to Joe in low murmurs at the door before he left. When Joe came back into the living-room, Jessica said, "I hope it wasn't awkward for you."

"Not at all," Joe replied. "He wanted to know what happened, and I told him the truth – that I didn't know. I believe he is almost as outraged as I."

Jessica stayed until midnight, then she insisted on seeing herself home. He hailed her a cab in front of his building and stood watching it until it disappeared from sight.

This was the first time Joe Weston had seen J.D. Marvel alone, and it was, Joe had to admit to himself, unnerving. All the more so, because Joe had been unprepared for the encounter. J.D. simply appeared

377

suddenly in his office, with Joe's secretary trailing behind, making nervous noises.

When they were alone, J.D. took a seat and gazed at Joe, who felt like a small boy being measured for discipline by his headmaster.

"Well, Joe Weston," J.D. began, "I've heard good things about you."

"Thank you, sir. May I get you some coffee?"

"No, thanks. Tell me about this granddaughter of mine."

It was a perfectly miserable Monday in June of 1962. Outside the air-conditioned confines of the Marvel Building, a leaden sky was pressing down humidity and heat onto the city. The shimmering buildings appeared to be melting.

"Something specific you wanted to know?" Joe asked.

"How is she doing? Does she understand anything about marketing?"

Joe paused to collect his thoughts. "I suppose," he said, "it would be, in some sense, more comfortable to report that she had deficiencies. Then I couldn't be thought to be currying favor with the Chairman of the Board. But I have to say that Jessica is absolutely first-rate. She possesses one of the quickest minds I've ever encountered."

"She's not twenty-two yet."

"Chronological age is beside the point where Jessica is concerned."

J.D. smiled. "She always was serious, even when she was a little girl. Where are you from, Joe? Boston?"

"Yes, sir."

"Don't ever lose that accent," J.D. said.

"I doubt that I could if I tried," Joe replied.

"I'm going to borrow my granddaughter for a couple of weeks, if you don't mind."

Joe did mind. Of course, he couldn't say so, because his reasons were personal. Ever since that awful night last November, when she'd come to him so terribly battered, they'd been dating. Perhaps "dating" was too strong a word. Rather, she'd allowed him to become a companion for theater, concerts, and dinners. He'd been amazed at Jessica's near illiteracy in art, music and drama. He'd delighted in being her tutor, and, as in everything else, she was a quick student. But they hadn't progressed past agreeable companionship, although Joe wanted a great deal more. Jessica had a way of forestalling his advances before he had a chance to begin them. But he cultivated patience. To force the issue, he knew, would be to lose her.

378

J.D. wanted to borrow Jessica for a tour of the West Coast. The Seattle Exposition, Century 21, had opened, and Marvel Scientific Machines had erected a pavilion there, as had most large computer manufacturers. When he'd been planning the trip it had occurred to him that he hadn't seen nearly as much of Jessica recently as he would've liked. Taking her along had the added benefit of introducing her to some important sales offices in the company, for the West Coast, with all its burgeoning technological industries, had come to represent a sizeable portion of the company's revenues.

They arrived on July 9, 1962, and were met at Sea-Tac airport by a delegation of nervous Marvel executives. The Seattle branch manager had arranged for a two-bedroom suite in a Seattle hotel with a view of the Space Needle from its sitting-room windows. On the street below the monorail train, which had been constructed for the fair, rumbled, taking passengers between the fair site and downtown.

J.D. and Jessica's tour of the fair had all the appearance of a royal entourage. Marvel field executives abounded, scurrying to open doors, fetching soft drinks, and generally getting in the way of Jessica enjoying herself.

The Marvel exhibit was housed in a modernistic pavilion designed by a Seattle architect. It consisted of an ATAC-S communicating, through an analog-to-digital converter, with a series of mechanical devices designed especially for the fair: a self-propelled vacuum cleaner that cleaned an odd-shaped bit of carpet; a mechanical arm (eerily suggesting a prosthetic to Jessica) that placed checkers on a checker board, and then lifted a 500 lb safe, to contrast the delicacy and the brute strength of its programming; and a plotter that, given certain simple data from spectators about a rocket launch, would plot the trajectory and orbit (if one occurred) of the rocket, and which caused a lot of good-natured kidding whenever the plotter announced that someone's launch had aborted.

The next morning Jessica and J.D. flew to Los Angeles where the rest of that day and all of the next was a whirlwind of activity. They visited branch offices and the site of a refinery where an ATAC-S with an analog-to-digital front end similar to the one at the fair was programmed to control a fluid catalytic cracker.

On the morning of their third day Jessica came into the sitting-room of their hotel suite to find J.D. already dressed, and with a gleam in his eye.

"I've ordered us breakfast."

"Thank you."

"And I've scheduled this day free. We can do whatever we like. I've rented a car."

"I've a feeling," Jessica said, "That you have something in mind."

"How would you like to spend the day at Disneyland?"

Jessica laughed. "I'd love it! I've wanted to see it for years."

"Well, so have I," J.D. replied, rubbing his hands together with delight.

The first thing J.D. spotted when they entered the gate at Disneyland was the Lincoln exhibit. "I've heard about this," he said. "Want to start here?"

"Lead on!" Jessica replied.

The Lincoln exhibit was in a theater and they were just in time for a "performance." The lights dimmed, the curtains parted and there, seated in an armchair, was President Lincoln. He rose, and gazed around the audience. At first Jessica thought it was an actor made-up to look like Lincoln, but as it began to speak, and gesture, it became apparent that it was a robot.

On the way out of the park four hours later, J.D. said, "I'd like to see that Lincoln thing one more time, if you don't mind."

"Of course not." Jessica couldn't imagine what he got out of it a second time. The first time had been interesting, but the second she found boring, since the robot didn't vary its performance one whit. But he appeared just as fascinated as before.

They ate at a steak-house on the way back to Los Angeles. Over drinks, prior to ordering, J.D. asked, "Do you remember that fellow you worked with – the one who used to help you with your programs when you were just a girl?"

Jessica's heart seemed to miss a beat. "You mean Tom Ryder?"

"Yes."

"Actually, I worked for him before he went to Huntsville."

"I'd forgotten that. Anyway, I thought you'd be interested to know I'm bringing him back to New York."

"Oh?" Jessica said, trying to sound casual.

"He got himself in a mess down there, J.D. said gloomily. "Maybe you heard."

"No. No, I hadn't."

"Damned near got canned."

"What happened?"

380

"Drinking," J.D. replied. "Couldn't leave it alone. His work slipped." J.D. shook his head. "I had my eye on that boy. I thought he'd go far."

"Why are you transferring him to New York?"

"You know me. Can't bring myself to fire anyone, particularly when they've got the talent of a Tom Ryder. He's on the wagon, and promises to stay on it. I'm giving him a second chance on a project of my own."

A week after she returned from the West Coast, Jessica was alone in the debugging room after hours when Tom came in with a thick program listing under his arm. The change in him was profound. It wasn't exactly that he had aged but that he had been somehow marred. He looked, Jessica thought, like a choirboy who had been seriously ill.

"Hello, Tom."

"I didn't know you were here," he said, starting to leave the room.

"Wait!" Jessica shouted. He stopped at the door. "Look, Tom – we're going to be working in the same building. We can't run every time we bump into each other."

He hesitated, then took a seat at one of the vacant tables, and spread his listing on it.

"I hear you've quit drinking."

"Yes. I belong to AA."

"That's wonderful, Tom."

"I had to," he said. "It was my last chance. If I blow this job, I'm finished."

"You're working for Grandfather?"

He nodded.

"A special project?"

"I can't talk about it. He asked me not to."

"I hope it's interesting."

For the first time since entering the room his eyes gave off some of the old enthusiasm. "It's the most interesting thing I've ever worked on!"

Marvel Scientific Machines passed the billion-dollar revenue mark in 1962. Profits were over $120 million. The board, at its annual meeting early in 1963, intoxicated by the treasurer's report, voted the largest executive bonuses in the company's history. J.D. received an even million dollars; Jesse, $600,000; and each of the group vice-presidents,

381

a quarter of a million dollars. J.D.'s request for a million-dollar budget for the coming year to, as he put it, "work on a little project of my own, that could lead to great things for the company," passed the board with hardly a murmur despite the fact that J.D. didn't divulge a single thing about it. The collective thinking was that a man who could turn them into a billion-dollar concern could do no wrong.

In April of 1963, Walter Hucko died. He was ninety-two years old. The death of his old friend did not affect J.D. as deeply as it could have, because, for the past three years, Walter had been in a rest home in New Jersey, functioning at a level only a bit above that of a vegetable, and J.D. knew that his death was a blessing.

Wanda arranged a small memorial service attended by their closest friends. She was almost eighty, but J.D. was surprised at how fit she looked. They talked together for awhile after the services, reminiscing about Walter, and then J.D. got into his limousine with Jesse and Clarise and as the car started forward he stared out the window at Wanda with the heart-wrenching premonition that he would never see her again.

Jessica couldn't have put her finger on the precise moment she decided to lose her virginity to Joe Weston. It was the culmination of several processes – her respect and regard for Joe; his devotion to her; and the rather sudden conviction that, at twenty-three, it was time she found out what the excitement was all about.

It would never have occurred to Jessica to be coy about her intentions, or to dissemble the reluctant virgin overcome by passion. She simply told Joe, one evening over dinner, what she had in mind.

For all his Boston aplomb, he couldn't help gasping. He managed to convince her that rushing out of the restaurant to his apartment to get the job done wasn't the way to approach the thing.

"You see," Joe said. "The first time is rather important. Don't want to get off on the wrong foot." He hoped to God he wasn't blushing. "We – we should have a whole night."

"Very well. And?"

"Well, you might – er – want to see a physician."

"What in the world for?"

"There is a certain amount of pain associated with the first time, you know." Now he *knew* he was blushing. "A doctor could – could prepare the way, so to speak."

"I've never heard of such a thing!"

"Done all the time, I assure you. Of course, if you'd rather not, I'm prepared to – prepared to –"

"Muddle through?"

"Wouldn't put it *that* way." He passed a hand over his forehead to find he was actually sweating!

"Good Lord!" Jessica exclaimed. "I didn't know it was so complicated."

They had agreed on the following Saturday night. Jessica arrived at Joe's apartment at seven o'clock, carrying a small overnight case and dressed in a black velour jumpsuit. Joe had laid in champagne, a tin of Beluga caviar, and two well-aged *filets mignon*. It was a snappish April night, with a harsh wind gusting off the East River, and Joe had lit his gas log. He took her coat and hung it up. Then he turned and kissed her gently on the cheek. "This way, darling,"

In the living-room the lights were low, and a bucket of champagne stood by the coffee table in front of the couch. He poured champagne and they touched glasses.

"Why, Joe," Jessica said, teasingly. "I believe your hand is trembling."

"If it weren't," he replied, "I'd be certifiably dead."

They finally slept, and didn't awaken until past eleven Sunday morning. Jessica stretched luxuriously, and said, "Wonderful."

Joe kissed her. "What, darling?"

"You. Everything. Tell me, does it just get better and better?"

"I think that's a question that needs investigation."

"In that case," she replied, "we'd better get started."

In April of 1964 IBM dropped the other shoe – the new line of computers that had been a rumor for so long became a reality: the System 360. The third generation of computers was born.

The 360 had taken them four years to develop. They had opened five new factories for its manufacture, increased their employees by fifty percent, and had spent $5 billion dollars. Besides being the third generation of smaller, faster computers with larger capacity, the 360 married scientific and commercial users into one line of machines.

Marvel Scientific, along with the rest of the computer world, reacted violently. An emergency meeting of the board was convened. The same men who, not sixteen months before, had been complacently handing out congratulations and millions of dollars in bonuses, were driven to near hysteria.

Jesse and J.D. formed a wall of reasonability. Jesse pointed out the research they'd already done with integrated circuits. The first prototype computer was only about six months from completion. J.D. told them how, in anticipation of IBM's announcement, Leslie Parks' marketing organization had, for the past eighteen months, been giving major customers special presentations on Marvel research in integrated circuitry, shoring up their allegiance to Marvel against the anticipated sales onslaught of the new IBM line.

"We can hold the fort until our new computer is ready," J.D. said.

"Computer!" cried one of the board. "IBM is announcing a whole new *line*."

"Yes," Jesse replied. "But you notice that there is only one IBM 360 that has a firm delivery date. We can match that – not now, true – but within six months."

When the meeting degenerated into an argument about what they should call the new line, Jesse and J.D. knew they'd weathered the storm, at least temporarily.

J.D. was now seventy-four, and Jesse wondered if he could take the stress of seeing a whole new line of computers into production. He talked to Clarise about it.

"He's in fine health," she said.

"So the doctors tell me. But damnit, Clarise, the man is seventy-four! He doesn't have the strength he had. And this new line of computers is the largest change we've gone through."

"Can't you take some of the burden from him?"

"The truth is," Jesse said, "he should retire."

"You know he won't."

Jesse nodded glumly. "They'll have to carry him out."

"You should be Chairman, Jesse," Clarise said softly. "You've earned it. Doesn't he realize that?"

"He might, if he ever stopped to think about it. But, for him, Clarise, it's simply a matter of survival. I'm convinced that the thinks he'd die if he didn't have the company."

384

34

The Marvels

THE NEW MARVEL LINE of third-generation computers was announced to the world in March of 1965. They were called, simply, "The Marvels," and the first of the line, the one on which the company had been working for nearly four years, was designated the Marvel Gamma. It was designed to be a middle-of-the line machine that could replace smaller ATAC-2s and larger ATAC-Cs and -Ss. Alpha, Beta and Delta models were in development. Like the IBM 360 line, the Marvels were intended to satisfy both scientific and commercial users.

In September of that year, J.D. decided that his private research project lacked proper security and he ordered that the rooms that housed it be walled in safe-quality concrete blocks and that the entrance door to the lab itself be replaced with a steel door with a combination lock. Jesse was goaded by these actions to try to find out more about what his father was up to. But the security around the project was watertight.

In October Duane Hopper came to see Jesse.

"Your daughter," he said, "is one of the country's leading time-sharing experts."

"I'm glad to hear it. But you didn't come here to please a proud father."

"I'd like to make her director of the company time-sharing organization."

"She's only twenty-five, Duane!"

"There's no doubt in my mind that she's the person for the job."

"I might agree on the technical end, but what about marketing? Are you sure she's capable of handling that?"

"I'd like to make Joe Weston Jessica's assistant for marketing."

"How would Joe feel working for a woman who is, what? Ten years his junior?"

"Joe was delighted with the idea."

"Well, then – I'd say you ought to do it."

In August of 1965 IBM announced their 360 Model 67 time-sharing computer. It was to be a large computer with unique features designed specifically for time-sharing, and it was Jessica's mission, and that of her department, to meet this challenge. To do so, they were working with the engineering group at Tarrytown to modify the Marvel Delta into a new machine to be known as the Delta-TS, intended for time-sharing. At the same time, Jessica's group also had the responsibility for designing and programming the time-sharing software to run on the Delta-TS, which was difficult to program for a computer which hadn't been built. To do this, Jessica first had her group create a simulation program, that would run on the ATAC-2 in the computer center, and that would simulate the Delta-TS in whatever its latest design configuration was.

While all this extremely complex work was going on, Jessica was also charged with developing Marvel's place in the time-sharing market. She had Joe Weston's assistance, but Jessica's nature was such that she couldn't be responsible for something and not take an active role in it. Besides, time-sharing marketing required deep technical knowledge, knowledge that Joe Weston didn't yet have to the extent required. Time-sharing customers were among the most sophisticated users of computers. They spoke of "conversational" computing and "on-line" and "real-time" applications, simple-sounding labels for complex and difficult programs that were understood by very few computer people.

As a consequence of all this, Jessica worked long, difficult hours. It was not unusual for her to get home at ten o'clock, and to be up the next morning at six, so she could get to the computer center and steal an hour or two of debugging time before the heavy day-time demand on the computer began.

It was during one of these early-morning debugging sessions that Jessica ran into Tom Ryder again. They were the only ones in the computer center at that early hour.

Jessica was surprised by his appearance. He'd put on weight, but was paler than ever. "Hello, Tom."

"Congratulations on your new job."

386

"Thanks." Jessica got herself a cup of coffee and sat down with her program listing.

"I don't see you anymore in the computer center," she remarked.

"We don't do much straight programming."

Jessica raised her eyebrows. "What is 'non-straight' programming?"

"You know," he replied vaguely. "Research – that sort of thing."

"Are you enjoying yourself?" she asked.

"I am." The light appeared in his eyes, the light that Jessica remembered so well. It was the light of enthusiasm, of commitment to a cause and, Jessica now realized, of obsession. But she still found it attractive. It seemed to transform him into the old, thinner, healthier-looking Tom Ryder that she had known. "Here's an interesting thing," he went on. "How many possible moves would you say there were in an average chess game?"

She shrugged. "I don't know. Millions?"

"Too low, by a lot. It's ten raised to the one hundred and twentieth power."

"That *is* a big number," Jessica said, wondering how this tied in with Tom's work.

"Now," Tom continued. "Suppose you could evaluate a thousand moves a second. How long would it take a computer to go through all the possible moves?"

"I could figure it out," Jessica replied. "But you obviously know the answer."

"There are ten to the sixteenth microseconds in a century, so it would take ten to the one hundred and fourth centuries."

"That's a long time," Jessica said. "But what does it prove?"

"What it proves is that if you were going to write a chess-playing program, one that could compete with a master, you'd have to do it some other way than iterating through possible moves. You'd have to use heuristics."

"You mean program in the rules and learning patterns of a chess master?"

"Or a group of chess masters."

There was a pause. Then, Jessica said, "Is that part of what you're working on, Tom?"

He flushed. "No. Just a thing of my own."

Jessica thought he was lying. Tom didn't work on "things of his own" when he had a project in hand. He worked exclusively on the project.

*

387

For 1965 Marvel Scientific had a billion and a half dollars in revenues and, despite the heavy investment required for the third-generation line of Marvel computers, had profits of almost $170 million.

1965 also saw the introduction of the first mini-computer by the Digital Equipment Corporation. The minis were smaller, cheaper computers than anything that existed in the third generation of machines, and they represented a stroke of marketing and engineering genius on the part of Kenneth Olsen, the head and founder of DEC. They filled a need that wasn't being met for the small user who couldn't afford the larger computers but who wanted to graduate from electronic accounting machines. They also found a market for what came to be known as "off-loading"; that is, mopping-up jobs that spilled from overloaded large machines.

Also in 1965 the world became aware of the enormous problems IBM was having with its 360 line, particularly in delivering the promised software. Delivery schedules slipped and IBM poured people and money into the problems that wouldn't be solved until well into 1967.

In 1970, the Marvel board of directors, in recognition of the importance of time-sharing to the company, made it a full division, and elected Jessica vice-president in charge, to report to Duane Hopper.

In the summer of 1970 IBM announced their new 370 line of computers. Instead of being the much-anticipated fourth generation, the 370 was an up-grading of the 360 line. Marvel management assessed their position and decided that they need do nothing to counter the 370. The Marvel line of Alpha, Beta, Gamma and Delta could compete handily with the 370. Instead, the board decided to press ahead with research for a new generation of machines.

Late in the year, Tom Watson suffered a heart-attack, and had to reduce his responsibilities at IBM. It therefore came as no surprise when, in the summer of 1971, Watson retired, and T. Vincent Learson assumed the chairmanship. Tom's brother, Dick, had retired early in 1970 to become Ambassador to France, so now, for the first time in its history, IBM was without a Watson.

Watson's retirement depressed Jesse. He remembered, in his early days at Marvel Scientific, how he had measured his own advancement against that of Watson. Jesse was fifty-four, Tom Watson only three years older. Having the standard against which he had once measured his career suddenly fade from the game gave him a little shuddering premonition of his own mortality.

J.D.'d passed eighty with hardly a pause. He hadn't allowed Jesse and Clarise to throw him the lavish party they'd proposed, choosing instead to commemorate the occasion with a quiet dinner at his penthouse with them and Jessica.

After dinner J.D. suggested that he and Jesse have a drink in the library. The women retired to the sitting-room. While his father was pouring their brandies, Jesse idly glanced at several books that were sitting on his father's desk. Then he looked more intently. "Are you reading Claude Shannon, Dad?" he asked.

J.D. came quickly to the desk, opened a desk drawer and swept the books into it.

"Are you interested in Information Theory, Dad?" Jesse asked. "Because if you are, we're doing some studies in the Special Research Section on artificial intelligence. I could ask the project leader to give you a briefing."

"I am getting goddamned sick of all this prying," J.D. said.

Jesse looked at his father in surprise. His face was pinched with fury. "Dad! What's the matter?"

"Don't think I don't know the spying that's going on," he said. "Ryder says you've been pumping him."

"I'm curious, Dad. We're putting a lot of money into your project, and it seems to me the board has a right to know about it."

"I will not permit this spying, Jesse! Is that understood?"

Jesse opened his mouth for an angry retort, and then something in his father's eyes stopped him. "Understood, Dad," he said.

They sipped their brandies in silence for a while. The wildness gradually ebbed from J.D.'s eyes and he began to speak to Jesse as if the incident had not occurred.

The year before, the Justice Department had filed a massive anti-trust suit against IBM. There was talk that the government wanted to break up the company, perhaps into as many as four smaller concerns. J.D. was worried that they might be preparing to spring a similar suit on Marvel Scientific and wondered if Marvel shouldn't unbundle. The previous year, in an attempt to blunt the Justice Department's attack, IBM had unbundled its prices. That is, it had set out a separate schedule of prices for systems engineering, education, software, as well as maintenance for leased systems. In the past all of these services had been included in one price for a computer system.

389

"We've talked to a couple of people at Justice, strictly informally," Jesse replied. "The feeling seems to be that the department has its hands full with the IBM case, and that no one wants to bite off another chunk as large as us."

"We should be prepared," J.D. said. "We don't want to be sitting ducks."

"The estimates we get from our contacts in Justice is that the soonest they could expect a verdict in the IBM case would be six or seven years. This time there's no question about a consent decree. IBM's going to fight down to the wire. The survival of the company is at stake."

J.D. was also worried about the economy. A recession had begun. For the first time in years Marvel Scientific machines were being cancelled for no other reason than that the companies who had ordered them couldn't afford them. The specter of the Depression still hovered over J.D.

"We need a cash position," J.D. said, returning to a favorite theme of his that Jesse had hoped he'd heard the last of.

"Dad," Jesse said patiently. "You simply don't run a high-tech company that way. We have to invest in research, in factory improvements, in marketing innovations. If we don't, we die. We can't do that and accumulate huge cash surpluses at the same time."

"If I hadn't insisted, in the twenties, on accumulating cash, this company wouldn't exist. The Depression would've wiped us out. It wiped out plenty of others."

Jesse sighed. "I know, Dad. But we're in different times, and in a different business. We need to invest heavily in order to maintain our market position. Our market position generates the cash flow to give us operating capital. The excess we have to pump back in."

"What about this research on the fourth generation? We're pouring millions into it. IBM doesn't have a fourth generation."

"That doesn't mean they aren't working on it, Dad. They're working as hard as we are on semi-conductors and large-scale integration. With LSI we could compress many circuits on one chip, thereby increasing speed and reducing the cost and size of equipment."

"Don't tell me about LSI. I know all about it. But is it something we need, to compete?"

"It's essential that we continue the research," Jesse said. "Otherwise, IBM will leave us in their dust."

"All right," J.D. conceded. "I believe you. But mark my words,

390

Jesse. This so-called recession is going to get a hell of a lot worse before it gets better."

J.D. was right. By the summer of 1971, computer companies were laying off employees. Several smaller companies failed. For the first time since the computer boom had begun, programmers were out of work in large numbers.

Jesse had always approved of, and followed, J.D.'s policy of no layoffs. In 1969 Marvel Scientific had gross revenues of $4 billion with profits of half a billion, the best year in the history of the company. In 1970 the figures were virtually unchanged; but in '71, revenues dipped by $100 million, and profits by nearly $200 million. There was a clamor from the board to change the layoff policy. Jesse was always amazed at the chicken-little mentality of boards of directors. In good times there was no tomorrow – they would authorize outlandish executive bonuses, limitless research and development funds, and generally behave like kids set loose in a candy store. But let them smell the faintest whiff of reversals, and they were all for running for cover. It took the combined efforts of J.D. and Jesse to fend off this latest attack of timidity. They won, in the end, by raising the specter of unions, the only thing the board feared more than a dip in the economy.

There was one rather surprising victim of the recession. In May of 1971 General Electric announced that it had sold its computer-manufacturing and sales division to Honeywell. GE would keep only its time-sharing division. After years of massive losses, one of the largest, most successful companies in the history of American capitalism was throwing in the towel and admitting it couldn't compete in the computer marketplace.

In September of 1972 Duane Hopper had a heart-attack. The damage to the heart muscles was minimal and the occlusion that had caused the attack dissolved. With proper rehabilitation, the doctors concluded, Duane could expect to resume a normal life. He was, they declared, otherwise in good health for a man of forty-nine with a sedentary job.

While Duane was in the hospital and, later, at home for several months of recuperation, his duties as Group Vice-President devolved, with a directing nudge from Jesse, onto Jessica. He was frankly curious as to how she would perform in the larger arena and it was an ideal way to test her, since it was understood that Duane would be back eventually to resume his duties.

Duane operated much of his group out of his hip pocket, on the run, as it were. He was an excellent manager, but he didn't leave much of a trail for a successor to follow. So Jessica had to grope her way along. But her instincts were superb, and her knowledge of the company, and her understanding of the fundamentals underlying the computer business, surprised even Jesse.

35

Secrets

In 1973 Marvel Scientific Machines broke the billion-dollar barrier in profits, with nearly $8 billion in revenues. At IBM Vincent Learson retired and Frank Cary took his place as head of the company. The cost of performing 100,000 multiplications on a computer which, twenty years earlier had been $1.62, was now one cent. And Duane Hopper had a second heart-attack.

Although, after a precarious initial ten days, it appeared that Duane would survive, there was no question of his being able to return to work. He was given a medical retirement, and Jessica was elected Group Vice-President of Research and Development. *Time* magazine featured her on one of its October covers under the heading "The New Woman?"

J.D. spent most of his time locked away on the third floor with his secret project. He'd had an office outfitted for himself there, and, since he spent more time in it than in his executive suite, he moved Miss Pribash and her files down. She was not, however, allowed into the inner sanctum of Tom Ryder's labs.

J.D. still took the time to make tours of branch offices. He enjoyed these trips, the attentions paid him by the branch managers and their staffs, the opportunities afforded to give his little inspirational speeches about the Marvel Way. The branch offices regarded him in much the same way as Indian tribes do ancient shamans – as a magical artifact of the distant and arcane past. The modern Marvel salesman was a tribute to training and technology. On his desk he had a cathode-ray tube terminal connected over telephone lines to the company's time-sharing computers in Tarrytown, from which he could instantly discover the status of his customers' orders, their installation schedule, his sales performance for the year, and through which he entered a record of how he spent his time, his expenses, and every other statistic connected with his job. The time-sharing computer printed out compilations of these data broken down in every way deemed helpful to the job of managing the company. Each salesman also had at his disposal a portable terminal with which he could, using an ordinary telephone, communicate with the time-sharing computer from any location in his territory, or from his home.

Sometimes it seemed to J.D. that it couldn't have been sixty years since he had first formed the Renovated Data Processing Company, that this amazing transformation he noted in the branch offices couldn't have occurred over more than just a few years. His past and his present seemed to be trying to collapse together.

His portrait still gazed down from the walls of every Marvel branch office. It seemed to him now to be an anachronism, misplaced among the green-glowing terminals on every desk and the chrome-and-enamel sleekness of the decor by some out-of-whack time machine.

But he still enjoyed the adulation, and the association with the young people. He took these occasional branch-office tours like some men might have taken, in a different age, the restorative waters of a spa. They gave a tonic lift to his spirits.

One day in the summer of 1974 Jessica came into Jesse's office and deposited on his desk a calculator. It was one of Texas Instruments' newest models, packaged in a plastic case, six inches long, three wide, weighing perhaps twelve ounces.

"Do you realize," she said. "That this has the same power the ENIAC had?"

Jesse gazed at the calculator in astonishment. "Good Lord! The ENIAC filled a room as large as a house."

"The point is," Jessica went on. "That we must accelerate our LSI research."

"You're right. I'll put it on the agenda for the next board meeting."

The board was in one of its kid-in-the-candy-store phases. With profits for the first time running to over a billion dollars, they could see no clouds on the business horizon of Marvel Scientific. The executive bonuses that year had been extravagant. Jesse's accountant had informed him that his personal fortune was over the $20-million mark. Jesse didn't know what his father was worth, but he knew it must be several times that figure, even with the practice that he'd continued of giving half his income to the Elvira Dinsmore Foundation. And

Jessica, with her sizeable bonus and her trust fund, was now a millionaire.

As he'd anticipated, the board approved the step-up in the development of an LSI line of machines with hardly a quaver. The work was being done at Tarrytown, and Jessica began to spend two weeks a month there.

When Jessica had been promoted to Duane Hopper's job, she had asked Joe Watson if he wanted her old job as vice-president of the time-sharing division. He declined. "I'd be a wash-out," he said. "I don't have the technical know-how to handle it. Besides, anyone who takes that job is going to labor under a terrible handicap. You did it so superbly, that anyone else is going to suffer by comparison." So Jessica ended up giving the job to the man who had managed systems design and programming for time-sharing.

Joe was due for a promotion. He'd done about all anyone could do with the marketing job in the time-sharing division. He was forty-four years old. However, Leslie Parks, the man who occupied the job that would be the natural one for Joe at this time in his career, was only fifty-three, and in excellent health.

Jesse had been aware for some years of the bond between Joe and Jessica and he couldn't help feeling that the relationship was a strange one. They had separate apartments and gave no indication that they were considering marriage, now, or in the future.

The problem of finding a suitable job for Joe Weston was solved through Leslie Parks' ambition: he left to head up a company that was going to make a new kind of computer called a "micro". It was a miniature, desk-top computer designed to sell for a few thousand dollars. Jesse didn't think there was much of a market for such a machine. But Parks' mind was made up. In October he left, and Joe Weston was made Group Vice-President of Marketing.

Jesse discovered, to his surprise, that J.D. did not share his skepticism about the market for micro-computers. "Parks is making a smart move," he said. "Micro-computers will make him a hell of a lot of money."

"I don't see that, Dad," Jesse replied. "Atari has already about cornered the games market which is a drop in the bucket compared to the macro-computer business. Besides, these games you hook up through your TV are sold in retail stores, and Leslie doesn't have any experience in retailing."

"He'll learn. And we'd better learn, too."

"You mean the toy market?" Jesse couldn't believe what he was hearing.

"Not toys," J.D. said. "But computers – desk-top computers. There's a market waiting for that, Jesse."

Jesse shrugged. "Perhaps. Very small companies might use a desk-top. But companies of any size will have terminals on their executives' desks, terminals hooked into a central main-frame computer. Like mine." He pointed to his own terminal screen on a console stand beside his desk, from which he could access, from the time-sharing computer in Tarrytown, sales and production figures for the whole company.

"I don't agree. We should start now."

"We've got plenty to keep us busy, Dad – with the LSI computer."

"Wouldn't cost much. My boys and I have done the research. We've got a prototype ready to roll. All we need are the plant facilities."

Jesse stared at his father. "You mean that's what you've been working on all these years in that lab?"

"That's it."

Jesse didn't believe him. His father had begun the secret research group in the sixties, before miniaturization was at a point where a micro-computer could've been conceived, much less designed. He didn't think his father was lying when he said that Tom Ryder's group had developed a micro prototype – just that he wasn't telling him everything.

"Could I see it?" Jesse asked.

"I'll have Ryder bring it up," J.D. said.

It was no larger than a good-sized suitcase, with a fourteen-inch screen, and a keyboard.

"Sixty-four K-bytes of main memory," Ryder said. "And another two hundred and fifty-six on tape cassette. See, the cassette drives are built right into the base here. But what you should eventually go to is floppy disk. More density, better reliability."

Jesse didn't miss the "you." Ryder was turning the micro over to Jesse, and seemed relieved to be rid of it. This was more evidence, in Jesse's mind, that the micro research was not the main concern of Ryder's group.

As Jessie had predicted, the large market wasn't there in 1974 when Marvel Scientific came out with its micro called, simply, the Marvel Micro. Jesse quietly reduced the production of the Micro and put its

396

marketing on the back burner. No one really noticed. The board was as complacent as cream-fed cats with the ever-growing profits. And J.D. had lost interest in the micro as soon as the board had given him the budget he wanted for his lab.

In 1977 IBM finally ushered in the fourth generation of computers. Although the 370 line had adopted some LSI technology, it had been hardly more than an improved version of the 360 line. But with the introduction of the 303X IBM took a quantum leap into the future. The 303Xs ordered in the first weeks after the new line's announcement represented four times the computing power of all previous IBM installations.

"Goddamnit," J.D. fumed. "Why are we always *reacting* to IBM?"

"Because," Jesse replied. "We've made a hell of a lot of money letting them pave the way. Remember all the trouble they had with the 360 that accrued to our benefit?"

"I suppose so," J.D. grumbled. "But just once I'd like them to eat our dust."

In 1977 the fastest-growing computer companies that year were ones that hadn't even existed a year or two before – Apple, Tandy, Commodore. And, although their revenues were still small compared to the industry as a whole, their success made a lot of people take notice. The micro-computer market had come into its own.

Jesse asked Joe Weston to prepare a sales plan for the Marvel Micro. Through Joe's efforts Marvel found a retail chain that was eager to market the Micro and had stores in every major city in the country. In November of 1977 the Marvel Micro went on sale, just in time for the Christmas business. The results, which Joe Weston presented to a board meeting in January of 1978, were gratifying – Marvel Micros had captured fourteen percent of micro-computer sales over the holidays. The revenue generated wasn't much compared to Marvel's total, but the board and the company executives were agreed – the potential for micro revenues might become enormous.

J.D.'s withdrawal into his lab left Jesse with a problem. J.D. still held onto the title of Chairman of the Board and Chief Executive Officer, but Jesse found himself doing that job, by default, as well as the President's job.

J.D., when he'd been active in the affairs of the company, had overseen essential functions, including management of the

397

all-important company finances – negotiating lines of credit, juggling cash flow and short-term borrowing to minimize the interest the company had to pay, deciding when it was necessary to ask the board for permission to go into the bond market to finance long-term capital expenditures and so forth. He had also been the liaison between the company and the board and until this duty had, in recent years, devolved onto him, Jesse hadn't realized how time-consuming it was. Then there were the myriad day-to-day issues that only the top decision-maker in the company could resolve.

The result of all this was that Jesse found himself working sixteen-hour days more often than not, and spending more and more of his weekends, when he was in town, at the office.

"You *have* to do something, Jesse," Clarise insisted. "I won't let you kill yourself."

"I have an idea," Jesse said.

It was a way of realizing, if not in name, then in practice, Jesse's dream of running the company with Jessica. At thirty-eight she had matured into one of the best executives to be found in the computer industry.

Over a lunch that he'd invited her to, Jesse presented his idea to Jessica on a chilly spring day in 1978.

"You'd be Executive Vice-President. All the Group VPs would report to you. In essence, you'd be President, without the title. I'd retain the title of President, but I'd take on the duties of Chairman and CEO."

"What a charade," Jessica commented. "Doesn't Grandfather realize what he's saddled you with?"

"I doubt that he thinks about it much."

"Perhaps you should bring it to his attention."

Jesse shook his head. "He's changed, Jessica. I'm worried about him. In any event, it would only upset him to try to get him to retire, and I know he wouldn't do it."

"But the board –"

"I won't start an internal fight. It would kill him, I'm sure of it. That lab of his is about all he lives for. That, and his memoirs. Miss Pribash told me he's begun dictating them."

"You said he's changed."

"Oh, little things. But disturbing, nevertheless. He's really para-noid about the third floor. The other day he raised hell with building maintenance because he thought some poor janitor, who was just trying to do his job, was a spy. I had to intervene to prevent him from firing the man. Also, he's becoming forgetful. The other day he came to work, impeccably dressed as usual, but without a tie or socks. And he forgets people's names – people he's worked with for years. I guess you have to expect things like that when a man's eighty-eight, but it's hard for me to accept in Dad."

"He always seemed so strong. So invulnerable."

"Do I have your permission to propose you to the board as Executive Vice-President?" Jesse asked.

"Of course."

He leaned across the table and kissed her cheek.

She smiled. "I suspect that's the only kiss a President will give a Vice-President in New York City today."

"Hell," Jesse said. "In the country!"

At the board's May meeting Jessica was elected Executive Vice-President of Marvel Scientific Machines, Inc.

TEN

O, slowly, slowly, run ye horses of the night.
Christopher Marlowe

36

Marvel vs. Marvel

JESSE AND CLARISE gave a small New Year's Eve party in 1979. Jessica, Joe Weston, Duane and Linda Hopper, and J.D. were there. Duane had never recovered fully from his last heart-attack. He was feeble physically, moving like a frail old man, but his mind was as acute as ever and Jesse, saddened by his appearance, nevertheless enjoyed his old friend's quick wit.

1979 had been a very good year for Marvel Scientific. Gross revenues of $15 billion, and profits of $2.3 billion. There had been a decided shift in the business. Revenues from main-frame computer sales and rentals were declining, while those of mini-computers, micros, software and peripheral computer equipment were on the rise. The nature of the computer business was changing.

The previous February Jesse had given to Clarise the latest Marvel Micro, which she'd installed in a spare bedroom. During the year she had been writing software. She had lost none of her old talents, and three of the packages she'd written were now in wide distribution among micro users. Since she was no longer a Marvel employee, Jesse had worked out a licensing agreement between the company and Clarise for the use of her programs. She was paid a royalty, and was on her way to becoming a millionaire in her own right. She referred to herself as a "hacker," a new term that had grown up with the advent of the micro computers to denote those who programmed them with the kind of obsession reminiscent of the first programmers who had the exclusive use of computers.

Clarise was sixty-six and suffered from arthritis, though her former beauty still shone now and then through the patina of age. Jesse at sixty-two had so far escaped any serious infirmities. His hair was almost as thick as it had been in his youth, but it was now entirely white. With his large, dark eyes, and his increasingly rugged features, he resembled the archetype of the American Executive.

The guests arrived at nine. Clarise had laid on a buffet. Jesse opened the champagne. J.D. sat by himself in a corner and gloomily surveyed the guests. Even Jessica couldn't draw him out.

A little before midnight Jesse cranked open the casement windows of the living-room so that, at midnight, they could clearly hear the church bells and the blast of horns, punctuated with the occasional discharge of fireworks. J.D. remained in his corner with a champagne glass balanced on his knee. He'd hardly said a word since he'd arrived.

After the guests had left, Clarise and Jesse had a last glass of champagne together. Jesse lit a cigar. He now confined his smoking to a good cigar on the four or five occasions a year that he considered special enough to warrant it.

"I'm worried about J.D.," Clarise said. "He didn't say two words all evening."

"He's moody," Jesse replied. "Sometimes he's energetic and almost his old self. Then he sinks into these glooms."

"He should see a doctor."

"He went two months ago – or I should say, I practically dragged him. But the doctor wasn't encouraging. He told me that, after all, Dad is almost ninety – you can't expect him to function like a young man."

"He shouldn't be working."

"I don't know," Jesse said. He rose to refill their champagne glasses. "It's something for him to do. And he doesn't get in the way, I have to give him credit. Titles aside, Jessica and I run the company."

"He only works four or five hours, with Ryder and his crew and is usually gone by lunch. Miss Pribash comes around afternoons at the penthouse. He's dictating his memoirs."

"Have you seen them?"

"No one but Miss Pribash has seen them, as far as I know."

Miss Pribash came to see Jesse one day in late January of 1980.

Typically, she did not beat around the bush. "Something has to be done about your father, Mr. Jesse."

"What do you mean?" He couldn't be sure, but behind Miss Pribash's thick glasses, he thought he detected evidence of recent crying.

"He must have care, I'm afraid."

"Care?"

"Nursing supervision."

"What happened?"

She sighed. "He's done it before. He – he removed all his clothes. But this time he tried to go out that way. I've always been able to persuade him to dress before he left. This time I had to literally cling to him until he regained his senses. Next time, I can't be sure. So, you see, he needs supervision."

"My God!" Jesse said, staring at Miss Pribash. "How many times before?"

She shrugged delicately. "A few."

"Are there any other indications?"

"He's forgetful. But, then, so am I." She smiled a smile that Jesse found heartbreaking. "We are all getting on, Mr. Jesse."

Jesse talked to Jessica about the matter. She was quite as shocked as he had been. "What can we do?"

"Provide care for him at home. Perhaps he could come into the office once in a while."

"What about Tom Ryder's project?"

"We won't persuade him to give it up," Jesse replied. "Especially now that the micro market is looming so large. The board thinks he's some kind of magician, and want him to keep doing whatever the hell he and Ryder are doing down there. I thought we could have Ryder report to him at the penthouse once in awhile. The main thing is not to let this become grist for the rumor mill."

Through a nurses' registry Jesse found a male nurse for his father – a burly, gently spoken man whose speciality was geriatric care. The man's name was Fedder, and Jesse liked him immediately. Fedder exuded competent kindness, but Jesse also detected a determination that he knew Fedder would need to deal with his father.

Joe Weston gave a party for Jessica's fortieth birthday. She had been working long hours on problems with the Marvel line of fourth-generation computers which had been introduced in April of 1980. The line, called Marvel IV, superseded the old Greek alphabet line that had been souped-up with LSI components in 1978 to meet the challenge of IBM's 303X. There had been large expectations in the company for the Marvel IVs which were, in design, a large leap forward with the technology. But IBM had itself come out with a fourth-generation line in 1979, the 4300s. This had set the Marvel board off into another one of its panics, and it had put pressure on Jesse and Jessica to get the Marvel IVs into production. Jesse had pulled Jessica off everything else she was doing and put her in sole charge of Marvel IV development. The new line was announced nearly a year before it had been planned to be. The hardware was exceptional. Through the use of VLSI (Very Large Scale Integration) the engineering department at Tarrytown had been able to design machines that had eight times the capacity of the old line, but that sold for the same prices.

The problems were with the software. The programming group at Tarrytown had been asked to design and program software for the machines before the hardware specifications were firm. As a consequence, the first customers to receive Marvel IVs experienced horrendous problems. They could hardly get a single production program to run because the operating system for the new machines was full of bugs.

Jessica ordered the entire programming staff at Tarrytown into the field to debug operating systems on customer sites. She coordinated this personally. She gathered all the fixes to the operating systems made at various locations, assured they were consistent with each other, that programmer time wasn't being wasted with duplicate work, and that a master program at Tarrytown was properly fed all the changes. By August 22, her fortieth birthday, she had the problems nearly licked. Orders for the Marvel IVs, which had dried to a trickle upon news of the troubles with the operating system, had begun to flow again, and Jessica was exhausted.

For the past several years leasing companies, which had prospered with IBM's unbundling, had been, one after another, going broke. The introduction of the IBM 303Xs had burst their bubbles. The new line offered so much more computing power, for less money, than the old lines, that customers had rushed to them, sending the leasing-company machines back to them in car loads. And the leasing companies were stuck with the machines before their lease income had amortized their costs. They drastically discounted the machines but found few takers for, not only was the price of the new lines fiercely competitive, but it had also become an axiom of computer marketing that few customers wished to suffer the stigma of using obsolete computers.

For Jessica's birthday party Joe had rented an Italian restaurant that was her favorite. Every guest was either an employee of Marvel Scientific Machines or somehow connected with the company. J.D. came, with Fedder in attendance, bringing him champagne where he had plunked himself down in an easy chair against one wall. A long table held the *hors d'oeuvre* and would later accommodate the buffet supper. A trio played softly and couples danced, including Joe and Jessica.

"How does it feel?" he asked.

"No different than thirty-nine," she replied.

"You're handling it well."

"I had you for a model." Joe had turned fifty three months before.

"This may not be the time," Joe said hesitantly, and then added, fiercely. "But then, damnit, when is! Are we ever going to be married?"

"I thought we were doing so well the way we are."

He sighed. "I suppose so. You aren't afraid of nepotism? Having your husband working for you?"

"No." She was silent for a moment, and he knew her well enough not to interrupt her thoughts. "I'll make you a deal. I'll marry you when I become head of the company."

"President, you mean?"

"Not if father is Chairman. I mean the true head, whatever the title."

"Your father looks likely to go on as long as your grandfather."

"He should retire."

"You mean your father?"

"Grandfather is retired, for all purposes. Father is sixty-three. I'm afraid his ideas for the company reflect that."

"What do you mean?"

"He wants to take the safe way. More government contracts. Cut back on research. You know that, Joe."

"I suppose he has become a bit conservative."

"A bit! He told me the other day that artificial intelligence is a pipe dream."

"A lot of very knowledgeable people wonder if it is achievable. I was reading the other day a paper by a fellow at MIT – one of the top boys – who was saying it's impossible."

"The Japanese don't think so. They're on the verge of launching a major research attack. If we don't keep up, we'll go the way of Detroit in the seventies."

"But, Jessica – machines thinking? I just don't see how it can be done. The human brain is such a different mechanism than a computer."

"Of course it is. That's why we have to come up with something different than the old binary, digital discrete machine that's been with us since ENIAC. Do you realize, with all the talk about advances in computers, that we still operate our machines under the same logical construct as the first computer? With the exception of micro-electronics, we've hardly done anything in the way of advancing the technology for the essential design of the computer itself. Marvel should be, can be, the leader in this country for that kind of research."

"Your father doesn't agree?"

"Absolutely opposed. Thinks we'd bankrupt the company."

"It is a damned expensive field. More expensive by far than anything we, or anyone else, has ever tackled. The Japanese will have government backing."

"You could say that about everything we've ever developed – each new advance, each new computer line, required a much larger investment than the one that preceded it. But I'm convinced it can be done, and the company that cracks the problem first will lead the world for a long time to come."

"What do you intend to do?"

"I don't intend to tear the company apart over it, if I can help it. I think Grandfather should name me as his successor, and then official-ly step down."

Joe gasped. "My God, Jessica! Do you know what you're suggest-ing?"

"It's not as dramatic as all that, Joe. Let's not make a Freudian sub-text out of it."

"Artificial intelligence began, really, with Claude Shannon's work on Information Theory," Jessica explained.

"Don't give me Claude Shannon," J.D. said. "I know all about Claude Shannon."

"That's good, Grandfather, because it makes it easier for me to tell you what I have in mind."

They were sitting in the living-room of J.D.'s penthouse. The maid had served tea and then departed. It was a brisk Saturday afternoon in the fall of 1980. Fedder was not in evidence, but Jessica knew he wouldn't be far away.

J.D. sipped his tea noisily, and said, "Just what do you have in mind, my dear?"

"I'd like you to name me Chairman and Chief Executive Officer of the company."

J.D. put his cup down with a clatter. "You'd what!"

408

"I've thought this through very carefully, Grandfather, and I hope you'll hear me out."

"*I* am Chairman of the Board."

"Nominally, yes. But we both know that you haven't handled the duties for some time."

He glared at her over his teacup. "Are you calling me a slacker?"

"Good grief, no! You've given your whole life to the company. But it needs direction now – day-to-day direction. We're in critical times."

"Tell me about these critical times."

Jessica described the research she had in mind. She described Jesse's resistance to it. She told her grandfather about the effort in artificial intelligence that the Japanese were preparing.

"We'll be another Detroit if we don't act," she concluded.

To Jessica's profound surprise J.D. broke into a wheezing laugh. "By God, Jessica!" he said. "You always were a bright one!"

"Then you agree?"

"That we should do something about artificial intelligence? By all means!" He grinned slyly. "Why don't you leave that to me? You may think I'm all washed up – a senile old fool, living up here with a keeper, and not good for much of anything. But, let me tell you, J.D. Marvel is not finished! Not by a long shot, he's not! So you just do the best job you know how to do with the job you have, and let me worry about what direction the company's going in."

Jesse never found out about Jessica's visit to his father, though he was aware that she disagreed with the direction in which he was steering the company – toward the development of better conventional computers, and away from what he considered the impractical pursuit of an all-out research effort in artificial intelligence. He wasn't convinced that a device could be built that would satisfactorily simulate the human brain. And he wasn't about to pour billions of dollars of the company's resources into such an ephemeral notion. He continued the research in the special projects section that had to do with Information Theory and artificial intelligence, but this was a microcosm of what Jessica wanted.

J.D. seldom came to the office any more. Tom Ryder went to his penthouse once a week. It eventually came to the attention of Jesse that Ryder was checking out video-tape equipment to take with him on these visits. The public relations department kept the equipment to tape sales presentations, and it was Earl Baxter who told Jesse about

Tom checking out the equipment.

"What does he do with it?" Jesse asked.

"I don't know," Earl replied. "All I know is that Tom's secretary told my secretary that she thinks he takes pictures of something in the lab to take to show J.D."

"Thank God for secretaries," Jesse said. "Or we wouldn't know anything that was going on around here."

In 1981 the Justice Department dropped its twelve-year-old anti-trust suit against IBM. In January Frank Cary retired as Chairman of the Board of IBM and John Opel took his place. At Marvel, Earl Baxter retired as Vice-President of Administration and Public Relations.

On July 11 of 1982, Jesse celebrated his sixty-fifth birthday by taking Clarise to a late dinner – declining her offers to throw him a lavish celebration. Actually, he wanted to downplay the whole thing and didn't want to draw attention to his having attained an age that at IBM, for example, was five years beyond their mandatory retirement. In fact, he'd let Earl Baxter linger on until his early seventies partly because he didn't want to seem to set precedences that he himself might feel constrained to follow.

For several years now he'd been Chairman of the Board in everything but name. But he very much wanted that final official recognition. If he retired before having achieved it he would feel cheated of something that he felt he had earned and that he deserved. He'd long ago resigned himself to having to wait until his father was either dead, or so incapacitated that to maintain the fiction that he was Chairman would constitute a patent farce. Still, he couldn't bring himself to wish for such circumstances. The possibility that the board would ever take the initiative was remote. They regarded J.D. as a near-magical, totemic figure; and the mythical quality of this regard had only been deepened by his absence from board meetings.

1982 came and went and J.D. showed no signs of either dying or deteriorating to an incapacitated state. His new, radical gerontologist seemed to have earned his lavish fees and there was no more bizarre behavior. Jesse tended to give credit in equal parts for this to the doctor's choline injections and to the watchful presence of Fedder.

Marvel Scientific Machines completed 1982 with revenues of $19 billion and profits of $2.9 billion. Jessica and Joe decided against attending any of the New Year's Eve parties to which they'd been

410

invited, in favor of a quiet evening of champagne and steaks at Jessica's apartment.

"I would hope," Joe said. "That this would be the year that I might address you as Mrs. Madam Chairman."

"I don't know about that," Jessica replied grimly. "But this is the year for a showdown with my father."

Jessica prepared the groundwork at the birthday party her grandfather gave himself on February 6, 1983; a dinner at his penthouse for the family.

"Grandfather, you favor research in artificial intelligence. Am I right?" she began.

"Of course!" J.D. replied.

"Then I want to quadruple our efforts in AI. We are barely scratching the surface."

"Jessica," Jesse said. "Do you think this is the place –?"

"This is exactly the place!" Jessica cut in. "Grandfather *is* Chairman. We keep forgetting that."

"I've heard," J.D. interjected, "that this debate over which direction the research should go has been dividing the company."

"It is essential to our survival that we pursue AI research," Jessica said heatedly.

"It's essential to our survival that we should not pour billions into an impossible quest," Jesse countered.

"There!" J.D. said. "There it is. Everybody choosing sides. I'm going to make you both a proposal. Can you patch this thing up for a year? Can you both promise me you won't do anything rash until a year from now, give or take a month?"

"What do you mean, Dad?" Jesse asked.

"I mean that a year from now, I will name my successor."

37

J.D.'s Memoirs

YOUNG RYDER HAS FIXED IT UP so that the tapes I record can be automatically handled, so I don't have to watch what I say for Pribash's benefit.

I guess I shouldn't call you "Young Ryder," should I? You must be what — well into your fifties? But, then at my age, everyone in the world seems young.

I remember when I called you back from Huntsville. (No, this is not a digression, Ryder — this should go into the Read Only Memory. Everything is pertinent, and you can just expand the damn memory, I don't care how many external units it takes.) Anyway, you were as bedraggled as a wet pup. Hands shaking, eyes bleeding. I'd had my eye on you for quite a time. But when you got your tail in a crack down at Huntsville, I knew you were my man. Now, this is important. It'll tell you a lot about how my mind was working then in regard to the project. I knew I'd have to launch the thing in camera, so to speak (an apt term, don't you think? Your lab is a veritable vault). I needed someone who had the brains to do the thing, but, at the same time, that I could trust beyond a shadow of a doubt. I read up on alcoholism. (Bet that surprises you.) The dependent personality. The passiveness typical of the non-drinking alcoholic. Ideal! Ideal! I said to myself. The only thing that worried me was that either the alcohol had damaged your brain to an extent that I couldn't use it, or that the passiveness had knocked the drive out of you. As it turned out, I needn't have worried. You have been everything I hoped for, Ryder, and then some.

Back to the topic at hand. You've asked me to recall how I first became interested in the project. Sometime in the fall of 1958 I read several articles by Claude Shannon of Bell Labs — articles that he'd written over a period of ten years or so — dealing with Information Theory. These articles, I don't have to tell you, are heavy slogging for someone who never had formal training in mathematics. But, then, not to sound immodest, I had educated myself over the years, in various fields, including math enough to be able to get a vague fix on what he was talking about. That, and a popular article I came across explaining Shannon's work,

412

along with consulting a professor or two, gave me a pretty fair understanding of what it was all about.

When the light dawned, I was damned excited! Here was something that could extend the frontier of the computer business far beyond the horizon. Shannon was talking about how *information gets passed,* what *information is, the redundancies necessary to prevent information entropy, and so on. (Anyway, Ryder, you have fed those articles into the system, so no need for me to go into them here.)*

When we got into the project, it soon became apparent that we were dealing with an even bigger area than subsumed Information Theory – that of artificial intelligence.

You know, I haven't felt better in years. I actually went to the office for the first time in a couple of months yesterday. Of course, I had to put up with Fedder tagging along, but he's not a bad sort, for a man who has the soul of a parole officer. I was amazed at the progress you'd made! Those video-tapes just don't convey the drama and excitement of the real thing.

Digressions! Digressions! What did you want me to talk about? Where the hell are those notes? . . .

I'm back after a brief absence. Found your notes, and mixed myself a stiff Scotch. Item one: Jesse.

Well, he turned out better than I'd hoped. Let's see – subjective view. I like him, most of the time. I don't know what the hell paternal love is, Ryder, so you can just strike that. How can I describe our relationship? Wary, I guess would be the word. He can irritate me, too. I can't tolerate the patronizing air he's adopted around me in the last few years, like I'm some kind of backward child who doesn't know enough to cross the street alone. Respect? Yes, yes! I suppose I'd have to give him that. He's turned into a pretty damned good executive. But I am sick of his sneaking around behind my back trying to get rid of me. SICK OF IT! Well, never mind. Have to calm down. One luxury you can no longer afford at my age, Ryder, is the luxury of blowing your top. Might quite literally happen, the quack says. Top of my head look like Vesuvius erupting. A-hah-hah!

Well, well – back to business. No wait! Before I forget it – the other morning – now I'm not saying this out of some senile, dirty-minded delusion, this is serious – the other morning I woke up with an erection. Quite an unexpected accomplishment for my age. But that's not the point. The point is that that side of my life, the – what do you call it? – sensual side? Now, that's important. I want that included. All that stuff on the tapes about the women in my life – I don't want you expurgating that stuff, Ryder, out of some squeamish impulse. Man is more than a brain. Well, I've lectured you about this before, so I won't belabor it now. You know what I want.

Back to your list. Let's see. Tapes. Yes, I have tapes of all their voices. Got the last one, Clarise, at my birthday party the other night. Wait! I gave you those tapes yesterday, didn't I? FEDDER!

Yes, sir, Mr. Marvel?

Fedder, those tapes I wanted to give to Ryder. We took them yesterday, didn't we?

Yes, sir. They were in the plastic box.

Okay. Get lost, Fedder. I thought I took you those tapes. Cross that one off. By the way, the tape of Jesse and Jessica at the party is better, I think, than the individual ones I've given you before. Anyway, you know how to sort them out. I leave it to you.

Back to the list. No, for Christ's sake, no one knows about the recording set-up. What do you take me for? I've changed the reels myself, when they've needed it.

The most important influences in my business life? Ah, Christ! There've been many. Beginning with Herman Hollerith. Then old Homer Medville Cranston, the cash-register king. Tough old bird, do anything to reach his ends. Couldn't work for him long. But he taught me a hell of a lot, I'll say that for him.

You know, Ryder, this is a funny business we're in. Ask the man on the street what the computer business is all about, and nine out of ten would say it was all science and technology. Not so! It was, is, and always has been, marketing. Good old-fashioned salesmanship. Oh, sure – maybe it's dressed up in new togs now, compared to the way we sold organs, Walter Hucko and I, off the back of a wagon. But strip off the fancy talk, and underneath is salesmanship.

Walter Hucko. Now there's an influence. Should've begun with him. He was the prototype of the old-time drummer. Wanda Agronsky was an influence. She was the polar opposite of Walter. All technical competence and incisiveness, wrapped up, I might add, in a damned attractive package. Here's an insight, or whatever you call it. The people who started the data-processing business in this country – the ones who are responsible for making it the trillion-dollar business it now is – I'm talking about old Tom Watson at IBM, Patterson at NCR, myself – a handful of men, really – what we had was this: we had the ability to blend together the Walter Hucko salesmanship and the Wanda Agronsky technical competence to come up with a new breed – the data-processing salesman.

I picked brains, Ryder. We all did. John von Neumann's brain. Ansell Farnsworth's brain. Your brain, Ryder! Here's the model: you look at the technology, pick the brains, then take a look at the market. Then you put together a sales force that will shape the market place to the technology. Technological Imperative. Learned that from Jesse. The term, not the technique. So, I guess you'd have to say he was a bit of a latter-day influence.

My management style was to throw up obstacles when anyone wanted to do anything radical. Like Jesse's Technological Imperative. I threw out every objection I could think of, and, in the end, he met them all. Finally, he threatened

414

to quit. And meant it. I knew he was serious then. Let him have his way. Which was the way I was headed anyway.

Now they're talking about the Sociological Imperative. The sponge-brains are, that is. Saying that we in the computer industry must adapt the advances of technology to the good of society. They'd never own it, but there's an old label for such soft thinking – Technocracy. Didn't work in the thirties, won't work now. Computer people have no business saying what's good or bad for folks. That's the job of government and maybe the churches. Our job is to take the output of the technology and sell it. Anybody worried about keeping personal records on folks on computers, or making control systems for nuclear reactors, or whatever the hell the sponge-brains worry about nowadays, they can write to their Congressman. The American Way is not, in the final analysis, Ryder, so much different from the Marvel Way. Complementary, they are. Downright complementary.

Influences. I suppose I'd have to say Joseph Falk Whittier was, in a negative way. Taught me to never trust a man with either your wife or your career. He took one, and damned near took the other, and nearly got me tossed in jail, to boot. Yes, I learned a hell of a lot from old Joe Whittier.

From the day I began selling organs, money never meant a hell of a lot to me. I always had plenty, I suppose. All dollars are counters in the bigger games. The more you have, the more your company makes, the better you're doing in the game. What is the object of the game? I suppose it's extending yourself as far into the world as you can. I'm not just talking power here. I'm talking two dimensions – space and time. You start out with nothing more than your health and your native wit, and you try to extend your influence into as large a circle as possible, and you try to make it last long after you've gone. (That's not a bad definition of the project, is it, my boy?)

The greatest advance I've seen. Well, in the technology, I'd have to say it was the transistor, hands-down. Took us off dependency on the vacuum tube. Those old tube machines had meantime-to-failure in minutes. Today its measured in months. The transistor also speeded up computations, lowered cost, and led to the micro-conductor as a natural progression. Those three fellows who came up with the transistor deserved their Nobels if anyone ever did.

The greatest advance in application hasn't occurred yet, so far as the world knows, has it, Ryder? But it won't be long. It won't be . . . it won't . . .

Jessica decided that the issue must be forced. Her grandfather had said one year, and it had been a year and more. It was time he made a decision. And she didn't intend him to make it without talking to her first. She knew what the right decision was, and she must make him see it.

She was forty-three, her father was sixty-six. She was in her prime,

415

as ready as she would ever be to take over Marvel Scientific Machines. Her father was past his. For the good of the company, he must retire, and she take over.

"Get your trousseau ready," she told Joe.

"What do you mean?"

"I'm going to see Grandfather. By this time next week I expect to be Chairman of the Board."

But Fedder was an insurmountable obstacle.

"I'm sorry, Miss Marvel," he said, keeping the door of the penthouse on the chain, and speaking through the crack.

"Let me in this instant," she demanded.

"He won't see anyone."

"He can tell me that himself."

"I'm sorry. His instructions were explicit. No one."

"Tell him I'm here."

"Very well. Wait here."

He returned in a moment. "He won't see you," he said through the crack. "However, he gave me this to give you." He passed an envelope out through the crack. "He said to tell you he'll be mailing one to your father and the rest of the board." The door closed.

Jessica ripped open the envelope impatiently. One sheet of folded stationery was inside. The handwriting was her grandfather's spidery script: *Be at my lab at 2 p.m. on March 9th.*

That was all. No salutation, no signature. March 9 was the day after tomorrow.

Extra chairs had been brought into J.D.'s office next to the lab. When Jessica arrived she found everyone there but her father and her grandfather. Tom Ryder seemed to be in charge. It worried Jessica that neither Jesse not J.D. were there yet; perhaps they were together.

Tom ushered her to a chair and offered her coffee, which she accepted. The board members greeted her with nods. Joe Weston smiled at her. There was an unnatural hush in the room. Tom got the coffee served and then sat on the edge of J.D.'s desk and fidgeted. He was pale and nervous, but there was a gleam of excitement in his eyes.

Time crept on. No one spoke. Eyes were pulled as if by a magnet to the combination-locked vault door set into one wall of the room, that they knew led to the lab, and in which no one present save Tom Ryder had ever been.

At seven minutes past two Jesse arrived with a briefcase in his hand. He took a seat, accepted coffee, and looked at his watch. Jessica tried

416

to tell from his face if he knew what the decision would be, but aside from the fact that he seemed a bit harried, his expression revealed nothing.

Tom Ryder cleared his throat, and said, "We can get started now."

"Where's J.D.?" a board member wanted to know. "I thought he was going to conduct the meeting."

"In a moment," Tom replied. "He asked me to begin."

"Is he going to be here?" another board member asked nervously.

"Please," Tom said. "If you'll just be patient."

"Let him speak," Jesse said.

"Thank you," Tom replied. "For twenty years now," he began, "I've been conducting a project under the direction of our Chairman. You've seen one result of the work – the micro-computer. That machine was a by-product of the larger work.

"What we've been working on is artificial intelligence." The board members exchanged looks. "The so-called fifth generation of computing. We started out very primitively. We thought if we could develop a machine that was capable of playing chess at the master level we would've taken a significant step. Today, of course, such a program is entirely feasible. But you must remember we're speaking of 1962, before *third*-generation hardware. The chess research taught us a lot about how learning goes on in the human brain, and how that might be translated into rules for the computer.

"We discovered fairly early that research into artificial intelligence could be separated into four areas: problem-solving – that is, how does, for example, a chess master make his decisions, and how do you reduce the process, through heuristic considerations, to steps that can be programmed? Second, speech and pattern recognition – the problem of designing sound-sensitive hardware that could distinguish among the various noises of human speech, and that could put these together into patterns that would be, in the human sense, whole sentences or, if you will, thoughts. Next, was the question of servomechanics, popularly called 'robotics.' That is, how could we build electro-mechanical devices that would perform physical functions? Turning dials, handling objects, and so on. And finally, the last, and by far the most difficult area of research – that of simulating vision. In other words, developing light-sensitive hardware that was capable of distinguishing among various objects of various sizes and color patterns."

Tom paused, and looked around the room. "Now for the results of our work. If you'll follow me, please." He walked to the vault door,

417

turned the large handle, and slowly swung the door open.

They filed into the lab. The room was dimly lit, and quite large, a rectangle fifty feet long and thirty wide. Work-benches lined the walls. At the far end of the room stood J.D. He was leaning on his cane with both hands and watching them file into the room with a small smile on his lips. After everyone was in, J.D. spoke.

"Welcome to our little dog-and-pony show. I must apologize for the light, but we have equipment in here that is very sensitive. However, I'm sure you'll find that you'll be able to see quite well enough." He moved to the benches. "We have on these benches a display of our work, arranged chronologically – that is, from the earliest development, to the latest. Here –" he pointed to a box with black coaxial cables running from it, and a checkerboard pattern of squares etched into its top surface "– is our first chess-playing machine. These squares are touch and weight sensitive. The white men are all heavier than the black, so that the computer can sense their positions. It outputs its moves on a typewriter. Pretty crude, but it worked! From this experiment, as Tom has probably told you, we learned a lot about heuristics – the rules by which people make decisions, the iterative processes you and I go through to finally come down to a choice.

"Here –" he pointed further down the bench with his cane "– is the first servo-mechanism we designed. It is a simple arm capable of radial, vertical and horizontal movement. It is similar to the robots developed for auto assembly lines. I won't bother demonstrating these earlier devices for you, because I'm sure you are as eager to see the final results of all this work as I am to show it to you.

"Next to the robot arm is our first crude attempt at speech recognition. It is, as you can see, an early model of a solid-state calculator. This box is the voice-recognition unit. The unit has a vocabulary of twenty-five words it can respond to. For instance, 'add', and 'total.' Simple stuff, but it was our kindergarten in voice-recognition.

"Here is an early version of a visual responder. These photo-electric cells were designed to recognize patterns of light. What we learned, first of all, was that the brain has an 'ideal' image of objects stored away with which it compares an object that the eye sees. For example, although every cow looks different in some regard, the eye is able to compare it against the brain's ideal of 'cowness,' if you will, and recognize the beast for what it is, rather than identifying it as, say, a deer.

"Now, those devices represent the four areas we were working in.

The goal of the project, of course, was to integrate them, after we'd solved the problems in each area. I'm skipping ahead over years and years of strenuous research, thousands and thousands of man hours from some of the most brilliant people it has been my good fortune ever to have been associated with."

He was standing still now, leaning on his cane, slowly looking at each person across the room from him in turn. "Gentlemen of the board," he said. "Jessica. I made a promise just over a year ago, that I would name my successor. The day has come. This research is completed. I believe that, whatever contribution I made to it, it represents my greatest accomplishment. It will live on after me.

"Before we get to my decision, I'd like to introduce you to someone else." His head turned toward the vault door, and all heads followed suit. "Please, come in."

Nothing happened. Eyes strained for signs of movement at the door.

"Please," J.D. repeated. "Come –"

"STOP!"

Jesse had advanced until he stood facing J.D. from only a few feet away.

J.D. seemed mesmerized by Jesse. His eyes gazed unblinkingly at him, his mouth was half open on the word he had been about to speak when Jesse had ordered him to stop. For a long, tense moment they stared at each other. Then Jesse turned to Tom Ryder.

"He's not coming," Jesse said quickly.

Now *Ryder* seemed mesmerized by Jesse. He stared at him, frozen, hardly breathing. "What do you mean?" he whispered.

Jesse turned to the other people in the room. "I regret to inform you," he said in an emotionless voice. "That my father died a little over two hours ago."

Someone laughed. "What kind of joke –"

"It's no joke," Jesse said. "Ryder – the lights."

Ryder, like a man awakening from a dream, walked to a wall and flicked a row of switches. Fluorescent light flooded the room.

All eyes were on Jesse. He was stooping by J.D., lifting one leg of his trousers. A black coaxial cable ran from inside the trouser-leg to a black box against the wall.

The thing, whatever it was, was still frozen in that demented-looking position, mouth half open, eyes staring unseeingly. A stifled sob escaped Jessica; Joe Weston put his arms around her . . .

Through a haze Jessica heard her father gather the board around

419

him while they examined the robot, and tell them that they must act now – the company was in peril. A new board chairman and chief executive officer must be elected. Joe held her tightly, as the board elected Jesse to his father's title by acclamation. Then she was being led from the lab, Joe on one side, her father on the other, to the elevators, up seventeen floors, and into her father's office.

Jesse went to a cupboard, got a brandy bottle and a glass, and poured a drink for Jessica. She took it with a trembling hand.

"How –" she asked. "How did he die?"

"A massive stroke. Fedder gave him CPR while Pribash summoned the ambulance, but there was nothing anyone could do. He died instantly, and, the doctors tell me, painlessly."

Jesse sat behind his desk and massaged his eyes. "When he died, he was dictating. All the papers and files for the presentation were spread out on his desk."

"That's how you knew how to stop that thing?" Joe asked.

Jesse nodded wearily. "The command had to be spoken at a shout; the word used in normal conversation wouldn't affect it."

"His choice!" Jessica said suddenly. "You must have found out from the papers who he was going to choose. It was me, wasn't it?"

"No, Jessica," Jesse said gently.

"I don't believe it! You've tricked the board. I can't believe he chose you!"

"He chose neither of us. Don't you see – he meant to go on for ever, through that device. For years Tom Ryder has been feeding father's reminiscences, his personality, into its memory units."

"My God!" Joe breathed.

"Jessica," Jesse said. He got up and came to her, and took her hands in his. "I've waited for thirty years to be head of the company. Give me a few years. I promise I won't hang on like Dad did. And I need you."

"I – I don't know," she said. "I could handle the job –"

"Of course you could. No one doubts that. But so can I, and I've been training for it a lot longer than you. I'm sixty-seven in July. I promise I'll retire when I'm seventy and you can have the job. Will you give me that?"

She shook her head. "I don't know. I just can't think right now."

"She'll stay," Joe said firmly. "I'll see to that. After all, a husband should have some say in what his wife does."

Jessica looked up at him. "I suppose it's about time, isn't it?"

"No," Joe said softly. "It's way past time." Then he bent and kissed her gently.

"You know what I want, don't you?" Jesse said to Tom Ryder.

Ryder gazed dumbly at him. They were standing alone in the lab. The board had long since dispersed and Joe Weston had taken Jessica home. The robot still stood in the same frozen attitude.

"Oh, God, Mr. Marvel. I don't know if I can."

"We won't lose the research. That's all documented."

"I know. It's just so damned hard for me right now – losing Mr. Marvel, and all. He was – he was my strength, you see."

"I understand, Tom." Jesse put his hand on Ryder's shoulder. "I can get someone else to do it."

"*No!* I – I can't stand the thought of someone else –"

"All right, Tom. But I want a thorough job. I want the Read Only Memory erased first. Then I want the thing taken apart."

Tom Ryder sat before the console in the lab for a long time before he finally put his hands on the keyboard to key in the command sequence. There was a brief whirring noise and then the robot came to life and began to speak and, as it did, a little smile appeared on its latex face.

"I was down by the pig pens when I first laid eyes on Walter Hucko. I didn't imagine how he was to change my life . . ."

Ryder depressed the 'Permanent Erase' button on the console. Then he put his head in his hands and broke down and cried like a child.